ENDGAME TRILOGY

By MJ Grigsby

The **Endgame Trilogy** Consists of the novels:

Endgame Symphony

Endgame Entropy

Endgame Symmetry

CONTENTS

<u>DEDICATION</u>

Dedicated to my family and friends and the idea of self-reliance

Without 16 - this would have languished, incomplete

For the preciousness of my Golden Mother, the supporting fortitude and example of my junkyard Brother, and for the respect and genuine admiration for my Sister and Nephew

For the Memory of Father, Grandmother, and Sally who would have hopefully been proud

PROLOGUE

The nighttime can manifest a temperament.

The city can sob, rail, rejoice, or despair depending on the whim of the moment. Evenings alter mercurially, becoming ardent reflections echoing the nature of their collective inhabitants. That is unfaltering.

The most accurate way to describe how that particular evening began would be to say that it was mundane. All around, the sky looked down with disinterest. Throughout the city, the mild Winter air moved reluctantly. Every building stood bleakly, shadowed, and unremarkable. The streets remained empty and muted. Nothing seemed to be especially extraordinary.

For some, an ordinary night was a thing to be avoided. That routine and monotony signaled a type of failure to them. For others, that kind of blandness was preferable. That meant that they could sidestep hazardous potentialities for one more night. Such was the case for two police officers that patrolled those streets.

Officers Anne Ingram and Mitchell Donaldson moved through their typical routes, having their typical conversations, and looked forward to the typical uneventfulness of yet another night shift.

Someone else was on patrol that night as well; someone who had taken no vow to serve or protect. His fists appeared sallow from gripping the wheel so tightly, even in the darkness. The radio asserted conspiracies and accusations from the conservative talk show that was his staple. That program, along with other exigencies never failed to compel the man to his purpose.

Winding his way around the city at a deliberate pace, his thoughts were fixed on a single phrase; There has to be a first-there has to be a first. The urge that was bred in him for the capture and censure of his quarry was entirely consuming. He'd stalked the somber streets relentlessly, searching for a soul that spoke to his need. He waited for the wind to whisper 'PREY' illicitly at the sight of the one intended for cleansing. But no one presented themselves.

That was wholly excruciating. His natural reaction to that fact took the form of a tantrum. A red stoplight and an empty road afforded him the opportunity to manically thrash first the seats, then the dash, the steering wheel, and finally his own body. He repeatedly struck his skeletal head against the glass and beat his chest as if the punishment he sought to inflict on others demanded release and needed an immediate outlet. His hoarse screeches were fraught and pitiful. His fear of being denied his right, let loose the frenzy in him. Then, he believed that he identified an offering. To his mind, his intentions were validated by what he saw. He acknowledged the desired whisper of his benefactors and moved forward.

Halfway up the block, he saw a lone man walking, passing from darkness to light as he went past each streetlight. Each time the light shone down on him, the image on his T-shirt glared like a personal insult to the driver. That image was of a clenched black fist with a field of white as a background. That image was inciting to his mind. Perhaps he'd found his first.

As the oblivious man walked to the edge of a curb, an awareness that comes from living in a big city prodded and kept him alive.

The car's engine tried to roar but instead released the whine of age as the white-knuckled man sped and turned towards his mark. Something, at the last second, whispered dissatisfaction to him and a jerk of the wheel came at the same time as a leap backward by the pedestrian. Only one tire hit anything and that was an unintended curb, but he'd come close, too close. Obviously, someone wasn't happy.

"What the FUCK! I have the light to cross! Are you tryin' to kill somebody?"

The response to that came from a sinister-looking mouth, "I didn't see you. Maybe you should smile, it's dark out."

For only a moment, the man on the sidewalk was taken aback. The attacks he was used to were often more subtle. This one was blatant; overt and unexpected. When the man reacted to it, his self-control was slipping away from him despite himself.

"What did you just say? What the hell is wrong with you?"

At that point, the driver threw open his door and sprawled out of the car. "I said that if you had skin a few shades lighter, you'd be safe on the streets at night."

"Look, my dude, you gonna mess around and pick the wrong one and get slept! I suggest you take your ass on outta here!"

Considering the appearance of the instigator, that warning should have been enough to end it. It was not. He fumed there next to his car, tall and lanky with too big hands and feet and too little, thinning, light-colored hair. What was there, hung limply down a long neck but neglected the top of his head. A jagged face glared back at his intended "first" as he continued his provocation.

"No! Recognize the Deliverer and the red tide rising! You should have rendered to Charon beforehand and kept me from the temptation but you refused!" He continued on while slowly moving to the front of his car, curiously circling away from his very confused target. "Fate begged for you on this island concrete and my triumph came that much closer! Twenty, twenty steps to Goodnight…"

Although he couldn't help but be mesmerized, he quickly recognized that he was dealing with someone that was unbalanced, so the man that had been minding his own business, decided it was best to continue doing so.

"Alright man, I'll go my way and you go yours." He said in a pacifying tone.

"You're of mud…"

"Whatever man, I'm giving you a chance now get the hell outta here."

"You'll soon return to it…"

"What?"

"Come to the dark butcher's block that I've picked for you boy!"

The attempts to control his anger and listen to an inner reason were all demolished with that one word. He'd been backing away from the crazed man but sometimes being baited was much easier than remaining restrained.

"Watch who you call boy mutha fucker, I will drag your ass up and down this block!"

"How simply controlled it is! Drag me! Come on… you ni…"

With just that one syllable escaping the ranting man's mouth, he found himself being charged at. His spin was awkward but intentional. He'd taken off down the darkened walkway between the two corner buildings nearest to them. That was his intention from the start, that's why he'd positioned himself to the front of his car; he'd gained just enough head-start to succeed.

Footsteps loudly filled the darkness, their echoes bouncing back off of the buildings as quickly as they fell. The only apparent witnesses to what was about to happen were small and scurried away. The chase was short due to the surroundings, but the lure was always the intention; escape was never desired.

"Now what?" was asked aggressively. "Where are you gonna go now Bitch-ass?" Coming up behind the pale lanky man, a forceful shove drove him face-first into old and ruddy brick. Then another shove came.

Despite the attacks, the pallid instigator refused to face the man he'd provoked into the conflict in the first place. His head sunk low in the dark and his arms closed around him, seemingly in an effort of self-protection.

"That's what I thought. You're a bitch-ass with a big mouth that can't back it up." he accused.

"That's not the moniker of the Blue-blood-the *superior*.", he responded over his shoulder in a low, warning tone.

There was a similar sensation that the two men shared; one who stood motionless, back turned and tense, and one man closing the gap, angered and intent.

What they both felt was anticipation.

Then, a purposeful hand shot out, grabbing most of a shoulder and some amount of stringy hair, spinning the thin man on his heels. To his surprise, that anticipation he'd felt a moment ago stalled in him; not from a sobering second thought, but from a chilling trepidation. That new fear came from the crazed expression that he was met with.

The dynamic had changed just that quickly.

Arms that before were thought to have been crossed to protect his body, shot outward followed by two distinct metallic 'schnict' sounds as blades were opened and driven into and between the ribs of the grim driver's intended "First".

With a ghastly inhalation, the man that was only moments ago walking toward the rest of his life saw the end of it instead.

Dismay and a punctured lung accounted for the weakened defense he tried to mount. An ineffective struggle to free himself ended before it began. The victim's aggression was stripped from him by the surprise, leaving only a terror-stricken look to counter the killer's crazed own. The clarity of hindsight made him try to turn and retreat back toward where he'd come from. That path was taken from him.

The almost careful manner in which he was guided down to the ground was contradictory to the brutal attack he'd just faced.

His assailant's grin was a giddy horror.

"Now, let me teach you the last lesson. You were the first toll-the premier sacrifice and the last insight. How does it feel? What must it be like on that side of the knife? Don't answer! I'll insert the aspects that I choose to complete this. As for what you called me..." he trailed off.

The patrol car rounded the corner, headed in the direction of the station with the promise of another unremarkable night nearly behind them and a familiar and heated discussion between them. The topic didn't matter to either as long as it passed the time and they got the chance to exercise their arguing skills.

They were halfway up the block before the scene ahead of them caught either's attention and put their friendly squabble on hold. Officer Donaldson was behind the wheel and reacted first by holding up a hand and then hitting the brakes. Their suspicions were aimed at the car ahead of them parked in mid-turn with the driver's door swung wide. They exchanged a leery glance.

Officer Ingram spoke first saying, "Pull up behind."

Both exited the car with the usual wariness. Donaldson circled around the rear end as Ingram made her way to the passenger side, hand on holster. A beam from the flashlight revealed nothing. The car was as empty as the streets.

DING-DING! A bell attached to the corner store's entrance rang loudly in the late-night quiet, startling three people. Two of them had guns.

"Whoa! Take it easy, I work here!" A middle-aged and somewhat round man raised his hands begrudgingly and offered information before he was even asked. "This is my store. I'm just leaving for the night."

Officer Ingram interjected, "That car, do you know where the driver is? Do you know who left it there?"

"No, I don't know. It's not my car..."

"Yes sir, we figured that." Officer Donaldson stated."But did you see somebody get out of it?"

"I ain't seen nobody. I mean, not really. I did see two guys out here a while ago but I didn't pay 'em any mind." the shop owner relayed.

Ingram followed up with, "What were they doing?"

"I'm not sure...they were talking. They did kinda look like they were getting a little heated though. Maybe they coulda been fighting, I mean arguing a little. I don't know. I was busy closing up."

"What did these two guys look like?" Officer Donaldson pressed.

"Uh, well, one was just a regular guy, kinda skinny I guess, and the other was a big col- uh, a black guy. I didn't really see anything else. I didn't pay no attention to where they went. Like I said, I didn't think nothin' of it."

"Ok, sir. Fine, you can go. Thanks." Officer Ingram ushered him away with practiced politeness. Then, the two officers scanned the area quickly and conversed non-verbally, deciding to move toward the walkway behind that shop.

First, they made their way casually, without cause for alarm; they were in investigation mode. They stepped on the plot of dirt/dead grass that you find along most city sidewalks and then crossed the cracked concrete.

At the building's edge, their bodies froze, straining to both identify what they were hearing and to rate the potential threat.

Several steps away, through barely moon-touched darkness, a conversation continued.

"You called me "Bitch-ass" before. You held no reverence in your tone." With that said, he withdrew the blade that he'd impaled the dying man with. The left side of his body spilled dark red down. His other side still had a blade buried to the hilt.

Continuing, he grimly stated, "Flay..." All he received back was a gasping breath and panicked eyes. The understanding he'd wanted didn't materialize.

"Flay! Don't call me "Bitch-ass", I'm to be known as Flay!" As before, he followed up his command with a cut. The anticipation he'd imagined in the preceding weeks paled to the experience and all restraint faded. With elation, cut after cut fell and with no life left to struggle, the first victim understood the intended meaning of the word "Flay". He knew and he cried.

It had, up to that point, been a relatively quiet attack and murder. That was before giddy laughter began to echo down the alleyway.

That's what drew the officers in.

Two brilliant beams shone on Flay and his first kill and then chaos erupted.

"Don't fuckin' move!"

"Hands up! Hands up!"

"Put the weapon down! Drop it! Drop it!"

The man calling himself Flay chose to heed the first command and made himself into a hideous statue. He knew that he had no exit and he knew enough to surrender despite his desires. With slow and deliberate movement, he tossed his weapon aside and submitted to arrest.

"On your fuckin' stomach now!" Donaldson ordered.

Offering no resistance, Flay spoke in a voice that contradicted the situation immensely, saying, "I won't fight you officer. Why would I?"

Donaldson pressed a spiteful knee into his back and began to fumble with his handcuffs due to the amount of adrenaline coursing through him.

"Shut the hell up, maggot." Ingram shot back at him; gun trained.

"There's no crime here. I did nothing worse than an extermination. Look at him. But look at us, we're the same."

"She told you to shut your..." Mitchell Donaldson trailed off before he could finish his thought. He'd noticed something. The forceful twisting of the perp's arm revealed an important puzzle piece.

"Annie, look at this." He directed his partner's gaze with his flashlight.

When she shone her own on the same spot, clarity hit her just as it had hit her partner. There, on his pale and boney shoulder, was a tattoo; a tattoo that resonated with the three of them.

Officer Ingram tested him by asking, "What have you got to say to us?"

"I only have **five words**..." Flay responded.

"I have **fourteen words** I always say myself.", Ingram called back to him. "Take the cuffs off Mitch."

Her partner's only response came in the form of a wicked grin and quick concurrence.

Without anything left to say between them, the man calling himself Flay got up, retrieved his second knife from the dead black man's side, and moved to leave. With a second glance down, he stooped, violently yanking something from around his victim's neck. Through gnashed teeth, he said, "You won't need this. Not that it did you any good. But-you can *rest* in it." Then, he stood to continue his exit. Nodding appreciatively, he strode back to the car he'd left on the road.

"Look at this bloodbath Annie. I haven't seen anything like this since that summer in holding a few years back."

With that, they both chuckled fondly.

"Yeah, he did a job on this boy..." She said without compassion.

"Fuckin' A. Probably deserved it. What play do we run?", Donaldson inquired.

"Same one that Shapiro ran about a year ago," Anne Ingram stated with familiarity. "Let's pull out one of the "plant guns", pop one into his black ass, and dig up some low-life gang-bangin' Homey to pin it on. You know that black-on-black crime is on the rise..."

They both laughed out loud, but the solitary figure that had been hiding deep in the shadows and out of sight did not; only the sound of a long-held gasp escaped.

At that, two bright beams were spun around and shone along the back of the alley. Those two searched for the source of the sound that could prove disastrous for the pair.

"Yeah, I thought I heard it too..." Ingram confirmed.

"You see anything?"

"No.", she replied. After a brief inspection, she cautioned her partner against letting the light reveal either of their faces. The fact that it was past too late for that didn't occur to either. Then, Officer Ingram decided to let a threat free to probe the darkness; a warning designed to dissuade.

Loudly she said, "You know, if anyone did witness anything that they misconstrued as wrongful, and they mistakenly linked either one of us to that, there would be nowhere that they could go that we'd be unable to find them!"

Donaldson understood and played along asserting, "Yeah, that's for damn sure. We can dig 'em up anywhere. But we'd just bury 'em again."

"Right next to anyone else they knew that might have been persuaded to believe lies."

Those words were left to hang in the air. It was meant to intimidate and it did just that, all too well.

They both began to move forward slowly then, intent on searching more thoroughly. Only the sound of another patrol pulling up the short distance away and sounding their siren stopped them from advancing. With a look, they mentally solidified their story and turned back to make an account of the situation.

A bated exhalation came softly from a dark hiding spot as the two turned and moved away. That went unheard; the witness went unseen.

SYMMETRY LOST

PART I: PREMEDITATION

The sorrowful ordeal of an unjust and involuntary transition wrought turmoil.

A jumble of disordered images and vague impressions surged at one time, erratically, resulting in unacceptable disarray.

"Stop!", came from a chorus of voices in unison.

"The sibling has a verse to contribute but her state is deficient. Her impressions and urgings cause undo discordance. Discordance impugns veracity. We desire that you, instead, start from the beginning and exercise clarity."

"Once!"

"Twice!"

"Thrice!"

The ruling body- *The Thrice*, stated their pronouncement authoritatively in their unique way of voicing their concurrence.

The desperation of the situation made the attempt to communicate the long series of events that had taken place chaotic at best. But, in the condition that Raquel, his twin sister was in, how could she be faulted for it. Their asses were on the line so, stepping up, he chose to speak on their behalf.

"I am willing to relay everything I can...as best as I can piece it all together." he offered.

"Rafael Dos Santos-We accept and encourage you to consider the import of rectitude.", the Thrice stated in response.

A host of concerns weighed on him as he took note of the figures surrounding them. All manner of intimidation seemed gathered around his sister and him; an assortment of figures exuding power and the threat of finality. In some ways, some of them were dazzling. Others only held depthless darkness.

The sides appeared to be drawn as each faced down an opponent. Each of them threatened others and they all threatened Rafael and Raquel.

He was not at all clear how he knew the exact depth of peril he was in, but the fact of it was not in doubt. His sister and his welfare were on the line. The combatants stood in readiness and Rafael was fearful; perhaps even more so of the Thrice; the judiciary body tasked with assigning judgment.

That faction had just demanded a thing from Rafael; his truth.

And so, he began.

"A little over a year ago, things took an unfortunate- turn. It started and ended with a blowout..."

The music was furious but fitting.

Opponents squared up and executed their attacks fiercely. One by one each threw powerful strikes with practiced technique and precision, only giving way once they realized that they'd been outmatched.

Rafael Dos Santos was at the center of it all.

His considerable skill was being tested. Masterfully, he'd execute a flip to escape a blow only to deal one of his own in return. Defying gravity, he outmaneuvered everyone that came at him.

Rafael's black dreads swung wildly, matching the way his arms and legs cut the air. His stocky V-shaped upper torso dodged attacks and responded quickly and obediently to his extensive training.

Without exception, he displayed superiority. That is until the last man leapt into the fray.

A lesson had just begun. Rafael did what he could, and he did it well, but the outcome was inevitable. He was going to be bested; and quickly.

"O suficiente!" was loudly declared in Portuguese.

Rafael's Mestre called it. The music stopped precisely on the beat and the combatants immediately followed suit. The mock battle was done. The players were all fought out.

The class was over.

With a unified cheer, the members of Capoeira Collective North reveled in what they'd just done. Their demonstration was one of their finest. Students and instructors alike performed at the height of each one's ability and were left drained from the effort.

Rafael smiled brightly behind a perfectly trimmed beard. He had cause to be proud. Everyone offered congratulations, back slaps, and hugs.

With all of the 'see you next times' said, a few of the academy's members hurriedly showered, dressed, and broke through the front door, determined to make the most of the rest of the night.

Footfalls echoed off of the concrete and grating as they ran, heading for the corner parking lot. The smell of fresh food wafting from the neighborhood diners overcame them and a setting sun highlighted the differing hues of their brown skin.

"It's ON!" a close friend of Rafael's named Mateo shouted at the oblivious pedestrians nearby.

"I've been waiting for tonight! Somebody is gonna have to pour me into my bed- if I make it home!" came from J.P. - the guy playing catch-up behind the first.

"Easy Bruh, let's all come out of this alive." Rafael tried to maintain his leadership role, as usual, at least initially. A knowing smirk between the three of them, repeated quite frequently in the past, broke that illusion.

Together, the friends chuckled as if they were kids again. The group was on its way for a much-deserved blow-out to start the weekend and to celebrate.

"Alright," Raf began, "The plan is to get to the bar, hook up with everyone else, and party our asses into the record book of oblivion!"

After a chortle and a pause, J.P. thought he'd try his luck by asking, "So, when you say 'Hook-up', does that include Raquel? 'Cause, if I'm keepin' it One Hundred, I've been tryin' to do that for a minute!"

A sneer and a warning were Rafael's go-to responses for anyone reckless enough to move on his sister.

"Do you want me to replay what just happened in class? Keep your shameful thoughts and hands off my sister." Rafael said it with a smile but meant it with earnestness.

"You know how protective he is of her man! What're you thinkin' bro?"

The three laughed loudly.

Rafael continued by saying something that they'd all gotten very used to hearing regarding his safeguarded twin sister.

He said frankly, "I just hope she shows up even somewhat on time tonight."

Doors were thrown open wildly at The Diaspora Dance Academy as a blur of a woman flew through them. That blur bounded into the open, and into a cloudless and unusually warm early March dusk.

Raquel Dos Santos had been brought on as an instructor recently, teaching others poise and polish. But class was over now and she moved gracefully, her long black braided hair trailing behind her, for a different purpose.

She was petite but her athleticism would have been apparent to anyone watching as she did a mid-air split down the remaining bottom stairs. The day was good, her mood was good, and her evening promised to be good as well.

Raquel had an appointment to keep.

With excited speed, she circled her car, threw her things and herself in (twice - because she missed the first attempt), and tore out of the spot with the sound of tires chirping. She was on her way but timewasn't on her side and neither was her driving
ability. Unfortunately for her, and her car, her grace was reserved for the dancefloor.

The front end found that out quickly as she hopped the curb turning the first corner. The rear end learned the day before on a different curb.

Raquel needed to make a twenty-minute trip in ten and she drove like it.

Over the next fifteen minutes, there were several questionable choices regarding intersections, multiple pissed-off drivers, a couple of tail-gaiting incidents with accompanying break-checks, and exactly two monstrous potholes. All-in-all not an unusual trip for her.

Coming to a customary screeching halt at the first spot she found, she failed miserably trying to jump out because of the seatbelt she'd forgotten to undo.

After freeing herself, she ran half a block toward a small brick building painted white that had a bright red and inviting awning over the entrance; the bakery where she'd had her appointment. That appointment had regrettably come and gone.

Raquel knew she was late but she wasn't easily deterred. First came a respectful but urgent knocking. Then, the kicking started.

"Hello! I'm sorry I'm late but this is an emergency! Hello? C'mon, it's only one minute (she lied, knowing it was more like ten). I just need to pick up my cake."

No response came from inside.

"Aw, man! Son of a flippin'...Monkey balls!"

The little shop was dark with the exception of a single light coming through what was assumed to be the kitchen; that must have been the back office. After the outburst that had just happened, that was turned out as well.

Turning away with a dramatic slump, Raquel had to question her next move.

A quick look to the right gave her no ideas. Another look to the left offered more of the same. That was the direction of her car so she headed dejectedly that way.

She was lost in her thoughts and aimlessly walking. There was no plan B. She'd missed the window to pick up the gift she'd planned on for a week. Raquel had never been known for her promptness and this incident only added to her already lengthy "tardy portfolio". Normally, it may have been laughed off. But Raquel didn't find it amusing at all. A few colorful mutterings flew from her tight lips as she went.

Preoccupied, she failed to notice the rumbling truck that had pulled up across the street and behind her. More direly, she also failed to notice the person driving it who'd been watching hungrily from the beginning.

Just then, in front of her, a door flew outward with no warning and a piercing scream flew out with it. That came from a rather tiny figure that hopped hurriedly down three small steps, landed awkwardly, and bounced off of Raquel's hip before plopping to the ground.

Before anything else could happen, the little girl sprang up again, unfazed and oblivious, and the shrill screaming commenced, followed by hopping.

"Honey are you OK? What's wrong? Are you...?" Raquel asked almost in hysterics. Her concern was two-part: why and what was the child running from and had she been hurt when she was knocked down.

That door burst open again and a lovely lady came out with a recognizable expression aimed directly at the hopping child. The woman was probably just a little older than herself, Raquel thought, but she had the "Mom glare" down pat. That look stopped everything, but only for a moment. The screaming started again.

"I'm so sorry! I didn't mean to bump her! She's OK...You're OK right?" rambled out of Raquel apologetically.

"Don't apologize, please. It's not your fault. She knows better than to run ahead of me like that!" At that point, the little girl ran over to her mother, never slowing her hopping for a second, and it became clear that she wasn't in pain or running away from anything; it was unbridled excitement that was on display there on the sidewalk. The cause of that excitement had just been revealed as well; a MEOW sounded and a tiny black furry head poked itself out of a purse at the lady's side.

The little girl had obviously just picked up her new kitten and her screams were of delight.

"OH-MY-GOD!" Raquel said as she began to hop, hand in hand with her new friend, equally excited.

"Mommy! Mommy! Mommy...!"

"What, Sweetie, what...?" the woman with her answered in a soft, lilting voice.

"Can I hold her? Can I?"

Looking down on the little girl put a smile on Raquel's face for a second reason. The child's eyes were wide, spirited, and light brown like hers. The girl's caramel-colored skin also matched her own. Two long and some-what wild ponytails flopped around with each bounce she took and the way she was dressed reminded her of her own youth; her blue tutu over pink denim paired with baby Chuckie T's and a tiny little black leather jacket screamed free spirit. Yes, Raquel saw herself in the girl and she loved it.

In contrast, the woman she only knew up to that point as "Mommy" projected all of the things that Raquel wished to be. The sophisticated Asian woman standing near her was dressed in a flowing ankle-length black skirt, slit up the side, that was intended to display both elegance and sexiness, and it succeeded. The hue of her complexion matched her daughter's and her own version of rebellious cool was on display in the black leather boots that showed when the wind blew. In her, softness and confidence were not mutually exclusive.

Then, her spell was broken when the woman responded to the earlier question: "No. Let's wait to take her out and play with this little one when we get home. We'll have a very long time to play with her."

"Okay." Came with an expected sense of disappointment.

"So," Raquel began, "Where did she come from? I mean the kitten not your daughter- I mean I know where daughters come from..."

A sincere laugh passed between them and then she was answered with, "We actually just picked her up from a woman who lives in that building."

"Awww." Was Raquel's response.

"It's actually kind of a special present." She continued in a more hushed tone. "You see, my husband is going out of town for a while soon, he does that a lot, and we both thought this might be a pleasant distraction."

"I understand. Separation anxiety and all that..."

"Yes, exactly." Just then, the lovely lady took notice of Raquel's outfit and her expression brightened even more. She fought to steal her daughter's attention away from the tiny black Meow machine so that she could make her aware, finally succeeding with, "Look, she's a dancer!" as she pointed at Raquel's attire.

Endgame Trilogy

That worked and the child froze, then she spun to look, instantly recognizing her as a dancer too. Then, the familiar little scream she made before sounded again, followed by a bearhug.

With another laugh, her mother matter-of-factly stated, "Yeah, she's not a shy one." Then, she continued what she'd been saying, "So, we searched and searched, but we only wanted to get a rescue or adopt a new-born..."

"Right, I know what you mean."

"Yes! Right? So, we finally found Mrs. Eyote, that's the lady upstairs, on an app. She had a fresh litter born recently and we have our very own little house panther now, don't we?"

"Yeah!" came from an elated eight-year-old.

A spark of inspiration made its way into Raquel then. "A little house panther...?" she repeated.

"That's- AWESOME! You've just given me the best idea! See, I was supposed to be here, well, over there, for an appointment and I was only late by – like – one minute. Okay, maybe ten minutes - but I was here! But they wouldn't let me in, and I know they were there, but they wouldn't let me in! So, now I don't have the cake for my brother!"

"Cake...?"

"Yes! See, there's a celebration tonight and I was supposed to get the cake. But now I'm empty-handed. Look at my hands...Empty!"

"I see that. What's the celebration for? What's the occasion?" the lady asked.

"It's for Rafael, my twin brother. Oh, I'm Raquel by the way. See, I'm a dancer, as you already know. I teach at the Academy downtown. He, my bro, also teaches. Not officially, up till now."

"Oh, so you both teach dancing?"

"No, he doesn't dance." She chuckled. "He says it's for girls. No, he teaches martial arts. He teaches Capoeira. Today, he'll move from Graduado to Formado/instructor at only 20 years old. Now it's official. OH! and, it's also our Birthday! So of course, we have to celebrate!"

"That sounds amazing! Oh, and I'm Kristina by the way. This wonderous kid is Sophia."

"Hiiii." Sophia chimed in.

"But I don't see where the kitten comes in.", Kristina admitted.

"Oh yeah. Well, like you said before, 'Now we have a little house panther'. Rafael is known as 'El Pantera' by everyone that knows him. See? Pantera...? Panther...? Pantera...? That means panther...Panther is a cat..."

"Ohhh! I see." Kristina said enlightened.

"So, since I couldn't get the cake-it was supposed to have this great picture of a leaping panther on it- you gave me the idea to get the actual thing!" Raquel relayed

excitedly before a realization hit her; "Wait, did the lady have any more cats?"

"It's a good thing you were late or you never would have met us and you never would have been able to go up those stairs and get the very last kitten that Mrs. Eyote had left.", Kristina said with a smile.

Then, simultaneously and without rehearsal, the three of them all began to jump and cheer a little.

Raquel exclaimed, "I'm so glad I'm never on time! One thing though; won't it be strange for me to go up there without letting her know beforehand?"

"No, no. It'll be fine. Just tell her that you know me and that I referred you to her. She's so nice, just the sweetest little old lady, and she'll be fine with it. She's on the second floor, apartment 208. See that window?" she said with the requisite gesture. "That's her place."

"You think, maybe you could come up with me and introduce me?"

"No, I can't Hon'. We have to get back now. Remember, I mentioned my husband was going out of town for a short time? Well, we're going out tonight and then we have a little celebrating of our own to do. Wink-Wink.", She spoke the gesture aloud.

"I know what you mean Mommy! You're gross."

Laughter erupted.

"I gotcha.", Raquel responded. "Okay, I'll go up and take that kitten off her hands. Rafael will be so surprised. It was great to meet you! You too Sophia! I hope we run into each other again!"

"I was thinking..." Kristina said pensively. "This little one has taken a few classes here and there over the last year and she's done very well. Maybe she could benefit from a little time at your dance academy."

"I know she'd love it! I'd love to have her!" Raquel said shooting Sophia an endearing wink.

With that, they exchanged each other's information as well as hugs usually reserved for old friends, and said their goodbyes, fully expecting to see each other again soon.

That was another's intention as well.

Raquel then made her way into the building, up the steep stairs, down the hall, and to the door of a certain Mrs. Eyote; cat owner. Just before she began to knock, a familiar tune began to fill the hallway. The music was coming, loudly, from inside the apartment. After an almost hesitant knock, the door was opened by a small and adorable Indigenous woman with dark skin and graying hair.

"Mrs. Eyote? Kristina sent me up. I'd like to take the kitten that you have and give it a home if that's okay?"

"Come in Dear. Come in." was her welcoming reply.

The air inside bore the faint scent of cleansers as she entered and the sound of Sinatra that had filled the hallway became muffled again as the door closed behind them.

"Clarity is more apparent in this iteration, would that it had started in this fashion.", came with a unified tone from the Thrice.

"This Body counsels continuation in like manner."

His and his sister's situation hadn't changed. She was at his back and he'd taken the same protective stance that he'd always taken for her; willingly. Unknown but seemingly formidable figures faced them and threatened them. He thought the group was motionless initially but they, in fact, oscillated where they were nearly imperceptibly. Then, the thought that they had also moved nearer to them occurred to him.

But a new illumination coming from behind stole his attention away. Despite his desire, he was unable to turn to see where the light was coming from. His focus again was ahead of him and on the prospect of conflict.

Conflict...he mused.

He went within himself for an unclear amount of time then.

"Yeah, conflict...I know you too well." He either thought or spoke aloud. The uncertainty of it wasn't given weight then and there.

A short life of vicissitudes had made the two siblings more familiar with conflict than they deserved to be. Two very unfit parents forced the twins into a system of tokenized adoption, force-fed religion, and what should have been criminal up-rooting. That up-rooting removed them from their home in Sao Paulo and irreverently dropped them into the suburbs of Chicago.

Their age left them unprepared for the relentless objectification that their brown skin and foreign tongues would face.

'Time can sharpen or dull', he thought, remembering wise words he'd heard. His life lessons had sharpened and strengthened him. His sister's experiences had not done the same. She was sensitive and delicate but she was protected without being naïve because Rafael had always seen to it. He always would.

Despite their many attempts, those that sought to hurt the twins were rarely if ever a match for them. Raquel's speed allowed her to escape the kids that underestimated her and her intelligence tricked them into following her to wherever her brother was waiting; the results of which was an inescapable beating for them.

As they aged, a natural if unintentional assimilation occurred and some sense of detente became the norm. Those many lessons in conflict were learned and ingrained by that point though.

"Yeah, I know all about conflict..." Rafael confirmed to himself.

"Oh, but this is going to be the pinnacle and paramount!" was offered in response to what he'd thought was unstated.

Just before those words were spoken, he realized that a rapid, pulsing, clicking sound had erupted. It was penetrating. There was no indication that anyone else present acknowledged it though, despite his feeling that it had been overwhelming.

The voice was new and menacing and contained too much excitement at the prospect ahead. Who'd said it? How did that person know his unspoken thought?

That was his initial question, but then...

"Clarity prevails.", was intimated by the Thrice. "All combatants will remain in neutral as that very thing is cultivated. The term 'blowout' was insinuated to be the impetus. Now, elaborate further."

Rafael gathered himself and reached back with the intent to take his sister's hand again; reestablishing their connection. He then offered, "Well, in this case, that can and does refer to a couple of things. See, the occasion was festive and the party was ragin'!"

There seemed to be a perfect balance to the room.

Anyone who's ever been to a bar or a club knows that the ingredients to a perfect atmosphere are tenuous at best. If there is too little background, then the conversations are stifled for lack of privacy. Suppose the entertainment is deafening; no one is able to communicate above the din.

That night, there was balance.

A group of students and instructors from the dojo were meeting to celebrate Rafael's promotion as well as the twins' birthday. The room was the kind of spot that told its long history by the things that lined the walls. Pictures of celebrated musicians, posters of infamous concert dates, stickers from an untold number of wannabe hopefuls, and various other items that shared their stories all spoke together, claiming a collective and undeniable reputation.

The lighting of the room suited itself perfectly to scope out the intended targets for the night. The level of conversation was loud enough to maintain intimacy but also allow for just as much raucousness as needed. Glasses clinked and the mood was upbeat throughout.

To the back of the long room, there was a band playing furiously. That group captivated the crowd with intense, and at times, aggressive sounds. The audience cheered and clapped without urging, and Rafael's table didn't hold back any enthusiasm at all.

The band's leader controlled the gathering masterfully and charismatically and the whole band followed his lead. Their skill capped off the symbiosis of the elements in that room.

The weekend had come, and with it, the drinking followed.

Rafael and his friends were having a blast and their worries were far from them then. The place was in perfect balance for at least a moment.

Raquel hadn't shown up though. But her unfailing lateness had taught everyone that knew her to reserve their concern for at least an hour.

Across town, Raquel was just finishing what began as a simple transaction and turned into a very lengthy but pleasant visit. Cat in hand, she bound down the stairs in both excitement and urgency because she knew she was behind, again and as usual.

The sun had long since set by that time and what had been charming in the daylight, was now unfamiliar in the darkness.

She made her way back, circled the car, threw open the door, and caught herself; she remembered the little one she was carrying and set him down, gently, in the passenger seat. Then, her usual hecticness returned as she flopped down on the driver's side, intending to speed away. Before both legs were in and the door could even be slammed, she noticed something was clearly wrong.

Either someone had tilted the entire road, or she'd inadvertently parked in a sinkhole. She quickly got out to investigate.

Eyes wide in disbelief, Raquel looked down on the two bafflingly flat tires staring back at her. The cussing flowed freely!

The first attempt to call for help ended with a redirection to voicemail and so did the third and the fourth. On the fifth attempt, her phone conspired with her tires and died. With that, her heart sank and helplessness began to overcome her.

Headlights came on up the street and across from her. Engrossed in her dilemma, she never noticed it. The sound of a diesel engine grew as it left the spot where it had been parked like something stalking. Pulling up akimbo, in the opposite lane, a loud voice called out to Raquel.

"You OK Miss? Is there anything wrong?"

She turned, startled, torn between wariness and relief. She responded, "Well, I actually have a flat. Arrghh!" Her frustration had gotten the best of her.

"That's terrible. I'm sorry about that. Let me pull around.", The man driving offered.

"No, no, thanks. I have someone coming." She lied, still unsure.

"I would feel like a horrible human being to leave you out here. Please, let me take a look. I'm just finishing my shift and it's perfect timing that I drove by."

That's when Raquel took notice of the fact that her would-be helper was sitting in a tow truck. Maybe it was an extremely fortunate coincidence that he'd pulled up. Options were limited. She needed help. He seemed nice.

"Yes, please and thank you."

At that, the corners of his mouth curved sinisterly. In the darkening day, that went unnoticed. The engine whined and rose as he spun around to park beside her. The tow truck's hazards went on then as it was parked just ahead of her car. As he stepped out, Raquel fought the urge to judge her rescuer on appearances.

He looked like a scarecrow that migrated from the deep south but hadn't adjusted to the city yet. He was lankiness and grime. But his manner contradicted that in every way.

"Well, let's take a look and get you on your way. I hate the thought of you being out here by yourself, waiting for who knows how long."

"Yeah, I hate that thought too." She replied with a nervous giggle.

"If you pop the trunk for me, I'll get the spare and have you fixed expeditiously." He offered.

"Here's the thing; I actually have two flats. Not one like any normal person would- but two!"

"Oh nooo. Talk about bad luck for you." He said with a forced concern that she couldn't recognize. "Well, how long do you think you'll be out here waiting for your ride to show up?" he probed.

"Honestly? I couldn't get anyone to pick up and then my phone died. Yes, my phone frickin' died! No one knows I'm stuck." At that point, she slumped down inside her car.

As he looked down on her, his true intent flashed across his face and narrowed eyes lost their disguise for just a moment.

But Raquel was looking away just then.

"The temp is dropping out here...You can't stay out here alone. What are you gonna do?" The question was only for her benefit. A hand moved to his inner pocket and one step toward her was taken then.

"I don't really know. I can't do anything without my phone. My bro's partying without me...I have to get this car off of the street..."

"I know what. I could drop you off if you'd like. And then... I can tow the car to a shop that I work out of. I don't mind."

"No, thanks, but I couldn't ask you to do that. I'd feel weird about it." She stated quite honestly.

"It's not a problem. I like to do good things when I can. I strive to do the work of the angels. It couldn't be that far."

"Uh, no. Really, I live pretty far."

"Really? What town?" he pressed.

Before she could think better of it, she answered honestly with, "Woodbridge."

"Woodbridge?" he repeated. "The shop I work out of is only one town past that. That's only another fifteen-minute drive. I'm not getting any other jobs and I was gonna call it a night. You're on my way home. Anyway, I wouldn't be able to live with myself if I left you alone."

His persistence was endearing. Raquel allowed herself to see more savior than threat. She began to welcome the ride. She started to accept but she first corrected him.

"Oh, I'm not totally alone..." she informed as she stood and faced him, presenting her new acquisition.

In mirrored panic, the would-be good Samaritan and the tiny house panther reacted to each other. For something as small as the kitten, it responded in the harshest most violent way possible. Without reason, the hissing began and something guttural rose out and was directed toward the man.

His response was to recoil in inordinate terror. He screamed a sound that shouldn't have come from a man and began to trip over his own large feet, trying to distance himself.

"Oh my God!" Raquel blurted out.

In a calculated attempt, a lie was constructed to save both face and the opportunity he desired. He claimed, "I...I...I'm really sorry. I'm really allergic to cats. Last time one rubbed up on me, I...wound up in the hospital."

With sincere regret, she offered an apology. Then, it occurred to her that the offer for a ride had probably just been revoked. She said, "I guess I'll have to find another way home."

"No!" he shouted, realizing that his reaction was far too abrupt. "Couldn't you just...get rid of it? Then we can be on our way."

"No, I can't do that! I just adopted this little guy and he's a gift. He'd never survive out here by himself. You're joking right?" Raquel asked.

The wheels had already been put in motion and his intent was something he found impossible to subvert. No, the opportunity presented itself and to his mind, the enticement was too powerful. His scheming mind decided on a new plan of action. In time, maybe a way to separate the two would be found.

"Of course, I was joking. I...I couldn't leave you here. If you would just keep it away from me..."

"Oh, I will. No problem. He's going right into my purse right now."

The pale and strained face he allowed to show through began to revert back to the contrived façade that he intended her to see all along.

"Great. You can go ahead and get into the truck and I'll hook up the car. We'll be on our way in no time."

"Ok. Thank you."

The door swung open with the sound of metal on metal. That was not a surprise considering the look of the truck. Climbing up into the rig was initially a challenge but quickly overcome. Being the first time in a truck like that, she had different expectations to be sure. But Raquel was amazed at exactly how clean and orderly that interior was; a real contrast to the outside.

While her car was being lifted, Raquel found that her curiosity got the better of her. The urge to snoop overcame her and she knew there wasn't much time to do it. Besides, she rationalized it; it was also a way to ease any insecurities she had about taking a ride from a stranger. And the snooping began.

Nothing was found.

The glove compartment was empty. The small storage under the armrest was as clean as new as well. Not even the requisite crumbled old fast-food napkins or wadded-up paperwork could be pulled from between the seats. That in-of-itself was a little odd to her. But his cleanliness did not equal a threat.

The only item of interest to be found was hanging from the rear-view mirror. Reaching up, Raquel playfully flicked the peace-sign necklace that swung there freely. The sentiment of it struck her in the moment as something to regard as reassuring. The truth of its origin would have proven horrific if it would have been known.

Satisfied for the most part, the window was rolled down enough to see behind. She put her head through and stated, "Um, you didn't tell me your name yet."

The sound of the towbar engaging cut through the air first, then an answer came, "Tucker."

"Ok, hi Tucker. I'm Raquel by the way."

No response came that she heard but it was quickly written off as being drowned out by the truck. She watched in the rear-view mirror as her new friend began to circle around to the driver's side. Before he reached the door, remarkably, her cellphone sounded a sharp alarm that scared her to her core, and a searing light that seemed to be reflected in the mirror blind-ed her and forced her eyes closed. In that split second, something more startling happened.

SACRIFICE!

The word seemed to be screamed-in her- at her- to her.

The distinctly feminine voice resonated inexplicably between her temples and forced a slight scream out of Raquel. Who it was remained unclear; the fact of it though was quite certain.

Understandably agitated, she spun in her seat, confused at how her dead cell managed to let out an alarm that she hadn't set, searching for the source of the single ominous word.

Only the driver's door opening snapped her back into the present.

"Did you..." she trailed off because there was no way at all to convey the question she wanted to without alienation. So, she thought better of it.

Preoccupied with an agenda of his own, the man climbed in without the slightest acknowledgment, asking, for the most part, rhetorically, "Ready to head out?"

Her answer came while staring, wide-eyed, forward, and wasn't much more than a distracted nod. Just like he'd said, the car was hooked up quickly, raised, and they were moving.

If not for each of their preoccupations, the stark silence between them would have been uncomfortable. But they both stared forward without question, lost in their individual thoughts.

A side glance from the driver's side eventually led to a cleared throat, and then to a silence-breaking question.

"You're not afraid, are you?" was offered.

"What...?" was said distractedly.

"Because, you shouldn't be, ya know. I mean, this will be painless." He said without inflection.

"I'm sorry, what were you asking?"

"You weren't saying anything, so I just thought you might have been having second thoughts about getting into a tow-truck, at night, miles from home, with some man that you didn't know even a little bit..."

A wary side-eye was all that Raquel could muster.

His laugh lacked humor despite his desires.

"Ha, ha. Just teasin' you. I...just wanted to cut through the ice."

His weak attempt had done nothing to make him seem less off-putting. Raquel tensed where she sat and he perceived that. The journey had just begun and he knew that it was far too soon for the level of unease between them. So, he tried another calculated tactic.

"Are you saved?" he posed the question reverently.

"Am I...saved? You mean...Oh, I'm not really religious. I mean, not that there's anything wrong with anyone that is." She added in an attempt to ward off any conflict.

"It's not too late for you."

"What do you mean?"

"Give yourself to your maker. Surrender. Allow his will to direct the rest of your life and you'll be set free." He entreated with a suggestive tone.

"I'd rather not get into a religious discussion, OK? I mean, it's just not something I usually think about."

As an indication of how unaware he truly was, the zeal in what he wished to convey only worked to effectively alienate his passenger further.

"Oh. Ok then. Your soul means more to me, I guess. I'll pray for it though. Rest assured. But I'll do it silently. I won't broach the subject again." He offered with another leering smirk that only created unease.

"Thanks for understanding." With that, she attempted her own distraction by posing the question, "Sooo...You been doing this long?"

"Doing what? What do you mean?" was fired back with a suspicious undertone.

"Umm...towing. Have you been towing long?"

"Oh, yeah. I've been doin' this for a long time I guess." He stated simply.

"What did you think I meant?" Raquel posed.

"Nothing. I thought that's what you meant." The lie was obvious but meant to be left unexposed.

It seemed that the awkwardness of it all had been agreed upon and accepted after that point. For a short time at least, they both rode in silence, aware that it was probably for the best.

MEOW!

That muffled little cry unexpectedly broke through and caused a minor panic in the driver. First, there was a violent swerve and then there was a pothole.

"I'm sorry!" was blurted out by both of them, simultaneously. That was followed by the slightest of shared chuckles.

"Jinx!" Raquel exclaimed first to counter their talking in unison.

"You got me!" was said in an attempt to both play his part and allay his passenger's fear.

"Yeah, good times..." came from Raquel then. She let out her own little semi-humorous laugh then. The mood had been inadvertently lightened and she wanted to keep it that way.

"Listen," she began with just a little hesitancy, "I know you mentioned taking the car back to your shop but, the truth is, I can't afford to do that. I don't want to be any trouble but, my brother can just take care of it. Can't you drop it, and me, off where I stay?"

A sincere attempt was made to hide the dismay she'd just caused in him. But, to reveal any amount of irritation at the request would have surely raised her defenses. That could not be allowed if he was to make his tithe that night. So, he complied with forced friendliness.

Raquel took some small amount of comfort in the fact that she recognized the areas they were driving through. She noticed the gyros place she loved as she passed by. Then the flower shop that she bought a rose bouquet for her grandmother was passed. The sound of the tires rolling over grated iron echoed through the cab as they crossed over a short bridge.

While they rode, they both settled and remained quiet; engrossed in their own respective thoughts. Neither sought to disrupt that peace.

She knew that they were headed toward her place and the thought of meeting up at the club began to excite her.

'It shouldn't be long now.' she thought.

Almost unconsciously, the third little black passenger in that truck was taken out surreptitiously and the scratching of tiny ears was begun. That was soothing to both.

"Waiting for my twin to show up was, historically, a past-time. Our group of friends was used to it as I've said, but it had been hours and we'd gotten restless by that point. The big difference that time was that it didn't seem like she was coming at all. There was no word from her. There was no outlandish texted excuse. The band was winding down and so were we. So, we made our way outside to get some air. It was a quarter to midnight."

"What a blowout!" one friend roared to no one in particular.

"Hell yeah!" came from another in response.

"Hey! Hey! What about Raquel? Remember her?" a close friend of hers named Shea asked soberly.

Raf initially offered her a furtive smile, as they so often exchanged, their mutual attraction yet to be explored. Timing was the issue and that moment was, again, off. He then answered her, "I still can't get through-phone has got to be dead."

One of their lesser evolved friends remarked, "I hope it's just the phone that's dead...". The alcohol was only partially to blame.

Just like many times in the past, they all peppered him with slaps and insults as payment. He wasn't surprised; he never was.

The ruckus they were causing just then took a turn to seriousness when the group began to notice a real issue that was beginning to go down.

Toward the end of the building, a slight, scruffy man began to raise his voice. The target was a much larger guy, dressed in a black coat and jeans that were tucked into combat boots holding a flashlight in one hand and the smaller man's neck in the other.

"Get off me man!" came in a pleading tone.

"I've told you already to get on! Get your raggedy-ass out of here! Nobody is gonna give you any money you bum-bitch!" was fired back in an unsympathetic tone.

Because they knew him well, the response from Rafael's group was as predictable as his intentions.

"Oh, here we go."

"Shit's about to pop off now."

"You know he can't help himself."

Raf turned in the direction of the struggle and they fell in step behind him. The funny thing was that he wasn't anticipating what was about to go down. He was still wondering where Raquel was. His concern was purely for her.

The clock on the dash read 11:25 PM and the ride was almost over. After being given a few directions, the tow truck turned the final corner, headed for the Dos Santos' home.

"Patience.", was muttered so softly by the driver that it went unheard. He was through biding his time. He reasoned then that it was dark, it was late, and the neighborhood was empty. There was a deep determination to reap some merited reward from the delay of that unwanted trip. He assured himself that the restraint he'd exercised would be rewarded.

The car was backed in, lowered, and unhooked hastily. All the while, Raquel sat quietly, not knowing that her acquaintance was searching for a believable pretense. When nothing came to him, he decided to go with pure deception, knowing he could rely on that.

"Well," he baited, "You're safely home now. I'm sure you want to go inside and let the day's woes pass, right?" Raquel, having been lulled by that point, couldn't agree fast enough.

"Yeah, I definitely need to chill for a minute or two or three..." she replied with a laugh.

"That...little one...with you must be very hungry by now. I'll let you go - so you can take it inside."

"I really appreciate everything you did for me. I don't know how to thank you enough." Raquel said.

"You don't have to. My reward is at hand.", came with a cryptic grin.

"Ok, thanks again."

To his horror, Raquel raised the kitten she'd been shielding the entire trip to his face and offered its goodbye in her most precious and saccharine voice, opened the passenger door, and stepped out, moving toward her house.

That elicited a reaction she hadn't anticipated.

Initially, it seemed as if the truck was pulling away. It moved down the short driveway and onto the street, stopping abruptly, only one house down.

With a twisted grimace, clenched muscles, and soulless eyes, the driver's side door was thrown open as he moved intently.

Raquel was unaware of the vile intent aimed at her as she wrestled with her keys and the door. Twenty steps behind...fifteen steps behind. The pace was steady and calculated, intended to match her entry.

He began to reach for something familiar then; something that pleaded for atrocities. He moved faster, obediently. He still hadn't been heard.

Just inside the doorway, with her body only partially inside and her arm twisting to reach for the lights, the distance was closed.

Simultaneously, the lights were turned on, the little black cat was set down, and footsteps from behind were finally noticed.

The reality of the situation became clear to her.

Before the door could be slammed, it was violently kicked against her. A scream was begun and stifled before it could fully form as she saw her attacker kick the cat, hatefully, under a piece of furniture.

"Finally! I had to subvert my instinctive nature for that entire ride! Finally, you were parted from your would-be guardian!" His rage then turned to her, and her scream found its opportunity.

He pounced.

She fought him intensely. She couldn't have grown up the way she had without learning how to put up a fight. Her spirit was strong and he was a weak excuse for a man. Despite her effort, he was crazed by that point and began to gain the upper hand. His bone-like fingers pressed over Raquel's mouth to prevent her outcry. They were filthy and the smell of engine oil assaulted her senses.

When he imagined that she'd resigned herself to him, he leaned close and sought to whither her resolve completely.

"Now, whisper your ending to me..." was snarled at her through gnashed teeth.

At that moment, to the surprise of each of them, the roar of an engine came from the driveway. In a thoughtless panic, the lamp nearest to him was violently thrown down, darkening the room again except for the revealing moonlight beaming through the opened entrance.

That mistake gave Raquel opportunity, and her shrill voice cut through the dark.

"No! No! Flay has you! I won't be denied! The time is now! Now! Don't think you can take my sacrifice! Mine! Now! Mine! Stop it...Quiet...Quiet..." her attacker rambled.

Those short moments were enough; a silhouetted figure burst through the doorway and threw itself at them both. Through the sounds of grunts, furniture being toppled, and curses being thrown, Raquel got to her feet and made it to another light. When that flooded the room again, she re-joined the fight.

Outnumbered and outmatched, her would-be killer broke free and hurled first a chair, and then himself through the front room's large picture window without the time to calculate the cost in pain.

Raquel started to run after him unadvisedly but was stopped and reminded of the foolishness by a familiar voice.

"Babe! Stop!"

Spinning around, the adrenaline faded and was replaced by recognition and joy.

"Casey!"

Initially, she didn't realize that he'd been holding onto her arm; tightly. When it became clear to her, she threw herself into him completely and he wrapped her up willingly.

Urgently, they both spun to find a lanky and damaged silhouette of a man rise and fall unsteadily, repeatedly stumbling toward the still-running truck.

"Mutha...!" the young man with her began. He was torn between the desire to ensure Raquel's safety and the desire for retribution.

"Casey, don't." Raquel urged.

She looked up at her unexpected rescuer; her grad-student boyfriend that swore to her the day before that he was completely overrun with work, that he couldn't get away that week, and that he'd have to miss her brother's and her party.

"Babe, are you hurt? Who the hell was that? Did he hurt you?"

"I don't think so. I think I'm good..."

"We have to get the cops here now! We have to get an ambulance! We've got to call..."

"No cops!" Raquel blurted out frantically.

"What?" Casey questioned. "What do you mean no cops?"

"No police! I don't want to talk to any police! Do not call them!"

He stared in bewilderment and she returned an unshakeable insistence back at him.

"Just get me to my brother...Please."

He didn't have to fully understand to know that she needed him to simply do it. Arguing the point was not going to calm her at all, so he rightly chose her well-being. Re-visiting the thought of getting the authorities involved could always be brought up again.

Outside the club, as the group of friends made their way closer to the commotion, it became clear that Rafael would not remain neutral. The larger man was obviously hired security for the nightclub, but the reason for what appeared to be pure harassment wasn't as clear.

"I got no more warnings for you, old man." He said with a shove for emphasis. For whatever reason, neither his size nor his threats made an impression on his scruffy-looking opponent.

"Who do you think you are, huh?" was the small man's defiant response. "What, you think I'm just some garbage or somethin'?"

"Leave- now.", The guard growled back at him.

"Kiss my entire..." was begun.

Before another word could be said, the club security fell on the man. From the beginning, he had no chance. His age, his size, and his insobriety all worked against him. The security guard snatched a dirty coat and shirt all at once in one hand and closed the other into a fist.

That was enough for Rafael.

Deftly, the distance was closed and he caught the bouncer's cocked arm in his own, preventing a pummeling. The surprise on the bouncer's face was quickly replaced with pure anger. But, to his credit, some degree of reason seemed to kick in.

With a relaxed arm and a relaxed jaw, he offered his advice to Rafael, "I suggest you go back inside, Sir, you don't know what's going on here and you don't need to get involved."

"Too late. Get off him."

For a brief time, the entire group of spectators silently agreed not to blink or breathe; waiting for what would happen next.

They didn't wait long.

Violently, with a thrust, the older man was pushed aside and a fierce right cross was hurled at Rafael. It didn't land. With the ease of experience, the martial arts instructor, newly promoted, ducked and side-stepped the next blow. He then saw an opening and he took it.

The kick stunned the bouncer but he was too big a man to be stopped with just one. He kept coming, and he was not completely unskilled himself. A jab landed on Rafael's chin that sent him into a rage.

The two men fought as members of the crowd both cheered and tried to stop it. Eventually, the animus spilled into the other on-lookers and several other brawls sprang up. The old man that was the cause of the conflict even jumped back in, wrapping himself around the bouncer frailly, only to separate himself quickly and skulk out of the scene again, heading toward a shadowed corner of the building; an inappropriate smile on his dirty face.

No one there witnessed the errant transaction that took place in that cloaking darkness. That man turned out to be little more than a self-interested instigator. His price was collected from a devious figure whose paleness was apparent even in that concealed place. That dispassionate individual extended an equally pale hand and dropped some small amount of money to the ground, followed by a bottle that miraculously survived the initial hit against the concrete, only to crack on the bounce as it hit again. Like something ravenous, the instigator pounced, clawing the ground for the money, and drinking despite the broken edges that threatened him. His bleak benefactor looked on with satisfaction as Rafael fought, reaching down to stroke the wayward man's head like a pet.

Not long into the fight, a car came around the corner on two wheels and screeched tires, stopping in the middle of the street.

Both Casey and Raquel knew their group was in the middle of the struggle. Immediately, they identified her brother and tried to reach him.

"Raf! Raf!" his sister called out. But he didn't hear her and he fought on. Casey took the lead then and pulled her through the raucous crowd. When they got close enough, she tried to reach him again yelling, "Raf stop it! I need…"

Her thought went unfinished as, like before, the phone that had been completely out of power flashed and sounded an alarm. In wonder, her attention was turned away from her brother as the sound of two disagreeing voices filled her head. Their conversation was piercing.

"You'll corrupt her natural essence!" came in a distant-sounding female voice.

"You reference the Nature in vanity! You yourself are corruption; she will imbue vision!" was retorted with conviction in a second dulcet and bodiless female voice.

As they continued, Raquel must have looked insane to those around her as she spun desperately searching for the source of those voices.

To her amazement, she found it.

At her back, she found two spectral figures inexplicably elevated above the crowd surrounding the brawl.

One of them was heavy-set and dressed in what could be described as a woman's business suit, although it was overly tight as well as overly revealing. It reflected several colors and seemed iridescent. Oddly, her skin was both a dark brown and also a pale whitish-pink combination. It quickly occurred to Raquel that it might be vitiligo.

The other was a contrast; she was petite with dark and flawless skin, large expressive eyes, and elaborate braiding in her hair. Her clothing appeared to be African-like attire, in white, with a flowing outer skirt over a shorter more fitted skirt. Even under that, she seemed to be wearing matching leggings. Raquel was spellbound. She would be stunning to anyone.

Then, the bizarreness of what she was seeing set in.

Raquel began to panic. She started to hyper-ventilate. She then began to scream as the two apparitions looked down at her and through her.

Several of her friends took notice of her panic and sought to make Rafael aware. Then, they got help in that task from an unwanted source.

Lights blanketed the area and sirens sounded all around as the police rolled up in force. The fight was ended immediately as self-preservation became much more important. Everyone began to scatter!

As Rafael sought to separate himself, the condition of his twin was pointed out. It was necessary to fight through the rush of bystanders to get to her.

"Did you see? Did you hear them?" she repeated to no one over and over. She appeared to demand a response but directed the question to the open sky around her.

Terrified and flustered, she could not be calmed.

Rafael quickly reached her, grabbing both of her shoulders, he gently tried to shake her out of it to no avail. Then, he recognized Casey, demanding, "What the hell is going on with her?"

"I don't know man! She just started freakin' out! It's been a fucked-up night though. You have no idea! We need to move- NOW!"

As the police fell on the crowd, their group, collectively, came to an understanding and split up. Each of them knew what to do. Rafael scooped up Raquel and followed her boyfriend back to the car they'd left open and running in the middle of the street. In seconds, they were off and avoided any and all police entanglements.

As they sped down the road and away from the night's excitement, Raquel remained detached. She continued to mutter quietly but inconsolably about the voices and visions.

It was a long, curving, and uneven gravel road that led back to his home. He bounced expressionlessly, stone-faced the entire length of that ride. Trees overhung the way and cast shadows like wicked fingers. Nothing but the engine broke the silence; it was as if nature shuddered frightfully as the vehicle passed through it.

Far from his more urban hunting grounds, the wooded and isolated area provided the perfect retreat. It misleadingly made him appear serene. But there was another thing that made him so intensely stoic; his earlier defeat. He hadn't remotely begun to express his displeasure at that point.

The truck crawled to a stop. The engine droned for only a minute and then was shut off. Then; nothing. There were no sounds of insects or animals and there were no other people to be heard. Not even his own breathing, because it was so shallow, broke the quiet.

Metal on metal changed everything as the door swung open. Yet, he still sat there; corpse-like.

A ranch-style house stared out in his direction with the expected amount of disrepair. No lights were on. No pets waited inside.

Climbing down from the truck, his body screamed out in malaise as he moved away from the front door and to the back of the lot.

There, surrounded by unkempt trees, was a shed. A padlock was distractedly fumbled with and eventually overcome. In he went with only the slightest of a creak behind him.

He stood in near-total darkness; unafraid because he was exactly that.

When lights were turned on, only three things were in the small space; one chair, one table, and in the corner, one human figure.

The figure had never been alive though. It was the kind of mannequin used for medical training, but this particular one had been crudely painted; darkened.

Grotesquely, it had been hung from the ceiling by the neck and splayed out, each limb ornately tied in a torturous manner.

Initially, Flay sat at the table. He sat there and began to allow the failure he'd experienced earlier to affect him. His chest began to heave and his head began to shake defiantly to no one.

Unable to maintain, his body jerked up to take only two steps forward toward the hanging effigy.

"I am an obedient servant! Please don't accuse me of that!" he pleaded. His protestations were not to the figure in front of him.

"Believe me, I will be equal to your urgings!"

His bowed head waved stringy pale hair back and forth in denial of some inaudible allegation. So, he sought a way to prove otherwise.

"As many times as you ask, I will provide your tithe. Each time you instruct me to, I will prove I'm devout. Watch me!"

With that, two blades were drawn and after a distinctly ridiculous bow, he attacked. The hung mannequin took stab after stab and slice after slice.

To his mind, he performed a fluid dance of death and precision, but the reality of it was solely and completely awkwardness and ineptitude. His limbs were graceless and his cuts were wildly inaccurate. It was the depth of his delusion that masked his perception.

Spent, he turned only partway back toward the table, apparently in deference, to look into the mirror above it. There, looking back at him, was a slight but menacing figure of a man. His paleness was obvious even in the dimness of that small shed.

Malicious eyes looked down and penetrated Flay but he seemed to be satisfied for the moment as the slightest of smiles came across his pointed face.

Peering out at Flay, the image behind the glass spoke to him then, silently. His mouth urged him soundlessly and his expression demanded his compliance without question.

Flay nodded furiously, his limp hair swinging wildly, unaware of how pathetic he appeared. His only consideration was the task he was being set on.

"I couldn't agree more. My new target is clear to me. I will redeem them both. I listened back there... I heard while I stood by...I know how to find them!"

Just a single nod was given before the figure behind the glass stepped backward and was erased from sight.

"Your inspiration is always my guide. Thank you. Thank you!" Flay said.

Given a new objective, his earlier failure was forgotten, at least for a time. His murderous purpose had been reignited.

"The house seemed different even in the few hours since I'd been there.", Rafael noted, continuing his accounting to the Thrice.

When they pulled up to their home, the events of the night had altered the twins' dispositions drastically, and the change was palpable. Rafael insisted on entering first, but that gesture was completely unnecessary because Raquel refused to go in at all. She was only persuaded not to bolt by Casey, as her brother walked toward the house guardedly.

Once inside, his imagination painted a picture that he prayed wouldn't be borne out by his sister's telling. As he surveyed the damage, the scene played out in his mind, and the thought that he hadn't been there to protect Raquel enraged him.

Overturned furniture and the shattered glass that covered the front room, as well as the grass, spoke to the ordeal she'd been through.

His anger flared. After countless times in their past that he was there for her, this was the most urgent and yet was also his most ineffective.

The initial impulse to allow his disgust to explode, as it had so many times in the past, had to be tempered for the sake of his sister. He knew he couldn't let her be any more upset than she'd been. So, he turned it inward and took on the strife of it as he so often chose to do; with the flask.

Trying to hide what he was doing, he turned away from her gaze and upended the small metal container long enough to subdue what he felt.

After the short task of clearing the rest of the house, he gave the signal that it was safe to the two waiting outside. Hesitantly, they went in.

"I need to know what happened here." Rafael stated delicately with attempted consideration.

She relayed the cake debacle and the flat tires. She mentioned the ride home by what she thought was someone decent, but instead turned out to be living evil. The belief that she'd made it home safe at the time was stated only to be dispelled by the attack that she described in uncomfortable detail. The telling of it all came from Raquel much more stoically than it should have. Casey attributed that to shock, having witnessed some of it himself, but he was wrong. Her preoccupation was the true cause.

She went on to tell of meeting up with her brother and wound down her story by absently saying, "And then the voices were arguing..."

"Wait, what...?" her boyfriend asked.

"...And the two of them looked down with, I would say, displeasure at me."

"Who looked down?" Casey questioned.

"At least that's how it seemed to me. Part beauty-part fury..."

Rafael and Casey turned to each other with justified confusion. The look they shared confirmed that they were missing a very necessary puzzle piece. Their concern had to go unvoiced for her sake though.

MEOW!

"What the...?" Rafael blurted out.

"Oh, did I forget to mention your present bro?"

A new member to join the conversation added his tiny voice as he came from under a chair and into the light. Despite his mistreatment earlier, he was no worse for wear. Hunger was his only concern just then.

"Que es esto Raquel?"

"That- is why I missed the party. This is your present. Now we have our own little house panther. I bought him today to surprise you. Flay didn't like him at all though..." she trailed off.

Both her boyfriend and her brother quietly agreed not to pursue the obvious then. The night had taken its toll.

"So, El Pantera has a mini-me huh? I love it!" Casey offered.

"Yeah, Raq, I love it too. Thanks. This little guy is just what I needed. But it's late. Don't you think it might be a good idea to call it a night?"

"Look at what he did. I have to fix this mess." Raquel countered.

"No, I've got this. Go on up and let me take care of it. Casey, take her up, would you?"

"Come on baby, let your man tuck you in.", he said, knowing full well that she'd never rest that night.

A week passed and a routine, seemingly, settled back into place. Casey returned to his college out of necessity, and his check-ins with Raquel came like clockwork, despite her insistence.

Rafael began to excel in his new position as expected and Raquel had turned her focus to her own students. There was a degree of order on the surface, but disorder was waiting to be uncovered. A crew of workers was hired to repair the front façade of their home but little progress was being made on the other façade that Raquel was presenting.

Her brother made attempt after attempt to relieve the burden of that recent night but she continued to withhold certain details; preferring not to re-live it.

Her forced smile was still as lovely but remained completely unconvincing. That fact amplified the regret and guilt that wrestled within him. His answers were, too often, sought in the wrong place.

So, a different type of dance began; one of avoidance.

The next morning, they exchanged the normal greetings, or sleepy grunting as the case may be, and headed off in their different directions as usual. Rafael watched as his twin got into her car and pulled off, in her usual rushed and reckless manner. Once out of sight, his hand slipped into his inner pocket and pulled out his first consoling of the day; his silver flask. Then, he sped off himself.

Since only the workmen were left to notice, with a roaring engine, a third vehicle slowly pulled away from the parked position it held several yards up the block. With no reason to suspect anything different, those men couldn't have recognized the treachery.

It wasn't a long drive to the Dance Academy and Raquel pulled up, parked, and turned off the engine. She'd gotten into the habit of sitting in silence, at least for a short time, before entering the building.

That effort was not for her in any way, it was in fact, for her students. What she felt could not be translated to those children she nurtured and mentored in even the slightest of ways. So, she worked to center herself.

The quiet lasted just long enough for it to be jarring when her phone sounded a piercing alarm. With a start, she tried to silence it, then she realized that she had no memory of setting it at all.

WITLESS BITCH!

She screamed at the sound of that voice.

It came to her clearly and hostilely and it wasn't completely unfamiliar. The night of the attack, Raquel had heard the same bitterness. Now, sitting alone in her car, it assailed her again.

Don't think that you can stave off your turning!

"What the hell!" Raquel began to panic.

Indeed- which Hell indeed...?

Spinning and twisting in the seat, she sought the source of what she was hearing, to, of course, find nothing and no one. Without thought of anything but distancing herself, the door was thrown open and a sprint for the building began.

She burst through the Academy doors, never once looking back, only narrowly avoiding colliding with two figures standing together. Initially, she was oblivious to her name being called out. Then her mind cleared.

"Raquel! Hey, slow down!" a familiar voice urged.

Recognition came then, as she saw her new friends, Kristina and her daughter Sophia. They'd been in contact and, just as they'd discussed, Sophia was registered at the school and had come for her first class.

"You can't be that late girl, it's not even 10 o'clock yet. What's goin' on?" Kristina asked with a smile.

"Uh, nothing...nothing." Raquel began shakily before gathering herself and displaying her usual infectious smile. "I'm so sorry. Just a...crazy...morning, ya know? How are you little one? Are you ready to dazzle everyone?"

"I'm SO ready!" Sophia responded with uncontained excitement.

"Awesome. You can go on in the rehearsal room and I'll be in there in just a minute."

Kristina ushered her daughter inside and then turned back to Raquel. With graceful strides of her own, she walked back to her with concern written in her expression.

"Hey, I didn't want to say anything in front of Sophia but I can see that something is obviously bothering you. Is it something that you can talk about?" Kristina asked, sincerely.

"I...well..." She began to respond honestly until she realized that she didn't know how to begin to relay what had occurred. How could she when the reality of it was something that she questioned herself? What happened only moments ago was, strangely, both removed from her as well as physically present in the form of an undefinable pressure in her head; or possibly her mind.

"It's nothing. Believe me, I would tell you if there was something to tell."

"All I can do is promise to listen.", Kristina assured.

"And I promise to let you if ever I need to. Thanks."

With those mutual promises, and a hug, the day was started, and their friendship grew.

The following days played out, for the most part, the same way. In short time, the two women began to meet before class for coffee, or in Sophia's case, various juices. They had become close quickly.

After class, they often stayed behind, talking and laughing as if it had been that way for years instead of several weeks. The mild Spring allowed for pleasant meals under the sun outside of their favorite local café. They would share stories of brothers and husbands, and boyfriends and sometimes, of little black kittens.

When it was time to go their own way, Raquel remained unaware of the vile shadow that had latched onto her. She never perceived the menace that had been following her from place to place. She never connected the sound of a whining, aging car engine to the threat to her safety.

After the standard gossip and giggling, Kristina and Raquel said their goodbyes and pulled out of the lot, one behind the other, headed for their respective homes. At the light, as they'd done many times before, one turned right and the other left.

The whining motor that had been invariably present, followed even more closely than usual, turned left, trailing the car of an unsuspecting mother and daughter.

Her car was pulled up to the curb and parked, unusually, without incident. The short drive was uneventful, which did nothing at all to explain away the foreboding Raquel was experiencing.

For a while, she made no move to get out. Her mind meandered between thoughts and sounds from recent days that had gone unexplained, to something like vacantness. The dusk outside framed her mindset and a slight chill began to convince her to find her way inside.

Once there, her belongings were tossed to the side without consideration and a somewhat purposeless wandering from room to room was begun. First, mail was picked up and set aside without being read. After that, a single stroke was all that was allotted to the resident little black house panther. Then, the refrigerator found itself opened but nothing was taken.

It didn't take long at all for Rafael to see that his twin was profoundly preoccupied. Assuming that it was something he had no interest in at all, his first thought was to ignore her. But he then thought better of it.

"Hey, wake up! What's the matter Raq?"

"Huh? Nothing...I'm just..." she never finished the sentence.

"What? Was there a problem at work?" he pressed.

"No, not at all. I was just feeling...I don't know...I can't explain it. I feel uneasy." She relayed somewhat exasperated.

"I told you about that volcano hot sauce! You're gonna go for one of those *plié* things at work and the crowd is gonna get something they didn't bargain for!"

"Shut up Jackass! You're so gross!" she pointed out for the millionth time.

She continued, "I was talking to my friend after class and she invited me to come by her place. She was having a girl's night and asked if I wanted to join her and her daughter. I guess they're alone for a few days."

"What does that mean? Who's usually with them?"

"Her husband. I told you before, he's a musician and I guess he's away, on the road again, gigging now."

"Yeah, and...?" Raf urged.

"And nothing. I asked for a raincheck and now I'm standing here talking to my dumb brother. I have some work to prepare for next week's competition anyway. I'll catch up with them next week in class.", She stated.

"Oh great, a happy ending!", he teased, only to be answered with a light punch.

"I still don't know why you're walking around all zombie-like." Raf pointed out to no answer.

"What?" came distractedly.

"You see my point?"

"What?" she repeated totally unaware.

"Raq! What's going on with you?"

"I don't know! Haven't you ever just felt- off?"

Before an answer could be given at her expense, she quickly raised a hand to silence her brother. The look on her face had changed from the prerequisite annoyance between siblings to concern and confusion, all in an instant.

With worry visibly noticeable in her eyes, she questioned Raf, asking him quietly, "Did you hear that?"

A shrill siren song broadcast through the cool evening air as an ambulance carved its way through the streets. An urgency just short of recklessness was surging through a racing heart as well as a racing engine.

It was a warm Spring and that brought people out of their homes, intent on enjoying the mild weather. That meant traffic needed to be overcome.

"Watch it, Ramirez! I'm not trying to be the one back there on that stretcher!" came from a nervous young EMT.

"*Cálmate* 'Rook', you can take a nap if I'm scaring you. I promise I'll wake you up when we get to the call." the driver replied.

Daniella Ramirez had been an Emergency Medical Technician for a number of years and had supervised a number of newbies. Each time, she had to demonstrate the difference between her real-world knowledge and their adherence to textbook guidelines. Each time, she brought them into the light, kicking and screaming if she had to.

She continued to their destination without another objection from her partner. The rig arrived at the scene with lights flashing but the siren silenced. Dusk was lingering, dimly highlighting the building as they pulled up. The three-story loft was in an old and scenic neighborhood on the Northside of the city. The area was well kept, but the residents were not wealthy. That block had, in fact, been earnestly fighting gentrification as best it could.

Ramirez and her fresh partner, Reese, maneuvered through the few police cruisers on hand and parked directly in front of the walkway leading up to the building. With purpose, they set themselves to the task.

The initial presence of the cops must have drawn some attention to the situation because there were a handful of people, presumably neighbors, gathered around. But there were still more police officers than observers as best as Daniella could tell.

Out of the rig, equipment in hand, stretcher in tow, they moved.

"Third floor, back bedroom." A random cop directed.

When the lift doors opened, the EMTs were moving quickly and were met by another cop keeping stride; he ran down the situation.

"We've got two victims in the far bedroom; we can assume that it's mother and daughter. Mom is approximately 25 to 30 years old and the daughter is about seven or eight I'd guess. We're getting them ID'd now. Massive trauma from a bladed weapon is what it looks like.", he rattled off before moving away to confer with another officer.

Daniella Ramirez directed Reese, saying, "You start on the child and I'll take the mother."

"On it!" was his response.

As they went about their efforts, the police kept enough distance as to not hinder their work, but remained close enough to see and be clearly heard.

Ramirez listened over her shoulder.

"This is the third attack like this in -what- a little over two months, isn't it?" One officer stated.

"Yeah, this does look similar to those.", her counterpart responded.

Another observer offered his take stating, "It does look connected; victims cut to bloody pieces and left for dead."

"First, it was that Indian guy-what was his name? Elijah Little Hawk, I think...Then, what was it... Ernesto Camillo, then there was the girl with that African name...", his partner interjected.

The first officer corrected their memory saying, "No, this is number four. You forgot the first one; the black guy four months ago- Darnell Brown. Remember, they found him in that alley..."

"Hey, uniforms! Break it up!"

Despite her concentrated efforts, Daniella's attention was stolen by the two new participants to join the discussion.

The woman that had just silenced the others was a squarish, unfeminine-looking woman with blonde hair pulled back in a tight braid. Her counterpart looked imposing and irritable under his stubbled jaw and crew cut.

She continued, "I'm Ingram-this is Donaldson. First of all, unless I'm mistaken, none of you have got a shield, right? So, keep your speculations to yourself. Second, that 'black guy' in the alley was just a banger offed by some other cholo or homeboy. There's no connection. Got it? Now, I want this room cleared if you're not in the process of saving a life."

The patrolmen knew their superiors, as well as beat cops could know detectives. Their ranks didn't mix. Despite that, they did know their position in the pecking order. They did as they were instructed and filed out silently.

Donaldson glared down at the last cop to exit and turned his attention to Daniella, saying dryly, "Hey you, what's her condition?"

"She's barely alive with massive blood loss from stabs and lacerations and I've done all I can here and now. We've got to move them both Asap if there's any hope of survival."

"HEY! NUMBNUTS!!"

Donaldson looked past her and directed sudden aggression toward an officer that passed them who'd seemed intent on remaining inconspicuous. His rant continued with, "We both saw who won that game last night! Pay me my money or you'll find yourself waking up in a hole somewhere!"

Daniella attempted to corral the distracted cop again.

"Listen, like I said...", she began.

"Watch that tone senorita! You're not runnin' nothin' around here. But guess who is."

Reluctantly, Daniella bit her tongue for her patient's sake and responded with self-effacing deference. She then stated, "I-need to get them out to the rig and moving. Is there any other info that you need to gather, or is it OK to take them down now- *Sir*?"

"Fine." He acknowledged, "Move 'em."

With that, the young mother and her lovely child were lifted and the transport began as Reese continued trying tirelessly to keep the two stable.

They moved out through the loft, past a beautiful piano, into the lift, and down and out past the reprimanded cops. By that time, a larger crowd had gathered. The sun was nearly set and faces were beginning to be obscured.

Ingram and Donaldson followed the EMTs down and after seeing the milling onlookers, began instructing everyone to disperse.

The crowd's response was sluggish due to the fact that some of those present had knowledge of the victims. Murmurs moved throughout them in somber tones filled with sympathy as they begrudgingly left.

Daniella heard some of the comments as they loaded the ambulance. She heard: "They didn't deserve this." and "It's a shame what they did to that poor girl."

The last things she heard before the rig's door was slammed shut were: "Where was the father? I think he was away..." and "What was their name? I think it was um...Goode...?"

With rediscovered urgency, the ambulance sped off toward the hospital.

Soon, most of the crowd had been ushered away. As Detectives Anne Ingram and Mitchell Donaldson surveyed the scene, their eyes met another's on the far side of the property.

A spindly, tall, and pale man with long equally pale hair stood a few paces behind the remaining onlookers, avoiding the notice of most. The two detectives were not so oblivious. Their recognition of that man went unacted upon and their knowing glance toward each other went unnoticed as the other officials there went about their investigations.

As the sun set fully, that cryptic figure stepped back into the shadows near him and wasn't seen again.

Endgame Trilogy

SYMPHONY:

PART 1: THE DESCENDING

Solitude brought out the worst in me.

The noise of life has a way of dulling the realizations of circumstance. "Everyday things" distract, often, from the damning truths that cause a person pain. When those things are taken away, and you're left with nothing but your own mocking thoughts, you can be suffocated with the weight of them.

That was happening to me.

I was ceasing part by part, like an orchestra winding its way through a sorrowful song, a section at a time ending its line, until the last tragic note. I was smart enough to see what was happening but too weak to be able to control it. That fact made it worse. Because I lacked the ability to control my fate, or myself, my self-loathing was fueled. All I could do was succumb.

So, I withdrew into solitude. The whirlpool is vicious.

For too long, I sat on the edge of the bed, head in hands, my mind desolate.

How long-how long had it been?

More than a year had passed since I confined myself to my cold loft with the bottle and a little black cat for companions.

And there I sat.

Because of that solitude, I'd become two very separate people; one man feeling profound emotions unwillingly- and one who was standing apart, cataloging the experience without any idea of how to effect a change for the other. One surrendered to numbing apathy and one to utter detachment, although it could be argued that those were actually the same state. The only truly common factor the two shared was that neither was whole.

And there I sat...

Without purpose, I droned my way through each hour I was unfortunately awake, just waiting for a dull and restless sleep to overtake me. That became my routine.

For the most part, I tuned out to escape my truth. Just like my spirit, my mind and body were lethargic and so I initially didn't notice when the phone rang. I had no intention of answering it though, and I let the machine pick up.

Over that small echoing speaker, I heard a grating voice say, "This message is for Mr. Devlin Goode. This is in regards to a past due- ". That was all I needed to hear, and I turned it off with a fist. It was pointless to humor the thought of paying bills because I had no money at all.

I hadn't taken a gig or sold a single sketch or painting for months. All the past due notices and calls in the world wouldn't change my account balance. So, my strategy of ignoring continued.

Aggravated, I stood and moved aimlessly out into the apartment to find a different place to sit thoughtlessly. After standing in the middle of the living room for a moment, fighting against my initial intention of avoidance, I broke down and went to sit at the piano. At some point that seemed very distant to me, I loved that piano. There were times when I played until I had only the strength to stand up and stumble away. There were also many times when I didn't play at all, but instead, stood there staring at it, etching every curve of it into my mind and spirit. This time was different from those. This time I felt reluctant to hear a single note. It had lost all familiarity to me. But the thought that somehow, I might recover some vague or lost part of me through the playing of that piano tried to make itself heard in the back of my mind. Eventually, I gave in and listened to that thought. With disinterest, I gave it its chance.

I touched the keys but didn't hear music. My fingers moved over that piano strictly from habit, from repetition, but there was no melody, only struggle. The feeling was like total emptiness. If I had been outside of myself at that time, I would have seen a man that appeared hollow. Out of frustration, I slammed my hands down repeatedly, until I noticed the pain, and ended my depraved concerto.

As I sat there, I questioned myself: was I truly unhappy, or was I stuck in a morass of self-pity? Did even being able to ask that question mean that it answered itself? No! It was just the opposite. The uncertainty was a symptom of a real problem, not some self-created drama.

'SHUT UP YOU FUCK! YOU DON'T KNOW SHIT!

That was what I heard me say to myself.

Maybe I was lost... Maybe I was outside of reality. But perception is reality, and my perception was the only one on the table.

I was alone, for the most part.

I had friends; I had close friends. But things were different.

How many people could say that they had friends for almost their entire life? Very few could. But I could. Although I never lost those few, the relationships had changed. How could they juggle their lives and problems, with my burden thrown in, without allowing one or the other to drop and shatter? How could I ask them to? How would they respond? Would they say that they really didn't have a use for me or my troubles? I'd never know because I'd never ask. No, things were different. They could never go back again. Circumstance had left me on my own.

So, I stalked my apartment like a wraith. All my efforts were put into escapism and admonition. I went from room to room without purpose, but I did not sit down at the piano again.

Instead, I grabbed a new bottle of vodka and stumbled into the bedroom to subdue my thoughts. There was never really any illusion that the drinking would make anything any better, far from it. Despite that truth, I felt that the blur of intoxication was preferable to complete clarity.

Fitfully, I slept.

For me, sleep and booze never equaled rest, quite the opposite. There were moments when I'd come around, admonish myself for it, then fade out of consciousness again. Still, I found no peace. The dreams saw to that. My dreams were as lucid as they were disturbing. When I woke up abruptly, I was on my back in an awkward position with Serenity in her usual spot, curled up between my legs. She almost seemed to feel for me.

It was dark; the clock read 1:18 A.M. Upset about being awake, I let out an obscenity.

The world around me was silent and sleeping as I was just coming to. I'd been trapped in that cycle for a while. My normal pattern had become disrupted and I suffered for it. Although I felt that it was unnatural, and actually hated the altered routine I'd fallen into, I was powerless to change it.

I'd stay up for a day or two at a time until I couldn't see straight, then I'd pass out and sleep for fifteen to twenty hours. When I did drag my ass out of bed, it was the middle of the night. The world around me was on a completely opposite schedule, which just heightened my sense of isolation. Then, that same sense of isolation found reasons to convince me that it was preferable anyway. There was always a reason not to leave the loft or communicate with the world on the other side of the door. The only thing I could have conveyed was anger anyway. I told myself that it didn't matter because I'd become leery of people anyway. I told myself that without being sure I believed it.

So, I took a drink and rolled over, back to oblivion.

The clock read 4:05 P.M.

The sound of the TV had woken me from a troubled sleep. I had to get up quickly, being a slave to my bladder, and disturbed Serenity. When I finished, I went to the window. It looked like the day in late October that it was. The wind was blowing a heavy mournful rhythm against the glass. The dark sky and rain empathically matched my sentiment. In the past I had found solace on days like that, but not then.

The decision had been made.

For all this time, I suppressed this one thought and turned away from its honesty. I treated it like a woman treats the scariest part of a movie. I now realize that I was peeking at it with squinted eyes the whole time. But it had become too demanding to be ignored. Maybe I had lost the will to continue ignoring it, or maybe I'd actually found the will to acknowledge it. Either way, it had finally burrowed its way into my mind.

The decision had been made, and I went about my plans with quiet resolve. I felt that distinct feeling again, of not being a single man going through it. Instead, I was a spectator again. Calmly, I imagined what should have been very disturbing to me. When I closed my eyes, I saw the most evil things being done by ...me! I was intentionally hurting the few people I cared about. They were being murdered, purposefully, by me. There was no reason for what I was thinking but it did verify one thing; my grasp of reality had weakened.

We began to argue with myself.

Our heart told us how unfair it would have been, but our head said it was only meant to save them pain in the end. I didn't want anyone to feel pain because of me, so taking any hurt away beforehand seemed logical; but not enough. How could I know what I would be stealing from them? There was no way! Let it go... Don't think you can decide for others and leave them powerless. That was the whole point of your own misery! Let it go. Which was rational and which was irrational? It wasn't a case of that line becoming blurred; it had become non-existent. It did seem to make sense but...

I didn't know who I was anymore!

What was I thinking? My original plan came back to me, and there was no contention about it. There was no thought at all- no "why" or "if"- only 'how". That came easily. If we all thought about it, we've all at least begun a plan of action in the dark privacy of our thoughts. I was no different. The extent to which we allow ourselves to travel is the only thing that separates us. I saw one way and set myself on that path.

So, I went about my plans because the decision had been made.

I turned the bottle I'd been drinking end-up to numb my body further and lower my resistance. Determined, I swallowed until my throat involuntarily closed in protest.

After recovering, I repeated.

Standing up as best I could, I went out of the bedroom and into the kitchen, there was a full bag of cat food on the shelf- I pulled it down, opened it wide with a sharp knife, and dumped the whole bag into Serenity's bowl. Of course, I'd become a little drunk and clumsy by that point and the food was scattered across the floor. I couldn't make myself care about the mess I'd made which proved that I wasn't myself anymore. Serenity looked up at me and seemed completely uninterested in what should have been a bonanza for her. I was a little surprised. She didn't eat at all but, instead, just followed me to my next task. Walking right at my side, she followed me to the sink.

If I didn't know better, I'd have thought that there was some degree of understanding in her eyes. But I knew better, I thought.

For a while, I stood there at the sink drowning in my own sad thoughts until a seemingly empathetic 'meow' brought me back. That made me remember myself enough to continue with what I was doing. I reached for the faucet. It was easy for Serenity to jump to, and so I turned it on and let it continually flow. She had food and she had water. I couldn't know how long she'd be alone but she'd have what she'd need.

With that done, I moved on to the next task at hand. There were a few things that I needed to get. As I stumbled my way to the bathroom, I took another gulp of vodka, and then I opened the cabinet and took what I needed.

The last stop was the living room. There was one last thing I wanted there.

Absent-mindedly, I stood there for a minute, just looking around, not focused on any one thing, until I remembered myself and saw what I'd come for. Then, I grabbed it, knocking over everything else around it, and moved quickly back to the bedroom. Sitting there on the bed, alone with a calm resolve, I took another long, determined drink.

After I set down what I'd brought from the front room, I began to fumble with what I'd taken from the bathroom. The alcohol was of course affecting my coordination, but I finally got it to cooperate. With an obscenity and some rattling, the pill bottle I'd brought in with me opened almost unwillingly. As I looked down into it, the pills and that bottle became distorted to me. It was almost as if I could have crawled inside of it if I had really tried. The sedatives that I'd been prescribed stared up at me, whispering a new purpose for themselves. They whispered their intentions and I chose to listen. Things had become somewhat less than realistic.

While I was staring down into that bottle, I found myself counting the pills inside... Why...? Did I think I knew the proper number to take and needed to make sure? Did I have some perverse desire to quantify the experience? Or, maybe the situation was doing strange things to my head.

"NO...YA THINK!" I heard me say in my mind. A laugh that was totally humorless came out of me then. That laugh was the sound of dissipated hope. If I could have seen myself, I'd bet that my face had twisted into what looked more like crying than laughing.

I remembered myself again. Then, I looked straight up and said out loud, "Thanks for fuckin' nothin'!" Then I looked straight down and said "Fuck you!" with hate and sincerity. With that said, I emptied those pills into my mouth. It was extremely hard to get them down; I gagged and I choked and hesitated and I spit them back up. But eventually, I forced every one of them back with that vodka and felt exhausted from the struggle.

I dropped the vodka and the pill bottle on the floor, both completely empty, and lay back on the bed. The only perception I had was a profoundly heightened body awareness. The sensation was strange. Somehow, I knew it was a kind of beginning of ending.

There was nothing else to do at that point but wait...

The quiet was obnoxious and, in a way, forced my awareness to, in fact, become more acute. In that short time, I felt a distinct weight from the top of my throat down to my stomach. My guts felt solidified. My heart was coming through my chest and my skin felt like it was trying to pull itself away. As uncomfortable as my body felt, the worst was just beginning.

Contrary to my expectation, my mind was racing! My first thought was to question what the hell I'd just done! That had to be natural for anyone to do in that circumstance so I tried to put it aside. Bit by bit, I began to slip away and my thoughts began to wander.

I wondered who'd find me. I wondered what I'd look like. I wondered what would be said about me. I began to question how many people might care and tried to count in vain. I imagined a fantasy of Serenity being so distraught that she never left my side. That thought was pure selfishness on my part!

Then, I began to notice the effects coming over me. My blood turned hot inside of my skin! My vision started to play tricks on me. At first, everything became more intense and brighter, and then a spotty haze settled overall I saw, quickly followed by countless pinpoints of light like tiny sparklers. Panic was creeping into my head and it was overwhelming. Although it seemed contradictory, my breathing actually seemed to speed up. But I had no idea if it was the pills or the panic. Soon, I felt like I was weightless and floating with nothing solid to hold onto. The feeling must have been similar to what someone drowning would feel I guessed. The sensation was completely opposite from what I expected. What it did was actually heighten the awareness of my ending rather than the dulling I had sought. That clarity didn't stop with my body; it was in my head as well. I couldn't stop thinking! Exactly the opposite was what I wanted though- then and forever.

Then, as if in response to that desire, my body seemed to, in effect, hit a wall as a lethargy spread through me. What had been clear faded and shrank. Everything that I was capable of acknowledging at that point seemed to be just inches from my eyes. My earlier uncomfortable awareness had changed but only into a different type of discomfort.

To distract myself, I reached over to the table next to me, groping for the other thing I'd brought in with me; a picture frame.

I stared at it but couldn't focus. I turned it in the light, moved it closer to my face and then farther away.

Nothing I did seemed to help me to see clearly and nothing allowed me to focus. But of course, it was my own fault. It was my fault that I couldn't focus on the picture of my beautiful wife and daughter. But it didn't really bother me because they were vivid in my thoughts. That fact would never change; I would never let it!

My eyes closed...

How long had it been...?

Had I been lying there one minute or one hour? My mind was now going the same speed as my body. Laying there on my back, waiting not to feel, an obscure memory crept into my head; a memory of a beautiful six-year-old girl. As I was putting her to bed that night, she tiredly said, "Daddy, do you know what I want to be when I get big?"

I knelt down by her bed and played my part.

"No, what do you want to be sweetie?" I asked.

"I want to be a miss unhairy."

"What does a miss unhairy do?"

"You know-we saw them on TV. They go to other countries and help all the people who are hungry or poor who can't help themselves."

"Oh!" I said understanding, "You mean a ' Missionary'".

"That's what I said daddy!" she defended.

"You're right, my bad." I conceded.

"What do you want to be when you grow up?" she asked me playfully.

"I want to be a person who tries to always do the right thing, just like you baby. At that, she giggled. Then, I told her, "You'll be the best missionary ever, I believe in you. Don't ever give up and don't ever stop trying. Promise?"

"I won't Daddy. You don't either, 'kay?"

"' Kay, I promise."

Thinking back on that brought out an emotion that was hard to define. We'd promised each other- and nothing out-weighed that in my mind. Then another clarity hit me fiercely. It was sobering-Was I breaking that   promise?

I don't know how long I'd been lying there. It was long enough to make every effort to move torturous, but not long enough to kill me.

Because it was such a struggle to roll off the bed, after I hit the ground, I quickly abandoned the idea of standing up. Weakly, I started to crawl to the phone. I was a mix of emotions, I couldn't help but be mad at myself. I didn't want to be considered one of those people who were just trying to get attention, this was no cry for help! In the past, I'd always thought those people were pathetic. But maybe those people were just as serious as I was and they'd also experienced something like I had. It made me rethink things.

But that was secondary. Although the effort was monumental, I did my best to keep moving and to remain conscious.

"You have got to get through this, you've got to get help!" made itself heard in my head. I did need help and I needed it fast. It was all I could do to pick up the phone and think clearly enough to dial three simple numbers, but I found myself fighting. In the time it took to get connected, I felt myself become somehow smaller, and I must have lost consciousness because the voice on the line startled me back to awareness.

She said, "911, what's your emergency?"

"...I..."

"911-Sir? I can hear you, what's your emergency?"

"...Pills...need help...I think I made...mistake..."

"Sir...?"

"I promised her..."

"Sir, you said you've taken pills? Do you know what kind they were? Do you need an ambulance?"

"...Yeah..."

"Stay with me. I'm sending help now but I need you to stay on the line with me..."

The phone dropped at that point. I wasn't able to understand what she was saying to me anymore. My hearing was muffled and my vision seemed to drift in and out. Trying to keep my head upright became impossible. My head seemed separate from my body and my neck wouldn't cooperate. It was as if the muscles refused to obey a simple desire to look up. Determined not to dishonor my promise, I started to crawl in the direction of the front door. More than once, I fell flat and had to start again. I would have suffered if I were able to feel any pain. Numbness had replaced even the slightest ability to feel. Had I gone too far? Did I have the time to stop what I'd begun? I wasn't sure at all. Everything seemed to be distant and the lights I saw seemed to strobe and flicker. Through it all though, I persisted.

'You should have reached the door by now' I managed to think to myself. For all I knew, I could have reached the door hours before but was unable to realize it. Then, looking up weakly, I saw Serenity sitting just a few feet away, there by the door that I had been struggling to get to. That's when I realized that I hadn't made it. That's also when I feared that I couldn't.

I felt myself conceding. It might have been too late to stop what I'd begun, But I still fought to keep my promise, the promise that I'd remembered possibly too late...

It was so hard to move...and it seemed so simple to just lie down.

'For just a second...' I swore. 'Just 'til I get some strength back.' I thought. Then, I closed my eyes...

In an instant, all rationales flew through my increasingly leaden mind-She was gone now, and did it still matter? What good could you do for yourself or anyone else anymore and why should you? You've already done the deed; you can't take it back now! Then, I thought I heard a voice...

-YOU PROMISED-

It was barely perceptible. Inexplicably, the sound of those words seemed to be, not in my ears, but in my mind.

'Impossible!' I thought.

My eyes opened reluctantly to see who was standing next to me.

No one was there... I was alone except for a new realization I'd just come to. But was it too late?

The TV sounded dully in the background...

I was aware....

The sound of a gasp, and deep breathing made me focus my mind and become aware.

White-everything was white.

I was blinded by it. We've all heard stories but could it be possible?

Was I...?

No-I was in a bed.

My vision became clearer. Then, I realized that I was being blinded by the abundance of light coming into the room I was in.

When I could focus clearly, I found myself in a hospital bed. I was alone and all I heard was silence and breathing; my own.

'I didn't kill myself...?' I thought. Relief came over me as I realized that I had somehow been given the chance to keep a promise that I thought had already been lost. That became the one thing that mattered to me. That became a pinpoint of purpose for me.

But — something was still unsettled; something was still unclear. Although I appreciated my reprieve, I didn't fully understand it.

When did the ambulance pick me up? Where had I been taken? How long had I been out? I didn't remember any of it. I couldn't remember anything after dialing the phone. I needed answers, especially to the question of what was going to happen next.

Since I felt that my thoughts and senses were strong, I made the mistake of thinking the rest of me was too. When I swung my legs over the side of the bed, I found out just how wrong I was. That was only my first mistake.

What I'd put my body through never crossed my mind before that point. I didn't consider what the toll taken on my strength would be after what I'd done to it. That price turned out to be higher than I realized. My feet touched the floor and my legs refused to support my weight. It was as if there was no muscle or bone in them and I began to go straight down as if I'd stepped in a hole.

Luckily, there was a tray table close to the bed. Through pure desperation, I just barely caught myself. With one hand on the edge of the bed and one on the tray table, I supported my weight through nothing but will, not strength. The thought of having to be picked up from the floor pissed me off. So, I struggled and sweated in seconds from the effort, barely making it onto the bed before someone started to come into the room.

For some strange reason, I tried my best to hide the exertion and appear as if I was calm and recovered. I breathed deeply to foster that illusion.

The person coming into the room was dressed in white from head to toe, obviously my nurse. I watched as she came towards my bed and began studying information from a machine next to me.

The first thing I noticed about her when she came through that door was that she wasn't smiling. In fact, she looked like her face had been pounded out of clay and   designed to scare children.

For a nurse, someone whose job it was to bring comfort, she seemed very unpleasant. She didn't say anything to me as she checked the I.V. I was attached to, so I didn't say anything to her either initially. I immediately didn't like her.

As she went to the other side of the bed, I took the initiative and asked her the most obvious and necessary question, "Where am I?"

"Cook county Medical and Correctional." she said without looking at me.

"How'd I get here?"

"Same way you people usually do..."

I barely heard her say it under her breath. She then threw back what little curtain there was blocking all that light coming in. I didn't want that.

"Could you pull those closed please, it's kinda bright in here and I..."

"It's very late. You have a new schedule to conform to now. You've slept long enough, despite your best efforts." She took pleasure in the fact that the light bothered me. I knew there was a reason I didn't like her.

"What? What is this...? You always talk to patients like that?" I asked angrily.

"I'm not here to be your friend; I'm here to do a job..."

"You do it perfunctorily."

She shot me a blank stare of misunderstanding and then a 'Thanks.' that she didn't know *not* to give. I didn't usually speak like that, I just needed to make a point. She'd seemed unnecessarily dismissive of me. She acted as if my inferiority was a forgone conclusion to her.

I'd always hated attitudes like that and I had every intention of challenging her. That is just what I did. The sneer that followed might have given me away though.

She stood there for a moment, probably wondering if I had somehow gotten over on her, and then with a huff, her face turned to a scowl. Then she took her big pink cheeks and her big ass out of the room.

That encounter made me really question what kind of place I was in. But I was much more uncertain about how and when I came to be there...

It was a total mystery to me. No matter how I tried, I didn't remember anything-except- trying to make it out of my apartment and...I couldn't help but wonder; was there someone else there...? Did I hear someone...? What did they say...?

No answers came to me. I was drawing a complete blank. So, I looked around me and tried to work with what I was sure of. I was in what looked like a typical hospital room; a bed, a table, a couple of chairs, and a lot of important-looking gadgets. The only thing that struck me as out of place was the bars on the outside of the windows. 'Not a good sign' I assured myself.

After taking inventory of where I was, I didn't know what to do next. Again, no answers presented themselves. The only thing I could think about was getting out of there and figuring out my next move. So, I made that my only goal.

My body felt drained and I knew my legs were still weak, so I tried to get some blood moving in them by bending my knees a few times. It was more difficult than I had expected and I couldn't help but think how unnatural it seemed. It was strange...It just didn't seem right.

Just then, the door opened.

A tall man with a bit of a gut came in holding what I assumed was a chart on me. He began to read from it out loud, never once looking up at me. He spoke with a completely insincere friendliness that did nothing to cover what was actually impersonal detachment. That façade insulted me. It said that he thought no one was quick enough to see through him.

He began reading, with a bit of a mumble, to himself. "Mr. Devlin Goode, extreme emotional disorder, thirty years old. African American, no immediate family, unemployed, no criminal record until now... O.K.! So, how we doin' buddy?" came with condescension and a slight drawl.

"Well...I feel a little..."

"That's good. Good! O.K., I'm Dr. Erlikson," He still hadn't bothered to talk to me directly, I quickly saw who and what I was dealing with, and remembered the one goal that I'd set for myself. It was time for me to move on.

"Listen..." I tried again. I must have said it forcefully enough to get his attention, "I realize that I'm in a hospital and that you people saved my life, but I would like to leave now." Again., his laugh was condescending.

"Hey buddy, you can't just get up and leave..."

"Yes, I can. I'm checking out...of...where ever I am."

"No, no, no. I don't think so. You don't realize what's happening here." He warned.

"it's illegal to prevent a patient from checking himself out of a hospital."

"It's also illegal to attempt suicide. Remember, I said you had no record-until now. This facility is correctional as well as medical. You're obviously not completely sound and you've done something very wrong, so, you're being held for observation and evaluation."

"I'm in a nuthouse!?"

"C'mon buddy, let's start off positively."

"I'm positively not staying here! This isn't necessary! Look, I admit that I made a mistake but I don't really need you to 'evaluate' me. It's okay now... I'm okay now, so I'm leaving. You can't keep me here against my will..."

"We can and we will. We'll hold you for as long as we feel it necessary to determine...what's best." he said.

I made a calming gesture with my hands and tried to steady my voice, and then I said, "I was confused before but I do feel a little better than I did, I mean I'm in a better frame of mind. I think I know what I have to do..."

He interrupted, "We're gonna do what we have to do, so just be cooperative and make this painless."

I didn't like the way he put that.

As he turned to leave the room, I made a serious mistake; maybe I should have stayed in that bed-but I didn't. Instead, I got up to go after him and stop him. Of course, my legs still weren't supporting my weight, and I started to go down. Rather than falling down flat on my face, I grabbed hold of Erlikson, which didn't go over well at all. He shook me off in a panic, and then he lunged, pressing a button on the wall by the door.

He had taken my stumble for an attack!

"Security! Security!"

"No, wait! I wasn't trying to...I fell!" I pleaded. But I was apparently unconvincing and two security guards burst into the room and came straight for me. I was pissed by that point and didn't feel the need to be thrown around without fighting back. But my anger couldn't possibly counter what I'd put my body through and I never had a chance. They grabbed me and threw me on the bed, pinning me down without much effort, no matter how much I struggled.

Erlikson played his part by sticking me with a needle, which had to contain a sedative I didn't need or want.

I protested, "You Mutha...!"

That was as far as I got before my world lost its solidity. The last thing I remember was the short fat guard who'd come in as Erlikson's lackey, nodding his head at me and licking his lips. Disturbing! His name tag said 'Lopez'.

My eyes opened a crack, just to find that I was right where they'd left me.

I moaned.

Then I heard the sound and saw the flickering of a T.V. – but I didn't remember there being one there initially... I thought that was strange.

The news was on and reporting about a conflict in the West Bank- "Israel opened fire on the crowd in response to what they called the "Unprovoked slaughter of innocents", referring to the bomb that exploded in a plaza yesterday, taking the lives of five Israelis. The Israeli government's response to the bombing has, so far, accounted for thirty-one Palestinian casualties..."

Then, I was startled by a voice-it said, "You like that?"

I jumped a little in surprise and rolled over to see who was asking.

"What? Who are you? Not another doctor...?" I asked.

"You like that? It's my work they're talking about. That's some ripe ground over there. Dead easy. Can you tell me who the real bad guys are? You'd be wrong..."

"You're not a doctor, are you?"

He continued, "They're like a well-played symphony, with a melody of zealotism, a counter melody of egocentrism, and the underlying rhythm of intransigence! Beautiful! I love it!"

I listened to what he was saying but didn't try to understand him because I thought he'd proved himself to be something to avoid, just that quickly.

Then, I took another guess and asked him, "Are you a patient n here with me?"

His eyes pinpointed my own.

"Do I look like a patient?"

His response made me take a good look at him then.

I had seen eyes like that before, penetrating and malevolent, betraying the forced smile he wore. He looked to be about six feet tall with a slight build. That closer look also made me realize that he definitely wasn't dressed like a patient. The suit he was wearing looked kind of nice but it was a little wrinkled. His hair was cut short, very short, and was so light that it almost looked white. The most troubling thing about him though was the look of his skin. It was so pale- almost grayish in color. It made him look unhealthy.

That fact made me answer his question, "Yeah, kinda..."

He turned his face into a threatening humorless smile and said, "Look again."

Instead, I bluntly asked, "What do you want?"

"Not what you'd think...But of course, how would you know what to think at this point? You couldn't. You don't know where you are, you don't know what's happening to you. You're helpless! Helpless and directionless...You might as well be an ant in an ocean. Think about it."

'Great! This is what I get! They sent a priest into my room to give me the catholic perspective on mortal sin! How appropriate'. I thought.

"No, I'm no priest..."

What the...!

"How did you guess what...?" I began.

"...You were thinking?" he finished. "I didn't guess. No, I'm not a priest but I do pick up tips from them from time to time. They can be so creative sometimes. You understand creativity don't you Dev? The process of willing your desire and perspective into substantiality isn't foreign to you. I'm a creator in my own way by those terms. I've got a mental picture and a chisel, and you- are my medium."

I realized then, that I had been staring at him with what must have been a completely confused look on my face. I had no idea what he was babbling about! I knew I was in a nuthouse, but I didn't think they'd be roaming around freely. That made me decide to call someone to get him out of my room.

Then he said, "Don't bother. I'm on my way out. As you know, the creative process is a draining one. I've got to work my way into this somewhat. Be assured, I will come back. I think I must chip away until the shape is revealed. You've heard that before, I'm sure. There is a form that exists beneath the surface, a true form. It is waiting to be exposed and freed. I am that liberator. That's the only way you can be helped. Dev, you do believe I'm trying to help you, don't you?"

I answered his question with one of my own, "Who the hell are you?"

"I'm exactly-who you think I am." He said cryptically. Then, without any further explanation, he began to step backward, going farther into the shadowed corner he'd been standing in, until the darkness enshrouded him completely.

He was gone! Just like that!

I questioned myself, my own eyes and ears, and I questioned what this place had been shooting me up with! What had just happened to me? Every waking minute seemed to provide another unanswered question.

I ran over the events of the past few days and ended up less sure than when I started. I never thought I could feel even less in control than I did before. I closed my eyes and hated how exposed I felt. But doing that only made his face and his words come back to me.

Who was he! Or-was he at all? My imagination was never that vivid! But I'd been through a lot, and maybe my mind was working against me the same way my body seemed to be.

Was he imagined? My experience taught me that being able to ask certain questions automatically proves them false. If that was true, then I'd have to accept that some creepy ashen psycho had a one-sided conversation with me and then just dissolve inexplicably into shadow...

Maintain Goode!

Keep this up and they'll book this little suite for you indefinitely. No, I'd just write it off as a combination of what I'd been through and everything that was in my system. That's what I decided. The only thing left to do was to roll over and wait for tomorrow.

The TV was still on...

He called me helpless...

There it was; that damn light again, invading blindingly through the window.

As I sat up in my bed, I realized that I had been taken off the I.V. and had gained my freedom. Taking advantage of that, I swung my legs over the side to test their strength. It might have been a minor victory, but I didn't collapse.

The first thing I did was make my way to those curtains! No light thanks!

With that done, I decided to learn what I could about the place I'd been brought to. Getting around was a little bit of a struggle and I was moving slower than I would have liked, but I was moving.

When I reached for the door, I got a strange head rush; a shot of adrenaline surged through me. I didn't know what to expect. Was I supposed to be on complete lockdown, was I breaking some rule by trying to leave my room? Maybe I was asking for trouble. But answers were on the other side of the door, so that's where I was going.

I opened the door tentatively and took a look around. There was another room directly in front of me, and six more like it to my right on either side. The room I was in was the last at the end of a long corridor.

There was no one around, so I went out into the hallway. For a short time, I stood there motionless, waiting for something to happen, for someone to discover me. But nothing happened and no one came. So, I made my way down the corridor with the 'slap slap from my bare feet on the tiled floor.

At the end, to my right, was a set of doors. I could see light coming through the cracks and through the small windows. Something inside of me seemed to urge me to avoid those doors, even though I had no idea what was on the other side. So, I turned away. To my left, there was a smaller hallway. Following the sounds I heard, I took the left and found myself in an open common area, but not alone.

My first reaction was to back away and avoid notice, but I didn't make it far before being spotted. A woman was heading my way. I didn't let that stop me though, I just kept retreating, hoping my demeanor would deter her. No luck though, she called after me, knowing my name.

"Mr. Goode! Mr. Goode!"

There was no escaping her, so I turned and faced the music. The look on my face couldn't have been inviting and neither was my tone when I simply responded, "What...?"

"I'm glad you came out of your room. Eventually, I would have come to get you. I'm Dr. Li. I'll be working under Dr. Erlikson on several case files in this wing. I'd like it if you'd come over and join the rest of the group."

Looking at her, her youth gave away the fact that she was probably fresh out of "Head shrink 101" but there was something else about her...I found her attractive, and most people would have, but that wasn't where my head was at. That wasn't it...I couldn't place it. But I wasn't feeling sociable at all and I had no desire to be "worked on".

I simply said, "No thanks." And started for my room for lack of options.

"Mr. Goode, I know that things recently have been very hard for you. That much is obvious. I'm not here to make things more difficult. Please come over, and maybe just listen. Besides, a certain amount of therapy and evaluation is requisite for your discharge."

She made sense, but I wasn't hearing her. Then I thought about it. She was polite when she could have come at me a different way, When I acquiesced, I told myself that it was only to humor her, never admitting to myself how fragile a lie that really was. I didn't say anything, instead, I just gestured for her to lead the way.

As I followed her to the other side of the room, I saw who she meant by the "rest of the group". They I were there waiting. None of them seemed too happy and I guess didn't look much different. It made me question if that was the best place in the world to "fit in".

Dr. Li brought me over, sat me down, and started the unsolicited introductions.

"Devlin, these are the other members taking part in our group sessions. This is Sid, Constance, and Egon. Everyone, this is Devlin."

Awkward pause-empty stares...

When I glanced his way, I saw that Sid was glaring at me intensely. He looked as if we'd known each other and had some bad blood. He was kind of a big guy, balding on top with a scraggly face. Under his heavy and hairy brow, were eyes trying to bore through me. I didn't flinch. People only flinch when they're trying to protect something. There was nothing this guy could take from me, and so our war of attrition began.

Dr. Li began her session with, "Egon..." But then he abruptly interrupted her.

"Just stop right there Mia. I know you want us to do tricks for our new arrival here, but that's not what I'm about. I'm not here to perform."

"So you've told me- as I've told you to call me Dr. Li. So, why are you here Egon? You seem to feel that you have a very singular purpose. Could you share that with us all?"

"Don't patronize me – Mia. I'm degreed as well you know that. Listen, I'll just put it out there, and then maybe you'll leave me alone and move on to one of those idiots. Hey new guy...! You've gotta die!"

His conviction stole my attention from Sid. I turned to face him. Red hair crowned his head and his superior smile let mocking seep through.

"The human race is irredeemable and I will find a way to effectively enact a mass extinction of a flawed and misguided experiment. So, you along with most everyone else will die. Some sooner than others though. It has to be a mass extinction because any person is potentially a threat, including you. Everyone except me of course...and maybe Dr. Li- I will need an 'Eve'. Maybe Constance...but, she is a little mousey. That's why I'm here-I have to decide between them. They're both fighting for me. We'll see who comes out on top in the end."

At that, Constance moved her chair farther from his but she never said a word.

"The obtuse think that I'm crazy, but what is more logical?", he continued. "I'm going to do it out of necessity and love. Not love of some person or something, but love for the ideal of perfection! Perfection that no one else is willing to sacrifice for. Why can't anyone else see clearly?" he said.

All I could think was 'What an ass this guy is!' But I never said it out loud. Just like the rest of them, I kept quiet after hearing Egon's ranting. I could only wonder why he'd concluded that I was a threat to him.

Dr. Li turned her attention to me at that point.

"Devlin, I see you're wearing a wedding ring, but your admit file says you're single. Are you married?"

I paused noticeably long and then flatly answered, "Not anymore."

"Are you separated?" she asked.

"No..."

"Divorced then?" she pressed.

"No!" Her persistence was irritating. "Look, Dr. Li, I don't want to talk about my family and I don't want to be a part of this group or any other group!" Without me noticing, my frustration had gotten the attention of the guards who were sitting at a station to the Dr's back.

"Devlin, this is obviously an important issue for you. All of this is for the purpose of healing. You can feel free to..."

"She's *dead* alright!"

At that point, Sid decided he wasn't content to just glare at me and opened his mouth when he shouldn't have. He said "Yeah, I know she's dead... I fucked her dead."

I don't know what he had against me, but he had himself an enemy! I felt the aggravation and anger over everything that had happened and everything that I hadn't dealt with boil over within a split second and I lost control. In a rage, I threw myself across the table and slammed into Sid. We hit the ground and rolled with threats and warnings coming from those around us. That didn't stop us, but we were about to wish it had. Just when I got the upper hand and was about to do some facial reconstruction, the guards stepped in. The shock of their taser was like a full-body muscle spasm. We separated, occupied by our own individual pain.

The fight was over and so was my first session with Dr. Li. I wasn't exactly helping my case for discharge. My eyes were closed as two people grabbed me under my arms and started dragging me back to my room, or so I assumed. I didn't put up much of a fight at all. At least I'd be away from those crazy people, for the moment anyway.

Once we got to the room, my head and chest were used to open the door. As much as I wanted to fight them, I didn't have it in me.

They put me in bed, roughly.

I don't know how long I was out, but I do know what woke me up-it was the news again.

"...and one hundred more displaced families were relocated into new homes by the not-for-profit agency that was able to side-step Washington's red tape and no-bid contracts...as well as, what some are calling, institutional exclusion..."

"He's not the only one with influence."

I was laying on my right side when that voice came over my left shoulder and scared the hell out of me. When I rolled over and saw the man it came from, I was a little shocked because, as dark as the room was, he seemed darker. It wasn't his demeanor; it was his appearance. This Brotha was darkness.

I remembered what he'd said and asked him, "Who?"

"Forge." He replied.

"Who's that?"

"My ashen counterpart."

"Your what...? Oh, him, His name is Forge?"

"Not exactly- It's more of a purpose than a name. For the sake of expediency, you can call him that. His true name would be un-intelligible to you."

"Whatever that means...How do you know him anyway?"

"...And don't let him impress you with that mind-reading. We can all do it. Although, his kind is very un-skilled at it. You see, there is an ineffable depth to ..."

"Who the hell are you?" I demanded, losing my patience.

"The irony of that question is lost to you. "He laughed.

"Well, who are you? You gotta name?"

"If you feel the need to assign me an individual identifier, you may call me Sheperd. I've come to discuss extremely important issues with you relevant to your present disposition."

"What issues? The only issue I have is gettin' up out of here!"

"Your Ascension...Exactly. So, then you do understand." He said sounding relieved.

"My 'ass-what'?" I couldn't have been more confused. Just like before, I was listening to someone who made no sense at all. I thought to myself, 'The last time I felt this lost was when...'

"...Forge contacted you...? Yes, I know."

He finished my thought! How the hell could he have...?

"But you must come to understand that confusion is his charter, while mine is clarity."

"Clarity? Yeah, that much is obvious.: My sarcasm seemed to bother him a little. "Look man, I don't know who you are or who 'Forge' is or what you want, but I'm beginning to think that I might just be in the right place after all. All I know is that I want to get out of this place and find a..."

"...way to keep your promise to your daughter?"

My mouth was stuck wide open.

"I assure you, that in the final beat, all will be clear and your way will be before you. And Devlin... you are not helpless."

Before I could ask for an explanation of what he'd said, the door to my room opened and the light from the hallway expanded to fill the corner he'd been standing in, seemingly erasing him as it widened.

He was gone inexplicably! Or, was this another indictment of my senses and sanity...?

It was nurse "Front Butt" coming through the door derailing my train of thought. She came toward me, stone-faced as before, and unceremoniously poured water into a cup, shoving it, along with a tiny container, in my face with the words, "Take this now.", Hissing through her teeth.

"What is it?" I asked suspiciously.

"It's nothing...just something to make your head feel better. Dr.'s orders."

Of course, I had never complained about being in any pain and I didn't want to take it regardless of what it was, but I'd resigned myself to the fact that I'd forfeited some degree of self-determination the second I got to that place, So, I took the pills and drank some water to send them down. They were tasteless, but I hated it just the same. I hated feeling like the pills were in some way forced on me. I tried my best to ignore what an incriminating irony that was.

"I see you've learned not to fight. If you had learned sooner, Dr. Erlikson wouldn't have had to put you on this sedative program. You'll be a bit more manageable from now on." With that said, she turned and headed out of the room with a kind of victory displayed in her smirk.

The effects came on quickly. I never should have taken those pills so easily! My thinking was clouded enough as it was! It was obviously unclear enough to let that nurse deceive me! Things began to lose their solidity. The haze that seeped through me was more familiar than I would have liked. I began to fade...

Keep it together! I had to stay alert.

Find something to focus on...

'...Sophia...' I thought.

As I tried to picture the pretty little face of my daughter. I saw only fractured images. No matter how hard I tried, I couldn't concentrate at all and I felt myself getting more and more detached with every second. My breathing got noticeably deeper and my bed seemed to suddenly become much more comfortable. They'd gotten me again!

They had gotten the better of me again and left me in a worse position than I was in before. But that was the last time! If I ever wanted to be cleared to leave, I thought, I'd have to have my senses intact and put up a convincing front. I wouldn't let them drug me anymore! I wouldn't be provoked again, And I wouldn't let them know that I was delusional and imagining incoherent conversations with the unreal.

"I've got to ...keep it...together..." My thoughts evaded me at that point.

It was dark and I was alone-again.

When I came around, I was too lethargic to be overly upset about all the light coming through the window again. Somehow, I found the energy to moan, and then I was only ambitious enough to roll over. I thought for a second and realized that that was the first chance I'd had to try to get my head straight in so long.

I'd spent so much time feeling the way I did just then; clouded in mind, body, and spirit and it made me want to find someone or something to punish for it. I thought back to the months I'd spent alone in my apartment, mourning and killing myself slowly, I'd fallen so far! I'd forfeited control; over my emotions and my thoughts and consequently, my health altogether. If I could just get that time back or start over again, would anything be any   different? Then I thought about my suicide attempt. The emptiness remained distinct and numbing still. The things I'd been through recently piled themselves on my back and beat me down. The more I thought about it all, the more very familiar despair resurfaced.

I tried to disconnect it. I tried, but I doubted.

With an effort, I sat up, rubbed my eyes and repeated my moan. After making my way out of bed and pacing the room for a few minutes, I realized that I was distracted and that I'd become accustomed to the darkness, so, there I was shutting out the light again. That was the one bit of power that I found I had left. I didn't want the light! For the briefest time, I felt like I exerted my determination and exercised control over something. It was a very small thing though and the feeling didn't last.

When I turned back around, I found I had an audience.

Through the small window in the door, I saw worthless Dr. Erlikson looking in on me.

We glared at each other until he realized that he couldn't match my disdain and he moved away. So, I stood there, arms folded in victory.

His mouth was moving as he stepped back to let someone I'd never seen before step to the window. Then there was another one and another one.

Apparently, Dr. E was doing rounds, and I had the distinct feeling of being a specimen. He'd made me his newest attraction and put me on display. All I could do was watch as they looked in on me, talking about me through that small window in the dor. I guessed that what he was telling those people about me wasn't good. That pissed me off. They had to have seen that displeasure in my face.

They had to have seen it but they never acknowledged it, with the possible exception of Erlikson. There might have been a hint of pleasure on his ruddy face...Although the door wasn't locked, he never came in, which was best for him. I felt like a cornered animal and would have lashed out if he had.

It quickly became more than I could stand. Being dissected by those clueless people was too much for me and I reacted!

It started with my jaw extending, then I let my arms fall loosely. My back arched and I bowed my legs outward. Finally, with the flailing of my arms above my head, I let out the loudest chimp sounds I could!

What a performance!

I went around the room throwing things and jumping on the bed having a monkey fit! The only thing I didn't do was hurl feces at them. If they wanted something to talk about, I'd make it worth it!

Those idiots crowded around that window in a panic. With their eyes wide with alarm, staring at me, I abruptly stopped, sat down calmly at the end of the bed, and, when Erlikson pushed his way into sight, I gave them all the   finger.

I got a certain satisfaction from that. Somehow though, the humor was lost on them. No one ever opened the door to come in though. That is, until a few minutes later when three guards and the nurse came in bearing unwanted gifts. They offered me a choice; the pills that woman had or the tasers they carried-and then the pills. Considering my last experience with those guards, I figured I'd do better with the drugs. I didn't see it coming the first time so there was no way to defend against it. She'd tricked me. But I meant to make that time different. I planned to out will their effects on me the way you can sometimes do with alcohol. So, after I cursed their mothers, I downed the pills.

I did my best to concentrate on staying aware and focused, but I was mostly unsuccessful. To say I stayed awake might be a slight overstatement. It would be better to say that I was conscious. There seemed to be a haze over most of my vision and as slow as my mind was, my body was two steps behind. For what seemed to be a long time, the best I could manage was to sit on the edge of the bed asking myself what I was supposed to be doing. I'd tell myself that I had to get up, then the thought would escape me and I'd continue sitting there mumbling to no one about nothing, slowly rocking back and forth dumbly.

I had no way of knowing exactly how long I was in that position. I do know that by the time I felt myself coming around somewhat, the room was dimmer. It must have been dusk.

Moving at about half-speed, I stood up and made my way to the door.

I'd been stuck in that room long enough, and my guess was that no one had thought about me all day. So,

I left my room for no other reason but change. At the other end of the hallway, I again took the left toward the sounds I heard.

It's not that I needed or wanted company at all, I just realized that If I spent all of the time I was forced to be there, alone and isolated in my room, that I'd just be reenacting the last six months of my life. Those months were what led me to my fate. Those months were too desolate to allow myself to repeat. The thought occurred to me that maybe the lack of outside influences led me to succumb to my own self-destructive inner voice. Then that same voice told me that it was all I needed anyway. Then I thought back to where that inner voice had led me before. It seemed like a good idea to try listening to something else. So, I made my way out and down the hall, stopping at the threshold of the common area to look around briefly.

On the far side of the room, to my left, was the guard station. Three guards were there talking with each other. They noticed me, looked me up and down, and then went back to their quiet conversation. Their look of suspicion didn't go unnoticed though. People like that never realize that they themselves are trusted even less by the very ones they condescendingly mistrust. What a familiar tune! I turned away from them with a scowl.

The table where I sat with Dr. Li was across from me but empty. To my right, on the other side of the room, there was a small seating area set up around a TV.

It was on and there was someone sitting there in the half-light but I couldn't be sure of who it was from where I was standing. So, I made my way over.

By the time I was close enough to realize who it was, I was already at the edge of the seating. I stopped dead in my tracks but it was too late. Just as I began to back away, a strange accusation was spat at me.

"You're transparent! You know that don't you?"

Sid sat there staring down at nothing, apparently anxious for another round.

"Transparent...!", he repeated, preoccupied with seemingly nothing.

"What the hell is that supposed to mean? No, here's a better question, am I supposed to care about what that means?"

"You tell me. Should you care?" was his reply.

"What's your problem man? From the second you saw me it's been nothin' but hostility...Do I know you...?"

"You couldn't know me! You'd have to be in my head for that! No, but I do know you though. I am inside of your head! Hostile? You think I've been hostile huh? Awww...you little bitch! Yeah, I'm hostile! I'm hostile 'cause I can be-because I should be! Or should I be a victim like you? That's all you're meant for. You're pray. The beast waiting to devour you whole is called

"Weakness". Yeah, you know that monster, don't you? You know 'cause it's already tasted your sorry ass. What you don't know is that it's cannibalistic. But I'm a predator took, you see. Rather than being hunted down by it, I do the hunting! Yeah...I know you... You're pathetic and everyone and everything like you is pathetic. I'm hostile 'cause I'm strong and you're weak and I'll eat you alive!"

Sid's intensity had shaken me a little. For a split second, I hesitated, second-guessing myself, then I replied.

"You're gonna 'Eat me alive' because I'm...weak? Well, if the "Beast" is cannibalistic, doesn't that in essence make you... "Weakness"?

Determined to match Sid's aggression, I refused to concede to him in any way. By that point, I'd moved nearer to where he was sitting, standing just to the right of him, Then, he suddenly jerked himself out of his seat without warning. I felt my fists clench in anticipation. But he didn't throw himself at me. I was never his target. Instead, he fell to the ground, scrambling on all fours for what I then realized was the focus of his attention the entire time; the biggest spider I'd ever seen. He came up with it cupped in his hands, continually shifting their position, trying to hold onto it as it worked for its freedom.

"You see this? This is exactly what I mean. I'm in control! What could this little bastard do if I," he moved his hands quickly up to his mouth, "just decided to eat it!

What if I closed my hands together! I have control over it. You are either powerful or you're powerless!"

With that said, he looked up at me challengingly. Then, with a sudden quick intake of air, and pain replacing that challenge, he dropped the spider to the ground. It had bitten him. It landed and took off at top speed. I watched it crawl several feet away, towards a wall, and then just stop suddenly, the way spiders do for no reason.

'Looks like your 'power' was an illusion. Looks to me like that spider chose to demonstrate where the true power was." Feeling like I'd won, I turned my back on him and started to walk away. Then, I heard him retort.

"Maybe so- but at least the spider didn't have to be told!"

That statement stopped me in my tracks. When I spun around, I went past him, over to the corner, and I stepped on that spider.

As I stormed out of that seating area and away from another confrontation with Sid, the sound of the TV followed me, reporting "... And from the BBC in Johannesburg- Civil unrest erupted as reports of a destabilizing influence by the CIA and a European counterpart came to light this morning. According to sources, the desire to slow the progress of the ANC by those groups stemmed from a lack of Western control within that governing South African party. Protests are turning violent..."

When I burst through the door of my dark room, I went to the bed and slammed my fists down in complete aggravation. Everything about my situation sapped my resolve. I felt my will fade as I stood there with my head slumped, feeling the beginnings of that very familiar despair again.

Then, I realized that I wasn't alone.

Lifting my head slowly, I saw him again, sitting at the corner table, legs crossed, arms rested and his hands-fingertip-to-fingertip, tapping in sequence.

He rose.

I turned to square myself to him but didn't say a word. Neither of us spoke for an uncomfortable amount of time- at least- it was uncomfortable for me. The smirk he wore, which I realized was natural for him, seemed to dare anything to try to make him uncomfortable.

His words jarred me from my trance.

"Still trying to decide if I'm real?", he asked rhetorically.

"It's Forge right?" I started moving toward him. "That's what the other one called you..."

He never moved an inch as I made my way over to where he stood, until, I began to reach out to touch him. That seemed to bother him.

"Don't touch me!" he warned.

"Why? Will you disappear into nothingness and prove you don't exist?" I challenged.

"No, don't be dramatic- I just don't like you things." He coldly added under his breath. "Besides, if I didn't in actuality exist, where would that leave you? A mental case missing his straight jacket...I'm as real as your dying breath."

"I want to know right now," my patience for word games had run out, "Who are you and what the hell do you want from me?"

"Aren't you demanding all of a sudden... You want to know right now, huh? Fine, then be prepared for my answers. What- I am, Dev, is an Angel." He proudly stated.

After that, nothing he could have said could have mattered, I was furious! It was obvious that some of the nut cases were roaming the facility freely and that I had been too willing to entertain a few insane thoughts myself. Maybe it was the drugs...maybe it was fatigue. Whatever it was, I'd come to the edge of my tolerance. Without forethought, I lashed out at Forge.

"Alright! Get the fu…!"

Before I could finish, he reacted so blindingly, so instantaneously, I could barely rationalize what I was seeing let alone believe it!

His response to me yelling at him was violent.

Two immense white wings sprang from his back and closed around him, creating a gusting wind strong enough to throw me and half of the room back against the wall. Before I could fall to the ground, he extended his hand like a shot. He was across the room and never actually touched me, but somehow, I found myself suspended as if I was in his grasp. Somehow, I had been pinned to the wall by – nothing; nothing that was visible to me. I was silenced by my terror. How was it possible? There was nothing to explain how I'd been thrown like I had been. The explanation for how I was pinned to the wall was even more impossible to come up with.

I stared wide-eyed at Forge as his expression went from anger to apathy and finally to amusement. His face softened and his eyes dropped their threat. He'd put back on his familiar facade. He then began to speak through his familiar smile. As I listened, Forge's voice was calm, almost placating, when he began again.

"Now, that answered your first question as to who I was. To answer your second question; what I want – is your discerning eye."

With that, he gestured, spreading his fingers which somehow released me. I landed awkwardly and struggled to get up.

'The din I made scrambling to get up must have been heard by someone outside', I thought.

"No one would've heard unless I wanted it that way Dev."

He knew what I was thinking again! He said it and I believed it. I was clearly powerless, so I just waited for his next move.

Endgame Trilogy

PART II: THE LANGUISHING

Cold is a depthless thing

All irrepressibleness can be immobilized by it

Cold is a formless thing

Is it material-spiritual or habitual?

Cold is an unforgiving thing

The point of its repentance is non-existent

Cold is a ravenous thing

Innocence-defenselessness-and nectar are synonymous

Cold is a mindless thing

Its own repercussions would leave it stricken if it were otherwise

Cold is a predatory thing

Its prey is kindness, respectfulness, loyalty, honesty, selflessness, and the undeserving

Cold is a transforming thing

What was once its prey, becomes distrustful remorselessness

Cold is a formidable thing

To defeat it requires the convictions of the as-yet-unrealized...

Those words from a favorite poem I'd memorized came to me for reasons I couldn't grasp initially. My situation didn't lend itself to rational thought and especially not to the poetic!

After months of isolation and despair so deep that it changed, fundamentally, who I was, I was led to a suicide attempt. After that attempt, I found myself convicted to yet another form of isolation, I was committed to aninstitution where everything I was seeing, thinking, and feeling conspired to draw me to a particular conclusion; that I'd tipped the balance away from sanity at some point without realizing it.

That thought left me cold, literally and figuratively. That was the correlation.

That cold made me lock myself away, alone in my apartment-that cold overtook my mind, my body, and my spirit. That cold made itself seem almost natural. Then that same cold turned on me and made me turn a pill bottle end-up. Now I seemed to get a sense of that same cold emanating from the enigma that was in front of me; this being called Forge who claimed to be an Angel.

That claim was something I wanted to resist intensely! How could I though after what I'd just experienced? What explanation could account for the way I was thrown against the wall?

Yes, I felt the strong need to resist his claim. But what would be the alternative to that resistance?

The alternative was a complete forfeiture of any illusions of sanity. That doubt lived in me like a parasite. As I stood there, with my back pressed hard against the wall, waiting for some indication of his intentions, Forge both glared and smiled at me. I thought I knew which of those to trust though.

He took a step towards me but I had nowhere to retreat.

"Listen to me Devlin Goode-I know that you're feeling confused and afraid, but I'd already told you that I was an Angel and yet you didn't believe me... and you mocked me. You will learn to trust me. You see, I am here to provide...clarity...to you. That is something you'll need very soon. You think that you know what you want or need to do, but your vision is limited. Let me show you. What do you see? No, don't bother to reply, I know your mind remember...Your first thought was a stammering' I don't know'. The second was 'A man'. It was a mistake to go beyond your first answer. You don't know!"

" I don't know' is the only answer you possess! See- watch- let's experiment. Where did I come from...? You don't know...Why are you experiencing this...? You don't know...Damn it, man, I'll give you what should be an easy one- Are you completely and irretrievably insane right now! Come on-you can say it- you can play your part..."

"...I don't know..."

"Good! It seems to me that you desperately need a degree of certitude right about now. Well never fear, that's exactly why Forge is here. Come with me. Your clarity begins now."

In a stupor, I followed where he led, out of the room, down the hall, and into the common area. Then, his questioning continued.

"How much of this facility have you seen thus far? This is it isn't it? Of course, I already know that." He pointed across the room. "See those doors there? There is an entire wing beyond them that you didn't know about. Let's explore!"

To the left of the small unoccupied guard station were doors that I had failed to notice before. On the other side of those doors, I found exactly what he'd claimed. There were several rooms in the corridor we stood in. We had entered another wing.

"You've now been given a larger perspective that, of course, you'd have been clueless about otherwise. But your edification has only just begun, Take a look... in that room..."

Forge faced me squarely and pointed, without turning, over his shoulder to a door at his back. Doing as I was told, I moved around him, cautiously, and made my way to the room.

He should have prepared me for what I'd see, but the fact that he didn't did seem true to character. He should have warned me about the disturbing scene I would look in on. But he didn't.

Through the small window, I saw a patient lying in bed, apparently sleeping. Somehow, he seemed familiar to me, but I couldn't place him. The room was too dim to make him out clearly. Suddenly, someone inside stepped into my line of sight and moved to the side of the bed. I recognized that little bastard. It was the guard Lopez.

He was standing there motionless, staring down at the man in bed. It wasn't clear what he was doing at first. But as the scene unfolded, it took on a disturbing tone.

When he began to pull the covers back, I expected the man in the bed to wake up. But he never moved. He couldn't have been sleeping...Was he unconscious...? ... Or dead...? I wasn't sure. Then, the ugly realization of what was really going on struck me as I saw Lopez begin to horribly molest that defenseless man!

I felt the need to act, but I didn't know what to do! What could I do? I was in no position to save anyone. But someone had to...The only thing I could do was to go in and stop it, any way I could. I started to reach for the door...

"Ask yourself if what you're about to do is wise Dev." Came from a voice at my back.

"Do you think you can honestly protect that man? Do you think that maybe this has happened before and will probably happen again?

Do you think that if you burst in there trying to help that poor bastard that you might just suffer with him in the end?"

"Here's the scenario; You bust in all heroic like, he promptly overpowers your doped-up lethargic carcass, calls for help, and puts you on trial for not only wandering the facility in an unauthorized area, but for also attacking a guard-and here's the grand finale- for the very perversions he himself was responsible for! So, I reiterate, is opening that door at all wise?"

"What the hell do you expect me to do-just ignore what I've seen-to do nothing? How could I do that! Someone has to stop it! Someone has to make him pay for this!"

Despite my anger and frustration, he smiled widely and matter-of-factly stated, "And that brings me to my point Dev. Let's walk."

Forge came up beside me, extending his arm forward, leading me away from that room. I was too weak, too scared, or too completely confused to resist him.

"Dev, everything is either a micro or macrocosm of everything else. Take where you are for example. Earlier, your perception consisted of only a few rooms and hallways; your whole world. Now you've been exposed to an entire area that you had been completely unaware of, which still isn't the whole. You can now imagine that there is a much larger structure to this facility although you haven't actually seen it. Your world has been expanded. Now it's a universe. But there is something more! The totality of that larger structure still resides somewhere; a building is erected on land in a city -in a country, etc. That figurative totality-of the rooms in the building on the land and all else-is-Existence. So, what does this all mean to you? I told you that I wanted your discerning eye and now you've seen why. You asked what I expected you to do. You were right about what you said before. There are those who owe a debt and there are those that collect. You wanted to "do" something, right? Well, "do" something for Existence! You're being put into a position to identify and punish those like that guard, on a significant level, which will, in turn, reverberate through all Existence!"

Initially, I didn't know where I was or how I'd gotten there. What I did know was that I was stretched out on a very hard floor somewhere. It took a minute to realize where that was. I was back in my room, lying in the wreckage that Forge caused the night before.

It could have been the chill of the floor or possibly the pain in my jaw, neck, and ribs that brought me around. I must have been sprawled on the ground for hours because my body was stiff and sore. Getting up was slow and painful. I squinted hard trying to deny the daylight as I pulled myself up and sat on the edge of the bed. There was barely enough time to be relieved before things took a turn for the worse again.

It began with her gasp, and then my favorite nurse unloaded a shrill barrage at me.

"What have you done!? You've destroyed this room!"

I looked around me and saw the remnants of my last encounter with Forge. The room looked like a battlefield. But there was no way to convey the truth about what had happened. How could I when even I didn't know what that truth was! So, there I sat taking the full blame for the chaos around me, knowing what it would cost.

"I will have the doctor prescribe so many drugs, you'll be chemically lobotomized! I'll...I'll..."

The threats would have probably kept coming if not for Dr. Li. Her entrance was perfectly timed.

"What is going on in here? I could hear the yelling outside."

"Dr. Li! I was just about to go get Dr. Erlikson! Look what this fool has done to this room! I think we should double his dosage immediately and place him on bed restriction until he learns to ..."

"Nurse, I'll take responsibility from here. You can go."

"I think I should get Dr. Erlikson involved. He needs to know about this outburst."

"Nurse," Dr. Li stated with added authority, "This is my patient and I'm working this case file and I promise you that I don't need to be second-guessed by you. Now, I have work to do and I'd bet you do too."

"Fine, Dr. Li..." was all that she could say, tight-lipped. She had found herself put back in her place. Thankfully, she left without another word or even a look back. When the door closed behind her, I felt myself slump, tired from the defensive posture I assumed around her.

Even without looking up, I was sure that the Dr. was staring down at me, wondering how to phrase her, undoubtedly, many questions. All I could do was wait. Then the Dr. commented, "Um...the room seems different somehow. Devlin...?"

I responded with a grunt.

"Will you tell me why you did this?"

"There'd be no point to it."

"Why? Because I wouldn't understand or believe it?" she challenged.

"Smart guess doc."

"Well, try...Listen, I feel it's safe to be direct with you. I want to talk to you and I want to help. We know that's why I'm here. What I need from you is some willingness. Neither of us can see the final outcome of things, obviously, we can only see our choices. For example-you chose to end your life. Why? Of course, only you know the fundamental reason but I'd say we touched on it the first time we spoke."

"Are you done Doc?"

"I'd just like to go a little bit deeper..."

"I don't think...'

"How did your wife and child die?"

Her perceptiveness surprised me. Although I was mad as hell at her for touching a sore spot, I kept my composure because it seemed to me that Dr. Li was the only one I'd come across recently without an ulterior motive. Her only agenda seemed to be in doing her job. Even if I could respect that fact, it didn't mean that I had to cooperate.

"My child...? I never told you that I'd had any children Dr."

"Well, you mentioned that you'd had a family. I know that your wife has died, you told me that. Since you obviously wouldn't abandon your child and then speak about it, I concluded that your child died with your wife. Tell me what happened."

I kept the acknowledgment of her skill to myself and answered her with a throaty whisper.

"My wife...and my daughter...were murdered."

The words sounded distorted to me as I spoke. Then I realized that that was the first time I'd allowed myself to say them out loud. A wave of grief rushed through me that must have been palpable.

Dr. Li began to speak, "I can see how much your thoughts are torturing you now, which tells me that you haven't worked through it completely."

She paused, but not to look for verification from me. She knew she was right. She paused out of respect.

"Do you feel like you can talk about it now?" she continued.

My first and my gut reaction was to explode all of my anger, grief, and guilt at the Dr. and ask her who the hell she thought she was to invade my thoughts and feelings with her learned intellectual rape! But I didn't. My second thought was to withdraw so deeply that I'd chase the Dr. away in frustration. But I didn't. I in fact, went with a third involuntary reaction-I made myself completely open and vulnerable to her. As surprised as the doctor may have seemed, it was nothing compared to what I felt myself. Although the grief came freely, it was closely followed by a slight degree of relief in the telling.

Dr. Li listened intently as I began to tell her details of my former life.

"I think...that...I was a pretty talented man at one point. There's a saying that goes 'Ability to do, comes from doing' and I really took that to heart. You see Dr., I can relate to and respect what you've had to go through to get your Ph.D. How many countless hours have you spent studying your craft? There must have been many times when you've sacrificed a lot to achieve. I know 'cause I've done the same thing in my own way. With me, it was art and music. I've studied all the best: Coltrane, Chopin, Living Colour...Galleries have displayed my art and I've toured the world playing music. That's how I've earned my "Ph.D.", through years of sacrifice. But where we differ isn't what we've sacrificed, but who. You're not married, are you? No children I'd guess? You probably don't even have a roommate because they'd interfere with your focus. Am I right? I'd say that's probably for the best though because that way the sacrifice is solely your own."

"But your sacrifices were shared weren't they..." she stated intuitively.

"You know the answer to that. I've had to work my ass off to provide for my family. That meant taking every job offered, every gig. There were times when I came home too late to be of any use to my wife and times when I wasn't around when my daughter needed me to be." I paused for a moment of recrimination. "I'd disappointed my wife and my daughter at one point or another, many times. Of course, I didn't want to hurt them at all-ever! But...I was conflicted..."

"Although you sometimes let them down and had to be away from them too often, you were also doing what you loved..."

"...Maybe I should have made different choices. Maybe there were times when I could have stayed. What if I was just selfish and justified it by telling them and myself that it was necessary!"

"You've been beating yourself up with those questions for a long time now Devlin. Hindsight is extremely unforgiving."

"Who said I deserve to be forgiven?"

"Who says you don't?"

"I do! I'm the only one that can! I know my failures... and I know what they've cost."

"And you'd determined that you would pay the final price...Do you believe that that price was equitable to what you saw as your failures?"

"What I believe is that if I'd been there for them, they'd still be alive and I wouldn't be here against my will and I wouldn't be forced to re-live that shit 'cause it never would've happened!"

At that point, I stood up with an obscenity that was filled with months of frustration and found myself throwing a chair across the room. Then, just as quickly as the rage came, it left, to be replaced by despair.

Despite myself, I began to cry quietly.

Dr. Li deserved a lot of credit because she never took my outburst as any kind of attack towards her. Instead, she sat patiently motionless until, I suppose, she felt I was calmer. She then simply said, "Tell me what happened to your wife and daughter."

"I was actually having a great night..." began my pensive answer.

"We had been traveling -my band-for a little over two weeks, playing clubs on the East coast and things were winding down. I didn't like the idea of staying away for so long and I didn't usually do it-almost never-but the money was good and I really needed it. Paying gigs were becoming harder and harder to find. Well, the last show we were scheduled to play didn't go so well." I gave a slight ironic chuckle thinking back about the place.

"It turned out to be a little shit hole called Penni's Pub. I disliked the manager of the place from the get-go. She was loud and aggressive and she had... Well, she accused me of staring at this skin condition she had but that wasn't the case at all. To make a long story short, we basically got stiffed by the owner. That kind of thing happens sometimes, but that time was a real problem for me. I expected that money, I needed that money and had already figured it into my bills. But because of that club, I was coming up short. I was lucky though because before I could panic about it, another opportunity dropped on us. Another job became available that would make up for our loss and then some. Kristina, my wife, and my daughter expected me back that night but I had to tell them that it wasn't going to happen. Although they were supportive of me, and Kristina said that she understood, the disappointment was clear, even over the phone.

I promised to make it up to them both and drove on to our new, last, stop. We had a good night-the band was tight, the crowd showed us love, and everything just went smoothly. It went so well, that when I collected our money, we were offered another night, another show, and I took it. The money we'd lost on the other gig was made up already but I thought that that would be the way I'd make it up to my family...I'd come home with extra money and they'd understand. When I think back on it though, I can't help but wonder if I was just doing it for myself...I could have passed on it and gone home to my family...'

"Before, when I said that I was having a great night, I meant at that last job. That last show was the best one. I was on cloud nine and I wanted to share it, so, instead of getting a room for the night somewhere, I decided to head home..."

"It was around four in the afternoon and I was three days late but I had made it back home. I thought I'd surprise my wife but it didn't turn out that way at all. Instead, I opened the door...and stepped into Hell."

"What exactly did you find?" Dr. Li probed.

"You know already...It was a breaking and entering... when I saw what was done to the place, I went into a panic, screaming and looking for my daughter and wife. Then, when I found them, I screamed from the bottom of my soul... There was no hope for my daughter. She was just...too little... too fragile...My wife was just barely alive after what they'd done to her. I was told later by the authorities that she'd been hanging on for hours-that's when the attack took place just hours before I got there! She was waiting for me! What if I'd left when I should have? I would have been there to stop them! I could have... I would have...Two innocent, beautiful people were murdered because I wanted to indulge my ego and stay an extra day. Two innocent and beautiful people were murdered but three people died that day."

"Devlin, I absolutely believe that it feels that way, but in fact, two people died and the last was critically wounded. You lived on, possibly marginalized, but you did live on. You've been going through a gauntlet of emotions ever since and you're in the most profound pain there is. But you have to realize that although that pain hurts, almost unbearably, it can be starved. You're doing just the opposite. You're feeding that pain by believing that your absence caused that tragedy or that your presence could have prevented it. The thought that you could have controlled an uncontrollable situation leads to self-loathing. You're intimately familiar with that. You can starve that pain by accepting the fact that you couldn't have changed things. That's not something that you want to hear or believe but that is the truth. I want you to take some time to think about what I've said. I know it's a lot to wrap your head around and it'll be a fight to accept it. I'm going to leave you alone for now but we're not done. We'll continue this next time. You've got a lot to think about-Devlin, don't feed that pain."

What she said did make sense to me but it also could have been a cliché psych line, rattled off and taken at face value by the gullible. For some reason, I didn't truly believe that though. As conflicted as I may have been, I wanted that simple little phrase to be a kind of life jacket for me. Although I did want that, there was no way that it would come so easily. So, I stayed where I was with just my conspiratorial sadness.

For lack of a better way to say it, I felt two-dimensional. All that I was, felt thin and without depth.

I sat, for what seemed like a long time, both thinking and not thinking. There are times when our heads are so inundated with thoughts that we're incapable of focusing on any one of them. That was one of those times.

At first, I sat silently. Then I rose but stood in one spot. Soon after that, the pacing started. Through it all, time went by unnoticed. Before I knew it, I was out of my room and in the hallway, engrossed in my thoughts. As I passed the room down from mine, someone fell in step next to me, although it didn't register initially, we were in the commons before I actually took notice, stopped, looked over at him, and offered one word.

"What...?"

Egon took that inadvertent queue and ran with it. "I've come to a pivotal turning point." He volunteered.

"You mean the end of the hall?"

"No! I mean the end of it all."

"Sounds serious...Let me know how that turns out for you.", I jabbed. Then I started to turn away from him.

"Your mocking comes from disbelief Goode."

"More like disinterest nut job. Now go away." I said it and meant it but he must have heard- "Tell me more you fascinate me"-because he continued on, oblivious.

"Like too many others, you don't seem to recognize the position you're in."

"My position...?" I responded before I could stop myself.

"That's right. You should realize that I hold your future in my hands. Well, it's in my thoughts anyway."

"My future huh? That's a lot of responsibility for you to have..."

"Your cynicism doesn't change the fact that your time is running out and I could be your tipping point.", he said.

"Don't care..." was my reply.

"That's because you lack foresight. You're blind to what's really going on right now."

"Yeah? That's great-now shut the fuck up! I didn't ask for you or your thoughts to come over here. I didn't ask for you to rattle off your stupid delusions and I didn't elect you to be the 'Decider of my future'!"

"Of course not...that's the point-the decision is mine! Just like all others are. Just like the final one is.", he insisted.

"What have I done in the past few minutes to make you think I want to hear this?"

Egon's reply was, "Why wouldn't you?", sounding genuinely perplexed. I answered his question with frustration.

"Could it be 'cause you don't make any sense and even if you did, it still wouldn't have a damn thing to do with me?" Having said that, I kept walking. Needless to say, I quickly realized that he was still shadowing me.

"What...!?"

"The end isn't far now Devlin.", was stated cryptically.

I definitely didn't want to credit Egon's persistence with wearing me down, so I attributed my response to my confinement and truly not having anything better to do and said half-heartedly, "The end? What are you talking about? The end of what?"

"The end of an incompetent system of failures and inequities. The end of mind-boggling inconsistencies and ill-conceived designs. The détente that has existed for so long has left people bereft of the ability to ascend! Imagine putting someone in a soundproof glass enclosure while the orchestra of Existence played on all around him! Now, ask him to join in, but in tempo and in key. Impossible! That's where you're all languishing! You're allowed to writhe loathsomely through your lives but told to excel, while handicapped the entire time with no true perception. As if being fatefully hamstrung isn't enough for you, you insist on reveling in your own ignorance. All the while you are all incapable of being infuriated by it the way that you should be. Now, think about the time frame of this entire mishap and try to imagine how it's been compounded. It will take a monumental effort to undo the damage! I alone am capable of taking on that effort and enacting a solution that will fix everything!"

I found that I was compelled to listen to him despite myself. His words didn't just hold my attention though, I found some indefinable honesty in them that eluded me. Rather than allowing myself to explore that, for whatever reason, I heard the disdain and sarcasm in my response of, "So, you're the new Messiah?"

"New Messiah...? I don't think so. There would have to have been an old one for me to be the new one." He challenged.

"That's a strong statement. What makes you think that if there wasn't one before, there is now?"

"Simply put, I fought for this and won." Egon claimed.

"What? Who could you possibly fight with for something like that? That's ridiculous..."

"No! No! It's not! You weren't there...you didn't choose a side or place a bet. I know when the bell sounded and when the tap was!"

I seemed to have a knack for agitating lunatics, so I attempted to cut my losses and end our little chat. Unfortunately, Egon wasn't having that and he continued on, intently.

"There was a time, when I was younger, that I was somewhat overconfident and self-involved...with good reason though. I thought that I was capable of anything and everything and that my will alone could see me through whatever obstacle. I showed little modesty and even less fear. It was my pride that made me throw down the challenge that has set the stage for the rebirthing...That challenge will ultimately prove beneficial. The end result will nullify the expenditure of achieving it. His efforts have failed! He did try though, but ultimately, I was proven right. It seemed that I wasn't vulnerable to his influence. He failed and I still stand defiant. So, I claim the right as the winner to re-design."

"'He'? Who, exactly, are you talking about? Who is it that you supposedly challenged?' I was in it too far not to ask.

"When I was younger, I dared the Devil to try to affect my life negatively. I begged him to presume to think that he had power over me! I stood there in my bedroom, arms wide in challenge, waiting to beat back his attempt with a snarl on my face!"

I had to ask, 'So...what happened...?"

"Nothing..." was all he said.

"Let me get this straight...You stood in a room-alone-and challenged someone -who doesn't exist-to a contest of wills...and of course, nothing happened. But you think you won that imaginary fight and now you're all-powerful. So, now you're going to "remake" the World into your idea of perfection...Is that right?"

"Except for the part about the Devil not existing... you're absolutely right."

"You're absolutely insane..."

"What justifies that accusation? Egon protested.

"Well let's start with the fact that you believe in the Devil!"

"But there...", he started.

'Next, there's a little problem with thinking that you could take him on even if he existed."

"I actually…"

"Then, let's examine the crazy-ass idea that you're all-powerful after supposedly winning." I challenged.

"As a matter of fact…"

"Finally, only a complete lunatic, who might happen to be in an institution, like yourself, would believe that he had the slightest idea of what perfection is or how to get it!"

"You seem to have everything worked out don't you Goode? How have you survived with such ignorance crippling you? Let's not bother to go back and forth about the existence of the Devine. Suffice it to say that you're wrong, agreed? So, then what becomes the most important point after establishing that they do in fact exist? I'll tell you-It's us; our role in the game-that's what. Or, I should say, *my* role in the game. I've put myself in the position I'm in."

"What position is that?"

"I've already told you that. I won the role of deciding peoples' fate." Egon said almost in boast.

"And how exactly do you plan to do that?"

"I'll do it by taking control! In any and every situation you must take control and this situation desperately requires me to do that. That is exactly what I plan to do."

"The weight and the fate of the World is on you huh? Can you be that arrogant? You're the same as Sid. Your concept of control is an illusion.", was my response to him.

"No! Your idea that you possess some autonomy that prevents you from being controlled is the illusion. Your concept of being the first and final conductor of your destiny is the illusion. You're not in control of anything and you never have been!"

"Bullshit!"

"You're not even in control of your emotions and reactions. I am! You've proven that more than once already. Of course, I might be wrong...Were you in control of things when your wife died...? Were you in control when you decided to make your way to where you are now? Are you in control of when and how you'll be leaving? Are you in control, in any way, of how you're feeling right now? Or am I...? Are you even capable of having such responsibility or should we leave it in my hands? Because, Devlin, if you were actually in control of things, and if you always had been, that would mean that you chose, either through ignorance or incompetence, every step and every outcome. Are you really willing to concede that?"

What I heard struck a chord in me. The tiny shred of self-assuredness that I'd been trying to hang onto since I came to this place was shattered twice by Egon's assertions. Once because I was afraid that those assertions were true and again because there was nothing that I could do about it but accept it. I had no defense. There was no fight left in me.

He'd asked me if I was willing to concede and, in a way, I was. But Egon had also succeeded in clouding my thinking and I couldn't be sure of exactly what I'd conceded to. If I wasn't in control like I had believed, then nothing I ever did made any difference at all, and consequently, nothing I would ever do would either. I might have spent a lifetime pointlessly trying to "purchase" my future through my oblivious decisions.

If I had been in control the whole time, then what did that string of sorrows say for me?

I wanted to be furious at Egon for affecting me the way he did, but all I could focus on was my new reason for self-hatred. There was no fight left in me because I was convinced that I deserved to lose.

"You actually seem surprised by this Devlin. That's just another indication of the degree of your ignorance. You see that I'm right though. You are another one of the flock. You're meant to be herded and penned for your own good, and you are. You're controlled by your teachers and your employers and your clergy! Media tells you who you are, who you can't be, and what you should want to be. Your complete lack of control is staggering when you think about it! You are even controlled into believing you have control by your government! And with all that staring you in the face you have the nerve to say that I'm unbalanced!"

"I think you've made your point Egon."

"Have I? I don't think so. My point will be made when my final choice has been made."

"Fine. Are you done?"

"With you? Yes. For now, anyway." He left me alone at that point with that veiled threat hanging in the air like a guillotine.

I sat down, alone there in the commons, and allowed every ounce of momentum to dissipate. The resolve that I thought I'd found was decaying in me. It was like looking into the eyes of a dying friend as they clouded over. There was no consolation to be found in that empty room. It had strangely gotten smaller and more confined suddenly. My eyes were directed aimlessly at a floor that stared back up at me unsympathetically. Soon, the direction of my thoughts began to manifest. I found myself anxiously biting my knuckles like I had since I was young in the worst times of nervousness and frustration; a bad habit that I could never fully explain. I must have appeared the same way I felt; hopeless!

Although it didn't really matter to me where I was, I did decide to go back to my room in hopes that the emptiness I felt would be less imposing there. Looking up, I saw Constance standing on the other side of the room. She was looking at me intently but expressionlessly. I walked over on my way back to my self-imposed isolation and stopped for just a moment near her.

Neither of us spoke.

I felt pointless.

Was I delusional and just fooling myself into believing that I could leave and accomplish anything for myself or my wife and daughter? The more I thought about it the less realistic it seemed to be. Purpose left my life the minute they died. Maybe I had known that all those months ago in the numbing solitude of my apartment. Maybe I had been too naïve to just accept it then. Regardless, whether I came to the conclusion myself or someone illustrated it for me, the reality of the emotion was the same; desolation. There was no escaping it. So, I stopped trying and began to settle back into a very familiar stagnation.

Again, it seemed that any sense of time had completely escaped me (although that may have been from the moment I was brought there), as I fell into a routine of being over-medicated and unproductively counseled.

I rarely got out of bed; for the most part only when I was forced to. When I did have to get up, it wasn't for long and it wasn't to do much more than pace. It seemed that I had just found a new location to re-live the time in my loft after all. But now my vodka had been replaced by mood-altering depressants. The effect of those apparently began to take a toll on my perceptions.

BLAM!

The sound of gunfire erupted and my life ended as a bullet under my chin tore through my besieged head...

But no...It was only my own finger and my own thumb as the cocked hammer. Of course, it wasn't real.

While lying there in just the half-light coming in from the hallway, I saw Serenity run under the table across from my bed. It never occurred to me to be out of the ordinary. I was just glad to see her. For some reason though, when I called to her, she wouldn't come to me, which was unusual...

Sometime later, I heard voices that were familiar coming from just outside my door. They were asking someone about me worriedly. Even though I couldn't put faces to them, they did seem familiar so I was anxious to find out who had come. So, I waited, but no one came in. In time, the nurse came in for her rounds and I asked her angrily, "Why won't you let my friends come in?"

"What?"

"Why won't you let my friends come in to see me?" I repeated.

"What are you talking about? There's no one here for you."

"Yes, there is! I can hear them just outside! Let them come in."

"There is no one here!" she said convincingly. But...I thought I knew what I heard...As she left, all she could do was scowl and shake her head at me. Our relationship obviously had not improved.

The only reasonable conclusion to draw was that I couldn't trust my own perceptions anymore.

Dr. Li thought that I had been spending too much time by myself and "suggested" that it would do me good to leave my room. I carried my isolation with me so I didn't care one way or the other where I was. So, I did as I was told.

It didn't do any good at all. It was a pointless exercise, like everything else, because there was no one else around at the time. Even if there had been, I would have been just as bad company for them as they would have been for me. So, I just sat there in the seating area in front of the TV, alone and uninterested, because that's what I was told to do.

But I didn't stay there alone for long. When I noticed her walking towards me, I just assumed that maybe she had been told the same thing I was told.

Constance came in, but she didn't sit down next to me. Instead, she walked behind and stood there over my shoulder. She was clearly a little different... At first, I was disinterested. But then after some time, it seemed strange to have her hover over me without ever communicating to me at all. It seemed strange but not enough to truly reach me. I looked back at her only once. She wasn't truly bothering me and I didn't really care where she stood so we left each other alone ironically. The television droned on.

Then, in time, I made an effort, "I wasn't watching anything in particular if you want to turn..." I told her. She had no reply at all.

"I guess maybe you want to stand up or whatever but you can sit down if you want..." Again, I was basically talking to myself.

"I thought it might be good to leave my room... actually, Dr. Li told me that I should get out and maybe interact with other people. She said I needed some outside stimulation from someone...she said it would be good for me... Same for you?" If Constance heard me at all she gave no indication of it.

"Guess the doc was dead-on with that one huh?" When I looked over my shoulder at her, Constance just looked down at me out of the corner of her eye. In all honesty, I couldn't be too upset by our one-sided conversation because I didn't really feel like listening to anyone's bullshit anyway. In fact, she was the absolute perfect person to have around me at the time.

Although she never said a word, I guessed that Constance wasn't catatonic. I got the distinct impression that she wasn't physically unable to speak, she just chose not to. It was a safe bet that the 'Whitecoats" had been trying to change that, but I chose to respect it. Besides, everyone else I talked to had either drugged, punched, tasered, or ruthlessly berated me up to that point. I was almost content to have a calm second or two.

Then, she did a funny thing; she reached down, grabbed the remote, and started flipping the channels continuously. She went from channel to channel, never staying on one of them for long. And then she just stopped abruptly when she got to the news channel. As I was looking back at her, wondering what she was doing, the broadcaster got my attention.

He was saying, "...and the first term Congressman from Illinois was able to garner enough votes to pass the historic healthcare bill through the Senate today despite resistance from the other side of the aisle as well as all of the major pharmaceutical companies. The bill is believed by many to be the first workable universal healthcare plan and is also believed to be the first milestone of a possible future President."

'Great news.' I thought. Then something hit me and I put two and two together.

"I hate to break up this party but I have to go. I'm expecting someone...I think." I excused myself to Constance and headed back to my room on a hunch.

Across the commons area and down the long hall to my room, an unlikely suspicion began to come alive. It seemed that I'd begun to notice something even if I wasn't sure of exactly what it actually was. Whatever that something was, it had been the only thing that was remotely able to touch my interest and drag me from my lull. At the same time though, it also seemed to scare me a little. For that reason, I stopped short, just outside the door. I'm not sure if my hunch being proven right or being proven wrong was scarier to me. Either way, I hesitated.

The room was too dark to see much through the small window, but it seemed to be empty. When I put my ear to the door, there were no sounds inside. Of course, the room was empty. Why wouldn't it be? What was I thinking? It was just one more sign of my state of mind. It was obvious that I'd bought into my own delusions.

Feeling pissed at myself, I exhaled deeply and decided to call it a night.

As I reached for the door, I froze instantly as it began to open by itself! I looked around but there was no one else there to tell me that they were seeing what I was seeing, or to tell me that I was just hallucinating. All I could do was stand there unsure and afraid. Then from inside the dark room, I heard him say, "Don't worry Devlin, I'll reassure you."

Sheperd stepped from behind the door and gestured for me to step into the room.

He looked the same as I remembered him; tall, well dressed, bald, and intimidating. The most apparent thing about him being the darkness of his skin. Although he did come across as physically imposing, in some way, he also projected peace. There was a definite duality to him. He was like a volcano that had gone quiet and grown a paradise over it. But no one would ever mistake the fact that the volcano still existed.

I moved inside.

"Don't look surprised to see me. You expected me to be here."

He was right of course, but I couldn't explain how. I had expected him, just like I also expected some answers.

"What's happening to me Sheperd?"

"Apparently a lot..."

"I don't understand what's going on! Am I completely losin' it! Why did I 'expect' you to be here?"

"It's part of a pattern-a rhythm of experiences that you're becoming attuned to.", Sheperd stated.

"What...experiences? The visits...? The news...?"

"Yes. The news; a solicitation to you-a diversion to others." He confirmed.

"A diversion? To who? Why?"

"To the Inimical."

"Who or what the hell...?"

"...Are the Inimical? Interesting phrasing of that question Devlin."

"And the answer to it is...?"

"They are the inverse of myself and those like me. They are the Abhorrent. All that the Inimical are is contrary to those like me.", Sheperd stated with seriousness.

"OK, I get that you're enemies but I don't fully understand about..."

"The solicitation...?" he finished.

"Yeah...and how do you...?"

He brushed past the question I started and began to explain further.

"It is necessary to limit our interactions with each other and at the same time, to distract them from what would be a common interest. We do this by forcing their hand. We use certain means of diverting them. They use similar methods of diverting attention away from their goals. You see, we'd both prefer not to communicate with you at the same time. We find it intolerable to be in the presence of an antithesis. So, we find it necessary to create situations that require their full efforts. Thus, the diversion so that we can speak uninterrupted while they scurry to undo our works. The same is true for us. We must turn our sights away for a time while we strive to overcome and counter their destructiveness. When you watch the news and see a positive, it's our work, either great or small. Of course, the opposite is true of them. The negative or horrific would be their calling card."

"Their...? You're talking about Forge. He's one of those In..."

"The Inimical...Yes, he is."

So, you're saying that you supposedly do good things to get their attention away from me, and they find out about it by watching TV?"

"No Devlin. They have the inherent awareness of us and vice versa. You are the one who finds out by watching TV." Sheperd clarified.

"Seems to me that I see much more shitty news than good.", I stated.

"Is it that more 'shitty' news exists or is that what you're force-fed, Devlin?"

"I don't know anymore." Was my honest answer.

"We'll work on that."

"What do you want from me? Why are either of you trying to talk to me at all?"

"The answer to that question begins the complexities. You must understand some things first before you can appreciate what we want with you."

I asked warily, "What 'things'?"

"First, that we do not want the same thing from you. Regardless of what Forge has said, what we would have you do is night and day!"

"Really? I don't know anything about you, but he claimed to be an Angel and from what I've seen, I'm not sure if I can deny that."

"Yes, I know. That brings me to my next point. You will need an understanding of The Nature to be clearer about anything from this point on."

I didn't question him right away because I knew that he knew my thoughts anyway and I was sure that he'd explain what he meant. Then, he gave his answer.

"The Nature is." Was simply stated.

I was still less than clear at that point.

"Yes, I know you're unclear. That statement is the simplest summation. By that I mean that if you were to ask me, one item at a time, what The Nature consisted of, my answer would be a "Yes" to each and everything. It is all things including nothing. The Nature is a single all-encompassing existence that simply put- "is", he continued.

"We are all part of it and all always have been. It is the totality of all. That means all matter, all energy, and all possibilities, which in actuality are the same things. That accounts for all life, and conversely, all death."

"You're trying to tell me The Nature is- God?" I asked.

"No. Don't belittle it by using such minuscule terms. A "God" is a thing created by men and women to fulfill self-serving purposes; to destroy an enemy, to reward a supposedly good deed, to dramatize an assumed superiority over another, and so on. The concept is fatally flawed because human desire is limited by its degree of perception."

"How many "Gods" have existed throughout the incredibly short history of your world alone? Weren't each of them the "True God" or "Gods". At one point, each of them was created to respond to a specific detriment within a given society. The proselytization began and became self-sufficient in each case and the religion of that particular "God" endured. It endured just long enough for a different group of people with different characteristics, different detriments, different self-involved needs, and thus, different "Gods" to surface. And so, the start of another brutal, subjugating conversion began." He elaborated.

"No, don't confuse The Nature with a religion or a so-called God." Sheperd admonished, "It transcends." He added reverently.

"Fine. Why are you telling me all of this? What does it have to do with me?"

"You are at a point where you require this knowledge, Devlin."

"What does that mean? Why would I?"

"As they say 'Knowledge is Power'. You need one to have the other. Power is energy, and energy is eternal. All things are and derive from energy. Energy takes more than one form but it is all interconnected. So, you too must be."

"I'm not following you…"

"You must and will connect."

"To your… "Nature" …?"

"Not mine, Devlin… "The"".

"Fine. Why?"

"The Nature is the summation of all energy-past, present and therefore future. It is the aggregate consciousness and intentions and experience of forever. You are not excluded."

What Sheperd said almost seemed contradictory. He spoke very reverently but at the same time, he dissed all religious faiths. Since I was never much of a churchgoer, I didn't find myself overly offended by

Sheperd's dismissal of organized religion. But it was contrary to everything I'd been taught to believe. He knew that.

"Devlin, don't get caught up in your Earthly faiths. They are all fleeting. Would the Israelis convert to Islam if they found out tomorrow that it was actually the only true religion? Would Protestants in Ireland become Catholics? Would Wiccans embrace any sect of Christianity? No. Not even if such a thing was possible. You are incapable of choosing and exercising a religion that is contrary to what you identify yourself with or as-whether it seems right or not. Religions suit tastes. Tastes change but the Nature does not."

My mind was racing trying to comprehend all of the things that Sheperd was telling me. One question after another sprang up to obscure the one before it. The first one I managed to get out was, "So, is the Nature a ... person...a male? I mean, not like I am I guess, but is there a gender?" It sounded dumb the minute I heard myself say it.

"Undoubtedly. It is all, and many, many men have existed to contribute. But, haven't many, many women also? Just as many, many insects and crystals and comets...?" he corrected.

"OK, I understand. But...what...?" I began to ask.

"...Does that make me...?" Sheperd finished.

"Well...yeah."

"I am a part of the whole just like you are Devlin."

"Just like me? How can that be? We're obviously extremely different."

"It's like I've told you. Energy takes different forms and frequencies, yet they are all interconnected. Your brain is completely different from your bladder and they each serve a separate function, but they are part of the same whole; of one body. I am a manifestation of the Nature and you are as well. The difference is that, normally, I function on a separate frequency than you. I am attuned to the Nature in a different way and therefore serve a different purpose than you."

"You look like a normal man..." As I said it, he began to walk around me, circling behind me.

"I look the way you'd understand me, Devlin. Would you understand if I looked like...?"

As he came back around me, in sight, he'd become what could only be described as a glowing, oscillating flow of white bands of energy. It was roughly human-shaped and extremely beautiful but at the same time, hard to focus on. He continued to circle, coming back around in his more familiar form.

What he'd done was incredible! Of course, I'd never seen anything like that before. I'd guess that no one had! But I didn't know how I could possibly trust what I'd seen. He'd illustrated his point very well but I knew that I still didn't have the complete picture. So, I questioned him further.

"And what about Forge and his kind? I guess he played me, telling me he was an Angel."

"Forge and the Inimical...They are another complexity.", Sheperd stated thoughtfully.

He continued, "The Totality is a spectrum-a range of "frequencies" for lack of a better way to adequately describe it. There is a particular range of the spectrum and an opposing range of it as well. The Inimical being on one end and We, being on the other. Antitheses-as I've said. The minutest fissure-physicality-exists as a separation between these particular two "frequencies" of the spectrum as the whole moves ceaselessly. Although Perfection is ultimately circular, it is the path chosen to traverse it that is the determination. The Inimical are the culmination of the choice of a path contrary to ours."

"So -they're bad and you all are good?", I tried to surmise.

"Of course, I have to say that that is an over-simplified conclusion, but I'd also call it accurate."

"And if I continue along those lines, then I guess that you could say that you're from Heaven and they're from Hell?"

"How do you define Heaven and Hell Devlin? Are you still using the dogmatic lessons you're practiced in?"

"I'm finding it hard to do anything else, Sheperd! You tell me..."

"I have. Your instinct is correct but you need to be broader. Heaven and Hell are neither a reward nor a deterrent. They are organic eventualities. What you'd call "Heaven" is what I've told you it is; a range of sympathetic frequencies, just as what you'd call "Hell" is as well. Neither conforms to the manufactured descriptions of anything you've been exposed to. The two are dissonant. The two are in fact opposing and confrontational."

"Why?" I asked.

"Because different ends are sought by both."

"What are those "ends"?

"Well...that's the crux. Forge and his kind would have the spectrum converted. They would have the so-called "frequencies" be converted to their own so that they might have a full range of the totality of energy that is The Nature."

My head was spinning! It was nearly impossible to process all of the information I was getting or the implications of it all. It was just so much to take in at once, especially with all that I'd been through still crippling me. As hard as it was, I still instinctively felt the need to try. I began to question him again, "And you want...?"

"We seek to maintain Balance."

"Why? Why don't you want the...the...full range... like they do?"

"We are attuned to a more complete understanding of the whole and understand that Balance is necessary to maintain purpose as well as form. Since we don't see any flaw in either its purpose or its form, we desire Balance."

Suddenly, I was afraid that I might actually be experiencing everything that had happened. It couldn't be possible for me to make it all up in even the most delusional state! Or maybe I was just that crazy...

"No, you're not." He said seeing my line of thought.

"Besides, how do you define "crazy" Devlin? Could it be in fact a judgment inflicted upon those that are misunderstood by the perceptually challenged?"

"Right. Tell that to the ones I've been dealing with lately.", I said.

"The message will get through..." Sheperd replied.

"You said that The Nature was everything that is or was right? If it's made of experiences...what about those things that haven't happened yet? They say not all things are written. Everything hasn't happened yet so..."

"Actually, everything that could possibly happen, and the variables of them, has. Everything that is or was is everything that will be. That is true because all matter and energy has always been. Nothing more will be added. You were once part of an exploding star as well as an ocean in a galaxy you've never heard of-and from only a single layer of the Whole. You have experienced everything physical in one form or another. No being has a new experience to contribute to the whole-just alignment." Sheperd stated.

"Alignment?"

"Yes...the only variable. One chooses the energy frequency they reverberate at with every newly experienced rendition. That consequently, enables the Balance to fluctuate."

"So, let's not even talk about whether or not I really understand all of this-let's just get back to what it all has to do with me."

"You will inevitably join a degree of the spectrum-The Nature-and you are entitled to knowledge of the final option. Forge would have you converted to his side under false pretenses. I want you to be aware and sober so that you can choose purely."

"I see. I'll inevitably join huh? You mean, eventually, when I die right?"

"Yes...when you die..." he agreed but hesitantly for some reason.

"I'm clear now. If I actually believed anything either of you has told me, I might be a little pissed right now. While I'm in the worst Hell of my life, the two of you are trying to ...recruit...me into whatever it is you're selling. You're trying to manipulate me to your own cause. Well, you seem to have misjudged one thing. Suppose I don't want to join or choose of fuckin' "reverberate" with either of you or any side?" I erupted.

"The Nature? Please! Why didn't "The Nature" have my back before my wife and daughter were murdered! Is it just the way of things to have an eight-year-old girl suffer the way she did? Well!? Why did I rot, from the inside out, for months and months, without any intervention from your Nature? Huh!? What-no answers for me now Sheperd? You were a damn Webster's Encyclopedia a minute ago! You think I want to be a part of anything- whether you try to convince me that it's supposedly good or bad? It doesn't even matter if it's all true or if you're full of shit. I'll pass either way. Hell can't help me and Heaven chose not to. So, I'll choose neither of them when the time comes."

Before I could turn fully, the door was thrown open and I felt a sharp pain in my head as I was struck from behind. I'd been surprised and I fell like a stone. Flat on the ground, I felt my senses dulling fast. Looking up with blurred vision, I saw that Sheperd was gone; he had disappeared. Then I saw two people dragging a third person in clumsily, dropping whoever it was not far from where I was sprawled and then leaving in a hurry. The only thing I could distinguish about them was their spotted white shoes. I also, just barely, made out a whisper from one of them to the other saying, "... We'll tell him in the morning..." I didn't know who they meant.

Something wet had worked its way to where I was lying... The last thing I remember seeing was the body next to me trying to sit up. Then, I lost consciousness, but not before I recognized the face of who had been thrown down. I recognized that face but the voice was a complete surprise to me.

She said, "I...am you..." and that was all she said. It was Constance.

The first and only thing that I was aware of was pain.

I felt it in my body and dully in the back of my head. Then, when I opened my eyes, I felt it there too. That blindingly bright light was coming through, burning my eyes again. I squinted hard and started to get up so that I could shut it out once again, but I didn't make it far.

My foot came out from under me and I went back down hard. I'd slipped on something wet. When I rubbed my eyes to clear them, I realized there was something thick and sticky covering my hands.

Blood!

Turning over slowly, I saw the trail leading away towards the wall and quickly realized what had happened. Afraid, I started to get up again, slowly. What I saw across from me made me unable to speak or even breathe.

Constance was slumped against the wall, her eyes wide but lifeless. She was in a pool of her own blood; blood that had emptied from her open, gaping wrists. They were horrible and sloppy wounds. I couldn't imagine her or anyone else being able to inflict wounds like that on themselves... Then, I remembered that two people had dragged her into my room...but I couldn't remember who...I had no idea who...

Before I could think about it further, I remember that the last thing I saw was Constance trying to sit herself up-and then I saw why. Across the wall, scrawled unevenly, were Constance's last words, the last words of a dying woman that never spoke except for a single puzzling sentence.

The reality staring back at me was unbelievable. She had actually written in her own blood as she slowly died! I couldn't help but picture every moment of her every effort to communicate using her spilling life. What message was worth that? What if that message had been communicated sooner, in a different way...?

That wall glared at me and scared the hell out of me, but it also demanded something from me. So, I read the message on it obediently like she'd intended. It said:

UNSEEN

INCONCEIVED

MOUNTAIN SIMULTANEOUSLY A GRAVE AND NURTURER

A BECOMING BEGINS WITHOUT SOLICITATION

THE BEGINNING THAT WAS A DESOLATE ENIGMA

NOW ASPIRED TO A RADIANT AMBIGUITY

THE HEARTBEAT WAS A SOLE COMPANION

DIVINED KNOWLEDGE AND AN AGED SPIRIT SOUL POSSESSIONS

AWARENESS WAS BEING CREPT UPON

UNAWARENESS WAS UNSURELY COVETED

POTENTIALLY DESTRUCTIVE POWER WAS IMPRINTED IN EACH CELL

YET DORMANT AND UNTESTED

BEAUTY WAS INHERENT BUT SUPPRESSED AND DISTORTED BY SEARING
PLUMES OF FLAME

FIRST STEPS WERE TAKEN WHILE WINGS WERE EXTENDED TO TEST THE
RESOLVE OF ITS REALITY

THROUGH ALL TIME AND INSTANTLY-THIS SINGLE EXISTENCE SPREAD IN
EVERY INFINITESIMAL DIRECTION OUTWARD

ALL WAS KNOWN BUT NOTHING WAS LEARNED

ALL WAS TOUCHED BUT NOTHING EXPERIENCED

ALL WAS LOVED THOUGH NOTHING CHERISHED

WITH EVERY SURROUNDING ACKNOWLEDGED

INTERNALIZATION WAS AN ONLY OPTION

THREE LEVELS OF BARRENNESS

FATHOMLESS BUT HOLLOW

REALIZATION WAS THE ONLY CONSTANT

THOUGH IT WAS TOO OFTEN OBSCURED

SEEING THE DUALITY OF ITS CREATION

THE PHOENIX SLOWLY DIED BECAUSE IT SAW THAT IT WAS THE ONLY ONE OF
ITS KIND

ASHES BECAME A NEST AS ITS SINGLE TEAR BECAME A CRYSTALLINE EGG

THE MOUNTAIN AND SKY WERE ITS COMPANIONS

THERE IT LAY WAITING

UNSEEN

INCONCEIVED

They were her last words communicated, but I remembered that they weren't her only words. She had said one thing to me before I lost consciousness, and I struggled to remember...She said...she'd said... "I... am you."

She was me?

I didn't understand what she'd meant but I didn't have the chance to dwell on it. As I knelt there over her dead body and in her blood, I was suddenly startled by the door being violently thrown open again. Dr. Erlikson was there frozen like a statue; except for the slightest curve of his mouth. He reached for the same alarm on the wall as before.

I screamed, "NO!"

The thought of trying to convince Erlikson that what he was seeing was not my fault never really occurred to me. It didn't seem possible that he would even hear me. So, I made up my mind and did what I had to do.

With panic in my eyes, I desperately fought to get up, slipping and falling back down, by that point, I had become covered in blood. Again, I struggled to rise. With one last look at Constance lying there, I broke for the door. Did her eyes shift...?

The Dr. never made a move as I threw open the door and rushed past him. He never made a move to stop me...At first, I couldn't get my footing on the cold tiled floor, so I bent low, hands extended to brace for any fall. Then, with the knowledge of what they'd do to me, I worked my way up to a full run to escape my fate. That's when the alarm sounded.

PAT! PAT! PAT! PAT! PAT!

My bare feet beat out a quick-time rhythm that echoed down the hall. When I got to the end, I turned right. To try to get away from the guards that were likely heading my way, I went through the doors that I'd avoided in the past. I burst through those doors and into a terrible and blinding brightness that completely blurred my vision.

Disoriented, I stretched out my arms to try to feel my way. How ironic it was to be surrounded by light and to be so blind and helpless! Like an invalid, I struggled for balance and direction.

I recklessly strived to move faster again because my desperation hadn't changed at all. First, I began to jog, and then I tried to run from that blaring alarm that followed me. With one hand on a wall, I made my way as best as I could but my vision never cleared and I couldn't judge my progress.

All I could do was follow that wall in whatever direction it seemed to lead me and hope. Because there was no other option, I kept running, stumbling often. Then, I came to something solid; very solid as I found out when I ran into it head-on.

Doors!

I threw myself through them and out into an area that was still blurred to me, hoping that I'd found my way out somehow. Wherever I'd made it to, the alarm was just as loud as it had been before. Although it took a few moments for my sight to clear, I never stopped moving. I couldn't! I had to escape! As my eyes cleared and I continued to run down a long hallway, I picked up speed.

Things began to take on an unsettling familiarity.

Then, I heard voices; the shouts of the guards. But I didn't know where they were coming from. I still didn't have my bearings. Unfortunately, I quickly learned that those shouts were coming from the worst place possible; directly in front of me!

Before I could stop and turn around, we met. It was a head-on collision. A group of them had been coming, moving fast just like I had been. We met right in the archway of a large room, crashing into each other violently.

A couple of them were hurt by that initial impact and a couple were hurt after I fought to get clear of their tangled bodies. My numbness was the only thing that probably saved me from that pain.

With every bit of strength I had, I fought to get away from those guards. One of them grabbed my leg and probably got a broken jaw for it. Another reached for my wrist but missed. Two others got up and began to chase me again. I threw chairs and hopped tables and swung out wildly to resist them. Ultimately, it proved futile.

With a horrible electric hissing, I was shocked within an inch of my life again. I seized and contorted and then just lay there. The fight was over.

Looking up, I saw Lopez impassively glaring down at me. At that point, all of the guards began to beat and kick me, shouting hate down the entire time. Those voices weren't new to me. That hate sounded just like what I'd heard many times before. Then, when I saw where I was, my spirit sank further as I realized numbly, that somehow, I'd only made it as far as the common area. How could I have gotten so turned around? How could I have been so lost?

Everything went dark.

"Ahhh!... Ahhh!... What...!?"

The face just inches from my own terrified me at first glance because I didn't know who it was, where I was, or even who I was. The unfamiliar darkened room I came around in just added to my confusion. In that instance, I somehow got the sense that I had died and was looking into the face of something threatening. And so, I panicked.

"Snap out of it!", came at me hatefully, along with a stinging slap in the face.

That troll of a nurse was there again, leaning over me, right in my face. That explained why I opened my eyes and panicked. Then I came to another realization; the bitch slapped me!

"You bitch! What the hell is your..."

SMACK!

She did it again! I tried to block her but found that I couldn't move. Then I realized how bad my situation really was. I'd been strapped down to the bed! Both my arms and my legs were immobilized! I looked up at her in disbelief and saw a smirk on her face that sent me into a rage. With the little strength that I had, I kicked and jerked and strained myself to get free. It didn't amount to much though; I wasn't going anywhere-they'd seen to that.

After I stopped struggling, she stepped back with a closed-mouthed laugh. Right behind her was Lopez, wearing a tense and anxious look on his face. I guessed that look was for me. Visions of what I'd seen him do to that helpless man suddenly resurfaced. That made me start struggling again even harder.

"Let me go! Let me out of here!", I demanded. "There's no reason for this! LET ME OUT!"

The two of them laughed to each other at my ranting like I was an inside joke of theirs. Then, she said, "No reason huh? I don't think that poor girl would agree with you. Why would you do that to an innocent like that? You're a sadistic bastard, aren't you?"

I tried desperately to defend myself, "NO! I didn't hurt her. Someone hit me from behind. When I came to, I found her there." They weren't hearing me at all though. Their inside joke seemed to have their full attention.

"Someone hit you from behind huh? Did you see who it was?" She was patronizing me.

"No, they were BEHIND me!"

"That's too bad. If only you'd been able to tell us who it was...", she said.

"It wasn't me! I didn't do it! Why would I? LET ME OUT!"

"So you can destroy another life, Mr. Goode? I don't think so."

She backed away from the bed and crossed the room, towards the table next to Lopez. He was staring at me. He never let his glare drop. It seemed to be a barely contained hostility. With her back to me, the nurse seemed to be working with something, but I couldn't tell exactly what. Whatever it was, I knew it would probably turn out bad for me. Then, when she turned to me again, I regretted being right. She came at me with a syringe and a grin; a grin that seemed to be dripping anticipation.

Although I knew that I was strapped down tight, I fought anyway. But again, it was futile of course. Lopez rushed over to fulfill his role and I suffered a quick beating for my efforts. There was no stopping them from what they intended to do. She jabbed me roughly with that needle and then bent down to lick away the trickle of blood she'd caused. It was disgusting! The two of them were equally twisted.

Both of them stood there staring down at me and there was nothing I could do. Their stares accused me of things. Their stares damned me for those things. But I'd lost the will as well as the strength to try to defend myself from them. Besides, I couldn't be sure of what I was defending myself from. Was I being blamed for just Constance's death?

It seemed that there was more to it than just that. There were uneasy feelings between all of us long before what happened to Constance. I got the feeling that I was being judged for other things as well...but I had no idea as to what. And so, they stood there over me, like gargoyles, still and condemning.

Through the haze of the injection, I saw them moving closer and closer to me. I felt that any recognition of reality was soon going to be lost completely. No matter how I fought it, I slipped down further and further into confusion until I didn't even know that I didn't belong there. They continued to come closer, remaining stone-faced.

Then the voices started. All around me and nowhere, voices stabbed at me. There was no origin for any of them, but they were there, just out of sight no matter which way I turned or how fast. Those voices shook with hate and blame.

They were saying:

YOU'VE WASTED A LIFETIME!

ALL YOU DESERVE IS NOTHING!

CONCEDE FUTILITY!

WORTHLESS LOSER!

I jerked my head from left to right trying to identify who or what I thought I was hearing. I never succeeded. There was no way to know what was really happening, just as there was no way to stop it. The shot they'd given me had succeeded in quickly erasing my clarity.

"You have a lot to answer for, don't you? DON'T YOU! Did you believe that you wouldn't have to face the music?", the nurse screeched at me. "You will suffer and you will regret what you've done."

"What...? I...didn't..."

"YOU KILLED THAT WOMAN!"

"No...who...?"

"You killed them and you know it."

"...wait...who are you talking about?"

"Oh, you know exactly who I mean Goode. You are completely responsible. How does it feel? You still have blood on your hands. You've always had their blood on your hands. It's as red as the mark on your soul."

"...Their? What...? Get out. Leave me alone you..."

CRACK!

Again, I was reminded by Lopez why he was there. My face stung from his blow and I hated him for it! I was helpless and they took advantage of that fact.

She continued, "Who's in control here...You or us? We're your judge and jury murderer! You know that if it wasn't for you, she'd still be alive."

My condition was bad enough with the amount of sedatives they'd been forcing into me to keep me lethargic and unmotivated but the last injection had left me nearly stripped of active consciousness. I watched, detached for the most part, as my two judges took turns beating and berating me. There were continuous accusations of my part in someone's death...

I vaguely remembered blaming myself for someone's death in my past... But I couldn't remember whose. Was it in my past? Or was it then? Did that just happen? I couldn't tell.

Was I completely responsible? Was I?

Through the fog I was in, I heard someone come into the room and say, "What the hell are you doing!"

With effort, I turned my head towards the door and saw Erlikson standing there. Who would have ever thought that he'd come to my rescue?

"I don't remember telling either of you to interrogate this patient.", he said.

"Help...me." I mumbled, hoping that he would be my unlikely savior. "They think that I...but I didn't...I didn't kill..."

"Both of you get out now. Your job is done."

Lopez and the nurse walked towards the door obediently. As they were leaving, something about them barely caught my eye; they both had tiny red spots on their otherwise perfectly white shoes. I saw it but couldn't rationalize the meaning of it. My attention turned back to Erlikson.

"I...didn't kill Constance..."

"I know that. I believe you, Devlin. Has anyone said you did?", the doctor replied.

"You believe me...?"

"Of course, you didn't kill her-they did."

"What...? How long...have you known.? I don't understand...why you're so calm...", I weakly muttered.

"They told me first thing this morning Devlin...and I'm calm... because they did exactly what I told them to do."

PART III: THE ASCENDING

Isolation was what I had been sentenced to.

Any ideas of struggling or pleading to be freed quickly decayed into hopelessness. Alone and immobilized, the feelings I was left with worked to lead me toward further desolation.

With only guilt and accusatory voices echoing through my thoughts, I suffered a very personal Hell. I was in Hell, Erlikson was the Devil mocking me with sickeningly white teeth, and his two demons were at his side. Between them, I was subjected to abuses that were meant to completely break me down and cripple me. Beatings, numbing depressants, accusations, and humiliation became standard prescriptions.

 Murderer! Murderer! They kept that mantra ringing through my head non-stop. I was constantly belittled and made to feel worthless. It didn't take long to begin to believe it and accept it.

Failure! Failure! Words meant to kill my spirit were soon made to feel natural to me. Those soon became my identity. Hope and my soul were being lost.

"Why is this happening to me?"

"Simple-because you deserve it.", the Dr. said.

"Why? Why am I in this Hell? If this is Hell, what have I done to deserve this?", I asked.

"That is precisely the question. What have you done? Apparently, nothing beneficial. You seem to have left a wake of negativity behind you. Dead family, substance abuse, suicide, institutionalization, murder... What haven't you done!? No one's to blame but you. How does it feel buddy? Lonely? Unfair? You've chosen your every step so you've obviously chosen to be here now. Therefore, you've chosen me. Those choices have led to punishment. That punishment will be assessed by me! You think this is Hell...? You'll wish it was Hell Mr. Goode. You'd be better off."

"I didn't choose this! You think I chose to lose everything I had! Are you insane!" I protested.

"Are you...? Ask yourself what you could have prevented if only you'd chosen differently."

"No...You're wrong. How would you know...?"

"You lack conviction. Your denials are weak. But let's consider the source.", he prodded.

"Bastard!"

"Now, did you mean me- or were you just talking to yourself-or both? I wouldn't blame you if you were. I mean really, I'm not surprised at your self-hatred after the magnitude of your failures. How do you live with yourself? Oh, that's right, you couldn't. How'd that turn out for you?"

'Leave me alone."

"You are alone..."

"LEAVE ME ALONE!" I yelled and then turned to confront the Dr., only to find out that there was no one there.

"Who are you talking to like that? You still haven't learned your place?'

When I jerked my head to the other side of the bed, I was shocked to see the hateful nurse glaring down at me. But I didn't remember her being there at all originally. I was yelling at...

"You'd have thought that you would have learned your limitations by now. But you do seem to be a bit slow Mr. Goode.", she said.

"You...made me this way!"

"Who made who Mr. Goode? I told you the first time you saw me that I was just here to do a job. Don't try to blame me for your condition. Did I make you into a worthless murderer! No, you did that all on your own and you know it don't you?"

"No."

"You should have been able to stop it...you should have been able to save them."

"Wait-you're confusing me...I couldn't save...?", I began.

"That's right, you couldn't save-and why not?'. She jeered.

"I...don't know...", came from the confused daze I was in.

"Because you never attempted to in the first place! Admit it, you're happy she's gone! You let her die on purpose-KILLER!"

"NO! STOP IT! I WILL GET FREE AND THEN I'M GONNA..."

UHH!

The dull pain of a hit to the side of my head stopped my threats cold. I turned to find Lopez there, just behind the fireworks he forced into my vision. He had hit me when my attention was focused on the nurse. He must have come in without my noticing...After I cursed him, I turned back over to finish my threat to his accomplice, but she was gone without a word.

It didn't make sense at all but I really didn't make much of an effort to question it. Too much had happened already. Instead, I turned to face what I'd come to expect from that sadistic guard. I waited, but he never moved or said a word to me. Maybe I should have been happy that he didn't come at me, but the threatening glare he refused to drop was just as disturbing. There was an unspoken debt to pay in that glare.

Between them all, each tried to break me down in different ways. Erlikson worked at distorting my mind, the troll nurse pecked away at my spirit, while the guard worked at pain. Although I was numb, I could still feel those effects to a degree.

Lopez started with slaps and moved on to a closed fist. There was nothing I could do to protect myself from him while I was restrained like I was. The beginnings of a very distinct suffering went through me.

"Stop...you can't do this."

CRACK!

I felt my head throb.

"You son of a...!"

Smack!

His blow cut me off.

"You will...regret...every time you've touched me.", was my warning to him. Then, he did something unexpected.

With no explanation at all, he stoically turned and left the room. Just when I thought that maybe I'd been given a reprieve, he quickly killed that hope. It was only a matter of seconds before he came back in with evil intentions.

Of course, I had been in the wrong position to be warning him of anything and he chose to point that out. His arms were behind his back, which made me begin to imagine the worst. Thoughts of tasers or clubs or possibly even blades flew through my mind. When he came up beside the bed and began to take his arms from his back, I started to panic. I struggled against my restraints as much as they allowed but got nowhere. 'This is it!' I thought. Then he made his move, pulling out what he'd been hiding. He threatened me with-a large dry sponge.

My breath came out loudly in relief. 'Maybe he'd reconsidered what he'd been doing to me' I thought.

CRACK!

He'd reconsidered nothing!

"What the Fu…" I started but never finished. He took me by surprise then and started forcing that sponge into my mouth! He beat me brutally the entire time I struggled. With every hit, he made a little more progress and I lost a little more ground and confidence. No matter how I tried, I was losing the fight against him.

I tried to clamp my jaw shut but ended up gasping heavily which just gave him more opportunities. Soon, he'd managed to force it far enough into my mouth to choke me.

It became lodged and I couldn't spit it out. He stepped back admiring my gasping along with the tears on my face. Just when I thought the worst was over, his real intention was revealed.

With that enormous sponge sticking from my mouth, he did something that redefined my true hopelessness; he reached onto the table and picked up the pitcher of water. As soon as he started to pour, that sponge started to expand in my mouth and throat. Of course, I became completely hysterical! As the sponge became saturated, it expanded fully, choking me tortuously. There was nothing I could do. That sponge was lodged and there was no spitting it out.

Lopez just kept pouring and pouring and all of the excess water went down my throat as I continued to struggle to breathe. It gave the effect of both drowning and choking. The combination of those two things sent me into a desperate panic. But it was impossible to maintain that struggle.

My energy was completely spent from too much fighting and my spirit had been severely dulled from too many nullifying things that were pumped into me. So, I not only eventually gave up, I began to blackout.

The last thing I remember was Erlikson standing where Lopez had been. Strangely, he was laughing and holding what looked like the sponge...

"The stronger the fight the weaker the faith.", I heard from across the room. His voice was neither a surprise or a comfort.

"That will be our sermon for the day.", he said with mocking in his tone. "Look at you. Your condition has deteriorated somewhat since I saw you last Dev. Why is that? Misguidance! That is the reason and I am the remedy. I seem to remember leaving off with something about "punishment" the last time we spoke. I'd say you have things rather backward though. You're choosing fighting rather than faith. Choose faith! Faith-in what I'm attempting to do for you!"

Forge's voice reverberated through the room and through my head. He'd come from out of nowhere, as usual, and started speaking in riddles the way he had before. But I wasn't listening to what he had to say because I had my own urgent agenda.

"Set me free…", I asked in desperation.

"That's always been my intention-but there seems to be a lack of cooperation on your part.", was his response.

His cryptic way of speaking only succeeded in aggravating me more, But I did my best to contain what I really felt; a lesson learned.

Forge continued in vain.

"Inmate or warden Devlin Goode?" he asked. 'What will you serve and how?"

"Serve? What do you serve Forge? I was told things…"

"You were told "things"? That's not an accusation that I hear in your tone, is it? You were told "things" … I know what you were told, I know who told you and why, and I know who and what I am! Can you say the same? Do you even know your own proclivities? Save your protestations-the answer is "NO!" I serve the One Motive!"

"Please, I don't really care, just set me free! I'm innocent! Why are you keeping me here!?"

"I am not the one who put you here. And, are you really innocent? Are any of you things?", he questioned.

"I don't need a theological debate right now; I need to get out of here! Let me out! Let me out! Let me out!"

He continued as if he hadn't heard me, "The answer to my question is again, "NO" by the way."

"Just help me…"

"Help yourself."

"Go back to Hell! Are you just here to fuck with me!? Leave me the hell alone if that's all you want."

My frustration erupted before the lesson from one of our previous encounters could stop it. Needless to say, he didn't appreciate what I'd said to him. He'd established my place in our relationship before. My outburst made it seem like I'd forgotten it.

Forge chose to remind me again; he chose to remind me severely.

From across the room, he exerted his power by closing his fist tightly and shaking it in the air several times furiously. My entire body clenched and strained and responded to every shake of his fist. It was as if I was something small and weak in the jaws of a vicious predator. Finally, he jerked his arm up which lifted my body, and in turn, the bed I was restrained to, off of the floor and back down again violently. My full compliance was his again, whether I liked it or not. When he began again, he had my full attention and I listened without interrupting him.

"What is All Devlin? All is one. "ALL" is singular. Yes, I know what you were told-but you've only gotten half-truths. It's a mistake to ignorantly try to make a distinction between an "Us" and a "Them" or a "Good" or "Bad". You don't have the tools to draw such conclusions. Again, "All" is one Devlin. Why do you believe a separation exists between what is an inextricable Singularity?"

"What are you trying to...?", I began.

"God and the Devil...", he said gesturing the quote signs in the air, "...are the same thing."

"I don't believe you."

"They are the same just as what you want to call "Angels" and "Demons" are the same. We simply have a less effective P.R. department. What...? Do you think that I once conformed to some vague description of "goodness" but either chose to or was duped into falling? I'm as I was made and I perform as I was designed to. What you feebly imagine to be "God" and the "Devil" are one, contradicting though it may sound to you. Let me illustrate. Look at where you are right now. There could possibly be all kinds of maladies within this structure; like someone with two very separate personalities but in one form. I told you before that everything was a representation of everything else with the only variable being its scale. This is no different. Dissociative Disorder is a condition that is a reflection of the state of the Singularity."

"Are you really trying to imply that God -is insane!?"

"Now ask yourself if you're in a position to be throwing that word around." He replied. 'No, not insane, but dualistic. How is it possible that a particular thing happens that appears unjust or out of balance? That is The All expressing itself whether it's regarded as positive or negative by the lesser. It can't then be taken back, because it was intended at the time by one of the pervading ends. It cannot be contradicted. And so...think about it...the appropriate mechanisms are in place to ensure that The Singularity does not contradict itself. We are those   mechanisms."

"We? You mean the Inimical?", I said refusing to concede.

"Yes...And you! *We*-Devlin! You only need to learn what you are!"

"Why should I buy this? I was told that..."

"The Chimerical are misguided." Forge interrupted impatiently.

"Who?"

"You know who I'm referring to-keep up! Sheperd and his kind-The Chimerical. As I've already said, I know what you were told. The Chimerical would have you believe that our motives are purely destructive but that's not true at all. We are judicious! How can that possibly be bad? Look at you. How do you feel Devlin? Justified or victimized? You're completely restrained, weakened, and impotent. I'm not stating the obvious to belittle you, I sympathize. You don't deserve any of this, do you? You don't deserve to be in the situation you're in do you?", he baited.

"No, I don't."

"Exactly! And I want what's right for you. I want justice for you. But someone has to receive that justice. Someone began this. That someone should be made to suffer as you've suffered."

"Hell yes!" I agreed.

"Hell yes is right! It's only a natural reaction to what is inequitable. The opposite would be illogical. So, how do you get equity back? By internalizing those injustices and allowing them to decay you? Or by re-focusing on an equally potent penance for the ones responsible?"

"I...don't know..."

"You do know. It's base-it's instinctive. You've got to hold their feet to the fire so to speak.", Forge said with a smirk.

"What do you want from me Forge?", I finally demanded.

He paused as he looked at me intently, apparently seeking and then recognizing a particular thing. Then he said almost thoughtfully, "Your sensitivity is more of a curse than a gift in your eyes. You almost wish that you weren't the way you are. You don't value it. That is because you've never exercised it for its real intent. It's not to be pointed inward to fuel self-degradation. It should have been extended outward, like feelers, identifying objectives-or should I say the tone of your objectives. You are a Harvester."

He said it like I should have epiphanied on cue. But of course, that didn't happen. I was a beaten-down soul, bound down and battered and his esoteric rants couldn't have possibly reached me then. Although he must have suspected it, that didn't stop him.

"The "Objectives" I'm referring to are those that attune themselves with a degree of the Singularity that needs, shall we say, direction. That sensitivity that you feel burdened with is the tool that will allow you to be effective."

"At what?"

"At harvesting for the Singularity! At gathering those that chose their frequency and thus sought out retribution. You will perform a service by contacting them and bringing them to exactly where they chose to be."

As I listened to Forge go on, I remembered stating that I was not interested in ever choosing a side. That's what he was actively trying to make me do. But I held onto my resentment tightly. Whether it was all true or not, I felt the same as when I told Sheperd that I wouldn't accept what he was saying. It didn't matter what I actually thought or believed. Nothing Forge had said up to that point had changed my mind at all.

So, I challenged him, "What makes you think I care about any of this? Why would I want to do what you're suggesting?" After putting the questions to him, the answers he gave made me regret I'd ever asked.

"Would you see your wife and daughter's killers punished Devlin...? Would you reject the chance to redeem the suffering of those just like you? Would you rather not take a position out of spite? That would be like turning your back on them, wouldn't it? We both know that you couldn't do that. You've repeatedly said that you only want a chance to keep a promise to your poor dead little girl, haven't you? Tragic... the way that she suffered...And of course your wife...most people would want justice. Don't you think that this might just be that opportunity! This is the means to set things right which will, in turn, allow you to come into harmony with your departed little family. You do want that don't you? Don't you owe it to them? Don't you have to make amends? Would you like to be reunited with them or would you like that last horrific sight of them to be their testament? Fine, don't do this for the countless strangers around the world that you could spare the type of pain that you've endured. Forget altruism! Do it for the man who lost everything. It's the only way to redeem their murders."

I believe that he'd had a dual purpose in tearing open the wound of my family, He definitely meant to hurt me. That much seemed clear enough. But he'd also meant to strike a chord in me that would resonate to his tune...He'd succeeded at both.

I'd been left alone with only the thought that Forge might be right harassing me. My perception of the things that I'd been told had evolved since the first time I'd seen him. That may have been a result of my own anger or possibly of some truth that I chose to inject into his arguments.

Maybe he was my way out-my unlikely savior. He'd been right about invoking the need for retribution for my family. I began to buy into it. Although I wasn't sure that I fully knew what Forge was offering, there seemed to be something desirable about it.

My bitterness began to take shape and was growing to the size of a monster. I felt that beast begin to turn outward maliciously. Forge seemed to be giving me an outlet and it was beginning to look appealing to me.

But was that outlet meant to condemn or redeem? Was I being skillfully manipulated or was I beginning to see more clearly?

The opportunity for what he claimed was justice occupied my thoughts. Those thoughts were still

somewhat clouded, but they had changed.
Unfortunately, my line of thought was the only thing that had changed. Nothing drastic had changed about my situation. I was still made to suffer. I'd remained confined and abused which only further illustrated his point.

'Would you see your wife and daughter's killers punished...?' That's what he'd asked me. That's what kept going through my thoughts over and over. Would I see their killers punished?

No.

I'd see much worse if I could! Punishment had the sound of ending, of finality to it-and that was far from my idea of equity. How could punishment suffice? No, they should be made to feel like they made their victims feel. They should be made to suffer the way I had been because of what they'd taken! I'd become furious again from Forge's prodding and reacted violently, fighting against my restraints, again in vain.

There was nothing left to do but let out a primal scream; that was also in vain. It was no surprise that it didn't make me feel any better. Actually, I half expected to be rushed and beaten for my efforts but thankfully, there was no response at all. No one came.

Forge had asked me something else- 'Would I reject the chance to redeem suffering?' He'd meant oth-er people's suffering as well as my own. The more I dwelled on that question, the more I felt myself pulling away from my previous resistance. If his idea of redemption meant what I found myself hoping it did, then I was beginning to welcome that opportunity. Despite the fact that I didn't know exactly how he intended to bring about his so-called redemption, I found myself becoming more and more drawn to it. My drastic shift in perspective did worry me a little though.

Then, a semblance of hope appeared unexpectedly and I clung to it. Dr. Li made an appearance.

Dr. Li came in with an empathetic look on her face. Maybe I should have been more appreciative of it but I was too preoccupied with my bitterness. My relief in seeing her was unintentionally obscured by rudeness.

I said, "What would be more helpful than that sad expression, would be for you to get me out of this..."

"That's why I'm here now Mr. Goode.", the doctor answered.

"Hurry-please!"

"It's not that simple. It's not within my power alone to make the decision to release you. If it were really that simple, you never would have been put in this situation.'

"Yeah, right, I guess we all answer to something or someone, don't we Doc? Maybe you could give me some answers now."

"I'll do whatever I can to...", Dr. Li began.

I broke in with, "Do I deserve to be in the situation I'm in now?"

"Devlin, I believe that there is a natural order to everything, whether we can decipher it or not. Since that is what I believe, then I have to say that although I'm not sure that "deserve" is the proper word to use-you are now, where you can only be."

"You're not sure "deserve" is the proper word? NO! I don't deserve this! You're trying to say that my own actions and choices put me in this Hell...I promise you that none of what has happened to me in a very long time has been of my choosing! You think I want this? You think I want to suffer?"

"But you do...on a level that you're either not able to perceive or are unwilling to acknowledge. Your self-condemnation brought about decisions, which determined direction, which naturally brought about a destination. Each hinged on the former. So, now, as a result, you are where you can only be."

"' Self-condemnation'...what are you saying Doc?"

"I'm saying that what you think, feel, say, and do are all connected but not necessarily in the way that you believe. You'd made the determination that you, in fact, did want to suffer for something that you felt was unforgivable. Not only did you come to that conclusion internally, but you also chose to administer the judgment internally rather than wait for some external source. So, you set about your self-destruction. Now, the question is-were you correct in your judgment? My answer would have to be-No."

"Why? How can you know that?" I asked.

"The question that should be addressed is this; would your wife and daughter hold you responsible for what happened to them? You believe they either would or should. That belief was the start of your sentence. But you needed to believe that because that was the beginning of your punishment."

"Punishment...? What are you talking about? Punishment for what?"

"Punishment for living after they'd both died, Devlin."

The truth of what I was being told was too painful to take at first. I was conflicted because allowing myself to embrace that idea meant that I wasn't really grieving for my family, but was instead, focusing on how the loss of them affected me. The thought that my selfishness played a part in the death of my family had pushed me beyond the breaking point. After hearing what Dr. Li told me, it seemed that my selfishness had just continued on afterward as well. That thought was more fuel for my shame. That shame made me raise the question; "Why should I be forgiven?"

"Devlin, you couldn't forgive yourself for not being there to protect your family, as you see it, but you're missing a fundamental point. To even be in a position to ask yourself whether or not you should be forgiven for a thing means that you are incapable of answering that very question. How can you forgive yourself on someone else's behalf? Your perceptions of failure and culpability would make your judgments imbalanced even if forgiveness was yours to decide. Of course, you are capable of forgiving yourself for a thing, but you clearly chose a different direction. You made the wrong judgment."

"If I accept that you're right, then the wrong person is being punished. That tells me that maybe I should be listening to...that maybe someone else should be judged and condemned."

"Does it seem logical to try to assign a sentence to someone else when you are incapable of exercising accurate self-judgment?", Dr. Li challenged.

"I don't know. I just feel..." I began.

"Yes-you just *feel*. Without complete accounting-all information possible-your conclusions are self-serving."

"Self-serving? Obviously, I'm not too concerned with myself or I wouldn't be where I am now."

"Exactly why you've chosen to suffer. Don't you see Devlin?', she asked.

"No! I don't see! You're talking in circles and none of it matters anyway. It doesn't matter because I don't matter anymore."

"To who?" Dr. Li asked.

"To me! To anyone! Look at me! Look at where I am!" Helplessness had gotten the better of me and I lashed out. "I'm done...I couldn't give you a single reason why I need to keep this up. There is nothing more that can be done for me and I can't do anything for anyone else! I don't need this anymore."

The doctor looked at me without expression for a moment, seemingly without a next move. But that wasn't the case at all. That was completely my misinterpretation. Her next move was to touch me profoundly by simply stating- "There is always someone who needs you more than you need yourself."

She'd left me speechless for a moment with the depth of what she'd said to me until my bitterness responded for me saying, "Just who the hell do you think that might be?"

"You know the answer to that...", was her reply before she turned to leave.

The point was well taken but with everything that I'd been put through, I was torn. I felt the need to retreat a little so I closed my eyes and allowed my world to become as dark as my mood.

"...And with this new evidence that has come to light, indictments of several cabinet members and an impeachment have become inevitable..."

I sat up with a start! My restraints were gone! Things had changed, but only back to a previous familiarity. I was back in my original room again, coming around to the sound of a news broadcaster.

The television played with shadows around the dark room but despite the realization that I was free again, I never moved to let more light in. Instead, I responded to an instinct and asked, out loud, "Do I have you to thank for this?"

"No. We definitely haven't progressed to that point yet.", was Sheperd's response from the corner of the room. My instinct had been right.

"How do you feel Devlin?"

"I don't know. Confused...frustrated...pissed."

He'd asked a question that I'm sure he knew the answer to out of politeness.

"I'm being pulled back and forth, violently, through intense emotions and I don't know how to get off of this ride. How do I know what to feel or believe after being torn in so many directions? You have no idea how much hurt I want to repay...how much anger I want to vent at someone else's expense. It would be so easy...so easy... Do I allow myself to go with those feelings? The offer was on the table to give me an outlet-and a part of me wants to welcome it! FUCK! Am I supposed to deny that I want payback out of some higher nobility!? What will that get me? Oh, but maybe it's not about what I want at all huh? I was told that I was still in some position to help someone else; that someone needed me. Can you believe that? Can I?"

"You can believe it and you can fulfill it. There is much that is open to you at this point but your time to exploit it is finite."

"Have you been straight with me Sheperd? I was told that I was only getting..."

"...Half-truths?"

"Yes. You know that Forge told me that. I can't say that I completely believe him but I can't say that I don't. In a way, I really want to trust him. For personal reasons, I want to but I'm just not sure if I can. But you seem to think that trusting you should be a given."

"Who do you doubt Devlin? Is it really me? I haven't told you half-truths. What you should consider is whether or not some of the things Forge told you were designed to fit a specific purpose. Just as he has been, I am aware of what has been relayed to you. He has been subtly steering you toward an outcome that suits his and the Inimical's desires."

"It was never subtle.", I said.

"I've told you that his kind want to control the totality of the Nature. They want complete and unopposed control. How do you gain control of any kind? You do that by taking away power. Forge is a Demon, regardless of his delusional ideas of our similarities, and Demons covet power and power alone. The Inimical take on power by first confusing and then converting. The act of confusing someone like yourself fulfills two purposes. First, the distress that you have to endure takes its toll by actually altering the "frequency" at which you vibrate. That process effectively lowers your reasoning and therefore your resistance so that the second function is achieved; your conversion. Once you are fully converted, your purpose is dictated by your corrupted frequency. That purpose is to expand, to create sympathetic frequencies, and to convert others, which ultimately means the confusion and distress of someone possibly just like you."

"And you and yours...?"

"The Chimerical, as he referred to us? The entities you would deem Angels empower those they provide choices to Devlin. That is the difference between the Inimical and Us.

I've given you information and direction in an effort to empower you. To what end? So that you can choose wisely."

"Yeah...You said that before. What choice could I have to make?"

"The same choice all make in the end; alignment."

"Alignment...? The end...? Right. You said that before too. I was called a "Harvester" by Forge, what is that?"

"It's a misnomer."

"A misnomer?"

"That is the Inimical's way of romanticizing their intent and existence. They choose to deceive others by claiming to do a service by gathering the so-called unjust and corrupt. What they fail to intimate is their own complicity in those same unjust and corrupt. The Inimical create disharmony, confusion, and suffering in an effort to convert all things to their purpose. It's referred to as "Harvesting" by them but the perspective is quite skewed. They are not gathering what has evolved naturally, but are in effect re-engineering and tainting all that they touch. It is a process that you have become intimately aware of. The end result is their propagation. This is what they call the "One Motive". The reference to you as a Harvester clearly reveals Forge's intentions toward you."

"Fine...You've told me your intentions as well. You want nothing more than to provide me with a choice?"

"What I want is not the issue Devlin. I'm bound by an understanding that is unquestioned. Our desire is, just as I've told you; to maintain a balance that will ensure the continuation of the Nature. We refuse and are incapable of the manipulation that our antithesis revels in. That manipulation is equitable to a violation! That violation is worse than even the physical defilement because it cannot be healed. We not only understand that fact, we honor it! The Inimical hoor only the subversion of it."

The imposing and powerful aspect of Sheperd that I knew existed surfaced through the passion of his words. Although he had never assaulted me the way that Forge had, I instinctually feared Sheperd more.

He picked up on that and responded, "Devlin! What you should fear is a ceaseless existence of damning others to hopelessness!"

Sheperd's demeanor had changed in a very short time. He seemed to become very agitated and aggressive all of a sudden without reason. I somehow knew that I hadn't said or done anything that would elicit that response from him, but I didn't know exactly what had. Until I heard him speak...

"EFFETE MARTYR!", Forge shouted from behind me.

"WHITED SEPULCHER! PHARISEE!", Sheperd accused in return.

Sheperd must have sensed the presence of his enemy and reacted to him angrily. I had been told that the Inimical and the Chimerical couldn't stand to be in the presence of one another and I assumed that if it did happen, the result would be disastrous. That was exactly what was happening right in front of me. From the change in Sheperd's tone to the overt hostility that Forge seemed to stop suppressing, their threatening intensity made me worry because I was in their crossfire. Although I couldn't be positive as to why Forge chose to appear while Sheperd was present, I had to assume that we'd reached some kind of turning point and that he'd had no other option.

The tension between the two of them almost had a physicality to it; a life. Eventually, I came to realize that what I felt was the power that they both possessed; smoldering. I had been shown incredible abilities by both Forge and Sheperd in different ways at different times, but I believed those powers were about to be fully un-harnessed. There was no way to predict what that ultimately meant for me though.

They stood motionless and initially, I just thought that they were waiting to see who would make the first move. But that wasn't the case at all. I'd misread the situation.

They weren't just standing still, they seemed to have become detached. It was like the bodies in the room with me were actually vacated, as if they had been in fact a kind of hindrance.

Their bodies never moved at all. There wasn't a single blink or breath, (I wasn't sure if they even breathed at all at the time). No one came forward or fell back which made it impossible to know who was winning. Although they never budged, their strife was illustrated in the frozen expressions they both wore. Those expressions told a story of horrible strain and depthless animosity.

There was no way to be sure of what was safe to do next. Should I try to leave, should I try to bring them out of it, or should I keep out of it completely and be the third statue in the room? I took a step toward Sheperd and waved a hand in his face to no response. When I turned back around, the thought of getting out quick came to me but that meant making my way past Forge and I found myself hesitant to try. That smirk he habitually wore had changed with his efforts into an evil scowl, which made me unwilling to chance it.

Anxiousness made my heart pound. I felt light-headed, like a person becoming suddenly aware that something very bad was about to happen to him and knowing that he was powerless to stop it.

With the exception of my own fear, there was a crypt-like silence in the room that I knew couldn't and wouldn't last. Somehow, it had to be broken.

Forge shattered it first by saying, "What has he offered you, Goode? Nothing! But I…"

"You are giving nothing! Your manipulation only seems to be redemptive!", Sheperd shot back without his normal quiet reserve.

I looked on, amazed at the fact that neither of them was actually speaking. Their words seemed to be echoing thunderously inside my mind rather than actually coming from the two bodies I saw on either side of the room.

"You take!", Sheperd continued. "You take from the foolish who then become your victims and you take from The Nature!"

"No! No! We give the ones you call foolish exactly what you refuse to-POWER!", Forge countered.

"Power comes through self-determination. What your kind does strips them of that irrevocably!"

"And what does your kind do? You leave them impotent and ineffectual."

"Not ineffectual at all, but non-malignant. They continue to contribute to the Whole through our path but without your corrosive effects. You'll never comprehend that fact.", Sheperd said with a tinge of pity.

"Have you ever questioned whether they prefer their newfound role of passivity to our non-abeyance? No, of course, you haven't because it's too late at that point!"

"Just as it's too late when your influence has corrupted their energies beyond repair?", Sheperd challenged.

"Our influence allows these things to set their minds at ease and to find their peace through retribution! How else can punishment be exacted? Who else should exact it other than them?"

Sheperd's voice rang through my head angrily, "You are in no position to weigh punishment or retribution Inimical! Do you know peace!?"

There was no doubt in my mind that they stayed apart from each other for a reason. Their exchange was intimidating and their hatred was palpable. I couldn't help but be afraid. With all that I'd experienced, I instinctually felt that somehow, I was at risk. One question did make its way through my fear though: what prompted the confrontation? Something must have happened to tip the balance and forced them to play their hands. My fate in all of it seemed to be ultimately at stake. Although I didn't understand how I knew that their struggle would somehow determine my future. I didn't like feeling so uninvolved in my own destiny.

Somehow, someway, I wanted to determine things for myself, but of course, I didn't know how to do it. That's when Forge and Sheperd's attentions turned from each other back to me. Forge's words began to sound in my mind again.

"I'll put the question to you now Dev-Would you remain a passive on-looker and refuse what should be your right?", he asked.

"How should I answer that Forge...?"

"Honestly! You don't need prompting from anyone! You have no more time for indecision. Say you want blood!", he prodded.

"I don't know what the hell I want anymore!! You think you know better than I do?"

Don't forget who I am Devlin Goode! You have no idea of what I know. Nothing you feel is hidden from me. You're transparent!", he accused.

Sheperd broke in at that point, "You've heard that accusation before haven't you Devlin...?"

Forge ignored Sheperd and continued to bait me, "You want to test what I know Devlin? Fine! I know that you weren't there for your wife and daughter..."

"Shut up..."

"I know that you blame yourself for their murders..."

"Shut up..."

"I know the fantasies you've had in your drunken stupors about what you'd do to the ones who did this to you..."

"SHUT UP!"

"I know what your bad decision then has cost and I know what the right one now can do..."

"Stop this. Stop it now..."

"Not convinced? Well, I even know the hint of pleasure in your wife's moan while she was being violated...it sounded just like...this..."

"FUCK YOU!!"

Forge had somehow mimicked my wife's voice. That was more than I could bear and I lashed out without regard to who I was dealing with or what the consequences might be. He'd gone too far. In a rage, I jumped at his motionless body still there with me in that dark room.

Then, I heard a warning of, "NO! STOP!", but from an unexpected source; Sheperd had spoken.

He knew what I felt and what I intended and he'd suddenly come around, blindingly moving to stop me an instant after I'd charged Forge. That instant was just slow enough to allow me to reach Forge and just fast enough to initiate what happened next.

In some way, Sheperd had seemingly completed a circuit- that was the three of us which ripped me from what I believed to be my world and into what I later came to understand was theirs. In the instant that we all made contact, that blinding light that I'd continually tried to shut out exploded through the room with an unbearable brilliance. It wasn't quite like it had been before; it almost seemed to have a density to it, a kind of weight. Trying to squeeze my eyes shut had no effect at all. That light penetrated me. It was like staring into the sun while sitting on its surface. In that flash, just that quickly, I'd lost all perspective. Initially, I thought that I began to go down to my knees, but the vertigo I was suddenly feeling made me unsure. Then, a sense of direction came back to me, but maliciously. I had the distinct feeling of rising quickly and uncontrollably; as if I had jumped up but continued to ascend.

My stomach began to remember the butterflies of a little kid riding in an elevator for the first time, but now those butterflies had grown into hostile dragons! The feeling was terrifying because I seemed to know that I was moving farther and farther from what I felt was solid ground, but I didn't understand how or why or if I could possibly come down safely.

Just like being blinded by sunlight reflecting off of snow and ice, my vision was painfully obscured. Desperate to get my bearings, I fought through it. Slowly, my sight began to clear a little, and gradually, the light was being replaced by blurry patches of vision. But the more things cleared, the more I began to panic.

Although reason seemed to have abandoned everything that had touched me since my suicide attempt, there could be no rational explanation for what I was seeing.

Was I in some intricate lucid dream?

But even being able to ask that question meant... Did it really mean anything at all? The only response I got at all to that question was my own anxious heartbeat and that held no answers.

When I was able to fully comprehend where I was, or where I seemed to be, I began to give up on rationality. The feeling of rising had proven not to be some trick of my mind. Looking below me, far below me, I saw the Earth turning. I saw every distinct detail under my feet; the mountains and oceans as well as the lights of cities and whole countries. It was incredible! It made me speechless! Then I realized that it wasn't just a matter of seeing the world beneath me, I was perceiving everything as well; Everything!

Wherever I looked or even thought about, every infinitesimal occurrence was known to me. There was a forest fire happening ...there were emotionally bereft children with automatic weapons...there was a light rain coming down on a smiling couple...there was a man wrestling with his kids...there was a landslide that buried a small village...there was a priest doing the things he spoke out against on Sundays...there was an antelope being killed bloodily by a pride of hungry lions...there were beautiful women laughing...there was a fissure erupting at the bottom of the Pacific...there was a sad woman mourning the loss of her father...

I was aware of everything! Somehow, I'd been exposed to some unimaginable power. It was overwhelming and amazing and I immersed myself in it. But then, I also questioned that newfound power.

Quickly, I found myself wondering if I was better off without it. I questioned how it was possible and whether it could even be potentially destructive.

Despite my reservations, I had to admire the beauty in the things I was witnessing. Even the raw brutality of nature elicited a kind of awe. The totality of what I was seeing was absolutely amazing! I thought that no sight could ever impress me more; until I looked above me. That sight was more than unbelievable!

Above my head in all directions, the entire Universe was on display!

Everything from vast dark emptiness to radiant suns and nebulas seemed to be within arm's reach. Galaxies spun and stars exploded and died at every turn. Somehow, I looked on as a meteor impacted on the surface of a planet that I'd never seen before. The destruction was awesome to watch! At one point, I saw a string of comets go by as if there was a race through the open roads of space.

I was just as aware of the entire cosmos as I was of the entire happenings of Earth!

Despite the experiences I saw and felt, I was still somehow removed from it all. Although I was total-ly aware and was somehow able to watch it all, none of what I saw ever actually touched me. But just then, something else did.

At the edge of my consciousness, something muffled but familiar sought my attention. That muffled and familiar thing was the ongoing struggle between Sheperd and Forge. I'd been understandably distracted from their fight, but was being drawn back in.

Being pulled back into "Reality" seemed to be a complete contradiction after everything that I'd just experienced though. What was happening to me!?

Beneath me was the world that I thought I knew, above me was a universe that I'd only seen in movies and books.

I was literally in-between.

I was suspended halfway between atmosphere and empty space. How!? How could I be where I seemed to be? How could I sense all of the things that I seemed to be perceiving? If I was actually where I seemed to be, how could I even be surviving it? I believed that my answers would come from either Sheperd or Forge, so I began to look for them through the haze of where I was, as well as the haze of my own confusion.

It didn't take long to find them. Their struggling had become louder and took on a more desperate tone. It was a total contrast to the immobile bodies that were left in that dark room. Then, one of the answers I needed made itself known; this is where they had gone to have their confrontation. This was apparently their natural battlefield.

This layer of reality existed directly over our heads and we were all oblivious to it. And I believe that I'd been transported to it by my attack on Forge, and Sheperd's subsequent attempt to stop it.

Realization was creeping up on me slowly.

As I zeroed in on what I was hearing or perceiving, I turned to find Sheperd; but not as I expected to. He had reverted to what I'd also come to realize was his truer form. Oscillating and brilliant bands of light formed the somewhat man-like shape Sheperd had shown me before. He glowed with energy as his power coursed down and around his form and out to the tips of what appeared almost like giant wings behind him. He reminded me in a way of an electric half-man, half-butterfly, but without any hint of the fragileness. Sheperd was anything but fragile in either his previous form or this form.

There, locked in combat with him, was something that struck me as malicious. If Sheperd had assumed his truer form, then it was only logical to assume that Forge had as well. That maliciousness I saw was Forge.

It was the true essence of what he was that he'd worked so hard to suppress until then. He was shadowy and dark almost like a kind of living smoke. He was, like Sheperd, roughly human-shaped with the exception of what resembled his own type of large jagged wings on his back. The surface of his skin was almost hypnotizing as it billowed and folded in on itself continuously.

Although he appeared intangible, just like Sheperd, there could be no doubt that Forge was also very formidable.

Watching them wasn't at all like watching a fight between two men. Gravity meant nothing to them as they turned and rolled and twisted against each other. I watched as they seemed to fight upside down and I watched them appear to fight vertically! The two of them struck each other over and over with incredible and inhuman speed. Sheperd and Forge threw each other and used as well as broke hold after hold. They were fierce.

It was brutal to see but not random. There was no awkward flailing around from either of them. They seemed distinctly practiced in their combat. Then the realization that they had been fighting for possibly all of time struck me. They both knew what to expect from the other and were well matched. Neither was gaining ground and I had to believe that that was by design.

As the two of them fought, I noticed something out of the corner of my eye, just at the edge of my perception. It was there and then it was gone. Then, some distance away, there was another one... and just that quickly, I'd lost it. I started to get even more anxious than I'd already been. Then, when it happened again, I was able to make out what it was.

Shapes very similar to both Forge and Sheperd were beginning to come into view all around me. A very few at a time appeared at first, and then the flood gates opened and they were like swarms everywhere I looked.

Sheperd and Forge's battle was not exclusive. This was war!

Chimerical and Inimical were now fighting all around me. There were now two armies locked in hateful conflict at every turn. A group of Chimerical flew near me at incredible speed like fighters in formation! An enormous group of Inimical rose up from the Earth looking for adversaries to engage. This "In-between" was now under full assault and I was helplessly caught up. It had to only be a matter of time before I became "collateral damage". One thought repeated over and over in my head, "Get clear of this! Get clear of this somehow!"

But I seemed unable to move significantly. It was as if I was a buoy floating in water. No matter how hard I tried, I made little progress. As they fought around me, I did the best I could to keep myself inconspicuous, although, at that point, that was probably a ridiculous notion.

I tried a kind of swimming motion and I attempted to walk with little effect. I barely moved. Then, I looked back at Sheperd, still fighting viciously with Forge, and thought that he would probably help me if he could.

Then an earnest threat came my way, "You don't need to move! Stay where you are and don't get involved!" Forge had extended an opaque limb toward me in warning after sensing what I was thinking I surmised. There was no doubt that he wanted me to stay out of it, but I did question his motives. How could I know if he was protecting me or withholding something?

"Do you have that same doubt about me, Devlin Goode?' I heard Sheperd's booming voice ask. I knew the veil had dropped long ago and I never questioned it again when either of them knew my thoughts. Although I didn't question it, I also didn't feel comfortable with it. They fought on as if they were oblivious of me again. Sheperd's question never was answered.

Both Inimical and Chimerical raced past me to join the battle and I dodged as best as I could. Everything sounded muffled as if by gusting wind, but the atmosphere was deathly still. Occasionally, when an Inimical came close enough, I heard a muted but shrill wailing that may have been the sound of true wretchedness. My feelings were beginning to plead for attention. They were warning me away from Forge and his kind. They begged me to open my eyes to the truth.

"...And what would you see if you could Dev?", Forge's voice sounded in my head. "You have no eyes! Your perceptions are weak and stunted! Don't try to comprehend what you see here, it's beyond you. Don't assume that you can draw a conclusion about us with so little awareness. Look no further than your own situation!

You are destitute in so many ways...will you confine yourself to that of your own volition?'

"What he's asking you to do is the worst kind of imprisonment because you take others in with you!", Sheperd countered. "The promise that you made was designed to benefit you, not your daughter! Believe me when I say that you should be trying to affect a positive outcome for yourself. Don't believe that you are at all capable of affecting them any longer. Your wife's and your daughter's alignments have been settled... Forge's urgings serve his needs, not theirs!"

Forge was infuriated, "And Sheperd's urgings serve nothing! I want you to provide equity. There is a need for natural and organic cleansing. Do you know how antibodies work in the human body? They don't respond with maliciousness! They're not thought of as evil. They only serve a purpose. They cleanse what is destructive so that a preferable state of health can be achieved. Their intent should not be wrongly misjudged! An antibody seeks out and eliminates that which is malignant. The task is a necessity! Ours is as well."

"Your metaphor is misleading. The Inimical are, in fact, responsible for the corruption they claim to remedy.", Sheperd said.

That statement seemed to further enrage Forge and he pushed forward aggressively. I watched them intently, never knowing what the outcome would truly turn out to be. All I could do was watch and wait. It was beyond belief! Their movements, as well as all the other combatants, probably distracted me from what I really should have been focusing on; depending on which one of them came out on top, what would happen to me?

Was I to believe that I had any say in what was going to come? I had no power to compare with what I was witnessing! How could I affect the outcome the way that Sheperd had suggested? Had the promise to Sophia really been strictly for my own benefit? Then, the thought occurred to me again that, in failing myself, I would also fail my wife and daughter.

"NO!" Forge's scream was so intense it threatened to shatter my mind. "Listen to me!", he demanded. All around us, existence seemed to shift into slow motion and my focus became pin-pointed on Forge and Sheperd. Their fight had paused, but they both remained in guarded stance for a moment.

Forge seemed to take a chance at that point and he turned his attention to me. My situation hadn't changed; I was still barely capable of anything more than "wading" there in one spot. All I could do was wait. Then, with his back turned to Sheperd, Forge continued with thinly veiled desperation in his voice.

"You would be making a monumental mistake in following your line of thinking now. The road back from it would be untenable at best. At the beginning of our encounters, I told you that you would be put into a position to identify and punish the misguided...like that sadistic hateful guard. Do his actions seem like the kind that should go without retribution? How about your favorite little nurse? Doesn't she deserve to choke on real justice? Who was it that eliminated your silent withdrawn little friend so brutally? All I want is for you to recognize things for what they are. Why do you persist in thinking that I harbor some ulterior motive?"

"That is exactly what he has Devlin.", Sheperd broke in.

"I've only been honest with you ...", Forge attested.

"From a certain skewed perspective.", was Sheperd's challenge to that.

"Nothing I've told you has been a lie! Nothing!"

"The lie rests in the withheld." Sheperd insisted.

"Devlin Goode...for the last time...will you turn a blind eye to your calling? You possess an inherent awareness, a sensitivity, which allows you to locate, with expediency, those remorseless doomed. Use it! You are an asset and you won't realize it. What other option could you have at the moment!? This is the closest thing to Salvation as you're going to get. And believe me when I say that you need to be saved. The product of your life cannot end with a whimper. What you are will fade, unceremoniously! And we both know that no one will be witness to it, don't we?

Who is left? So, what does that mean for you? It means that you will and must become something different. It's not at all surprising that you can't fathom that "something" right here and now, it's just beyond you. But believe that it is a power that even your creative imagination hasn't begun to touch on..."

As Forge spoke, I unconsciously began to respond to what he was saying. My defensiveness began to break down. He was like a masterful musician performing with his favorite instrument. I assumed that I hadn't hidden that impression from him judging by the sound of anticipation in his voice. Sheperd stood by soundlessly, not protesting or challenging in any way. I also assumed that there was a reason for that.

"You have no idea what you'd be capable of. Want to find out who's responsible for the worst thing that has ever happened to you? Want to locate them? Instantly! That is what you're being offered! As well as the ability to exact justice...! I know you still want to be altruistic so I'm not asking you to do this for just yourself or your murdered family, I'm asking it for the many like you who will suffer just like you have. They may not be so willing to let those responsible go without a reckoning. Redeem them and you move towards the redemption of your wife and daughter as well."

"Justice is not exacted Devlin, it is administered. As far as the others that may be like you-do you know what you'd be stealing from them? Don't think that you can decide for others." Sheperd seemed to pick his spots as well as he made his points.

I listened passively until I felt that I'd reached some vague conclusion. They'd both made points that I couldn't help but respond to at some level, but I also had a point to make of my own.

"I...am tired." I calmly stated. "You may not understand this, but I honestly can't remember being happy. It would seem impossible for me not to have been, I know that, but it's so distant...It's like a favorite picture you once had that has become sun-faded. It was made into an ugly thing. Looking at it corrupts the original impression and makes the thought of it hurtful. I suppose my spirit was killed when...my family was. Now there is nothing left but emptiness. That emptiness is all-consuming. It's crippled me. It's crippled me to the point of not caring if I recover and not looking to. Yeah, for a time there, I thought that I could possibly change things and maybe fulfill a promise I'd made. That was me being naïve, I guess. But not anymore. You might not understand, or you might laugh, or say I'm being silly and dramatic, but understand this; I'm done. Neither of you has said or done a thing that would take away that emptiness, not one thing! Neither of you has given me an alternative to what goes along with that emptiness either. Emptiness and loneliness go hand in hand and I have been lonely for a long time. What I'm trying to say, what it all means, is that despite your efforts, the best

I can be right now is apathetic. I don't need lectures on what I need or should want or how I should feel. Don't you think that I can rationalize that out myself? What I can't do is pretend that I actually feel something different or that those feelings are unjustified. I didn't make this situation, it made me! What do you expect from me? What do you really expect me to do? Who knows what you're even proposing Sheperd? I just don't know. Not that it really matters much to me at this point."

"Forge, you think that you've made me some kind of miraculous offer that will appease my soul? Well, I'm numb just that deep. Why do you think that I'd believe you or respond to an insane appeal to some deep-seated feeling of responsibility for all man-kind? That doesn't exist in me at all anymore! Altruistic? No. People are irredeemable. Altruistic? No, I've lost that childhood quality. Maybe if I could go back in time and start all over somehow...and get it right from the start...But now I'd just as soon see a natural disaster solve the world's problems. I'm prayin' for rain...Hope the few good ones learn to swim. The fact is, I don't think I could make myself care about whatever the two of you are selling. So, I'll tell you again-I'm done"

I'd communicated exactly what I thought and felt sincerely, in the hopes that I'd be taken seriously and then be shown a way out. What I said was not taken well at all.

"Unbelievable weakness! You worship at an alter called Sanctimony! You're no different than any other zealot! You fall short of your faith Dev. You think you're done? You've given up once before haven't you Dev? Is that all you know how to do?", Forge jeered.

"It's not giving up!" I tried to defend. "I'm being realistic."

"What you think is reality is malleable!"

"I can't! I won't!!"

"You can, and you will! You don't get to decide! You are in no position to dictate what you will or won't do! You things are subordinate!" Forge insisted.

"No Devlin, you're not. This is exactly what I offer you; the ability and right to choose for yourself!" Sheperd spoke up.

"It is not truly a choice if your options are defined for you Dev. You are not to choose; you are meant to acknowledge an eventuality- a natural course of events and where it has led you. Recognize the path you've already chosen!" Forge urged.

"No." was all I said in response.

There was a tense pause after I'd refused and I couldn't be sure what it meant. Had they accepted what I'd said? Was that the end of it? Then, Forge removed all doubt when he said, "Think again..." Nothing had been settled. He went on, saying, "Would you go back? Would you go back to that existence of being subjugated and suppressed by those with an agenda of their own?"

"What?"

"The good doctor and his lackeys would love to see you again...There is a lifetime's worth of pain they'd like to prescribe to you. You can look forward to suffering at their hands...for a very, very long time."

I thought I heard barely masked pleasure in Forge's voice.

"It doesn't have to be Devlin.", came from Sheperd.

"Quiet! You've said enough Chimerical!" Forge warned.

"You possess no means of intimidation to me Inimical! Devlin, listen to me. You need not suffer under self-loathing anymore..."

Forge attempted to dissuade Sheperd again, "You will say no more!"

"Self-loathing? What are you saying...? I asked.

"I'm saying, Devlin, that...", Sheperd began.

"Enough! You will stop!" Forge persisted as Sheperd continued.

"...you have the power within you to overcome what you face in the guise of the doctor, the nurse, the guard, and any other impediment because..."

"Do not...!" was all Forge could get out in time.

"...they... are you, Devlin Goode.", Sheperd said with a tinge of relief sounding in his voice.

He'd floored me with that statement. Although I didn't understand it at all, I felt that an essential but elusive answer had been laid out in front of me. I began the awkward questions with, "What? How? How could that even be possible? What the hell does that mean?'

Neither of them spoke up immediately. Sheperd was suspended there, a small distance from me with Forge between us. The Inimical had been facing me, until that moment. Although Forge had taken on a grayish, semi-human but faceless appearance of living smoke, at that instance, I recognized him for who and what he truly was. When he heard Sheperd reveal what he himself had apparently been content to hide, he paused, just long enough to gauge my reaction, I assumed. Then, in seeing what that reaction was; my desire to know more, the stalemate was broken and he made his move.

I saw Forge begin to turn toward Sheperd. But something had changed. I was perceiving everything differently. I'd seen it once before; when I was watching the warfare of the Inimical and Chimerical. In that instant, everything I was seeing began to move in slow motion, including myself. Then, I began to perceive an incredibly deep, booming, and resonant sound. It was as if millions of timpani had been struck at one time! Turning my attention back to Forge, I saw him spinning toward Sheperd with the obvious intention of attacking. But Sheperd hadn't moved to prepare himself for that attack at all. He seemed completely vulnerable. If he didn't move, he'd be struck down.

That couldn't happen!

I needed to find out more from him. I needed to know what he'd meant when he said that 'They are you'. I'd heard that statement before...I needed to understand!

I found that I was unable to speak when I repeatedly failed to get out, "Forge-Stop! No!" So, I tried again to affect my movement. At first, I struggled like a newborn in a crib, but slowly, I made progress. I was moving at a slow speed just like everything around me, but I was moving. Gradually, I could hear myself yelling at the top of my lungs, trying to be heard over that incredible booming. It was quickly obvious that I wouldn't and couldn't make up the distance between us to stop Forge, even if that was possible to do. That didn't stop me though.

I wrestled with the nothing that I was suspended in, to move forward and to prevent Forge from possibly eliminating my chance at getting to the truth. I fought harder, screaming at the slow-motion Inimical the whole time. But Forge was too close to Sheperd, who still hadn't prepared himself for the attack. It seemed to be inevitable. But still, I fought harder.

Just as Forge closed the distance between them and looked set to begin a killing strike, I saw Sheperd move. He didn't do the expected; prepare to strike or block, instead, he spread his luminous white arms wide. He knew what was about to happen and he intentionally made himself vulnerable to it!

That made me panic and desperately try to reach Sheperd. Then, the series of events that happened next made everything that I'd seen, experienced, and been subjected to since I found myself in that damned place, pale by far in comparison.

Over that terrible booming that was all around and everywhere, and through diminished perception, I heard Sheperd say to me, quite clearly and reverently, "This...is the final beat."

Then, as Forge moved to strike at Sheperd with what once had been his arm but had transformed into a barbed stabbing point, I reacted.

Without warning or reason (that I understood) my slow-motion subsided and I lunged forward in a blur of light, placing myself between Sheperd and the inimical a single moment before he struck. In that moment, I somehow blocked the Inimical's thrust and found myself face to face with him. As I began to yell "Enough!", the word was accompanied by something unexpected; a brilliant and intense light that came from-me!

That light shot from my mouth and into the smoke-like Inimical, burning and incinerating him there where I held him immobile, sending pieces of his form floating away like charred paper. I couldn't or didn't stop until there was nothing left of him but small singed bits and the memory of his shrill scream in my head. He never had a chance. It appeared to be extremely painful. But when I thought about it, I didn't mourn his loss.

As I looked around me, the fighting between the Inimical and Chimerical began to subside as they either separated from each other or began to simply fade away into nothingness right before my eyes. Soon I was left there "In-Between" with the panorama of Earth and the Heavens that I'd marveled at before. In that moment, I was overcome with peace. All was still and silent and I was alone...or so I thought.

"I told you that all would be clear Devlin."

I heard it from over my shoulder. I spun around, easily to my surprise, to find Sheperd there facing me, unharmed and beaming.

"You're wondering what and how everything just unfolded, I know. All will be clear to you now. Come with me, Devlin Goode."

"Come with you? How? Where? I don't even know where *this* is- how I got here, and I definitely don't know how to leave! Yes, I'm wondering how everything just unfolded! I couldn't move, and then I was like... Everything was in slow-mo, but then it all...how could I do that with the light-thing...And what was with that loud-ass booming sound...Man! What was that about?"

I heard a deep resounding laugh come from Sheperd suddenly. That laugh became infectious for some reason that eluded me and I soon erupted in it myself. To say it was strange to hear myself laugh would be an understatement. The last time I did it seemed more than a lifetime away. That thought made the laugh trail off even though I would have chosen to hold onto it forever if I could have.

"Devlin," Sheperd began, "take a good look at yourself. You'll begin to find answers there."

For a moment, I hesitated. Maybe I was afraid of what I'd find. Maybe I was afraid that I wouldn't find anything at all...Then, it was clear that answers and questions would become intertwined.

What I saw didn't make sense to me. But, nothing had recently. I had become something different. My body was transformed and I was almost a glowing replica of Sheperd. I maintained a human-like shape, similar to the body I'd always had, but it was now luminescent!

The light that made up his body was now what I saw when I looked down at my own hands and at my legs and feet. On my back were huge and brilliant wings that seemed to support me without effort or movement. I had become something drastically different from what I was! I was similar to him, but still very different because we truly were very different. As he'd told me, I found my initial answer with that first look at what I'd become.

"That, I think, explains how I was able to move like I did...How I was able to block the Inimical...the light from my..."

"Yes. It's as you've already guessed. You endured all and, just as I told you, in the final beat, you made a choice and were transformed. In that instant, you broke free from your mortal trappings and became something more. Your decision to defend me was the lynch-pin circumstance that determined your conversion. You recognized the Inimical's intent and its inherent wrongness and you acted according to instinct. For that, you have my gratitude."

"But you didn't defend yourself! You could have been destroyed! Why did you do that?"

"I admit, it was a gamble..." he replied.

"What!? Are you serious? That's insane! Why would you risk that?"

"Listen, Devlin, things aren't so different from the physical to the Frequency you know. We take risks and gamble to get a worthy payoff. This time, I happened to be fortunate."

"But..." I began.

"Don't worry too much, I was never in any intractable peril. Our kind wage war continuously and when one or the other is defeated, we return to the Nature and are reconstituted; as our essence is energy. Energy cannot be destroyed. This is the Balance."

"But what if I had...made a different choice?'

"It is true, that was always a possible eventuality. If that had happened, your energy would have been converted to match the resonance of the Inimical, therefore adding to their influence on and within the Nature. It is not an unheard-of event; you must imagine that we've faced it many, many times throughout the span of existence. When that does happen, the Balance is tipped, if only for a time, toward their negativity. But experience has proven that those imbalances are extremely short-lived. Balance is always a breath span away. That is to say, it is to our perceptions. Earthly senses may view that period slightly differently than we do."

"That is why there are especially dark periods within our history..."

"That is correct Devlin. You're adjusting well."

"There is something that hasn't been explained to me yet. I'm sure I have many things left to understand, but let's start with this; What did you mean when you said 'They are you'. I need you to explain that to me."

"Of course, but as I said, you must come with me. Some answers require visual aids, Devlin."

That was a puzzling response but I did as I was asked. He began to slowly circle around me, then he extended an arm downward, and within a blink, like a beam of light, he had descended. It was incredible to watch! Then I heard his voice saying, "Follow me. Your answers are here…"

I didn't question or hesitate. I instinctually extended my new wings and "opened" myself to where he'd gone, and just like Sheperd, I became a blinding flash.

Everything was black.

Disorientation overcame me. By complete contrast, the brilliance that I had been, was replaced by-nothingness-or so it seemed.

The complete darkness made what I believed had happened to me appear to be a lie. It didn't take long at all for my faith to be shaken.

Was I right from the very beginning when I doubted my own sanity? Could It have been a...? But a dream could never be so distinct and involved. The experience seemed so detailed!

The sadness...the pain...the anger...and the awe that I felt. It had to be more than I was capable of imagining! I wondered if I had done something wrong or If, despite the fact that I'd come to accept everything that had happened, I really had misled myself the entire time. What if everything that I had refused to accept, and subsequently convinced myself was in fact true, had been the most elaborate and realistic delusion of all. Could it be that I had been in that hospital bed, drugged and out of my mind the entire time?

"Must you always doubt yourself, Devlin? Get up... open your eyes and get up."

His voice immediately reassured me and I was glad to hear it. I wouldn't doubt again. That sense of assuredness was invaluable but it was not an antidote for shock. I found that out when I did as I was told; I opened my eyes.

How could I be!? I was back in my loft!

I did as he'd instructed and rose.

There I was, standing, facing my front door, looking down at my little black cat Serenity. She seemed intently focused on me, staring up at me as she sat there. It was so good to see her. As I started to bend down to pick her up, I received the first shock of many to come.

"MMMRRr...I...love...you...rrroooWWW."

The voice was a soft but somewhat gravelly whisper, strangely accented.

"Did you...? Did you just...?" I started to ask out loud in disbelief. Then I heard Sheperd speak again, this time from directly behind me.

"Of course, she did. She always did. Serenity spoke to you constantly but you just couldn't ... hear... very well. That is, until now. Things are and will be very different from now on, to say the least. You have achieved something monumental. But you have not been fully enlightened-yet. Devlin, prepare yourself and turn around."

His seriousness warned me to do exactly what he'd said, so I steadied myself and began to face him, slowly. But nothing I could have done and no amount of preparation could have made me ready for what I saw behind me.

"HOLY...! What the Hell!? I yelled In initial fear. As I turned and looked down, I saw my own body there sprawled just feet from the front door!

There I was, curled in a semi-fetal position with my own clouded, dying eyes looking back at me. That sight would make anyone pause.

Then an unexpected reaction came over me. The feeling that I'd lost the last chance to honor my daughter overcame me. The thought of my failure to keep my word ran through me and I yelled down, "YOU PROMISED!", angrily.

'This is where Sheperd led me? This is what he brought me to see?'

Those thoughts entered my mind first but were soon followed by another, previously unimaginable thought; 'The sight of me lying there dead should be even more horrific than this really is.'

"Yes, you would think so." Sheperd began. "But you are not what you were. Therefore, you would not respond the way you once would have. The reason I've brought you here is because this is the beginning and the end of that. All of the answers that you want and require will be given now.

You have even begun to answer some things on your own I'd suspect."

"I succeeded...I actually did kill myself...the suicide didn't fail."

"That is correct Devlin. You did intend to take your life and after you acted on that decision, and then in fact question it, you crawled to that spot, where you ultimately and very recently, faded. Your suicide most definitely did not fail."

"Then...does that mean that everything that I just experienced was in fact a dream?"

"That term is subjective Devlin. Dreams and dimensions are virtually interchangeable terms. You will come to understand that. For your purposes, let's just say that it was all very much real."

"You said that the doctor, the guard, the nurse... you said that they were all me. I need to understand that now! What does that mean?"

"It means exactly that; all of them, as well as what you perceived to be Dr. Li, Sid, Egon...All of them were manifestations of you. Each was an aspect of your thoughts and feelings that demanded a voice. Each voice had a will and a persona and each had an agenda, but they all contributed to and also stemmed from the whole that was you."

"The whole that *was* me...And what about Constance?"

"Well...that voicing was your consciousness. Symbolism and reality are intrinsically intertwined."

"But-all of those horrific things that happened..."

"The depths of one's despair determines how to manifest itself.", Sheperd stated.

"You're saying that I subjected myself to all of that-that I tortured myself?"

"In effect, yes. Your own concepts, opinions, judgments, and dispositions worked together to create what was your final act. Nowhere is it written that it must be harmonious. It is as you make it."

"Yes, I recognize the truth in what you're saying. I suppose I recognize it because, as you've said, I'm not what I was. What about you...?"

"I know-Am I what I've said they all were... a manifestation...a remnant? The simple answer is "NO". I am what I've always maintained I was. I am exactly what I've explained myself to be."

"Then that would mean that Forge was real as well.", I said rhetorically.

"Yes." Sheperd simply affirmed.

"So, the only true players in my "final act" were the three of us."

"That is accurate.", he confirmed.

"Yes, I understand it now. As fantastic as it seems, I accept the truth of it. It's clear to me with the exception of one aspect. What I'm unclear about Sheperd, is the point behind everything that has happened."

"The 'point' as you call it, was an organic means of working towards the decision that faces you all. There is no need for euphemisms any longer so I will say it plainly. At your death, a resonant frequency must be decided upon. Your experiences form the means through which you play out that decision-making process. Your life, especially of late, has been hard and so the Endgame, the final act was, unfortunately, reflective of that fact. The moment you faded significantly from the physical, you began to play out the illustrated ideas, so to speak, that formed what you were. Those illustrated ideas led you to a final pinpointed option; what will you choose to serve. You see, when you choose something consciously and freely rather than dogmatically or through coercion, that choice is cemented and your resonance is selected. That choice can only come at death because there is no further branching off of essence. There is no more left of physicality, which is the only separation between the Inimical frequencies and our own. In the physical, you could vacillate back and forth recklessly, randomly, with only a particular mood or indulgent desire to guide you.

Death is the first and only opportunity and the moment you swallowed those pills, you began dying."

"From that point on, my final choice played itself out of course. Ultimately, I apparently chose wisely and sided with the Chimerical. Although I don't doubt the rightness of that choice, I don't exactly remember making one, to be honest.", I pointed out.

"That choice came with the acknowledgment and acceptance of a truth; either his or mine. You tried to defend me from the Inimical's attack and in doing so, you aligned yourself to our frequency and to us. His urging became self-defeating and dissonant and mine held promise to you. Thus, you acted and the Inimical was put down."

"And if I hadn't tried to defend you...?"

"It is as you can imagine. I would not have come out on top, he would be leading you to continuous ruin, and you would be forever obscuring the final decisions of others the way he did to you. Some of them would have chosen the way that you just did, but some would have faltered and fallen. That is the way of things. That is the Balance. It's so much better when they choose me."

I smiled and laughed lightly. My last question was, "So, what happens now?"

"Ah yes. What happens now? I love it when I'm asked that. Now, you are rewarded and your pleasures begin...

Afterward, the real work starts.", he said with an uncharacteristic grin on his face.

Apparently, I hadn't gotten all of the answers I'd need but I was unconcerned. The idea of pleasure was too enticing, after all I'd gone through in death, to lightly overlook it.

I asked Sheperd with anticipation, "What pleasures are you referring to?"

Then, everything became worth it instantly. All that I'd been put through and all that I'd subjected myself to obscured and faded from me.

"That's when, of course, I heard your beautiful voice call out to me. That's when I discovered that pleasure had also been transformed in death. Its pureness became almost indescribable! I suppose that rather than "feeling" that pleasure, I had "become" pleasure! Nothing I'd ever imagined could measure up to that experience. No dream was ever more perfectly fulfilled! Then, to actually see you there...Well, of course, you know exactly what I felt and what I mean..."

"Yes, I know, I felt exactly the same way, Daddy... I just wanted to hear you tell it.", Sophie Giggled.

"Come now, Devlin. We are needed.", Kristina said in her soft voice.

That was very true, we were needed and it was time to move on. I'd finished my story and turned toward Sheperd. As he looked back at me, he winked and the droning television behind him that had been left on the entire time blinked out and fell silent.

With a smile and a bow to us, he extended his arm, guiding my wife, my daughter, and me up and out on our new path.

That was only the beginning...

Endgame Trilogy

SYMMETRY SOUGHT

PART II: EXAMINATION

The background of stars and expansive darkness both intimidated and astonished Rafael Dos Santos.

Yet, conflict remained imminent.

"We see, clearly, the damaged cornerstone of the edifice that is in question here." the Thrice interjected.

"I don't think I like that statement.", Rafael refuted in an attempt to defend his sister.

"Your disapproval does not negate the definitive assessment."

"Your circumstance also precludes all protestation."

"Your impetus is to remain on the task of concise conveyance."

Each one in the overseeing body offered their direction individually, and then the collective affirmed with their characteristic; "Once, Twice, Thrice."

With the understanding that he had no influence that could possibly be exerted against them, Rafael did as he was instructed to do. Sufficiently put in his place, his relaying of what came before that point continued.

"We came back from the funeral heartbroken. We were, both of us, devastated in our own way."

Somberly, the rain that fell on the Dos Santos twins painted a picture very much reminiscent of the emotional landscape within them. As they pulled into their driveway after the somber service honoring her friends, neither of them rushed to leave the car immediately. Rather, they sat quietly together in unvoiced agreement.

Rafael found himself staring forward at nothing. Raquel, sitting in the passenger seat, was turned awkwardly, peering up and out at either the grey sky or the drops on the glass.

At that point, the entire world seemed devoid of color.

"No, I don't want to talk..." Raquel stated in anticipation.

"I didn't ask." He retorted.

"What is there to say anyway? Nothing! I guess most people would ask 'What's the purpose of their deaths?' Should I say 'There is a plan to everything and that nothing is done by mistake'- she said with growing agitation in her voice.

"No..." her brother began before being cut off.

"I guess that little girl had seen and done all that she needed to in only eight years, huh! And Kristina, I suppose her poor husband had enough of her!"

Hysterics overtook her at that point and sobs flowed as heavily as the rain dropping down on the car.

He knew well enough that his role then was not to engage, but to provide silent support as well as a, figurative, safe place to fall if it came to that. So, stilly, her brother sat without trying to comfort her. That attempt wouldn't have been received even if he had tried.

Her emotions ran their course in short time.

"What you're feeling is justified, and it's gonna last. After what happened to you back in..."

"Don't!" Raquel cut his thought off blindingly.

"Yeah, OK. I only want to say that you're like an exposed nerve right now. No one blames you for feeling so upset."

"And what about you Raf? Are you gonna try to remain stone-faced and unaffected? I know better. You're hurting too."

"I never claimed...Listen, with everything that both of us have gone through in our lives, I can't afford to stop moving, and allowing myself to get emotional would stop me in my tracks. So, I'll keep it together; because I *need* to."

Although she could have argued the point, she chose not to because, without wanting to admit it, she relied on that very characteristic in him.

Whether by providence or coincidence, the sun broke through above them and the last drops fell down to newly sunlit puddles.

Rafael suggested, "Hey, why don't you go inside now? What have you even eaten today?"

"I've had as much as you have, brother."

"You got me. I don't deny it. Why don't I go pick something up? What...? Uh, Mexican?" he asked.

"No, that's too heavy. I don't even have an appetite, but I don't really feel like going back and forth with you about it right now. What about Chinese? I can pick at that enough to keep you quiet." She gave her brother a sly wink then.

They both offered a half-smile and a head-nod, opened the car doors, and went toward the house. The scent of moisture on grass and fresh air mingled as they moved together thoughtfully. When Raq saw Raf begin to trail behind her, she understood what he was about to do. He opened the garage and began to further cement her opinion that he was sometimes a profound dumb-ass.

Unadvisedly, Rafael's Harley Davidson was brought out onto the wet ground. That illustrated the point she'd recently made. He was, in fact, at least somewhat distraught and the ride he was determined to take was his way of practicing moving meditation. That was the reason that she refrained from openly criticizing him.

The model was a Breakout, the engine was a 114ci, and the pipes were aftermarket and raucous. She knew those things only because he'd repeated them so many times before.

Unlocking the front door with one quick look over her shoulder (a habit she'd very recently developed), she stooped to pick up a kitten before the door was closed securely behind her.

She didn't bother to watch Raf speed away.

He didn't bother to wave as he left.

 Rafael was already rolling toward some small measure of peace. What he needed a respite from was his own past, his memories, and his recrimination. The stresses of recent weeks raised demons in him. Each higher gear shift helped to subdue them.

He'd find though, that it would be transitory.

The effects of the attack on his sister were obvious and weren't only felt by her; some small amount of responsibility troubled Rafael as well. As their first line of defense against all assailants, his role went unfulfilled that night. To add to the dismay of that, the incident reignited memories that were better left repressed.

The ride was an attempt at push-back, but it was no small task. As a memory flashed in his mind, he tensed and felt the bike lurch as he missed a gear. A mild but self-directed curse came in response to that.

A second flash of memory stole his attention, just briefly enough to require a last-minute swerve from an imminent pothole. His concentration was divided between what he was doing then and what he had done.

Thinking back half a lifetime, he continued his ride on auto-pilot.

Immediately, the Thrice concurred with each other about the clarity and quality of Rafael's remembrances. Up to that point, he'd been sharing a collective past. The information was first-hand in this instance. A history began to play out as he rode.

The world his sister and he came from was chaotic. The part of Brazil they lived in had the type of veneer over it necessary to entice tourist money. Under that illusion was a bereft wilderness. The lifestyle they were forced to live was- detrimental- to a couple of twelve-year-olds. An ever-rotating parade of foster parents did nothing to provide stability for the twins.

Too many took advantage.

His memories didn't linger overly long on any given abuse; though they did include several different instances. Drunken women without husbands seemed to believe that it was their obligation to beat Rafael just enough to ensure that he would never consider himself a man. Drunker lascivious men seemed to hint too anxiously at the development of Raquel. Priests and nuns assaulted their minds with platitudes that they themselves rejected and were unfulfilling to them regardless. Other children that were much like them, struggled with them for necessities as well as attention, all in the effort to be saved themselves.

The worst of them all though, by far, was *O Homem Sombra*- the Shadow Man.

Everything about him seemed to be designed to scare children. His skin leaked sweat uncontrollably, and his eyes cut through souls with bloodshot redness. He smelled of smoke constantly. The sound of his voice was rawness and strain and his size was the basis for the name everyone called him. By intentionally towering over everyone, an oppressive shadow was cast that stole courage from anyone under it.

For two years, the Shadow Man had been taking advantage of the twins. He'd initially presented himself as a friend to many of the orphans. He'd offer some slight amount of change to a child that had none which purchased more loyalty than it should have. Sometimes he would have something irresistible for them to eat. Ultimately, they'd each be preyed upon by any means that would prove effective.

Once a child was enlisted, the object was to teach them the many varied ways of stealing and cheating the tourists to their large city. Everything was done in secrecy and with the threat of pain as well as the deceptive promise of liberation. The children feared just slightly more than they dreamed.

But although they were two of the top earners for him, Rafael and Raquel were difficult to control, even at twelve, and found themselves within the shadow too often. The last time was two days before they were to find out that they'd been adopted.

While Raq distracted what they thought was a clueless couple with her prettiness and dancing, Raf did as he was taught and quietly slipped into the purse of the beguiled woman. It went wrong when he became overly ambitious and tried for her man's wallet. He was unsuccessful as the man deftly caught him by the wrist and held him where he struggled.

From a balcony not too distant, their Shadow Man watched it all.

Maybe it was both of their pleading (despite the inability of the foreigners to understand the language), or maybe it was the naïve liberalness of the couple that caused them to take pity on the would-be thieves. While they could have involved the police if they'd wanted to, they did not. Instead, they chose to take back what was theirs and scolded them to their own satisfaction before letting them go.

The children ran.

It wasn't long before their reprieve was torn away from them. They were forced to meet up with their lying, criminal benefactor after each score. That time, they were empty-handed.

The three made their way to a back alley behind a hovel of a hotel where they always turned over whatever they were able to grab. With nothing to offer, Raf put himself between his sister and harm.

In that grating voice, he posed a question that he knew the answer to, "What did you get from those branquelos?"

No answer was given at first because experience had taught the twins what came from failure. The punishment for not answering could be equally bad as well. So, Rafael began to speak up through his fear.

"Well, we…"

With a backhand, his equivocations were stopped.

Raquel let out the scream to be expected from a young girl as her brother hit the ground. Then, the Shadow man turned on her. He blamed her for the loss.

"If you would have done your job, I wouldn't be out of my take!"

Like a shot, he snatched Raq up by the arm violently. Her brother fought the explosions in his head and set himself on the monstrous man. Wrapping himself feebly around him, it was all he could do to hold on. Twisting and spinning, still clutching Raquel vice-like as she struck him, the behemoth landed a poorly aimed blow that was more than enough to stun the boy. He landed heavily, a second time.

Raf rose unsteadily, prepared to beg if he had to, and prepared to bargain if he could.

"Please, it wasn't her fault! I didn't do it right! I messed up! I won't do it again. We'll leave!"

"What did you fuckin' say you little dog? Where could you possibly go? What makes you think you can leave me?"

"We might...someone might...maybe we will be adopted and we'll be taken away. Then I won't mess up anymore. You can get someone better. We won't make you mad anymore. We won't tell anyone what you do!" Raf offered, trying to placate as best as a pre-teen could. Of course, he'd miscalculated.

The look in that demon's eyes was something that they'd seen before. It was will devouring. It was soul-stealing. With Raq still struggling within his slimy grasp, a deliberate motion was started as the Shadow Man reached for something at his back, a thing that everyone knew he always carried; a monstrous knife...

Spitting a loud curse at the past, Rafael snapped himself back into the present. The remaining memory was beaten back; for self-preservation.

Still roaring through the streets on his Harley, Rafael fought against the memory he'd been reliving. All he could ever manage though was to post-pone them for a short time. The results of that day haunted him despite his resolve. They had for years. They would again.

Once inside, with the locks all double-checked, Raquel set the kitten down gently. Following a recently established pattern, she moved from room to room turning on lights to comfort herself.

Her next attempt to allay her fears was at the front window. For some time, one eye alone was allowed to peer out of minimally pulled back blinds. Nothing went through her mind when she did that; just the search for something, anything, that might be unwelcomed. This was a routine that she never shared with her brother; this was done when she was alone; solely to placate her anxieties.

When nothing at all unusual or troubling occurred, a hunger she'd underestimated pulled her away. She moved to get a snack to tide her over until Raf came back with their dinner; an equally hungry cat trailing behind. Passing by a mirror, eyes that seemed too dark and weary stopped her. Her skin looked dull and her mouth showed only tenseness. She drew closer and stared.

The sound of a startling cell phone alarm changed her weary features to fright. Again, she'd never set an alarm and she didn't understand. Reaching for the phone, the distraction of a sudden and quite loud POP! held her where she stood. A flash from a lightbulb blowing out in the room at the end of the hall was the source of her fear.

She voiced her frustration, "Son-of-a- Mother!"

Tackling the first issue, she worked to stop the obnoxious alarm, but it ended on its own. As she started to make her way down the hall to check the light that blew, she stopped as if frozen, tensed as if her chest was constricted and her breath stalled as if she'd forgotten how.

A figure was emerging from the darkened room.

"You doubtless remember seeing me young one"

Screaming would have been appropriate if she were at all capable of it. She wasn't.

"No need to cultivate that kind of response. I'm not a thing to dread."

Raquel's beating heart resisted that suggestion and sped its pace. As she looked on, she realized that she had in fact recognized the figure in front of her. It was the same woman she'd seen the night of the...in the parking lot; the beautiful woman in white.

Inexplicably, the woman was only partially visible. The shadowed blackness of the room cradled her and seemed to only allow her upper torso to be seen. Raquel was petrified enough without any part of an apparition appearing to her.

"Allow me to, and I will inspire more than fear child."

"What...?" It came from her meekly, but that was also the full extent of Raquel's courage then.

"Ah, so can we talk now?" the beautifully coifed lady in white asked gently.

"What...?" was all Raquel could answer.

"You've been through much. You will endure much more. But you are also a rather fragile individual. That is not surprising and does not have to be detrimental. The truth of it is not accusatory. What's necessary is that you persist."

Her accent was captivating and her mannerism was intended to be pacifying. Those facts helped the fear to subside, but only somewhat. Raquel then found, if only in some small measure, her voice again. The questions came without pause.

"Who are you? How did you get in here? What do you want?"

"Glori – here and there are invariable- and - the preservation of the constant.", was uttered in answer to her questions.

"What...?" Raquel repeated, truly confounded.

"I've actually, in fact, blurred it all completely with precise clarity haven't I Raquel?"

"How do you know me? Who are you?"

"Again- Glori. You may refer to me with that name. I know you, essentially, through the frequency of you. But, for now, I would like you to know me; at least to the point that you can accept my urgings."

Eyes wide with apprehension, Raquel realized that she still held the phone in a clenched hand. Despite the apparent lack of threat, recent happenings informed her actions and she responded with, "I want you out of here now! I'm calling..." the threat went unfinished as, suddenly, the phone in her hand began to ring loudly, drawing her attention away, only momentarily, from the woman who'd intruded into her home.

After looking away for a millisecond, she turned back to the dark room and found that the intruder-Glori- had disappeared into the blackness soundlessly.

Quickly, the flashlight from the phone was pointed that way. Nothing and no one was there to be seen. The exception being a little black kitten that was sitting just outside the doorway, motionlessly, staring up into the empty room.

Instantly, her self-assuredness came into conflict with self-doubt. She questioned how something so unreal could actually, possibly be imagined so vividly.

Taking notice of the persistent ringing, Raquel answered the cell she'd been holding in a death grip, hesitantly, timidly saying, "Hello?"

She'd been too slow. There was no one there. Her arm slumped thoughtlessly from distraction. Then the rest of her body did the same.

The dial-tone filled the quiet.

"Raq!"

Sudden awareness of two firm hands shaking her shoulders began to pull her from a haze. At first, there was nothing but unfocused blinking. Then, recognition crept up.

"Raq! C'mon, snap out of it." Casey urged.

"Hey, baby- I'm hungry, where's the Szechwan?" Raquel asked blithely.

"What? Raq, what's up with you? I've been trying to get you back to the living for a while. You were completely zoned. What happened?"

"Glori...? I...saw... something." came from her tentatively.

"What do you mean you saw something? What?"

As she attempted to make sense of it herself, the telling of it was that much more of a struggle. Ambiguity and hesitancy only confused her boyfriend more. Besides that fact, something else distracted him despite his clear concern for her. She noticed and gave up trying to legitimize what was likely a delusion.

The sound of an aggressive engine pulling up stole both of their attentions then. When Raf came through the door, he put down the bags of take-out and greeted Casey with more enthusiasm than the situation called for at that moment. Raf took notice.

"What...? It wasn't that long of a ride. Do I stink?" he asked, hoping for a laugh.

"No man, read the room." Casey gently admonished. "Something happened to Raquel."

His demeanor became instantly serious at the suggestion of trouble with his sister. Flashes of the recent turmoil she'd been subjected to, and some more distant ones as well, scrolled through his thoughts as his expression became guarded.

Casey continued, "When I came in, Raq was somewhere else-and looked like she'd seen about a hundred horror movies at once."

"Raq...", Rafael gently attempted, "What's up? Did something happen? You good?"

With eyes averted, distantly locked, her voice sounded between quivers as she responded, "Hey, haven't you left yet?"

"What are you talkin' about?"

"I thought you were going to get food..."

"I did. That was almost two hours ago. I'm just getting back." Rafael clarified.

"Really? Good, 'cause I'm starving." That said, Raquel awkwardly moved to the far corner of her bed and collapsed herself into a fetal position, her arms wrapped around her like something to ward off the world.

A look passed between Casey and Rafael.

Casey tried to draw her out again, "Babe, you said you were hungry. Don't you want to eat now? I'll even let you steal from my plate."

"Hungry? I never said I was hungry...", she contradicted. A deep breath was drawn and released peacefully as she closed her eyes and uttered one last bit of confusion to her brother and boyfriend. She said, "... the preservation of the constant..."

The concern the two men in her life shared was clearly evident on their faces. Quietly, they withdrew and moved downstairs to talk.

Casey began, "I found her like that-detached. It took a little coaxing to snap her out of it. She told me she saw something."

"Something? Or was it someone?" Rafael asked sincerely.

"She said 'something'. What are you saying?"

"That night...the night that bastard tried to hurt her, she was acting the way she is now."

"Yeah, I remember.", Casey agreed.

"She was talking about something she'd heard, or seen then. I didn't take it too seriously at the time."

"I didn't either. Of course, I thought the stress of that night had naturally overcome her. I *saw* that scarecrow lookin' asshole. What have the police said about him? I haven't heard anything about him being picked up yet."

Not wanting to be directly dishonest with someone who was so close to his sister, but was also a good friend to him as well, Raf chose to be evasive.

"I haven't heard anything." His answer was true, in a way. What wasn't touched upon was that they'd never in fact reported the incident to the authorities and had no intention to.

Casey seemed to, fortunately, write it off as the inaction of bureaucracy.

Raf continued his line of thought with, "I don't know if she was reacting to someone she saw in the crowd, or if it's leftover from the things we've been through in our past. Whatever this is, it's real to her."

Casey thought for a moment and then ventured, "Neither of you has shared much about that past Raf. Care to elaborate?"

A grim look came over Rafael at that prodding. But he allowed it to pass without letting it dig itself in. Casey picked up on the weight of the reaction and knew enough to move past it without pressuring. Changing the focus back he continued thoughtfully.

"Could be stress-induced trauma-panic attacks."

"Ok, Dr. Freud!", Raf jeered softly.

"Hey, I'm putting this degree to use, bruh!", came with a slight chuckle.

Then the seriousness of the moment returned to them both.

Raf admitted, "I'm afraid that all of the bullshit she's had to dig herself out of lately is breaking her. She took the death of her friends hard, man. They got close quick. The...attack. That night...It's still an open wound."

"She's stronger than we think.", Casey defended.

"She has no other choice.", came from her brother, speaking from experience.

Rafael was grateful that his sister had someone that would defend her. Casey was someone that could be counted on to have his sister's back when he himself couldn't. He found that he hoped that would remain the case for a long time to come.

"Casey, we have to watch for anything that is out of character in her. I see her slipping away a little and I'd be a liar if I said it didn't scare me. We're all she's got."

"We got this. Summer is coming and this semester is almost over. I'll be around to smother her with my brilliance and handsomeness! I'm not going anywhere anytime soon."

Enshrouded by the shadows at the top of the stairs, Raquel listened to the conversation, crouching unseen; a death-grip on the railing and a tear slipping down.

As each week on the calendar went by, anticipation took two different paths. The first was the dispensing of it, from those that had been anticipating the worst. Without anything negative happening, something approaching complacency was allowed to settle in.

The second path stemmed from the urgent anticipation of, in fact, *doing* the worst; of committing that negativity. Instead of complacency, turmoil festered.

That turmoil left one soul in particular, ravenous in a sense.

His thoughts were on a continuous loop; fetishizing (in more than one way) the chosen tithe he failed to sacrifice. It was a wound that wouldn't heal. It was like a splinter in his spirit.

The unbearableness of it drove him to act.

The time of the year meant that the sun wouldn't set until late evening, forcing a nearly non-existent patience to be exerted before another attempt could be made. And so, a slow deliberate circuit was wound on the streets surrounding his target.

Waning daylight closed the circle. Dusk quickened the hunt. The sunset ushered in the approach, and the moonrise cloaked his vice.

Flay sought to fulfil the obligation he'd been given by adding the one and only escapee, Raquel Dos Santos, to, as he saw it, his assigned list of culled fodder.

To do that, he'd have to be stealthy. The darkness was on his side, in more ways than one. The night sky helped to conceal even his paleness and the darkness within him spurred him on.

Being familiar with the area, Raquel's would-be murderer sought the shadows between the homes as he crept upon where the twins lived. He moved as stealthily as his gangly form allowed, finally eyeing their home from directly across the narrow street.

Few lights were on, which bode well for killing. But, being unmethodical would reap no benefit as far as he was concerned. So, he watched. He watched and waited. Death required an invoking, a provocation, for it to yield the sweetest reward. No one had provided him with that final ingredient as of yet. Undeniably, it was to come. He just had to bide his time.

Blending invisibly between tall bushes and the unlit brick of the house where he stalked, Flay did little more than breathe for hours. Then, his desired beckoning to kill came in the form of movement in the same front picture window he'd so ungracefully leapt from.

The blinds that hung there separated, only slightly, and swung slowly back and forth until their momentum subsided. To his deluded mind, he'd been engaged.

Whether it was manic obsession or conceited bloodlust that propelled him then, his attempts to conceal himself were abandoned. He practically strode across the street, directly to the window; unabashed.

Giddiness began to overwhelm him at the thought of finalizing his crusade.

Kneeling where he was, he strained to identify any movement inside the house. Although he couldn't spot his target, he believed that she had to have been inside because of the swinging he'd seen begin and end. With pleasure filling him, he closed his eyes, only briefly, to absorb the moment. Unexpectedly, a thumping on the glass directly in front of those closed eyes drew him back from reverie.

His expression contorted in terror.

Not two inches of glass and distance stood between Flay and the glowing green orbs of an unflinching black cat. Those eyes pierced; they penetrated. As that cat regarded Flay, his only indication of living was a heaving little chest and palpable hatred that could be felt even through the glass.

As malevolent as Flay was, fear grasped him at the unexpected sight and transformed his blood into something frozen. His phobia was profound. His terror was inherent in him.

Flay recognized that black cat as an implacable guardian that was beyond him.

Too irrationally afraid to bolt, he timidly began to back away; never breaking his gaze. When his opponent began to deliver a guttural rumbling, perceptible even through the pane that separated the two, Flay let a pathetic whimper escape.

That was the impetus for aggression. The black cat opposing Flay, for the second time in its life, hissed and released a sound through the window, intended to send the intruder away in terror.

It did just that.

Flay abandoned grace and coordination at the sound and fled as if no barrier was between them. The irrationality of his horror be damned. It existed in him and he sought safety.

As he sped away, the thought that the sound the cat spewed at him was actually the word 'LEAVE!' wound itself around his mind, and refused to let go.

With a vigorous shake, that little black house panther circled, curled, and sat regally down on an earned place of comfort, stoically reengaged as the protector of his home.

Flay retreated, denied a second time of his tithe, fearful of reprisal from the very ones that set him on his task to begin with, and fearing that his desired Appointment had been put in jeopardy.

Blissfully unaware, not two miles away, the Dos Santos twins were enjoying each other's company. The season brought traveling carnivals to town and they hadn't missed one since they became old enough to make that decision themselves.

Rafael and Raquel, Casey, and friends were parked at the far end of a field, sitting outside, in the warmth and comfortable breeze that wove between them. They sat on the trunk of Raf's car, a '91 Firebird that looked faster than it was, their feet hanging into the back seat, convertible top down, teasing, laughing, and relaxing. Parked next to them, J.P., his latest conquest whose name no one cared to commit to memory, Shea, and Mateo (the odd man out) sat on the trunk of J.P.'s car, exchanging drinks as well as insults between the group.

The sky couldn't have been clearer. The stars couldn't have been arranged better than they were. They provided the most impeccable tapestry to highlight the explosions. Above them, the colors bursting from the fireworks mesmerized as the biggest were just beginning to be launched.

The smile Shea displayed beamed at the sight in the sky, and Casey and Raq exchanged a perceptive wink between them because they recognized exactly why Rafael was beaming.

Raq gently prodded her friend then, "Shea, come sit with us...you can see better."

Without thinking, Raf teased his sister as a standard, go-to move, saying, "What are you talking about? You can't see the open *SKY* any better over here."

"I mean...the reflection off of the lake-those trees are blocking the reflection more...from their car! Dumbass! Shea, just get in this car!" Raquel blurted in exasperation.

Shea was quick enough to understand and began to move. Raq and Casey's shared expression voicelessly called her brother dense. That's when he finally grasped Raq's intent.

Raf made room for Shea next to him, extending a helping hand. Timidity was not his shortcoming. She took his hand and settled next to him, allowing an arm to stay wrapped around her.

"Ya know," Rafael began, "The third is good, but the best explosions always go down on the 4th. I can pick you up tomorrow and we can make some- *WATCH*-some, I mean."

An innocent, light laugh, one not marred by cynicism, passed between them. Rafael had managed to divert Shea's attention from the brilliant sky she'd been admiring. She knew her feelings, but held him off just the same, hoping for a measure of endurance.

She replied, "Maybe…"

Rafael took it as it was intended and looked forward to seeing her again, despite the fact that she was right next to him.

What was developing was a long time coming and Raq readily took credit for expediting it; even if no one else recognized it.

BOOM! BOOM! The finale was at hand.

The sparseness of the display began to take a turn as the colors and concussions were increasing by the minute. The OHHs and AHHs rose with the claps and everything seemed in harmony.

"C'mon, let's get closer.", Raq suggested to her man and jumped from the car. Heading closer to the water, Casey, Rafael, and Shea in tow, Raquel held them in a tether of her enthusiasm; concerns of her episodes believed to be far from her then.

The sounds of the crowd, the carnival, and the brilliant sky show collided as the group navigated through the few trees present and toward the water's edge.

As if it had been conspired upon, the crescendo overhead hit as soon as Raq reached the lake, and ominously, she stiffened and washed pale.

Staring down into the reflective water, Raquel became a statue.

Having been steps behind her, none of the others saw the look come over Raq that would have otherwise chilled them.

Fiercely, Raq's head wrenched back, and her clenched mouth strained violently. Her stare was directed up, not at- but through the fireworks, to the outer reaches beyond them.

As if it was agonizing, she forced her gaze down, where the water held the dual image of the bright explosions above it.

THE BALANCE WANES BITCH!!

The sound of a hate-filled voice overtook all of the combined revelries around her and felt as if it had weight enough to crush her. It seemed to crash down with concussive force on the water, sending waves impossibly high into the air, only to fall back down on her like a judgment.

But was that real?

Unable to contain it, Raquel shrieked-desperately.

That sound immediately engaged Casey and Raf, and they broke into an all-out run. They had been only a few steps behind at that point and caught up quickly. Casey reached her first, catching her as she collapsed. Rafael was only a stride behind.

Unconsolably, Raq twisted in Casey's arms, distraught. Mumblings and cries were being wrung from her by something none of them could identify. The men had, in the past, seen something akin to what they were witnessing then, but the severity of it had them shaken.

Shea, having been in some kind of slightly heeled shoes, came through the trees then, visibly annoyed that she'd been left.

Only the two men in her life had any inclination of what was happening to Raquel, and they, at her wishes, sought to shield the others from the knowledge. The look they shared was a decision in the making that took less than a second.

"Shea! Stop! Don't come over here!", Raf said commandingly; more so than he had intended.

Shea was understandably taken aback and simply said, "What? Why?"

Casey interjected then, stating, "There's...a...snake over here. A humongous snake! It scared the shit out of Raquel! Don't get too close."

"Yeah, we... lost sight of it...It could be anywhere.", Raf added to the necessary deceit.

Shea willingly conceded, "Oh, hell no! I'm good. I'm not moving! Raq-are you OK?"

Raquel was anything but; she was panic-stricken. The concern her friend had for her couldn't be acknowledged in her state, as she teared and shivered, mumbling softly about voices and visions.

"The heavens are battling! Look at the water-look at the sky! The energy careens all around. This looks like the warfare always above! Omni-present! Eonian!" Raquel's words were desperate and confounding!

With Shea's concern still hanging in the air, her brother answered for her, to allay suspicions, "She's good! She's all good! Just got scared. Listen, why don't you go back and I'll catch up with you tomorrow. I'm sorry...", Rafael offered. "I'm sorry...I yelled.", he said, actually regretting something entirely different.

Shea accepted the situation, knowing that the mood had been obliterated, and turned around to backtrack to her other friends. She mentioned something about calling the next day to finalize their meeting up, but that never happened. Whether it was the derisiveness of fate, or randomness alone, the timing for them was, again, wrong.

With the worsening condition of his sister requiring an increasing amount of his attention, Raf wondered if perhaps it wasn't for the best.

In time, Casey was able to calm Raquel.

Soothing words failed. Firmly gripping her failed. Intentional teasing from her brother failed. Although the dismay Raq had been in made the gesture seem untimely,

Casey ultimately calmed Raquel by doing what he'd intended to do that night.

As she became more composed, he reached into his pocket and produced the ring that she'd been eyeing for months.

Recognition slowly reflected in her eyes and tears quickly followed. Her episode had passed and she sunk into his embrace, comforted for the moment.

The show was over at that point, all of the rides and games of chance were ending, and back at the car, Mateo noticed the sound coming from the backseat, where the others had been sitting. Reaching down, he picked up a cell in a bright-colored case that he knew to be Raquel's. As soon as it was grasped, the continuous, urgent alarm that had been sounding, went silent.

The days shortened and darkened. Leaves turned and then fell. Winds gusted and chilled. In time, the skies opened and soaked the ground. Then, a soft white blanket transformed the streets and homes into something serene.

To Rafael, snow was never a thing to be annoyed by. Too often in his childhood, he wished that he could play in it just once. But Sao Paulo rarely gave him that chance.

Now, he was in a place that was famous for its winters. Although he was, for the most part, past playing, he still liked the snow just fine.

A light but lasting sprinkling of powder covered the city and began to glow in the coming night. His footfalls were nearly soundless as he made his way to the parking lot. His desire to pack and then heave one *perfect* snowball was irresistible and had to be done. It hit his mark perfectly!

The New Year festivities had come and gone, and he and his partners in crime had celebrated, perhaps a bit too hard, and the recovery process was begun in earnest. Raf was finishing his duties at Capoeira Collective North and was headed home to suffer with his sister and Casey.

Then, he was stopped in his, literal, tracks.

Rounding the corner building, Rafael watched a slight and hooded figure as he huddled and struggled with a car door. Rafael couldn't help but shake his head, questioning how he found himself in those situations.

Without concern or urgency, Raf walked up behind the would-be jacker and watched, initially amused.

Ultimately, his mood turned toward annoyance, He let himself be known then, stating, "You're doing it wrong."

Understandably startled beyond reason, the person spun on Rafael and allowed an already demonstrated penchant for bad choices to display themselves again. He took a swing at Rafael with the slim piece of metal that he'd been using.

The move wasn't unexpected and Rafael redirected the attack, spun him, and disarmed him without effort. That's when he realized that he was dealing with a kid. That didn't stop him from shaking the shit out of him.

"C'mon man! Get off me! Get off me!"

"Shut it! What are you doing, huh? Why the hell are you out here tryin' to steal stuff?", Raf demanded.

"What's it to you punk! Let me go!"

Rafael did just that, and the kid went down in the snow with a grunt.

"What are you, like ten? Raf jabbed down at the failed thief.

"Hell naw! Do I look like a baby to you! I'm 14, you...!"

"Watch yourself!" Raf warned, and reason settled in the kid's voice again.

"Fine, man. What now? You got me. Do what you gonna do."

"I intend to, kid." Raf stated matter-of-factly. Then, he reached down, grabbed a handful of the kid's hoodie, and dragged him roughly to his feet. He continued then saying, "Let me ask you a question. There is only one right answer to this so think before you spit out something stupid, got it?"

"What man? What?", came back begrudgingly.

"Alright listen. You can choose to claim that you make the wrong choices and are misguided and lack both the necessary opportunities to develop- and the proper outlets for your energy because the *system intends* for you to remain crippled and dependent - **OR** – you can just say that you don't buy into *any* of that and you just chose to be a piece of shit menace to those around you because you didn't care enough to be any better. Which is it?"

The question visibly irritated the kid, and his expression indicated that he meant to react poorly. To Rafael, it was clearly evident. So, he squashed that.

"No, no, no. I told you to think before you answered and trying something stupid right now wouldn't be you thinking. Now, which one is right?"

"I'm not some piece of shit!" was sincerely stated.

"THEN STOP ACTING LIKE YOU WANT TO CONVINCE THE WORLD THAT YOU ARE!"

For a moment, each of their eyes reflected fury. Then, acknowledgment softened the young man's face, proving that he had internalized the message. Rafael let him go then.

"Listen, what's your name?", Raf asked.

The answer came back simply, "Anthony."

"Alright, Anthony. Monday, come back here, around that corner, to the training facility and I'll show you how to do something better. Fair enough?"

The offer hung in the air for a short time, the young man apparently not used to positive opportunities. Then, an affirming nod came.

"Alright, I'll talk to you later. Now, move your ass so I can get in my car."

Anthony watched in astonishment as Raf opened the door to his Firebird and began to back away.

"This was *your* car the whole time?! Why didn't you say so? Hey!! Can I get a ride?"

Rafael flashed a smile and said, "Nope."

Back at the house, Raquel stood just to the side of the front window, musing at the appearance of the newly shoveled sidewalks on the street.

Casey sat silently, facing but not really looking at the TV. He'd driven up to spend the beginning of the New Year with Raquel. He'd been quiet that day, but the assumption was that his partying had gotten the best of him.

Across from Raq, a group of children played, loudly, throwing crude snowballs and running frantically. The snowfall had accumulated just enough to make the requisite angels, and they fell back to form the shapes.

Raquel smiled but wondered when was the last time she'd done the same thing.

After being called inside by a parent, Raquel continued to look wistfully at the angelic outlines the children had left behind.

Confusingly, the world outside her window brightened. The thought that it was street lights was dismissed immediately. A glow began to emanate from across the street. The source was the snow angel that she'd been staring at. It was suddenly radiant!

Raquel stood motionless.

As if something was being poured into a life-size mold, the outline began to fill and take shape before her eyes. From that snowy figure on the ground, a fully formed and recognizable entity rose inhumanly.

Glori appeared, regarding Raquel with an amiable smile.

"Casey...Casey...Casey...", Raq fought to vocalize.

"Casey! Do you see her?!"

With effort, he moved to her side as quickly as he could, but all he saw was a snowplow, violently kicking the contents of the street up and over the area; nothing more.

Raquel saw it differently; she saw Glori-*erased*-for lack of a better term, by that snow-drift.

"You didn't see that?"

"See what Raq? I didn't see anything unusual.", Casey stated distractedly.

"It was...It was..." But she couldn't articulate. It was in part because she resisted the improbability of it, but there was also a physical component to it. She struggled to communicate.

The insanity of what she doubted herself was being brushed aside by Casey. Raq felt that it was not done out of maliciousness, something was wrong. Instead of taking offense, she turned to what might be causing Casey's preoccupation, saying, "You don't look good. What is it?"

"I'm sorry, my head is hurting so bad- it feels like something is trying to push through my skull."

"How long have you been in pain?"

"It started Tuesday morning on campus and stayed with me the whole drive up. After yesterday, I thought it was just payback from the celebration. But it's gotten worse. I'm trying to ignore it though-mind over matter." Casey said, intending to be cheerful but only conveying discomfort.

Raq fought against her own preoccupation, even though it was like a dissipating dream at that point. Casey noticed and attempted to uncover what was bothering her again, asking, "Babe, tell me what's wrong."

Before she could respond, her twin walked in, noticed the mood that seemed to be pervasive in the room, and asked, "Did I miss something?", with sincere concern.

"No, Bruh. My head...is..." Casey began but couldn't finish.

"Hey, go upstairs and lay down for a while if it's that bad. Raq, take him up there! What's wrong with you?"

Her brother's question was rhetorical and would never have been asked if he'd been aware of what she thought she'd seen. Despite that, she didn't need to be told to help her man.

"C'mon babe, let your girl take you upstairs and make you feel better."

They went up without Raquel telling her brother about the apparition that she feared she'd seen.

That was a Thursday night.

Early Friday morning, nothing seemed to have improved. That included Rafael's mood, Raquel's preoccupation, and most notably, Casey's condition.

A fever joined a worsening headache overnight. Although Casey attempted to downplay it, his discomfort was obvious. Raquel and Rafael discussed it and decided for him; he was going to see a doctor.

The three of them left for the nearest hospital late in the afternoon, not urgently but concerned. As soon as Casey stepped outside, he lifted an arm up to block the sunlight from his eyes. With a grimace, he hunched and practically dove into the back seat. That didn't go unnoticed by his friends. Raquel sat next to him, holding his hand, trying to be present but lost somewhat in her own concerns.

As they arrived at the hospital ER, exiting the car, his aversion to the brightness was repeated. Again, it was noted but none of them realized that there was in fact a puzzle let alone that they'd seen the pieces.

The overworked front desk staff was routine, the repetitive paperwork was routine, Casey's lack of health insurance was routine, and the subsequent waiting because of that fact was, regrettably, routine.

At first, the Dos Santos twins sat as patiently as they could with Casey. Then, Raf excused himself, claiming the need to relieve himself, but using it as an excuse to wander. By the time he got back to them, still waiting exactly where they'd been, Raq decided that the same tactic could be used by her. She, also, had another agenda.

As she moved through the bright corridors, she searched. Raquel sought an answer to a question that she hadn't even fully formulated.

Hovered over the counter at a nurse's station, a doctor scribbled furiously away at a chart. To Raquel, an opportunity to settle her mind seemed to have presented itself. Despite some small reservations, she took the chance.

Going over tentatively, she began, "Doctor...?"

Curtly, the woman she'd approached began to cut her short with a dismissive response, "I'm extremely busy right now young lady. Please..."

Then that doctor managed to look up from her work, to notice the plaintive look in Raquel's eyes. Some iota of decency returned to her mannerism after seeing that. She cleared her throat and began again. "Yes, what seems to be the problem?"

"I was hoping I could ask a, very quickly, ask a really, kinda, weird question." Raquel struggled.

"Fine, be brief." was the response.

"Well, what would you say might be going on with someone if they were…"

"Before you continue, if this is something that you're experiencing, I suggest that you…"

"No! No!" Raq interjected. "This is something that my-ahh-*Father*-told me. See, he's seen some strange things."

"Seen?" the doctor asked. The expression on the doctor's face gave Raquel pause. She then attempted to come across as a concerned advocate.

"Well, what might be the reason for hearing - voices. He said that he's, only a couple of times, heard someone saying- things."

"Auditory hallucinations?"

"Yeah, and he saw- something- too. Once or twice. What does that mean? Probably nothing right? Maybe it's stress."

"Well, listen, I can't give you medical advice without a proper examination ethically, but I will tell you that auditory and visual hallucinations are often attributed to some degree of schizophrenia. I would take the proper steps to have your father evaluated."

The magnitude of what she was told struck Raq and stifled a response. Then, the disinterest of the doctor returned as if she'd reached the limit of attention she was willing to expend. At that point, a very cute little girl walked over with her parents. That gave the doctor the opportunity to separate herself from the unsolicited pestering and advice she'd been asked for. She nodded unceremoniously and turned away from Raquel without another word.

Raq watched that doctor move to greet the parents and the girl. She listened as she addressed them without warmth saying, "Hello Mr. and Mrs. Tunney. I was just going over your daughter's file."

Two things struck Raquel as she lingered; the way that the girl, all of roughly twelve, brightened the room and, in contrast, the way that the doctor's distinctly plain and undistinguished presence seemed to work against that. Remembering why she was there in the first place, Raq worked to hide her new concerns and made her way back to her brother and boyfriend.

Finding her way back to the waiting area, she found her brother sitting alone.

"What, you get lost?" he said rhetorically.

"No…" she began, not aware that an answer wasn't necessary.

They'd all been there for hours and while she'd been gone, someone had obviously and finally come for Casey. The siblings sat in silence for another hour waiting for him to be brought back.

When he eventually did come back, he seemed to be in roughly the same condition.

"Let's go." was all he chose to say.

"What happened man? What did they tell you? You got an infection in your uterus?" Raf said joking.

With that, Casey tried to punch him but missed. So Raq gave her brother a quick kick that he couldn't see coming. She connected and her boyfriend thanked her.

Casey led them out, relaying what had happened as they went. After a perfunctory exam by a distracted doctor, he was told that he'd come down with a mild case of the common flu, given a shot, and discharged with the instructions to stay hydrated.

"It's fine though. Yeah, maybe it took forever but now we know that it was just like I said. I'll be fine after I get some rest back at school."

"What do you mean? Why wouldn't you stay up here until you feel better? Why go back?" Raquel asked, trying not to allow too much need to sound in her voice.

"I have to get back to class. I have to be there first thing Monday. I never intended to stay past the weekend. No worries. Besides, do you think I'm gonna stay here and get you sick too?" he insisted.

The drive home was decidedly tense. Rafael felt like an unwelcomed observer to the disagreement his sister and Casey were having. As he listened to them go back and forth, obvious openings for jokes were passed up, wisely.

"I'm not trying to be a pain in the ass right now Raq, but this isn't helping my headache."

"Well, what about mine!" Raquel shot back.

"You have a headache now?"

"No! But, I could!"

"What...? That doesn't even make sense!"

"Neither does you driving back to school!"

For the rest of the way home, the bickering stayed the same. Casey's face became more and more taught and Raq became more and more emotional. By the time they'd reached the house, they'd reached a fever pitch.

"I can't deal anymore. I don't have the energy to do this right now. I think I'm just gonna head out." came from Casey then.

"You're not even listening to me, Casey. I've been trying to tell you..."

"What? What?" came in a tone that Raq instinctively pulled away from.

"Never mind! It doesn't matter. Nothing happened! Go back to school."

By that time, pride had taken control. She stormed into the house defiantly, unable to tell him that the real reason she wanted him to stay was because of what she'd seen before. The visitor she'd had was far too real to be imagined but far too surreal to accept as fact. So, to her mind, if he'd simply agreed to stay, she could have cared for him and he could have watched over her. Somehow, the exact opposite was allowed to happen.

Casey had gone up the stairs to get the one bag he'd brought with him. When he came back down, he was   moving stiffly but that went unnoticed by his girlfriend. She had her back turned. With one kiss on the temple, a feeble attempt at détente in her eyes, he left, headed back to his college dorm.

"I'll call you when I get there, babe. Sorry. I'll make it up to you next time I see you. Love you..."

Raq didn't return the sentiment from as much hurt as spite.

After a tiring drive of a little over two hours, Casey pulled onto the street that led to his school. Winding his way along the quaint roads, he drove faster than he should have in anticipation of the rest he craved. He pulled up to his usual parking spot, threw the car door open, walked at a quick pace, and shielded his head from what remained of the setting sun. Fumbling with the keys for longer than he could stand, three loud pounds brought his roommate to open the door.

Casey greeted him brusquely and said wearily, "Listen, man, I feel kinda like shit right now so I'm gonna crash. Don't wake me up unless the building is on fire or it's Monday morning and I'm late for class. Whichever comes first."

A disinterested "Yeah, yeah", was his roommate's response before going back to his standard ignoring.

That was late Friday night.

In his room, under the covers, and in the dark, Casey curled up with the expectation that he'd sleep it off.

That persisted through Saturday.

With his roommate out of the apartment, presumably staying with his girlfriend, no one heard the level and frequency of Casey's moans. No one was there to notice that he hadn't gotten up in more than a day. No one monitored his increasing fever.

By Sunday, Casey was dead.

Despondency took hold and shook her ruthlessly.

It was a brutal and violent thing and, in its grasp, all she could do was inwardly beg for help.

For what seemed like a lifetime, Raquel had been a shivering heap at the foot of her bed. First, whispers brought confusion. Then, bodiless voices carried fear with them. It didn't matter that she couldn't identify where they'd come from. There was no consolation for her; she was alone and it was happening again.

Terrified eyes darted back and forth without blinking; blood-red and tearful. Anxiety was making her heart race nearly beyond the point of what she could endure.

The voices accused her; they threatened her.

You're a burden!

Get up!

Don't bother getting up!

You deserve what you get.

They all know you're worthless.

What do you think you can provide?

Pray for the end!

Each word seared her soul. Every one of them was a blow that forced her to turn and cower within herself. Then, through the blur of her emotion, she feared that she'd caught sight of another presence in the room and that held her frozen.

Looking from the corner of her eyes, she believed she saw a figure in the dim room with her. At first, Raquel couldn't make herself turn to look head-on. She only allowed the unclear ghostly shape to brush her awareness. Tightly closing her eyes did nothing to lessen her knowledge that she wasn't alone any longer.

It wasn't courage that finally made her turn, it was the voices.

Weak and ignorant!

Face the fear!

With only the slightest of turns, recognition came. Raquel knew the woman that, somehow, glared down at her from inside of her dressing mirror. With every taunt that she heard in her head, she saw the apparition mouthing them. It had been her the entire time. She recognized that same vitiligous face from the night that she was...that she was...

To her horror, the woman peeled away from the glass then, stepping through it, out into reality, never once removing her baleful stare from Raquel. No scream could overcome the panic.

Far too much time went by uncomfortably between them before Raquel found voice, timid and cracking, to speak.

She pleaded, "This isn't real!" only to be answered with scoffing.

A look came over her scornful face, imposing and hateful as if to show how loathsome responding to Raquel truly was.

"The veil between your perception and Totality is thread-bare Miss Thing.", She accused.

With no indication that she was understood, she continued, "You quite ignorantly spoke of "real". What the Purgatory is REAL anyway, Thing? Don't bother, you have no idea. You'll know when I tell you what is. Going forward, I'm just going to refer to you as Thing by the way; because that is what you are."

Nothing more than breathless bewilderment could escape Raquel. The other continued.

"Here's where you say, '... And you are...?', but you'd pathetically sound much more -trepidatious - I'd bet. And then I'd reply, "I -am- Diva!"

"Diva?" was predictably questioned by Raquel in misunderstanding.

"Don't bore me bitch! That is how you are to refer to me. Try to be more than you are for even a short time. See if you can manage a semblance of composure and understanding."

Raquel tried to steel herself, not at the behest of this "Diva" but because she desperately needed to get out of the situation.

With a condescending tone, the imposing woman leaned over and asked, "Where do you think you will go? You're alone. How does that feel?"

Some amount of opposition rose up in Raquel at that accusation. The strength to challenge welled up in her chest and she spat back in defiance then.

"I'm not alone I have my brother!"

"Witless bitch!" was the answer to that. "Where is he? Where was he the last time you needed him? My wager is that he's staring at the bottom of a bottle right now. And you think he's here for you...? He has a number of shortcomings of his own to deal with. How is he supposed to carry your weight too? Don't you think he's held you up long enough?"

Just as the thought to object came into Raq's head, another barb left her reeling.

"How are you handling that rather, ruinous, bit of news that you just got? Hmm?"

Raquel had been called "fragile" in the past. That was certainly accurate up to a point. With the ordeals she'd experienced, damage would be inevitable. She was, possibly, encased in somewhat thin armor, but it was most definitely armor and her spirit was incited by Diva's attacks.

She began her counter with, "Who the fu--! "

Regrettably, the contempt on Diva's face indicated that Raquel's attempt at resistance was both expected as well as feeble. Before it gained any momentum at all, Diva struck; blindingly.

With her spotted face stretched forward, almost like a maw, she let out a sound that was like countless crying souls. That noise froze Raq and, it seemed, peeled back her skin where she huddled. Somehow, the scream was like a gale force against her. Looking through squinted eyes, Raq saw hands begin to morph into claws, a back begin to take on an arch, and eyes begin to darken like coals on fire.

What seemed like endless time to her was in fact only an instant. Then, it was over.

"Do you see the complete futility of you?" Diva posed with some minuscule amount of pity. "Never approach me like that again." She'd added that warning with her usual harshness.

The attempt to rationalize what had happened to her didn't even begin to take shape. It was accepted. It was too frightening to doubt. She simply shrunk from it.

"Now, I'll let you think about all I've told you. Judge the solace that you'll receive when your sotted savior returns. Let me know how secure you're made to feel. Gage where he places his efforts. I'll see it in your eyes the next time we speak. Trust that. Know that we're not done, Thing."

For a moment, their eyes locked although they conveyed two drastically different things. Then, Raq's attention was pulled away by the slamming of the front door. Looking away and turning back happened in a blink, but in that blink, the stout and spiteful figure of Diva disappeared. Scanning the room furiously, no sign to prove that the encounter had been real could be found. From the corner of her eye, the tall mirror, seemingly, shifted almost imperceptibly just as her brother entered the room.

Raquel looked manic and her brother fell to his knees when he saw her condition.

"Raq! What's the matter? Look at you! What happened?" His concern was not misplaced; her hair was disheveled; her clothes were drenched with sweat and her eyes still held the same anguish. She was slumped at the foot of her bed and focused on the mirror in front of her, but not her own reflection. The last thing noticed was the cell phone that she'd been holding the entire time in a death grip. It had been sounding an alarm that suddenly stopped. He couldn't pry it from her.

"Sis, talk to me. What the hell is goin' on with you?"

"I...got...a call. Casey...is gone."

It came from her, far too matter-of-factly. Her brother stared back in stunned speechlessness. Her meaning was taken. He didn't question the word "gone". As he reached out, unsurely, to grasp her shoulders, the ordeal struck her fully and she broke; completely.

Raquel erupted in desperate sobs. To describe her as inconsolable would belittle her pain. Her twin brother pulled her to him and simply stayed there.

In time, "How?" was all he allowed himself to ask.

Unable to detach herself from her welling emotion, his question went unanswered. Instead, she began muttering softly of guilt and remorse at the part she played in the way that they parted.

"We fought...the last thing we did was fight! All I did was push him away...I was so...stupid...Why? Why? Now, I'll never be able to...we were going to get..." She withered then and her brother consoled her by simply being near her. In time, the natural course of Raquel's sorrow played out and some slight semblance of composure returned.

She pulled away and continued to cry through the telling of the conversation with Casey's father and the true extent of his illness over the past weekend. Then, weakly, absently, she lifted her head and saw the way Raf appeared. She saw some small amount of bruising and blood on his face, quickly surmising that it didn't happen in one of his classes.

"Have you been fighting again?"

The second thing she noticed was the distinct smell of alcohol. The outpour of emotion she'd been exhibiting began to turn. Despair and anger clashed after her maddening realization.

"I...needed you and you weren't here! You have no idea! I needed you!"

"I'm sorry! I got into a little brawl. It was mostly the other guy's fault. I'm here."

"I needed you! I needed you! You're not fighting for *me*!"

The look on her face, so very much like his own, weakened him. It was all that he could do to keep from shrinking away. As he started to protest, to defend himself to her yet again, it became clear that she'd become detached.

He did have the smell of liquor on him; he had been fighting again but there was a purpose that he couldn't admit to himself or verbalize to her. It was inexpressible.

Before his sister's disturbing encounter that night, Raf had just finished a class and the night had gone well. His mood was upbeat as crude jokes and farewells were exchanged with J.P. and Mateo as they parted ways for the night. His only objective then was to head home. It was a short and usually uneventful walk to the car, but fate had a different objective for him. It was unavoidable.

Only two cars were on the far side of the lot; one of those would ruin his night.

On the passenger's side, a loud, large, and infuriated woman towered over a sobbing little girl. Curses and ridicule intended to humiliate came out of that mouth. The will of the girl seemed withered. A meaty and noticeably spotted, blotched handheld the child's tiny wrist painfully as its match drew back to strike.

"Is all that necessary!" shot from Rafael before he could contain himself. The scene was too familiar and too abhorrent for him to truly want to try.

For no more than a beat, the mouth of the woman was silent and gaping at the interference of someone else in what she considered her business. Of course, that ended with her turning her evilness toward Rafael.

"What the fuck did you just say?" she spat. "You don't know me! Don't say shit to me...!"

"Stop. Just stop! I'm not about to go back and forth with you, just leave the girl alone." He'd said it and considered himself reasonable for expecting that she'd end her torment. Two steps away, he pulled out his consoler; his flask. His mood was ruined and he drank.

With his words still in the night air, that meaty hand drew back and connected against young skin with an echoing CRACK! The berating continued despite the wailing and in spite of Raf's warning.

He was enraged.

He was also a stranger being forced to come between a "mother" and her child. Quickly, all the ways that that could go wrong for him played out in his mind. Inaction was never a possibility for him though. Spinning back on the cruel woman, he saw her reach for a very large cup that was on the trunk of the car which he hadn't noticed earlier.

She was too bold for her own good. She screamed, "What the hell are you gonna do? Huh? What's this got to do with you, you little bitch!" With that, the drink was awkwardly thrown at him, missing wildly. That might have been the reason that she upped her attack and let an open-handed slap fly. That missed as well, dumping her to the ground on her bulbous ass with a thud.

A quick look at the little girl showed the delight in her expression at seeing that fall. He thought the situation had resolved itself but he was very wrong.

At his back, he heard footsteps.

"Whoop his ass!" came up from the mother of the year.

Spinning quickly, Rafael caught a weak but well-placed sucker punch to the jaw. The irate beast's man had been in the driver's seat and chose to back his woman over the child; undoubtedly his usual pattern.

The feeling of swelling and the taste of blood sent Rafael into a fury as he quite completely pummeled that man.

Sirens sounded and lights could be seen in the distance. Nothing about the situation was anything that he'd asked for, but the prospect of explaining a bloody heap of a man to the police with the smell of Hennessy on his breath was never going to happen. He went rapidly to the child and softly told her two things. She nodded her understanding and then began to walk away toward the authorities.

Rafael hastily got in his car and with lights off, put distance between his run-in and himself; the wretched woman was ignorantly spewing hate at him, too boldly, the entire time. But he never looked back. If he had, he would have questioned why another heinous-looking woman was grasping and shaking that mother's wrist like a puppeteer, and where the hell she'd suddenly come from.

His anger never subsided, regardless of how removed from the situation he got. His feelings were a torrent in him and his mind was anchored to his sister and his former lives and abuses. As he had so many times in his past, he reassured himself that he did what he had to...just like he'd done the night before they left Sao Paulo.

"She told me you'd disappoint me..." Raquel mumbled.

"Who said that?" Raf said defensively.

"I told her I had you...you had me... I thought she was wrong..." Raq continued to speak as if she was alone with her thoughts, instead of with the one person that had   always supported her.

"Who are you talking about? I've got you! You know I've always got you. Tell me what happened here."

"*Mano*, something is wrong with me. You won't believe me..." she began with one tear descending.

"I will. Talk to me."

"You don't understand. This is insane- *I'm* insane. I...saw things, and heard their voices. They appeared and they said...they said...things to me. I heard."

The possibility that his sister was mistaken or even worse intentionally lying was unthinkable. His belief was unconditional as it always had been. But he had no explanation for what she was saying. He couldn't rationalize it away and wouldn't try. That would only work to unsettle her further. Belief didn't require understanding.

The two sat together for a very long time. Piece by piece, Raquel relayed what happened to her and Rafael took it all in without judgment. She began with the night of his fight at the nightclub and ended with the belittling she'd received from Diva. When she'd said all she seemed to want to, he took his time before finally reassuring her.

"Irmã, we came in together and if need be, we go out together. Believe that. Don't ever let anyone make you doubt that."

"I never used to doubt it." she said distantly.

Raf was hurt by that more than he showed.

"But...you doubt it now? C'mon, maybe you think I'm off my game a little but I promise you I'm not. Alright? As far as what you've told me, could it be stress or panic attacks or lucid dreaming that only, I don't know, felt real maybe?" he asked before consideration could stop him.

A slap to the back of his head quickly followed with the question, "Did that feel real?" His sister was genuinely annoyed with the suggestion that what she'd experienced was chalked up to an errant emotion.

"Ow! Ok! It sounded stupid as soon as I said it. You tell me-how do you explain it?"

"I don't know! All I can tell you is that it was real to me! The voices, the women, the taunting...They want something from me. Or, they're trying to keep me from something."

"Do... you hear 'em now?" Raf tentatively asked.

"No. I don't hear them now!"

"OK, OK, don't get upset. Sorry. Well, right now it just seems like it's messing with your head. Maybe these two-voices-or women aren't really a threat to you." When he suggested that, it seemed to Raq that he was primarily trying to reassure himself. She picked up something indistinct in his tone that concerned her. But her attention was fleeting and so was that perception. Her distress was consuming. As her brother continued, she struggled to focus on his words.

"I don't have the answer to any of this. I don't understand any of this. I'll do what I can to be there for you. All I can do is promise to look out for you." her twin assured her.

"All I can do is promise to let you."

For a moment, they let that bargain hang in the air. But Raq knew that she had to insist on an addendum. She needed one other reassurance.

"The only thing that I'm worried about, is your pastime. You have got to stop fighting."

There was no misunderstanding on Raf's part despite his need to play it off. So, with feigned obliviousness, he claimed, "I fight for a living. What do you want me to do, go broke?"

"I'm not talking about your class! Don't play dumb. You know exactly what I mean! I don't know what you need to prove or if it's just for pleasure, but you are constantly getting into it with some other jackass on the street. You get off on it?"

"No! I really don't. I don't like to hurt people and I don't do it for no reason at all. It's never for no reason. I only fight when..."

Raq only somewhat wanted the rationalization to be finished. It was never something that she would be able to accept regardless. But he never did complete his thought.

"Listen, Raf, I'm...scared...more than I've ever been before. If you got me, for real, then make sure you got me. Compreendo?"

Considering all that they'd been through, the weight of that admission was not lost on him.

"Yeah, I got it. I will do better. I promise." Came from her brother sincerely. The likelihood of that sentiment enduring was something that they both doubted silently.

Weeks bled into months and Rafael did what he could to maintain stability for himself and his sister. He'd continued to teach his Capoeira students just as Raquel continued to teach her dance classes. Their lives maintained the outward appearance of normalcy but despite any promises made by Raf and all attempts to mitigate what Raq was going through, nothing had significantly changed; for either of them.

Although he had no intention at all to disclose what he'd been doing to his twin, Rafael had done little to stop his extracurricular brawling. He hadn't been able to express himself freely to his sister as to why he did what he did, but to his mind, his justifications were clear. If he had been as clear with her, she might have identified the need that he himself was so determined to overlook.

He hid the fact that he fought. He rationalized each by the necessity of circumstance. He also considered the larger size of every opponent as something to offset the indiscretions.

'Each one of them was bigger, almost like...' he thought to himself without daring to allow completion.

The second most crucial fact that he chose to cling to was that he never sought out the confrontations. Not one time did he initiate conflict. As he saw it, he was stepping into existing hostility with the intention of mediating. If the others wanted to escalate it and in turn, learn their limitations, then so-be-it.

Regardless, he'd promised to do better and to be more available to his sister and he'd failed her consistently; whether she was aware of it or not. His clashes stacked up and his guilt followed suit. That, in turn, brought about the constant attempt to mask it with the flask. That pattern continued through the summer and into the first months of the fall.

Raquel's unnerving occurrences only seemed to multiply. Spiteful voices continued to assault her regularly. Some days, it was unbearable. Some days, to curl up defensively was all that could be managed. Some days, she wandered throughout their house untethered.

There were occasions when a very different energy was felt and heard. In those times, her voices and visions were far more encouraging but not any less unsettling. Regardless of the motivations, a disembodied urging or a threatening apparition had the same mental effect on her. It soon got to the point where the physical affects became apparent as well. It became increasingly difficult for her to communicate clearly; her speech became a jumble. Raquel began to look disheveled as a rule. Her eyes darkened and appeared sunken from the stress.

When her work began to suffer, there was an agreement between them that something had to be done.

The early Autumn air had a touch of the coming crispness to it but the day was still nice, and the beginning sunset was a pleasant one. The drive Raquel and Rafael were taking began to elicit emotions that had been kept subdued. They were on their way to the same hospital they'd visited months earlier with her ex-Casey. This was their second visit, in as many weeks. The first involved a series of tests that Raq protested, uncharacteristically, rather aggressively. The blood tests yielded nothing unusual. CT and MRI scans failed to provide any physical answers at all. The attending doctor chose to pursue the issue despite the lack of definitive evidence and he referred Raq to a psychiatrist. That appointment was set for that day.

Raquel's mood had remained uncharacteristically grim. Rafael couldn't help but notice the tension his sister failed to mask; her entire body was tensed. That was soon mirrored in his own temperament. The wait to be seen did little to help the situation. The outer office looked to be designed to soothe and reassure, but without needing to voice it, they both found it to be a wholly inadequate attempt.

Shortly, after a deep and justified frustration had begun to set in, a nondescript assistant led them back into the inner office.

"Good afternoon, let's begin shall we." The doctor that welcomed them in, spoke in soft, un-threatening tones by design. He was immediately despised.

"Raquel, we seem to be having some difficulty, don't we? Now, I do have my suspicions but I'd rather not put the cart before the horse. What I'd like to do first is…"

Nothing that he said past that point was either heard or understood by Raq. As the dull man droned on, she'd become preoccupied with a profound apprehension. It was something that she'd learned to recognize. That feeling usually proceeded distinct angst.

BUZZZ-BUZZZ-BUZZZ!

An alarm, set to vibrate, sounded from her phone.

"Please, if you don't mind, kindly turn off all cell phones during this evaluation." the doctor chided them both.

With a hint of agitation in her voice, Raquel protested that her phone was not, in actuality, even on. The man across the desk took no notice and continued his self-absorbed dissertation.

Her denial didn't go unheard by her brother though. Her expression of panic was also clear to him. He watched as her eyes darted back and forth around the room. A racing heart quickly sent perspiration down her temple and a familiar fear manifested in a twitching, restless leg. The doctor continued on though, seemingly oblivious.

None of it escaped Raf's notice.

He watched as she, almost inaudibly, began to mutter. It seemed like the things she was saying were actually responses. He'd heard about the voices and the ones they belonged to. He'd seen the dismay those voices caused Raquel, but this time it was consuming her.

There was nothing that he could do to affect her obvious struggle. That fact twisted his own face into a helpless mask. Raf could only imagine the dialog taking place internally. Taking her hand, he tried to support her in some small way as he feigned interest in the psycho-babble they were being bombarded with.

As his sister worked to contain an obvious struggle, Raf's expression shifted from concern for her to anger at the doctor and back again.

A tear slid down her cheek from where had been welling, and that fact brought the first acknowledgment of the verbose doctor.

"What are you feeling right now Raquel?" he asked. No answer came as she sat there detached. His statement did reach her as he followed instinct and experience by saying, "The voices you're hearing are not real. They don't hold sway over you and they are not powerful. They are not real Raquel."

That assertion was beyond her limit of endurance and the little composure she'd been able to maintain abandoned her.

"They are real! They're real and they're stronger than me! They demand! They hurt! Even when they are soft, they hurt!"

Rafael simply stated, "I know they do." He then turned to the man across the desk from them, looking for an immediate solution.

The rehearsed calmness he tried to convey was obvious. The doctor's "solution" came in the form of pills that he strenuously insisted she swallow. She was near panic and sought her brother's guidance. His face left little doubt. He assured her that taking those pills would be the right thing to do and she deferred.

Eventually, the two were able to leave the office in somewhat calmer states. Raquel had been sedated to the point of near insensibility. Distant, unsettling phrases were all that she could manage to convey. Rafael worked to hold her steady as they went, his mind racing from what he'd been told.

Schizophrenia was the diagnosis assigned to Raquel.

They were given explanations, instructions, prescriptions, and reassurances and then sent on their way.

The two moved silently through the hospital, each engrossed in unspoken thoughts about their distant past, their recent past, and the coming unsure future.

As they went, they passed a stern-looking doctor working on something that was undoubtedly tedious. She glanced up in their direction. Something sparked the slightest hint of recognition in her at the sight of Raquel, but it was too indistinct. A very common and pervasive dismissiveness returned to that doctor then, leaving the matter unpursued.

Waiting for the elevator, Rafael wrapped a protective arm around his twin after noticing the teary redness of her eyes. That made him turn away and push the call button repeatedly, impatiently. An orderly came behind them loudly, pushing a cart full of food trays. His blond man-bun was piled on top of his head like a euphemism for his unlikability. Rafael took little notice of him. Raquel didn't seem to initially, but when he leaned his weight against his cart, struggling to lift his foot to tie his shoe, Raquel released the wheel-lock he'd set. That sent him and those food trays sprawling down the corridor.

Raf missed what his sister had done. No explanation for her action was needed. The doors opened, Raf ignored the clamor, and they went down.

Moving toward the entrance of the hospital, the area was energetic as patients and workers came and went hastily. Just to the side of the doors, a man paced a tight pattern into the rug. He was fumbling with something small he held; staring intently at it. Despite seeing him clearly, Rafael collided with that man as he turned to begin his pacing again; as if it was unavoidable.

"My bad, sorry Bruh." Raf offered.

"Doctor…" was the response given.

"What…?"

"It's Doctor."

"OK-sorry Doctor." Rafael amended, feeling some degree of tension pass between them. The doctor looked too young to be filled with such pomposity. Although, the greying at his temples cast some doubt to that.

Reaching into his pocket to put away what Raf then saw had been a tiny black box, the doctor exhaled deeply, trying to release his tension.

Seemingly becoming conscious of how he'd come across, the doctor attempted to course-correct saying, "No problem. It was probably my fault. I'm preoccupied."

A nod passed between them and each returned to their purpose; Rafael's was seeing to his sister and putting that day behind them both.

Once outside, a short walk through the parking lot revealed the beauty of the day's sunset. Engrossed in their own anxiety and concern, neither acknowledged it. They got in the car silently and Raq sunk into herself.

Traffic was light. Turning out onto the main road, headed home, their progress was hindered. The sound of a siren was to be expected considering where they were and they heard exactly that as they pulled up to the intersection. From the right, halfway up that block, he noticed the ambulance weaving its way through the stopped traffic. The light in front of the twins had turned green but no one moved in deference to the coming emergency. Rounding the corner, being the first car in the far lane, Rafael took notice of the driver of the large red and white vehicle. Even in his current state, he had to notice the beauty of the woman behind the wheel. Her long black hair bounced as she turned. Her face showed the gravity of her job, even at that distance. The rig roared past them on the other side of the divider, headed for where they'd just left. He wondered who was in the back and what they were going through.

In the time it took to cross the intersection and fade away behind them, the light turned red again. As they sat waiting, anxious to be home, Raquel began to speak distantly.

"She should be upset...But she should also see..."

Raf allowed her to go on without question or interruption. She continued on cryptically.

"...He did want to assert his power...but he also loves her...and she knows it. She feels the same. She doesn't know what he intends to do today...his vision is blurred but...he could turn again and find a way back..."

An annoyed horn from the driver behind them alerted Rafael to the newly turned traffic signal. As he lurched forward, the next thing he heard his sister mention was curious.

"...He said, 'Wai!'. She can't help herself."

"... Three...Two...One...Boom! I knew her. Now there's only smoke."

It sounded ominous. Rafael listened without any understanding. It was unclear who she was referencing but when she spoke of someone 'turning and finding his way', Raf was forced to question if she meant him. He doubted it though and drove on.

Looking behind them, he suddenly saw a plume of dark smoke rising. It was clear that there had been an explosion. It was also clear where it was coming from.

More sirens began to sound near them, coming from multiple directions. Something horrible had to have happened. He had no intention of looking for answers. His only objective was to seek some small measure of security at home; for both of them.

His focus was reclaimed and redirected ahead. That clarity may have allowed him to finally hear something that had been at the edge of his perception before.

The muffled sound of an alarm had been underneath everything that had happened since they got into the car. Straining, he could recognize that it was coming from Raquel's pocket.

In a distinct moment of clarity between them, she shot her brother a knowing and troubled glance as the phone went quiet.

ENTROPY ORDEAL

PROLOGUE

It had been an unseasonably stifling day. The sun heated the air enough to make moving a chore. But there was always so much that needed to be done. To be idle was an unaffordable luxury. There was laundry that required folding. There were dishes that needed washing. There were those things and so much more to do. While some would take the opportunity to indulge in a bit of harmless laziness, others kept decidedly busy.

One task at a time though, that was the plan.

Unfortunately, when you are elderly and live alone, even one small task can become overwhelming. That was the case that day. Frailty was always an obstacle at that stage of her life. Forgetfulness and COPD were also enormous hindrances to her otherwise industrious nature.

Although a woman came once a week, hired through an agency by her grandson, that help was often lacking. That help could also be undependable at best.

That help also chose the worst day to be absent.

Just like times in the past, the no-show of her helper did not excuse the tasks at hand. Letting chores go undone was never in her nature. The aggravation outweighed the exertion in her eyes, so, she set herself to it.

After that preventable over-exertion, the woman felt herself wilt a little where she stood. With some effort, she was able to take her usual measured steps to the nearest seat. She fell into it. Her sight seemed a little dimmer than before and her throat became dry. Only seconds later, she slumped forward.

It was unclear how long she was unconscious. She wasn't even sure if it was simply sleep that had overcome her. With effort, she lifted her head slowly.

For a time, she sat there still, focused on nothing at all.

Her thoughts were not on her work. Her face was emotionless, and her gaze wandered without aim. Then, something changed. That aimless gaze became a pin-pointed stare as she focused wide, fearful eyes a short distance in front of where she sat. She'd been alone, as she usually was, but something held her scrutiny. Something forced her to leer intently.

"My kinda town…" came from her then in a weak voice. "My kinda town…" she repeated.

As she sat, dazed, her hand rested on the table next to her. She began to slap the table, lightly at first, then sharply. The familiar song lyrics were repeated. Initially, she spoke in a hushed and hurried way, but that changed.

Her voice climbed as the words were repeated until she was yelling them. There was no melody to what she was doing. Words came in a strained and urgent way.

No one was there to witness, and no one was there to help. Her breath came in gasps and the tenseness she felt was painful, although she had no one to convey that to.

Abruptly, the episode ceased.

The ragged singing ended and her strikes on the table did too. Only to be replaced by something more troubling. Small skeletal hands shot forward, knocking over countless knick-knacks on the table, sending them across the floor. The tablecloth was being torn from its place as she clenched with unusual strength. Her head slumped as she no longer had control enough to stay upright. Then, with an exhalation, she relaxed and became calm.

With glazed eyes, she tried to recognize where she was. All she heard then was her own wheezing. Back and forth, her eyes tracked, unable to focus on anything in particular. She stayed there in confusion.

As the little lady tried to straighten herself, she began to mumble a different tune to no one.

"The time to hesitate is through...no time to wallow in the mire...Come on baby light my fire...Come on baby light my fire...Try to set the night on..."

The song trailed off, but her actions sought follow through.

One hand moved across the clutter on the table, possibly searching unconsciously. A lighter was found and a steady "flick-flick" began as she thoughtlessly sought to light it.

Her other hand crept up to her breast, perhaps, again unconsciously, to the pendant that she'd worn for many years. With minimal awareness, she pressed the red button on it for the first time and closed her eyes.

There was an accompanying unit for the alarm pendant she wore not ten feet away. It flashed its urgency and almost immediately, the phone rang. Unable to answer, of course, it went to voicemail.

"Mrs. Eyote...This is Red Guard Services. We've received an alert from your location. Mrs. Eyote if you can hear me and you're in distress, we have dispatched someone out to you and we'll be there shortly. Mrs. Eyote...?"

It wasn't long before the siren sound filled the air.

Endgame Trilogy

PART I: THE CONSONANCE

Endgame Trilogy

Confusion was immediately apparent.

Through blurry, tear-filled vision and a piercing ringing in his ears, consciousness fought for its footing. That footing was elusive. That consciousness seemed unwilling. When it did come, it came empty-handed.

Where was he? What happened? Why didn't he know? Nothing was clear except that confusion. Coming to out of oblivion with no concept of the most fundamental answers of your circumstance is, at best, troubling.

He found himself lying flat, face down on unforgiving concrete. With effort, an arm was untwisted and brought up to a haze-filled and clouded head. That light touch provided the first answer and was the initial beacon through the fog.

He was injured.

A reflexive reaction overcame him as he began to survey his extremities and torso. No broken bones - no bad contusions - no major injuries - just a head wound. That seemed to be minor. His probing was deliberate and practiced. Somehow, he knew his method was accurate.

There was no doubt in the process. He'd known what he was doing. Yes, he knew that much for sure, but he didn't know the basis for that certainty.

Something to be added to the shortlist of what he did know, was the fact that he felt a distinct heat all around him. That hinted at an unidentified threat.

Working his way up to his knees, with his hands stretched down in front supporting him and his heavy and murky head, to crawl a few feet forward was all he could manage. That effort paid off with an answer to a second question. On the ground, partially melted at its edges, was a laminated badge. Picking up that photo ID sparked the recognition of his own face looking back at him from within that plastic.

Nathaniel Ash, M.D. - that was his name and title.

At least a degree of clarity had been recovered. Rising unsteadily, Dr. Nathaniel Ash began to put the pieces together slowly.

As he got to his feet, one realization followed the next, painting a grim and desperate picture. Where was he? He was at work, at the hospital, and specifically in the ambulance bay. What happened? That was still not clear but seemed unmistakably bad. Spread out in front of Nathaniel Ash was wreckage and flame. The source of the heat that he felt was of course a fire that surrounded him. Directly in front of him was the burning shell of an ambulance. Beyond that, he could see the broken pillars that had supported the overhang to the bay. They were snapped and smoldering, obscuring the twilight outside. The whole of the ambulance bay was gutted and burning around him. How could this be? Had the vehicle crashed? Why did he seem to have only minor injuries in the middle of what looked like a strike on Kabul?

Staggering closer to the carcass of the ambulance, Nathaniel caught a glimpse of himself in the side mirror. He decided to look a little more closely. The reflection he saw of course matched the ID he'd found. He took notice of the deep darkness of his eyes in relation to his light-brown skin as if that was the first time he'd ever seen the contrast. His goat-tee looked as if it had grown slightly wild from its usual neatness. Black wavy hair on his head was cut short but thick. The small white patch in that hair at his right temple, which belied his age, was both familiar and novel to him. But the slow turn of his head, revealing his left temple, showed what looked like a deep laceration. There appeared to be only minimal bleeding though. He seemed to have gotten off lucky.

Without any recollection of what caused the scene staring back at him, speculation took the lead. Was the damage confined to the bay or was there more to the situation than could readily be assessed? It was very possible that the damage was much more widespread throughout the facility and that there were people that needed him. But if that were true, it meant that he would be putting himself in danger by entering the building. There was a reluctance that felt unusual to him. Fear was not the factor that motivated him, logic was. That's what he believed. That's what mitigated his reluctance. His logic was that any of the doctors inside would be working to triage, to evacuate, and going in would add to the confusion. That was reasonable and well thought out, but the fact is that reason and logic can sometimes be the outer armor that fear and weakness don.

Any person that claims to have the courage to act without hesitation in desperate situations has never actually been in one. That was what Nathaniel realized as he surveyed the Hell he'd found himself in the middle of. He was trained, and he was capable, but he was also well aware of the fragileness of humanity. At that time, his was in the balance.

He hesitated, as most would have. Then, a lesson from his past came through loud and clear from his subconscious. Nathaniel remembered an instructor telling his class of a very distinct and inevitable eventuality that would arise in their future practices. That instructor knew that all doctors face fear at some point. Skill didn't prevent that fear. Knowledge didn't prevent that fear. The other thing the doctor communicated was the fact that hesitation always trailed fear closely. But the secret to overcoming both fear and hesitation was conveyed as if it was an undocumented piece of wisdom not found in any of the texts in existence. Everyone in the class was made to huddle close to receive that sage wisdom. With shushes for every student and feigned paranoia, one word was quietly uttered- HELP. That instructor stated, in the simplest terms, to always think help. Always help... It was a thought that seemed unnecessary to communicate to a group of people devoting years of their lives to the idea of helping others. The groans and sighs came out loudly, replacing the false reverence that had been created. With searching eyes, the doctor found and met the gaze of the only person not preoccupied with some kind of mocking. Nathaniel and his newfound future mentor studied each other. Instinctively, Nathaniel thought that there was more to it and his assumption was quickly proven right.

"H-E-L-P." his instructor spelled out loud. "Hesitation-Eventually-Loses-People". The restless jeering stopped and was replaced by understanding and appreciation. "In each of your futures, when you feel afraid and naturally and humanly hesitate, remember- H.E.L.P."

That was his first day of med school. The doctor's name was Malcolm.

Dense and dark smoke obscured the entrance to the Emergency Room lobby. It was entirely possible that through that veil, everything was as it should be...but he sincerely doubted that and considered that wishful thinking. Moving decisively toward the door, his left temple began to pound, demanding attention. Nathaniel stopped where he was, waiting for it to subside. But the throbbing of his head ultimately won his full attention as he stood there. For what initially appeared to be an insignificant wound, he was experiencing an inordinate amount of discomfort it seemed. More questions presented themselves at that point. What if there was more than met the eye to his head injury? Was it possible that his judgment was impaired? He was aware of the possibilities involving head wounds. That may have been another solid reason to look past his earlier logic and go into the facility; what if the person that really needed to be helped was the one on the ID and in the mirror?

Whether that was true or not wasn't given much consideration. That possibility had to remain secondary. "Pain doesn't hurt" he told himself. Nathaniel's intention was to look beyond it, to refuse to acknowledge it. He also chose to ignore the odds of accomplishing that little feat. Regardless, he did what he could to steady himself for what he intended.

Staring out beyond the burning rescue vehicle, into the receding sun, gathering clouds filled with colors that billowed like the flames. The skyline would have normally been considered beautiful. But the waves of heat misled his eyes and made what he was seeing into a corrupted thing. He felt it necessary to turn away. Doing that revealed something that had almost gone unseen. It had escaped his notice earlier. To his right, at the rear of the vehicle, was a small and singed thing. One shoe... One charred shoe sat there smoldering about five yards from him. Moving closer, with a hesitancy based on fear not self-preserving logic that time, Nathaniel made his way over. Whose shoe was it? It wasn't his... both accounted for. He came to it, bending down to investigate closer, and there was a shock there waiting for his curiosity. There on the ground, just behind the ambulance, missing one small shoe was a ruined little figure of a woman. She was frail and elderly with large, open eyes. Obviously, she'd been caught in whatever had happened. Nathaniel rushed to her to assess the extent of her injuries. A learned response went through him as he looked her over. There was no visible movement, there was no ascertainable pulse, and no breath sounds. There was nothing to be done.

She was gone.

As he looked down on her, there was a fleeting familiarity that came and went so quickly he failed to capture it. She was a pretty lady. He felt that she must have been very likable too. But the recognition eluded him. So, he let it slip away without further thought. Hanging over both of her ears was a thin tube that ended, dangling ungraciously, under her nose; the remains of a breathing tube. Nathaniel reached out to remove it respectfully.

Her eyes shifted!

The movement was sudden and surprising, but what was even more startling were the expressions in them that kept him transfixed. Those eyes conveyed some un-named agony initially which then turned into seething anger.

It was only when lifelessness again replaced all else that Dr. Ash was set in motion. Immediately he began chest compressions. One step of CPR followed the next as he fought to revive the woman, he felt he should somehow know. "Non-responsive...! Non-responsive...!" was all that he repeated to himself. Reluctantly, he gave up his efforts. Although he wasn't at all sure how long he'd worked at it, he was positive that he'd had no effect. Those intense emotions she displayed in her eyes had been last gasps.

For whatever reason, Nathaniel felt like a target. He felt like the specific target of those eyes and all they intended to convey. There was no logical reason for the inference that he could come up with, but it bothered him just the same. It would have burrowed its way into him if it had had the chance. But a distraction delayed that from happening. A sudden burst of static sounded near him.

"A radio...? Of course..." He moved to investigate what he'd heard.

From where he was at the rear, he could now see the other side of the burning ambulance, the passenger side.

"Daniella!" he screamed.

Daniella had been her name, Daniella Ramirez. She was an EMT at the hospital. Her long black hair was pulled back in a tight ponytail now but he remembered it flowing beautifully free. He preferred it that way. She'd told him before that her work required her to do it up that way, but she did keep the promise to wear it down on their first date. That was not too long ago it seemed... but he wasn't sure. They liked each other more than either admitted. She teased him about being arrogant and he teased her about being naive. He remembered her...He cared for her. Now, she was sprawled brokenly near the wreckage, her lower torso resting in the fire. Her eyes never shifted.

The static made itself heard again through the feelings he tried suppressing. That snapped him back to the dilemma at hand.

"What the hell happened here?" he questioned vacantly. All he could do was to stand there frustrated with his inadequate conjecture.

Inadequacy was not something he'd been used to. Nathaniel Ash was an accomplished doctor, well aware of his abilities and dismissive of his limitations. But just then, there in the midst of an inexplicable occurrence, he'd already proven to be incapable of helping the only other people he'd come across. That feeling was bitter to him. He had no intention of allowing it to become familiar. But intention and outcome can be regrettably opposite. He'd learned that in his past. That lesson played out in his mind then. He thought back to the time.

Near the end of his first year, Nathaniel allowed himself to become somewhat complacent. He'd lulled himself, through routine, into disbelieving what he'd been told was inescapable. Even though he'd been cautioned against it, he chose to disregard. The inescapable truth he'd disregarded at the time was that every doctor would eventually kill.

It had been a sunny and unusually warm Saturday in early January. The New Year had just started, and everyone was either recovering from or foolishly trying to continue their celebrating. Lack of seniority landed Dr. Ash the long and unwanted shift through the New Year's celebration. That period was without question the least coveted slot and any intern that pulled it was renamed "New Shoes" for the extent of it. They were called that because that was exactly what everyone needed to buy afterward due to all of the spewing revelers. Nathaniel was exhausted, and he was frustrated, but he was near the end of his shift and ready to proclaim that he'd lived through his first New Year as a doctor when Casey came in. Casey was his first name but his last regrettably escaped him. Dr. Ash did remember the kid's face though. He was a good-looking young man of college-age with dimples that, if he'd known him well, would have contradicted his mischievous wit. Unfortunately, when he came into the hospital, he wasn't feeling overly playful. As bad as he felt at the time, the only small-talk he was enthusiastic about was regarding the fiancé he'd come in with. The doctor engaged him on that subject curiously, without feigned interest.

Casey had come in complaining of a headache and soreness. He'd driven himself in and that drive had been a long one that he would've, of course, avoided if at all possible. Like so many others, he didn't have any insurance and that fact meant a very long wait to be seen at the County Hospital. He'd sat there in the ER for hours, in quiet discomfort, watching everyone around him come and go. Some were there before he'd ever gotten there, and some came after. The intricate details of each of their lives imaginatively played themselves out in his head as he waited there stoically.

Regrettably, both Dr. Ash and Casey were unfortunate victims of the time, although Casey was undoubtedly more so. Dr. Ash was a victim of overwork and of nonchalance, and Casey was, subsequently, a victim of those as well. Neither could have foreseen what was to come. Neither would have ever intended it.

After a perfunctory examination, the slightly elevated fever and soreness Casey presented was attributed to some common form of the flu. It seemed a simplistic diagnosis to make and after all, Nathaniel was only minutes away from being off for three days. No further investigation seemed necessary. So, after a long and painful drive, waiting for hours to be seen, and a dismissive exam done by a disinterested and distracted doctor, Casey was given a shot and told to go home, get some rest and drink fluids. The initial problem with that was that Casey hadn't been taught the proper and often usual lessons in cynicism that he should have been by life. Thus, he did exactly what he was told without a second thought. That proved to be a fatal mistake.

If a more thorough examination had been done, and more thought had been given to the situation, Dr. Ash would have concluded that Casey had driven from a nearby college-a college where a handful of similar cases had presented themselves recently. Those cases all began with the same flu-like symptoms but quickly escalated to something else very different and deadly; something which had already claimed lives. That possibility was never considered and consequently was never explored. Casey suffered because of that. Dr. Ash's suffering came soon after.

Meningitis was the proper diagnosis.

Meningitis was the viral disease that attacked the protective membranes around his brain and spine. It went to all of his joints and caused crippling and painful swelling. It elevated his body temperature quickly and lethally as it went to the fluid within the lining of his brain, causing it to both swell and compress as well as to literally "cook" that most vital organ due to the degree of fever. That disease had seemingly come out of nowhere. Although there were only one or two cases that were treated at other hospitals, a more experienced and a better-rested doctor probably would have pieced it all together. Meningitis was what Casey had mysteriously contracted. Meningitis was what caused the severe pain, disorientation, and delusions that he suffered through, alone, for a day and a half before an ambulance was called by a dorm mate.

Meningitis was what soon killed him.

Nathaniel's guilt insisted on carrying the blame for that. Coming back from his off-time, he discovered what had happened. After reviewing the follow-ups on his previous patients, he realized that his eagerness to administer to his own needs and not those of Casey led him hastily to a fatal conclusion. Entering into his profession in the first place meant that he possessed a naturally resilient ego, but this was his first death and that ego hadn't been entirely steeled yet. So, he bore the weight of that for a long time afterward. Of course, none of his peers assigned any wrong to what had happened. Unfortunately, the likelihood of misdiagnosis was all too common for interns. That misdiagnosis also sometimes led to the worst outcome. That fact did nothing to lessen the damning sense of personal responsibility that Nathaniel felt. His intention was never to do harm or to be un-thorough or dismissive. He had been all of those. But, thoughts of his own intentions were self-serving and didn't help a dead man in the least. The lesson learned was that intention and outcome can absolutely be inverse. That lesson bludgeoned him. It was an extremely hard first lesson to learn. But it was also one that had served him since. One way or another, he knew it would likely present itself again at some point.

The promise of that eventuality brought him back to his present circumstance. He'd hesitated before momentarily, but he'd been acutely reminded of what was required from him. He was needed. Although the outcome was impossible to predict, his intentions now were to be of use to anyone he could. To do that, he'd have to go inside.

As he turned to go into the building, the opaque veil of smoke grew and billowed as if it meant to restrict Nathaniel to where he was. But there would be no dissuasion. He began to move forward. Then, static erupted again unexpectedly. That sound was coming from near where Daniella had fallen. Reluctantly, he moved closer. Quickly, he found the source of that static. It was just as he'd thought. Lying next to her body was her radio. The second thought to come to his mind was that he'd possibly be able to contact someone, anyone, inside with it to assess the situation. The next thought was a promise to mourn this beautiful woman appropriately at some point in the near future.

Circling around and through the blaze, he made his way over. As he bent down to get the radio, it hissed static at him again like a defensive cat, startling him. At first glance, it seemed undamaged. But when he picked it up, it became obvious that the radio hadn't escaped damage completely. Urgently, he pushed buttons and turned dials trying to tune it in, attempting to contact someone.

"Hello! Can anyone read me? Is anyone inside the hospital picking this up?"

The only response was that aggressive static. There wasn't much hope that he'd been heard, and he accepted that immediately. The bottom half was partially smashed as well as being somewhat melted from the heat. Of course, that meant that Nathaniel wouldn't be able to speak to anyone using it. The upper section did seem to be intact though. Again, he fumbled with the controls in an attempt to tune in a favorable frequency. At first, it was little more than a syllable, then it was a word, and finally, he was able to lock in a channel. He'd done it. He could make out, although quietly, a voice, a voice of someone on the other side of that curtain of smoke obscuring his way. He reasoned that he would at least be able to listen in on any communications. Of course, that was based on the assumption that the signal would last and that there would be further communications to listen to at all.

There was a panicked dialogue between an undetermined number of EMTs coming through. He picked up the pieces of conversation as he listened in. "...I've got one here in the bay...We've got a blunt trauma here...Send this gurney to the O.R. stat! Code Blue...Got a Code Blue down here...Get down to the Burn Unit as fast as you can...! Find a Doc!" The men traded urgent requests back and forth, painting a detailed picture of the need for help. The best-case scenario of it being restricted to the ambulance bay had just been rendered wishful thinking.

Whatever happened had been widespread and devastating. Listening in longer didn't provide the answer to what exactly went down though. That answer, if it came at all, would have to wait.

Nathaniel looked toward the ER doors. Something caught his eye. It was so quick that it almost went by unnoticed. His angle now showed that the billowing smoke rising in front of the entrance was actually coming from inside. Nothing could be made out through it. No one was visible beyond it. The lobby was completely obscured. To his surprise, a figure moved hastily through the entrance despite the danger and away from the wreckage in the bay. It was beyond reason and there was no opportunity to prevent it. Nathaniel got such a brief glance that he couldn't distinguish any recognizable features of the person. He called out urgently but in vain.

His mind raced to make sense of what he'd found himself in the middle of. Logic dictated that if it had been another member of the hospital staff, they would have made that fact known to him. Since that wasn't the case, the Dr. had to assume that the figure was more probably someone disoriented and in need of immediate medical attention. It was a given that Nathaniel had to follow; that he had to act. To gain access, he'd have to jump blindly through that shroud as well.

"If that's what I have to do to help, that's what I have to do.", he said to himself confidently in the hopes of sounding convincing. A quick check of his possessions showed that he in fact had none. He was carrying nothing at all with him, which consequently meant that he had nothing that could be of use to anyone injured. The thought occurred to him to take whatever salvageable tools and instruments he could find from the wreck, but the fire rose up suddenly to dispel that idea. All he had was the will to help and a partially melted, only somewhat useful radio. Although he needed and certainly wanted more than just a radio and slight resolve, that was all he possessed. Those would have to suffice. He'd get whatever else he needed once he was inside no doubt. There was also little doubt that he'd be tested once he was inside.

With another look around him, a profound thought came to mind. His surroundings were an amazing and ironic contrast. Not far from him, but just out of reach beyond the collapsed overhang, was a picturesque familiarity that was safe and desirable. Opposite that, on the other side of that choking cloud was bleakness. There he stood between them both. That position was, without question, unsustainable.

As he stood there, in a writhing garden of flame, a somewhat perverse desire for a cigarette came to him. The absurdity of that brought an un-humorous and curious chuckle. But the desire persisted. The strange thing about that thought, was that Nathaniel wasn't a smoker. Then, suddenly, the head wound that he'd concluded to be minimal began to throb intensely, causing Nathaniel great discomfort. His previous concern that he might have needed further evaluation returned. But strangely, it subsided quickly, bringing him back to focus on his task at hand; he needed to get into that hospital. One more hiss from the radio was a final incentive to replace inaction.

"...We've got several injured in Emergency, find another doctor..."

The tone was desperate. Then, a panic-stricken scream sounded and was his final motivation. With only the radio and urgency to lead him, Nathaniel moved toward the entrance. It started as a jog and then broke into a run. That running was as much propelled by determination as it was threatened by fear. Either way, he threw himself through that blanket obscuring the Emergency Room entrance resolutely.

Clouds that had been steadily building, chose that moment to roil and shudder. The late October day had turned. The instant Nathaniel leapt through the unknown, a downpour began morosely. The heavens seemed to be unleashing.

He was on the other side...

But it wasn't right...It wasn't what he expected at all. The situation that he'd been listening to had taken on an undeniably imperative tone- that contradicted what he was witnessing just then.

How could it be possible? How could there possibly be stillness and silence inside the ER after what he'd heard? Couldn't he trust his own senses? "I know I heard it..." he said out loud unconvincingly. Stillness and silence...? That was exactly what he'd found himself surrounded by after taking that blind leap forward. He scanned the ground floor, as much as could be seen from where he stood, from end to end looking for any indication that the panic in the voices he'd been listening to was justified. But there was no one there to confirm that it had been. The room was typically a large and modern hospital lobby with common and non-distinct hospital furniture placed throughout. The wide and low front desk stood empty and austere in front of him. On either side, the seating areas looked disturbingly unnatural in their vacancy. There were no patients, there were no injured, and there was no hospital staff there looking anxious and fatigued administering to anyone. He stood alone.

The room itself gave every indication that something devastating had in fact occurred and had subsequently fallen silent. He'd expected to find hysteria on the other side of the hell he had just come from. The room stood dark and solemn, but it was disheveled and smoldering. A conflagration had ripped through the area, but from the look of it, it seemed that it had happened some time ago.

Evidently, it had somehow been extinguished, leaving just its charred fingerprint. Some time ago? "Doesn't add up..." Nathaniel concluded. The timeframe didn't seem accurate at all. He'd just leaped out of wreckage and flame that seemed like a freshly opened wound. He'd seen the billowing dark wall that spewed out from the entrance. He'd just thrown himself head-long through it! There was no congruency to what he'd come from and what he'd found himself in the middle of. Suspicious, he made his way forward, searching for a rationale as he went. The place was cast in shadow due to the emergency lighting and almost growled in unwelcoming. Above him, several hanging lamps swung slowly, unbidden. Overturned chairs and up-ended artificial potted plants were noticed around the room. Nathaniel began to quietly whistle the most haunting tune he could think of as mood music.

The situation had come across clearly over the radio or so he'd thought. There should have been some degree of frenzy from patients who'd been caught up, mixed with an atmosphere heavy with urgency from any medical staff present. But the ER looked, as well as felt, abandoned. But...he thought he knew what he'd heard...

Continuing on, he found upended gurneys, wheelchairs, and machinery. The conclusion that his original line of reasoning had in fact been accurate came to mind. Anyone inside must have been working to evacuate the building and were now far ahead of him, moving toward the rear exits. That meant that it had been determined that the building was unstable. So, that also meant that Nathaniel definitely couldn't linger either. Evacuating an entire hospital was no small task! Catching up to and helping whoever he could, became his priority. That was all he could offer. That became his purpose.

Dr. Ash began to act on that intention when his training again came through, reminding him to be thorough. So, despite the possible danger, he began an earnest search for the one that had jumped through the now barred and charred entrance, as well as any stragglers or left-behinds.

Methodically, he made his way around the ER and the surrounding areas. Then, he made his way along a short corridor toward the first of the examination rooms at the rear of the ER. The chairs outside the door were empty. The table inside stood stark and solemn in the center of the room. The instruments hung from the walls, without purpose for the moment. Suggestible imaginations could have easily been tempted and teased by the dim cast of the lighting. But there was nothing to be found. There were no charts to be found either, which in-of-itself could be taken in more than one way. Had all of the papers and files been taken along with any patients? That would make sense and would be procedural. Or, was it simply that there were no files present because there hadn't been any people present? But...He was *sure* that he'd heard...He thought he knew what he'd heard.

His pragmatism spoke up at that point, telling him that he was misreading the situation. Logic would state that he'd simply misheard the location when he was listening in earlier. He only needed to make up ground, to catch up to everyone else somewhere in another part of the hospital. "It makes sense." he told himself. He would quickly finish his search of the area and move on, counting on the fact that a larger group couldn't move as fast as he could alone. He'd catch up and be of use soon, or he'd meet them in the rear of the building. Either way, he'd be serving a purpose by confirming that no one had been overlooked or by eventually lending his skills to the evacuees. Determined, he continued on.

As he moved through them, the hallways echoed in emptiness. The rooms surrounding the ER were each checked and then checked off of the mental list he was keeping. Then the speculations began to stir- could it have been an attack? Why would anyone hit this place? Might it have been a natural occurrence? He wasn't on the coast!

There were no earthquakes here. Nothing much worse than a heavy and scary storm usually happened around Chicago. Even the occasional but powerful, albeit rare, tornado wouldn't account for the way things had unfolded so far. What then?

Across from the first three exam rooms was a large file room. He'd never looked inside before then. Behind a secured door, which his position gave him access to, was a room of contrasting curiosity.

One side, the left side, was cramped and overrun. Badly stacked and overly-filled files were splayed on and around misshapen cabinets with sharp and rusted edges. Old files, undoubtedly from forgotten years and experiences, did their best not to tumble over from neglect. Worn boxes, stacked high, let paper histories peek through them. Dark metal cases stood partially open and accessible while some seemed sealed, dented, and implacable. The space was lifeless and bleak.

To the right, on the other side of the room, it seemed that there was still some use to be gotten from that area. One overhead light still glowed, although palely as if it was struggling for power. There was evidence of a degree of organization on that side as well. The files had not piled up as they had on the left. Those files hadn't spilled over to that side at all. A table stood against the far wall,uncluttered, with fresh paper, pens, and supplies on top, unused and unnecessary just then. The contrast was unmistakable and striking.

Nathaniel walked in, going to the dimly lit right side first, mindlessly running his hand over the table, flipping through the pages laying there. Glancing down at the first piece of paper, he saw a single word that had been only partially written; it said "Confusi..." incomplete, with the last letters trailing off illegibly. Nothing else came after that on any other page. The rest were blank. Although it appeared ready to be utilized, it hadn't been. He acknowledged the strangeness but quickly let it pass as inconsequential.

Then he made his way to the opposite side of the room, maneuvering through a forgotten paperwork forest, trying not to make a mess within a mess. There was no telling how many years were cataloged or how many facts and figures were recorded within that darker corner. But none of it was accessible.

Looking up, something out of place caught his eye. More evidence of the unknown happening that had taken place became apparent. Coming down from the ceiling, at an awkward angle, was a thing that didn't belong there. It extended down from the floors above. It was wrapped in shadow but it was clearly a large and heavy piece of metal from the inner structures overhead. From the half-light barely seeping over from the other side, the metal took on the look of a weapon.

Moving nearer to it, he first heard a dripping, and then, reaching out to touch the closest pile of boxes to him, discovered a liquid seeping from the scar in the ceiling above him. The initial and logical assumption would be that a pipe running between the floors had collapsed and fallen through, dripping down what it held, washing over, and entirely erasing whatever usefulness was beneath it. It wouldn't be long before there was absolutely no chance of recovering anything at all. That thought was the catalyst that set him back on his task. Without a second look, he turned to continue his searching.

The empty hallway he walked through echoed his aloneness. He'd covered a large section of the wing quickly and wanted to catch up to the others as soon as he could. He made his way down corridors coded and marked with arrows and colors along the floor and walls meant to help the unfamiliar navigate. There was no need for him to follow those guides though. They'd become obsolete through the repetition of hours of practicing medicine within them.

Through a set of heavy double doors was another empty station. Thoughts of nurses, some attractive and others not, came to mind. Regardless, the flirting flowed freely, and it was not at all one-sided. But there was no one there now; no patients, doctors, or nurses. Only darkness hadn't abandoned the area.

As he searched, his thoughts turned on him and became less and less cooperative. The eyes of the old woman in the ambulance bay bored into his thoughts troublingly. It disturbed him deeply for some unclear reason. Although he hadn't been able to place her, the sight of her felt just as unsettling to him as if he'd known her intimately.

How did he get in the situation? Why was there a certainty in him that he should have been much more aware than he was? No answers came. He would remain in the dark figuratively as well as literally. The fact that he'd been unable to resuscitate the lady bothered him. It aggravated him. He had the type of ego that fought tooth and nail with what most would call the inevitable, and that persistence meant that he would often come out on top. Nathaniel Ash was a fighter. But there was no doubt that he'd lost the opening round and that the unnamed   elderly lady had paid the price. "The next round is mine." he promised himself. His voice sounded strangely hollow to him, but he hoped that the promise would not turn out to be as well.

His thoughts were distractions that slowed him down and kept him separated from the others he believed were ahead. With some effort, he worked to put them aside so that he could make better progress.

He was coming up on the rear exam rooms. The first two were in shambles but proved to be empty. Whatever took place there was over and whoever was involved had moved on. The third looked as if no one had needed it for the entire day. It remained prepped and pristine.

Nothing overly eventful was found except damaged overhead lighting that flickered erratically, making the place uninviting, but it did appear that there had been some type of incident there earlier. The gurney was   disrupted and bloodstained. Instruments on the floor lay waiting for a cleanup crew to retrieve them. I.V. bags hung drawn and empty, spent where they swung, like bodies in gallows.

With the extent of damage that was found, there was no way to accurately gauge if the rooms had been in use at the time of or after the fact of the destruction.

It looked like the ceiling had collapsed. That debris was obscuring most of the area, covering the entryway, table, and four corners in dust and ruin. The door lay partially inside the room at an awkward angle, torn from its hinges. No lighting shown out from inside.

The minimal light leaking in from the corridor illuminated only a partial sliver of the area inside. It had to be concluded that there was nothing to be found or done there.

One last room in that section remained.

It was a short distance down, at the end of the corridor. Somewhat unusually, that door was closed, unlike any of the others. The standard procedure would be to open the door of any room that was not being occupied by a waiting patient. A pulse of anticipation ran through him then. That quickened his pace. It may have been nothing at all. It may have been everything.

Either way, his answer would come momentarily.

He moved to reach for the doorknob. The doctor was set in motion by necessity and determination but then he was stopped by surprise.

HSSSSSSSTT!!!

"SHIT!" he said, startled. The radio he'd been carrying, which had remained silent and unconsidered up to that point, suddenly erupted. The quiet that he'd been enveloped in was burst like a thin bubble floating on the air. That brought about a sudden and unexplainable self-consciousness which made him feel exposed and vulnerable. Clumsily he fumbled for the radio, bobbling it and nearly dropping it more than once.

HSSSSSSSTT!!! It sounded again.

A conversation began to come through over the half-charred radio. It was the same EMT that had been relaying desperate messages before. This time, the tone had changed somewhat. As he listened in, Nathaniel stood frozen, waiting for any information that would provide direction to him. He picked up partial sentences - "...this one is shook-up but will be fine with just...good news over here, he'll be back with his wife again soon I'd bet...keep on moving...O.R. soon...good news..."

A fairly clear picture could be interpreted from what had been said. The first bit of positivity had finally reared its head! People were being helped and were in the process of being evacuated. Someone somewhere was being spared the sentence of this still undefined catastrophe. Whoever that may have been, they were apparently not far ahead. Nathaniel had been able to discern the term "O.R." being mentioned.

The operating rooms were only two sections away from where he was. His intention of catching up to the others hadn't changed at all. Now he had every reason to believe that it was just a matter of closing the gap. He'd be on them quickly if he kept up his pace. He let that positive information bolster him and drew encouragement from that. Re-energized, he turned his attention back to what he'd been doing before, going a second time for the doorknob to verify that Exam Room had in fact been cleared.

An unexpected resistance kept the door from swinging in freely. With his shoulder against it, he pushed hard, creating enough of a gap to fit his head through. A quick look showed that a toppled wheelchair on the other side was wedged between the entrance and the exam table, barring his way. The right side of the room was visible and clear, but the partially opened door was still jammed up against the chair, preventing a definitive look to the left and behind it.

First, he tried pushing harder, and then he worked his leg in to kick the obstruction away. It took a combination of those two efforts to finally gain access. Nathaniel was eventually able to squeeze inside.

The first impression was of normalcy. Like an earlier room, this one seemed to be undisturbed and with all things in place. From what he could see on the right side, everything was as it should be. Only the fallen wheelchair seemed to be out of place. No other signs of disruption were apparent to him. But there was still part of the room that he hadn't seen. Moving further in, he bent down to attempt to set the fallen chair upright again. Only then did one of the other unaccounted-for areas within the room, behind the exam table, reveal what it hid.

Someone was sprawled on the floor!

Baleful eyes stared back at him.

Those eyes shifted, chilling Nathaniel where he knelt.

As Dr. Ash dropped it back down, the crash of the solid metal wheelchair reverberated out and down the hall. Bounding to his right, he moved to circle behind the exam table. A man was there, unnaturally positioned and completely still. He was on his stomach, with his neck at an awkward angle facing toward the hallway. His appearance put his age at about fifty or so. He was largely undistinguished and average. No readily available evidence indicated what his trauma might be. A quick check uncovered no broken bones. Unceremoniously, Nathaniel grabbed the fallen man's clothes and pulled, trying to roll him onto his back to begin the prelim-evaluation of his condition.

His learned thought process was set in motion. The attempt to identify the pulse and heartbeat came first. No breath signs...Pulse indeterminate. All of the probabilities began to rotate through his mind, one by one. He skipped nothing, going through each logical and ingrained step. His duty had driven him to look for stragglers with the intent of doing his job, of helping whoever he could, and now he had found someone. Determination compelled him, and past failures reproved weak effort. His focus was complete. It was so complete that he didn't realize that the side of the room he'd been unable to see before, the left side, demanded his attention as well.

Two chairs that had been previously obstructed stood against that left wall. One of those chairs was empty. The other chair in the corner was occupied by someone unseen by Nathaniel. That someone went unnoticed,quietly but intently watching his every action.

His eyes seared, though Nathaniel was oblivious.

It was only a matter of time before all attempts at revival proved ineffective. Only frustration resulted from the energy spent. Combined with his other recent failures, an incredibly disturbing pattern was developing. A strong determination to break that pattern was developing as well.

Nathaniel Ash sat on the floor with his head hung, next to the body of the man he'd tried and failed to revive. A dull throbbing had begun at his left temple and his ineffectiveness joined with it to darken his mood further. He knew that he didn't have time for admonitions, but he also felt the weight of his circumstance. Despite that, there was no questioning what was required of him. Like he'd had to do so many other times before, he did what he could to rally himself. 'Get your ass up Dr. You've got to keep going. You've got somewhere to be...' was spoken within his thoughts.

"Yes, Nathaniel- but the final destination and the route taken are still very much in question."

"What the...!" Nathaniel exclaimed, taken by surprise.

He jerked his head up towards the direction of the voice he'd heard and saw the man it had come from. He was sitting in a chair against the wall with a combination of stoicism and amusement playing across his face. Had he been there the entire time? If so, why hadn't he said anything or helped? Most importantly, what could his seemingly arbitrary statement about a destination and a route have possibly meant?

"*Meaning*... That's the crux, isn't it? I am here for that very purpose. I intend to convey all I can to you toward that end." the enigma staring down at him said in his resonant and accented voice.

"Who are you? Why are you still in the hospital?"

"I know how necessary it is for your frequency to individualize, so you may call me Aegis."

It seemed a strange response to a simple question to Nathaniel, but it was accepted and quickly set aside. Getting to his feet, he examined the man across from him. That man seemed unmoved by the state of affairs that had naturally left him quite shaken. That man sat still and calm at first, in a relaxed and un-anxious position. Then, he rose smoothly, almost with the intent of being non-threatening.

His Asian features were angled and distinguished with a calmness in his amiable smile conflicting with the intensity that shone through his eyes. Nathaniel estimated him to stand at just over six feet tall which put him just a few inches taller than himself. Aegis's shoulder-length hair was so black that it almost seemed reflective and hung just past the collar. His clothes looked distinctly Asian as well, with loose-fitting jet-black pants and coat over a white mandarin collared shirt. To Nathaniel, Aegis possessed an antiquated air about him, to say the least. He also seemed to be strangely intuitive, appearing to guess at what his thoughts were.

"Your name is Aegis huh? Well, what ...?"

"...More of a purpose than a name really." he broke in, his point going untaken.

"Whatever...you shouldn't be here. Something disastrous has happened and we're unsafe here. That should be pretty obvious. We've got to go."

"Destination and route are intrinsically linked.", Aegis responded.

"What are you talking about?"

"Not only what, but also who..."

"Listen, we don't have time for this. I don't know who you are or where you came from, but we don't have time for this. My name is Dr. Ash and I work here at the hospital. I've been making my way through the building looking for...someone... and any other stragglers that might need help. Obviously, I'm trying to save anyone I can and catch up to the others. This place is unstable and deteriorating rapidly. Running into you was unexpected. So, I want you to stay with me and give me a hand. Can I count on your help?"

"More than you know Nathaniel."

"I...didn't tell you my first name... do you work here? I don't remember ever seeing you before..."

"You wouldn't have-until now. And you're right about many things. The situation is disastrous and unstable, and we don't have much time at all. You definitely have someone to save, but you're looking in the wrong place. Therefore, I need you to stay with *me*." Aegis quizzically answered.

"OK...You must have been injured I'm guessing. So, sit down and I'll take a quick look at your head. Then we'll have to move on."

"I'd say that you're mistaken to worry about my head. I'm not damaged and don't need assistance. You, on the other hand, have some things to sort out in your own head Nathaniel Ash."

"What the hell are you talking about? You haven't said anything coherent yet. You're talking in riddles! Just trust me. Let me do what needs to be done and I'll see you through this OK?"

"Well put-that last part. Actually, I couldn't have said it better myself." Aegis complimented. "I would in fact say the same to you."

"Listen, Aegis, I really think you..." Nathaniel began.

"...should allow you to do your job?" Aegis completed.

"How could you...?" Nathaniel started.

"...have known what you were going to say to me?" he finished again. "Simple. It's just one of the things that we must cover in the short time that we have.", he stated. He continued but almost seemed at that point to be thinking out-loud as he spoke. "The fortunate news is that we've, fundamentally, reached you first. The negative influence of our counterparts would impair your ability to stabilize your frequency. That would be unacceptable. Now the probability that you'll make the proper decision has risen. Though, all things flux."

There was no response from Nathaniel at all. He simply stared blankly at the obscure and rambling man in front of him, feeling unprepared and untrained to deal appropriately with the situation. Nothing he'd heard made any sense to him and no relevance could be assigned to any of it. Multiple possibilities might have applied. This man could either be possessed of some profound knowledge that should be heeded or much more likely, he was from a wing of the hospital that most doctors tended to strenuously avoid. Nathaniel tended to believe the latter based on all the incomprehensible things he'd already heard.

Aegis chimed in at that point, speaking directly to Nathaniel, who'd been preoccupied with his own reasoning.

"I'd go with the former thought if I were you."

"How is it that you seem to guess what I'm thinking?"

"That answer falls lower in order of consequence Nathaniel. It will eventually be clear to you, but with the time that we have you'd be better served with other answers."

"First, the task you've set for yourself, to search for and save those that you can, is in fact, self-defeating. You only undo your transition. Any that you encounter here have had their final acts played out and cannot be affected by you anymore. That time is past. So, you must turn your attention to where it can be beneficial-here and now; to yourself. That is your only redeeming course from this point on. It is the one tangible, graspable option that is still obtainable for you.", Aegis stated soberly.

"...turn my attention to myself? You're telling me not to help anyone? What the hell is wrong with you? Look around you! What kind of situation do you think we're in right now? Despite the fact that I've already told you, it should be incredibly obvious to you that I'm a DOCTOR! Who else is going to help anyone still here... You!? Whatever you're on about is not only incomprehensible and unhelpful, but it's also aggravating! So, do both of us a favor and SHUT UP FOR A MINUTE!" He paused then to reconsider his tone. "Look - I'm sorry about that. Just stay close to me. I'm just making my way through this disaster as best as I can, trying to get to the other side intact."

"We have a similar objective, even though you are actually unconscious and unaware Nathaniel."

A look of exasperation was allowed to show through before Nathaniel responded, "Fine- Whatever you say, man. We're falling behind so let's get moving."

"But who's with whom?" Aegis asked.

"What? I don't know what that even means."

"Let me re-phrase; am I staying with you or are you staying with me, Nathaniel?"

"We're in this together. We're getting out together, OK.?"

"That doesn't sound as promising as I'd want it to be. Your "GETTING OUT" is still very much an under-defined concept at this point. Your destination is yet to be determined. By your compass, you might remain off-track and fail to realize that destination. Although it is in actuality yours, only one of us here knows the way." Aegis then clarified, "It's implied that I don't mean you, of course."

The stare on the Dr's face held firm as he waited for what he'd heard to unravel. The man in front of him seemed disturbed, or perhaps traumatized. What he was hearing was as chaotic as the situation was. Regardless, there was no miscomprehension about what needed to happen. It would be necessary to endure Aegis and his puzzled ramblings long enough to see him clear of their predicament. Urgency was still at the forefront of Nathaniel's mind, so he attempted to placate Aegis.

"Fine, whatever you say. Let's keep moving and eventually we'll get you to that destination you're talking about. Where ever that is, it's ahead of us. Let's move."

But Aegis didn't move at all. Instead, he knowingly responded by saying, "There is far too much that I haven't explained yet for this to be clear to you. So, I understand your attempts to placate someone that you'd perceive to be unhinged. It's easy to make a misdiagnosis without all of the relevant data, isn't it? Once you have a much more complete understanding of what lies ahead of you, I'm sure you'll grasp the need for and the importance of more sober judgment. I'm confident that clarity will come before the last gasp."

At that point, Nathaniel reached the end of his already limited patience.

"I'm done going back and forth with you about this. We're leaving! You seem like you're, physically, uninjured so I'm sure you'll be able to keep up. I want you to stay on my ass. We'll make our way through the hospital toward the rear of the building and continue to search as we go. If we don't stop for any more of your word games, we'll catch up with the others and be out of here, O.K.? Now, let's get moving."

"Destination is..." Aegis began.

"Tell it walkin' man. Let's go!"

With that, Nathaniel turned to leave the room at a quick pace. His aggravation was displayed noticeably. Out of the door and only a few steps down the hall, the slightest of glances over his shoulder was all he wanted to spare to verify that he'd been heard. With that side glance, he caught sight of Aegis standing in the doorway but not following. His frustration ignited his arrogance, causing him to yell back over his shoulder, "Don't be an idiot! C'mon! You want to be buried where you stand?" He kept walking without hearing anything from behind. Two more steps were taken without another look back. Then, as if on cue, as if it had responded to his urgings, things worsened drastically.

Without warning, a thunderous crashing sounded behind him as the upper level came down through the crumbling ceiling as if it was made of paper and sand. Spinning on his heels, he saw that the entrance to the room he'd just come from was now obscured by debris. The destruction was working its way down the corridor quickly and almost calculatedly towards him! In seconds he'd be overtaken. He had no time to think. There was no sign of Aegis, but the thought of moving in any direction other than away from the collapsing ceiling was irrational. He couldn't go back for him. He turned and took off at a full run.

His shoes gripped the floor desperately in response to his need. The crashing chasing him down from behind sounded like the growl of a predator. Down the wide corridor and around the turns of it, he moved as if he was prey. He was fast, but so was the collapse that threatened to overtake him. He had to imagine that the fire had worsened and made its way throughout the building, bringing the upper level down as it spread. A fire that large would not be contained. Destruction like that would be complete. He knew eventually the whole of the structure would be lost. He'd made a vow to save whoever he could as he went but the thought faded and died in his immediate desperation. His former sense of agency turned to self-preservation. So, he kept pushing himself on.

Behind him, there was a mixture of smoke and plaster and dust and darkness. Everything above must have come down! Nothing higher must have remained. Still, he ran. Turning a corner blindly, he collided with an errant wheelchair left unfortunately in the wrong place at the absolute wrong time. He went down in a tangled heap. Scrambling backward on the ground, still fighting to keep in front of the dust and darkness, he saw that wheelchair disappear under the rubble. It was no less than it deserved he thought. But that was also going to be his fate if he didn't continue on. A roll and a desperate thrust got him to his feet and bursting through a set of heavy double doors.

He didn't stop immediately. He didn't stop until he recognized that silence surrounded him. No crashing deafened him, and no falling rubble threatened him. Tentatively, he stepped closer to the doors he'd just burst through, intending to look through the small windows to see what he'd escaped. Edging closer, he stopped short, afraid, and looked through at nothing but smoke and darkness. Everything behind him was obscured.

The situation demanded that he abandon his searching and get out immediately, but the nearest exits were now behind him, unavailable in his urgency. Without a doubt, there would be no going back.

He accepted that and was resigned to the fact that nothing had been overlooked or left behind. Then yet another demoralizing realization struck him suddenly.

Someone actually had in fact been left.

The man calling himself Aegis was yet another victim he'd allowed to slip from his grasp and failed to pull to safety. The sting of another inadequacy enraged Dr. Ash and he exploded, taking the extent of his emotions out on the heavy doors directly in front of him. As fast as that anger surfaced, it faded. He was a pragmatic man and knew the futility of unrestrained emotions. He remembered himself. His goal was still ahead of him.

Resigned, he turned to continue on.

The heavy doors he'd come through were the beginning of a section of the hospital that was not accessible to the public. He'd entered the Imaging department. The area mirrored, in mood and stillness, the deserted section Nathaniel had just come from.

The dimness kept him on edge and the silence magnified that. Immediately, he recognized a chill. There was coldness throughout the area that began to permeate. He took a few steps. 'Strange' he thought as he considered how much his remembered perceptions of the place had altered. Were they altered? Or, was he forced toward better awareness by his circumstance? How many times might he have been through the same area and not paid attention? It was as if he'd gone blindly through before without notice of detail, preoccupied and self-involved. Now though, the actual lack of light seemed to illuminate things in some ironic way.

Again, he took notice of the surrounding chill. That cold was palpable. If he'd have let himself, if he'd have been just a little less focused, Nathaniel Ash would have been deterred by it. But he kept moving forward, however slowly. He reasoned that the fire that was raging throughout the facility hadn't gotten that far yet.

That fact didn't comfort him. He knew that it was just a matter of time before things would devolve. But for the moment, he was intact. As he walked, he tried to force some recall of how his situation came to be. Nothing beyond the moment of waking on cold hard concrete was clear to him. Anything before that point was as clouded as the ER entryway had been. He began to reach up toward the injury on his head; the thought that it may be the reason for his diminished memory immediately came to mind. It hadn't given him much significant trouble, but it had remained a constant and dull awareness. He was concerned, but he was also distracted from that by the objective he'd set for himself.

Continuing on at a slower pace, thankfully, emergency lighting still functioned. Directly in front of him about ten feet forward was a desk area that was short and ordinary with a large windowed section; a reception station. Along opposite walls, chairs stood empty or lay awkwardly where they'd fallen on the floor. To either side of that area, branching off like a Y, were hallways. Those led to the Imaging rooms. That was where he was headed.

That section of the building was, not at all, his favorite, and for very good reason. Whenever he came that way, that reason pestered his memory until he eventually acknowledged it, however briefly. Taking the right passageway, he was reminded of a time in his past that he both valued and detested. It was during the final stage of his internship.

Dr. Larena Ahern had been the kind of Attending MD that frustrated her interns to the point of breaking. The problem with that method was that it wasn't intentional. If she had had some concept of toughening students through harsh interactions and hard lessons, then her ways could have been rationalized when those lessons were finally learned. That was not the case. She had no such honorable motive. Every word and every action was by nature contradictory and infuriating. Everything about Dr. Ahern was short, from her size to her speech and mannerisms. Nathaniel often thought that if she had been a man a Napoleonic complex could have been attributed to her. Her short brown hair was unflattering and dyed. The glasses she wore were uninteresting. Plain was the most complimentary description that suited her appearance. None of that would have mattered if her focus had been on betterment. It was not. Regrettably, Dr. Ash had the misfortune of being assigned to her. That turned out to be a double-edged sword at best.

Regardless of the fact that her skills were as average as the rest of her, Dr. Ahern was overly arrogant and was known to believe that nothing worthwhile could be expected from anyone she worked with. Despite the definite promise that Nathaniel showed, he received no better treatment.

Entering the section, brought him back to the bitter memory of Ahern and the case of Rachel Tunney. It happened every time he went through that area. This time was no different. It was unavoidable. His thoughts pulled him back to another time and another lesson learned. Rachel Tunney taught him that lesson.

She was the kind of girl that would have been the perfect mold for all little girls to be made from. Her sweetness and her playfulness were more than a match for all of the adult stoicism and cynicisms around her. Her spirit was like sunshine. That fact made her condition much more disturbing.

Twice she'd been brought into the hospital after fainting, both times to be sent home undiagnosed. When she was brought in the third time, Dr. Ahern and Dr. Ash were given the case. The previous files were examined. A series of current tests were ordered. Results were thoroughly scoured. All of that was done with little consultation between the two of them. There was a distinct yet unsaid expectation that Nathaniel was there to observe and not to be heard.

"Dr. Ahern, what if the..." Nathaniel would begin.

"Wait Ash- I'm busy here. Why don't you go to lunch?" Ahern routinely said dismissively.

That pattern repeated itself regularly for two days. He wasn't allowed to contribute constructively, and he wasn't learning anything other than complete un-professionalism. He continued to be understandably aggravated while Rachel continued to be undiagnosed. Despite it all, he held his tongue and continued to defer to Ahern's decisions.

"Dr. Ahern, is it possible that she..." he tried at another time.

"Look Dr. Ash, several doctors have been through the files and examined this case top to bottom. So far, no answers have come up. Do you think that any of those doctors were un-intelligent? Do you think they were novices? You're an intern. I am not. Why would you think that you have anything constructive to tell me? Could you possibly have anything to contribute that is unthought of or original? ...Doubtful- right? That's just the truth of it. It might not be what you want to hear but that's not important right now. You want to be useful? Go down to Imaging and light a fire under those idiots and bring me back the current films on the girl." She said those words and turned away from him, never expecting any contradiction.

So, with a clenched jaw and closed fists, Dr. Ash turned and left the room. A sense of futility began to smother his will. His anger exploded further down the hall as he passed a cart of unused bedpans and plastics. The noise carried as each one hit ground. Everyone around him stared but also understood, knowing who he'd been working with.

Nathaniel thought back to how he'd fumed through the halls all the way to Imaging that day. He also thought back to how he'd held his tongue, not from any degree of respect, or even less likely, fear, but due to some misguided perception of an accepted modus operandi.

That day, he'd gone down to retrieve the latest films of pretty little Rachel as he was told, with no intention of attempting to provide any further input on the case. A long wait down in that department gave him time apart to cool off somewhat, which was best for any bedpans he might have come across later. During that time, a theory began to take shape. Spontaneously, an idea started to form in the back of his mind, but it remained incomplete. A possibility that might explain Rachel's fainting presented itself.

Anxiously, Dr. Ash waited for the x-rays to develop. That time worked against him. The un-solidified theory he'd begun was being hampered by the thought that Ahern could've been right when she stated that he had no new insights to present that hadn't already been covered. He second-guessed himself.

That realization upset him again. The small amount of calm that he'd been able to cultivate was lost just that quickly. The annoying wait for the x-rays only worsened his doubts and clouded his mind, taking his thoughts away from his original theory. His focus, unfortunately, turned away from Rachel and to his own feelings, at least for a time.

Eventually, his wait was over as a tech came out to deliver the set of films. Dr. Ash's curiosity was peaked, and he decided to go over the results right then and there. He didn't bother going back to the department to view them properly. One by one, he pulled out each individual x-ray to hold up to the natural light. His idea began to become more and more implausible. Nothing showed on the first. Nothing showed on the second. After several, his confidence waned. Then, with just two more left to view, something showed up.

In a rush, Dr. Ash went back into Imaging to view the film the correct way. The picture was of the chest of the young girl; of her heart. He looked at it once, then again, and then a third time. In an effort to be thorough, he searched for and then found previous films to compare against the most recent. After comparing each round of pictures that had been taken, he surmised that a thing had been horribly overlooked.

Twice, Rachel Tunney had been discharged without an answer and twice she'd returned under the same set of circumstances. He felt that it was probably unlikely that she'd be given another opportunity. So, the desire to be absolutely positive fought with his eagerness to share what he believed he'd discovered.

Convinced, he pulled the films from the wall and took off at a run, back to his despised Attending. Along the way, the thought of being able to help a very much loved twelve-year-old filled his thoughts. But that was also joined by the self-centered thought of upstaging Dr. Ahern.

When he'd gotten back to the room where he'd left Dr. Ahern, he was winded and excited which did little to force a change in perception of Nathaniel for the Attending.

"Dr. Ahern! I believe I've found something important that would explain Rachel's condition! Take a look at this film. It's one of the last of her heart."

"Ash, stop. I've already…"

"Wait Dr., there is something different here. Look. There is a contrast in this film that wasn't in previous ones.

See? There is trace blood- now I realize that it's only a very small amount but..."

"Ash! We've been through this before. There's nothing there. That spot you think you see is negligible. The fainting can most likely be attributed to poor dietary choices and hypoglycemia. I'm cutting the girl loose. Now, go discharge her and make sure she has an appointment with the dietitian before she leaves."

Dr. Larena Ahern, Attending MD, turned and walked away at that point, satisfied with her conclusions. The probability that she never thought again about the case or Rachel was very high.

Dr. Ash couldn't say the same.

He'd deferred his own judgment again and watched the girl leave the hospital. Then, in less than a month, he watched her come back. This time though, he hadn't been given a reprieve; a third chance to help her. She'd been brought in DOA. The so-called "negligible spot" that he'd detected had in fact been, at the time, the smallest of tears in her heart which leaked blood intermittently, but then finally erupted, in essence exploding her heart within her chest. Nathaniel had been right but had let himself be dissuaded which may have cost the girl her life. He both hated and valued the lesson he'd learned. The hate spoke for itself. The value he took from it came in the form of a tragically earned and abiding lesson in self-reliance and determination.

Rachel Tunney taught him that lesson at her own expense.

Not Rachel Tunney's parents, her friends or family, nor she herself had been given any indication of the seriousness of what she faced. None of them were prepared. None of them could have been. Their mourning would have been just as profound even if they had been.

Nathaniel made an effort to bring himself back to the moment. He'd allowed himself to become immersed in his past thoughts long enough. With reprove, he reminded himself of his obligation. Though he may have been distracted from it for a short time, he hadn't forgotten completely.

With the recollection of that poor young girl newly subdued and some slight sense of immediate security, Nathaniel allowed himself to revisit his original motivation.

Leaving Imaging brought Nathaniel out into an enclosed atrium. It was as if someone had sliced a section of a park away and set it under glass for preservation. The area was a relatively small passage between the main sections, designed to combat the sterility one might feel in a hospital with a kind of calculated and contrived "naturalness". There was a hard and uncomfortable bench with grass underneath. Two small but real trees grew on either side. At times, birds could be seen flying freely throughout the area, but there were none to be seen then. He turned and looked to his left. Night darkened the glass and the lights overhead made his reflection apparent. Those lights were dim, which cast his features in a dull and transparent way. He didn't recognize his own eyes. Attempting to, he stared intently.

For an unknown amount of time, he'd stood motionless. Still, nothing could be made of what he looked at. Something that wasn't quite him looked back from the other side. That something was altered. That something was aberrant. The calm peace he should have felt standing in the atrium was made into distinct apprehension instead. That feeling and that reflection made his desire to move on more urgent. For some reason it was hard to pull away, he turned slowly, still intent on recognizing something of himself.

HSSSSSSSTT!!!

Startled again by static breaking silence, he jumped suddenly. Something was coming over the radio again. He started walking as he listened and waited for any piece of information that could be added to the puzzle to come through. Before he could take more than two steps, the unexpected happened. Beyond the glass doors of the atrium, on the other side of that walkway, he caught sight of a figure moving away from him quickly. Could it have been the same figure he'd initially seen outside the ambulance bay and followed inside? Dr. Ash took off at a full run. His footfalls on the stone path echoed off of the glass around him.

His first yell to the silhouette went unheard. The subsequent ones did as well. The dark figure on the other side was moving quickly out of sight. Dr. Ash came to the doors hurriedly, clumsily fighting against them to get out, not remembering whether to push or pull. Finally, with an obscenity and a pull, he opened them forcefully.

Directly outside the atrium was a large waiting area. The area was under a skylight, but no moonlight shone down then. Couches with expensive appearances but inexpensive comfort were centered in the room, back-to-back, bookended by two fountains, and surrounded by rock landscaping. The figure he'd been running after disappeared behind one of those fountains. Darkness enshrouded the room just like it had the others before. Only the same dim and insufficient emergency lighting allowed him to see. This was the outer area of the hospital's Operating Rooms.

There were only a very few ways that the evasive silhouette could have gone. The obvious question went unanswered. Who was it? Could it have been a patient roaming lost and confused? Could it have been a staff member trailing behind the others, possibly attempting to do exactly what he was trying? He *had* seemed somewhat familiar... Whoever it was, he had to be found in a hurry. That much was obvious. So, Nathaniel continued on to the O.R. rooms.

HSSSSSSSTT!!!

What he'd been listening for chose that moment to come through over the radio. That distraction forced him to neglect the figure he was chasing. He had every intention of catching up but for the moment he'd lost sight. Reluctantly, he allowed his attention to be stolen away by the hissing.

He heard, "...I'm losin' this one! I need some help here!" "...time of death on him is..." "...She won't make it to O.R. unless we move her right now..." "...estimate the count at two dead and soon more will..." "...son of a bitch! We need a doc or else all..." the last part of the comment was cut off but easily guessed. Nothing more was audible after that. Considering the grim tone, that was just as well he thought. Again, his temple throbbed in response to the news he'd just heard. He felt the anger over the situation growing and tried to maintain as best he could. Everything around him conveyed a need for distinct urgency! All of the resoluteness he felt was antagonized by the message he'd just picked up on. The determination to help was stifled by his inability. He had no idea of how to reconcile those things. All he knew for sure was that moving forward was the only option.

One unshakeable problem stayed with him. The problem was that there hadn't been any indication of where the group he'd been listening in on had been at the time. There was nothing to judge his progress by. The separation he felt worked against him. The isolation he experienced disheartened him. It also threatened his intent. That couldn't be allowed. He stepped up his pace.

A single central corridor stretched out in front of him separating eight large rooms on either side; the main O.R. Nothing turned up and there was absolutely no sign of his mystery figure anywhere to be found. At the end of that corridor, now directly in front of Dr. Ash was the largest and last operating room. This room stood apart from the others because it was sunken, with an observation deck overlooking it, for the purpose of instruction. He made his way to the entrance on the right and through one of the doors leading inside.

Beyond that door was a modest viewing area, almost like a skybox at a sports stadium. Thick paned glass separated the sterile atmosphere eight feet below. There were many times in his past that he'd gone there to watch some particular procedure being done. The lights inside were curiously bright just then but the room beyond the glass stood in faint and dim contrast.

Making his way down the few steps toward the glass, he pressed his face against it to get a better look. Down in that lower room, the lights flickered on and off as if they intended to prevent his attempt. For a second, he thought that he'd seen something...but he lost it just that quickly. Then the flickering allowed another glimpse. But not long enough. There still couldn't be any real certainty.

Then, for no longer than three seconds, there was a reversal. The observation deck went dark and the erratic flickering below stopped, revealing a body down on the table!

What he'd seen was a silhouetted form covered completely by the light blue sheet of the O.R. table. That brief illumination confirmed it. But then his initial alarm turned quickly to disappointment with the realization that if the body had been covered there was nothing left to be done. Another unsaved person mocked him from the other side of the pane.

"Too late again." he said in admonishment. With a touch of dismay, he stepped back from the glass. He felt drained. The layout of the hospital flashed through his head then. He'd covered a good amount of ground up to that point. Then a quiet thought appeared in the back of his mind. The thought that he'd possibly done enough; that he'd more than done his part, stopped him where he was. Hadn't he already done more than most would have in the same situation? Couldn't he feel contented with the decision to get out, to leave without putting himself in any more danger? It seemed that he'd assumed enough risk without reward for his taste.

Suddenly, the brief reversal of the lighting between the rooms ended as the observation deck brightened again.

"Oh, shit!" was blurted out at first sight of the figure that was standing next to Nathaniel, only inches away. When the lights suddenly came back on, it made it seem as if the man had appeared from out of nowhere.

"Where the hell did you come from?", Nathaniel said with a racing pulse.

"There is someone down on that table." was stated in a deep monotone.

"What? Yes, I know that...Who are you? Are you the one I saw from the atrium? Listen, I'm glad I found you...I've got to assume that you're aware of the situation we're in, so let's not waste any..."

"Time wastes you, Ash. It's not the other way around. There is someone down on that table."

With an open-mouthed stare, "What...?" was all Dr. Ash could muster.

"Discouragement doesn't serve you, Ash. You must be more. Your intentions can't be so easily disrupted. From the start, you've been reminding yourself of what you have to do here. Can you say for sure that there is nothing you can do down there without any verification at all?"

"How do you know me? Who...?"

"Riven." he said interrupting.

"What?"

"Riven." he repeated.

"I don't know what that's supposed to mean. This is the second time this has happened to me today...Do you...?" Ash began.

"Yes, Ash. I am infinitely familiar with the one you're thinking of. He goes by "Aegis" and also claims it as his purpose-just as I go by Riven."

"I see...that's your name. OK - Riven –It's actually Dr. Ash and I'm going to try this again. I'm not sure what's going on here, but you need to listen to me. It's not safe here..."

"Yes, I know Ash. I'm well aware of what is happening. You're correct in your assertion that we need to move on. But you're also correct in the acknowledgment that you don't know what's going on. To that point, I intend on educating you."

For the moment, Ash was standing dumbstruck, staring without any degree of comprehension. In that time, he looked at Riven intently. His appearance was intimidating. He had the look of someone that should be given sufficient space, of someone not to be challenged, of a hardened fighter. Pale colorless skin seemed stretched over a bald and heavy skull. That head was hairless with the exception of thick and light-colored eyebrows overhanging shadowed eyes. He was dressed in a suit jacket and pants, the deep rust color of it reminiscent of dried blood. He stood there looking down on Ash, almost a foot taller. His arms were behind his back in a relaxed manner, but his heavy brow showed none of that.

Then the thought of Riven's statement snapped him back and he questioned, "... Educate me...? I have no idea who you are. Who are you to educate me? What could you have to teach me? And don't call me Ash, it's Dr."

"You will learn who and what you are, when and where to act appropriately, and why and how those actions can be your only possible salvation." came as the response.

"Enough! My God this is insanity! Am I the only one that understands the severity of what's going on? You're just like that other one earlier; you ramble on about nothing, incoherently. You're not making any sense at all. Are you injured somehow? Were you hurt? Is there at least anything that you can tell me- anything coherent- about what happened here to cause all this chaos?"

"It was The Nature." Riven replied.

"The Nature...? Are you saying there was some kind of natural disaster? What do you mean by Nature?"

"And so, your education begins. You think you know the entirety of your circumstance, but you don't. Necessity requires that you are made aware now. Your intent has become singular. A decision is before you that you must be made conscious of. It determines the difference between meaning and misguidance. It's been some time since you first started your work of protecting, healing, and guiding. You should be complimented. How many owe you for what you've done for them? It is necessary, and desired, that you continue."

"Ya know, I'll be honest with you- I'm really not used to being out of the loop, I'm usually at the head of the class but I gotta tell you, I feel like I'm playing catch-up now and have been all day! But I'll humor you for no other reason than to keep my eye on you; why don't you break it down to me slowly, as if I was ignorant. What are you talking about and what do you want from me?", Ash said.

"I don't want anything from you Ash; ask me what we want *for* you..."

"Fine! What do you want for me?"

"All we want is all you've wanted. We simply want you to continue doing what you've already set out to do. Continue to help. You have unique skills. That fact has been recognized. You've already defined your path with the   intent to help those you encounter. Simply fulfill that intent and leave no soul un-aided, Ash."

"Why? I know why I'm doing what I'm doing but what's it got to do with you? Do you have some vested interest in me doing my job that I'm unaware of?" Ash demanded.

"We do."

"You keep saying that! Who is "WE"? I don't see anyone else around. Is that the problem...? You do...?" was asked with a degree of seriousness mixed with no small amount of sarcastic frustration.

"I'm referring to those like me. I am not alone and soon you'll find that same truism applies to you too."

"Who are you...?"

"Don't make me repeat myself, Ash. You've been told who I am. You've been told what I want. Pay attention!", Riven commanded thunderously. For too brief a time to be sure of, the room itself almost seemed to buckle and distort as if in response to Riven's annoyance. Dimness came and went to the lights quickly enough to leave doubt that it ever happened. Riven had lost his composure for a brief second but that time was long enough to confirm to Ash that the impression he'd originally gotten from Riven was accurate.

Riven continued in his original and regained monotone, "The veil has dropped. The All is intent on you. Don't deviate from your objective. Continue doing what you've begun. It's just that simple."

"I don't need to be coerced into doing my job."

"You'll find that situations will come up that test your dedication. Those situations will play out in such a way that will make you falter and doubt. The architect of that doubt will be Aegis. Don't be misled. He has an agenda that isn't what it seems. That agenda, he will claim, is for the purpose of your own self-preservation."

"First of all, Aegis is most likely dead now. I saw him buried under..."

"Did you?"

"Did I? Yes. I did!" Ash insisted. "I saw the ceiling come down right on top of...Wait...Well, I didn't actually see him, but I did see the upper-level collapse, and there could be no way that he or anyone else could have..."

"...Survived?" Riven concluded the thought. "There is no question that Aegis is undamaged and that he is still very much intent on fulfilling his purpose. Don't allow his languid manner to deceive you."

"Why? Assuming for the moment that I believe anything I'm hearing now, why would he even be here in the first place? Why wouldn't he have evacuated a long time ago? What is it you're claiming he's trying to do?

"He intends to dissuade you from action to protect himself and those aligned with him. That is the Nature." Riven indicated.

"You mentioned that term before- "The Nature"- what do you mean by that?"

"It's a misnomer. But that explanation is for another time, Ash. Your instruction will continue in its entirety soon. For now, you should focus on his deceit. When the time comes, and decisions require certitude because a single chance is an only chance, ask yourself who truly needs protecting."

"What does he have to protect himself from? What's he hiding?" Ash asked.

"He's protecting the fact that he and his kind are actually responsible for the devastation you're traversing now." was Riven's response.

"What?! Are you serious?! He caused this?" Ash questioned with astonishment.

"He and his affiliation are culpable. The indicators are quite clear. Their influence is detrimental at best and destructive at worse. This particular instance would be an unfortunate example of the latter."

"What affiliation are you talking about?", Ash asked.

"You're involved in something much more complex than you've ever spent much time thinking about Ash. I'm here to enlighten you because I sympathize with you and those like you. I feel for you-for what you're going to experience, and I believe that you can in fact be emancipated through enabling redemption. I fight for that. Some others fight to nullify that. This is the first crucial aspect of many that you must come to understand before you can fully grasp the truth. Those like me strive for your redemption. Aegis and those he is aligned with strive *against* that."

"Why do I feel like I'm caught in the middle of something that has nothing to do with me? First, you imply that there was some kind of natural disaster here, then you start talking about something that sounds like some kind of...I don't know...religious war or something?

Redemption...? What are you sellin'? Are you a priest or something?"

"The priesthood would be a demotion for me." was Riven's puzzling response. He continued on, saying "No I'm definitely not a priest but their work is greatly appreciated. Before you ask your next question, no, I'm not an escapee from the mental ward either. Who I am, is the single voice of reason at your side in the midst of this, and the only one that has a pure motive."

"I guess I'm in too deep to get out now without getting the full pitch. What motive are you talking about?" Ash hesitantly asked.

"As I've told you, I only want you to help everyone you can. That is my one motive for being here; to help."

"You want to help? Fine, I can appreciate that but what about Aegis? Are you saying he wants something else? Are you claiming that he's here for some other adverse reason?"

Riven paused and smiled almost imperceptibly before answering, "He and his want you incapacitated and nullified."

"Why would anyone want that? What have I done? What do you mean by "his kind"? I still haven't heard you name the groups that either of you are actually part of. Who are you claiming did all of this damage and why, and who are you really working for Riven?"

"His kind is called the Anathema, among other names, by us."

"Sounds like some kind of terrorist faction... Is that it? You work for the Government, don't you? What are you...CIA...FBI...Homeland Security...? Which is it?"

No answer was verified or denied by Riven. He simply looked down impassively on Ash with an unreadable look on his face. That lack of denial fed into Ash's preconceived concept of how an elusive government agent might act, therefore, confirming the suspicion.

Riven continued on intensely, "You've asked for their reasoning. Their actions are dictated by their Illusory Nature. They are governed by misconceptions and unrealistic conclusions that corrupt everything they do. Fanatical beliefs distort any and all actions they undertake, leaving a multitude of abandoned souls in their wake; The Amiss. We find that to be unacceptable. You and I share a purpose. That purpose is to help those we can to the best of our abilities so that a preferable state of health can be achieved. Aegis doesn't see things the same way. Hasn't he already advised you not to help anyone?"

"Well, yes he did. How did you know that?" Ash responded.

"I'm well aware of his actions. It's part of his pattern. He's shown his colors. Who would suggest that helping someone was "self-defeating"? Does it make sense to ignore anyone in the middle of all this bedlam?"

"No, it doesn't. I'll give you that. But, how would you know that he said that to me?"

The question was ignored by Riven. He brushed past it with the statement, "He's dangerous. I want you to ignore anything he's told you and have no further contact with him. If he should show himself to you again, disregard whatever you hear purely as misinformation and manipulation."

"This doesn't add up to me. Simply put, you sound nuts. The fact is that I don't know who he is and I don't know who the hell you are either. Should I just go by whatever you tell me? For all I know, you both came from Psych. I won't humor your delusion. So, thanks for the advice but I'm sticking to my original plan. Just stay with me 'cause we've got to keep moving."

"You're mistaken, Ash."

"I've wasted enough time here listening to this." Ash answered with unhidden irritation in his voice.

Riven also displayed a degree of irritation in his own voice when he said again, "There is someone down on that table."

"I know! I can see you know? You know what I see? I see a body completely covered by a sheet. That's usually not an encouraging sign! So, stop telling me that there's someone down there alright?" Ash had lashed out through frustration at Riven, quickly realizing that he'd probably done so unwisely.

Riven was a towering presence compared to Ash and physically intimidating, but he'd been, up to that point, considerably mild despite that appearance. The only physical indication of anger from him surfaced on his heavy brow. A deep furrow developed between his eyes that only helped to further obscure already sunken, darkened, and intimidating orbs.

The perception Nathaniel had earlier of a distorting of the room returned for a more perceptible period of time as Riven stood there motionless in front of him after his outburst. Without any discernible source, Ash realized that an unbearable heat had suddenly come between the two of them.

His analytical mind had attributed the room's distortion to the degree of heat that he was feeling, but what he couldn't have possibly known at that time was the fact that that was only a partial explanation. The full extent of it would stay hidden for some time.

He began to panic.

Had the fire made its way that far into the facility?

Riven seemed oblivious to the sudden heat that threatened to overcome Ash. How could that be? But before he could consider that fact any further, the situation took a turn for the worse.

Without warning, the glass of the observation room buckled outward, recoiled, and shattered explosively! Ash turned away to shield himself from harm as a wave of unbearable smoldering heat threatened to put him down. He was unaware of the fact that Riven had not flinched at all. There was no explanation for what had occurred that Ash could grasp.

"There is someone down on that table." Riven annunciated purposefully.

Mollified by what he'd just witnessed, Ash offered no resistance. He turned slowly toward what was left of the obliterated glass next to him, and then warily peered out and down to the operating theatre below. The lights failed again, casting dim shadows throughout.

Initially, there was nothing different about the room. Then, something startling happened. There was movement! The previously still body on the table below him shifted under the sheet that draped over it! He'd written that person off for dead and nearly ignored his responsibility. Riven had repeatedly encouraged him to attend to whoever was down there. The lesson was learned. Ash didn't hesitate. He began to turn to go down the stairs to the O.R. behind him but stopped in his tracks. He couldn't believe what he was witnessing. That person wasn't simply moving at that point, that person was rising! The body under that sheet sat up with a lurch and swung unsteady legs to the floor. The darkness prevented clear identification of whoever it was, but it was unmistakable that the person was stumbling away from that operating table toward the door at the far side of the room!

"Are you seeing this?!" Ash exclaimed to no response from Riven. Swinging back around, he beckoned, "Hey! Wait! Don't leave the O.R.! I'm a doctor and I'm coming down to you!" he shouted down to no acknowledgment. Either he went unheard or he hadn't been understood. Either way, there was only one option to exercise. "Riven, come on, follow me!"

With that Ash turned urgently to go down the stairs. He simply expected Riven to acquiesce. He never bothered to turn to verify the fact.

The staircase was short and steep, and his frenetic pace nearly caused him to take a fall. As he made his way closer to the swinging O.R. doors, negligible light escaped from inside. The room looked like bleakness from what he saw through the small windows. He burst through the threshold. As fast as he'd moved, he was still too late. The figure he'd seen had already left the room. At the far side, the doors out of the O.R. were still swinging slightly. At a run, Ash took off, knocking over an instrument table in his path that filled the emptiness with metallic crashing. Weaving his way through the room around machinery and tables, he made it to the other side and put a shoulder to the door.

A wall directly ahead of him stared back, leading away in either direction down a long dim corridor. A choice stood before him. One direction was wrong, and one was right. The two directions were disparate. Glaring brightness obscured his vision in one direction, and relentless dimness enshrouded the other. He'd always thought differently than most people regarding such odds. To get it wrong with so few choices would have heightened the sense of failure to him. At that point, he turned with the intention of asking for Riven's input, only to be confronted with the realization that he in fact hadn't been following and that yet another individual had been allowed to be left in harm's way. In an infuriated fit, Ash let out a reverberating obscenity. Just then, the pain in his left temple returned to exacerbate the situation that much more.

The wound he'd been distracted from began to throb again. As he reached up toward it, he winced as he touched it, bringing his fingers away with a small amount of blood on them. Although some concern went through him, he downplayed that and stuck with his intention of relegating it to secondary importance. His attention shot back to what he was doing. He had someone to find. But which way should he choose?

Instinct led him to his right. That choice was less than scientific, and that fact bothered him but he followed it just the same. He started down the corridor to his right at a jog, with every footfall making his head shudder.

The direction he'd chosen led to the post-Op ward. Although there were few rooms in that area, the person he'd been chasing could have gone into any one of them, if he'd even gone that way at all. Ash began calling out in earnest as he went. No answer came. No one was found in any of the rooms. His calls grew louder and more desperate but remained unanswered.

The thought that he'd taken the wrong way of course came to him then. It seemed obvious that he'd have to turn around and search the other way. But he feared the amount of time he'd already lost. If he had to backtrack in the opposite direction, could he catch up? Before he could act on that fear, something caught his eye.

At the edge of his perception, he saw the light blue-colored material of the operating table dressing sticking out partially between the two doors leading out of the post-Op area. It had almost escaped his notice. Immediately, he took off in that direction.

On the other side of those doors was the same dimness he'd seen throughout. The emergency lighting offered little assistance to his need. The corridor he stood in was lit with only small islands every twenty feet or so. That fact slowed his initial haste down to a staggered pace. He'd have to be mindful of the dark places ahead of him and choose his steps carefully.

The blue sheet from the O.R. was there on the ground at his feet, spotted with ocher, stretched out and almost pointing him in the right direction. From where he stood, just beyond the double doors, he began to call out.

"Hello...?" The sound of his own voice seemed timid to him. He tried again.

"Hello! I saw you in the O.R. and followed you... Where are you? I'm a doctor and I'm here to help..."

No response came at all. The possibilities ran through his mind then. Could he even be heard? Was it possible that the unknown figure simply couldn't respond? Was the person in actuality a threat and seeking to avoid discovery? The setting began to affect Nathaniel's mind. He shook his head to clear it of any imagined stupidity running through it and tried calling out again.

"If you can hear me, stay where you are, and I'll come to you!"

He started down the corridor slowly, leery of the voids between each island of light despite himself. The only sounds to be heard were his footfalls and heartbeats. On either side of the hall were darkened rooms that needed to be checked as he passed. Nothing and no one was to be found in any of them.

Nathaniel went down the hall alertly, sure that he was close to finding who he was searching for. There was no basis for his surety, he simply had a feeling that he'd responded to. The problem was that the certainty he felt was coupled with some undefined dread that put him on edge suddenly.

HSSSSSSSTT!!!

The static of the radio at his side breaking the deadness around him sent his heart racing. As much as he hated that thing, he accepted the necessity of it. It remained the only link he had to the unreachable world just beyond him. For that reason, he listened to it intently.

As he listened, he was encouraged by what was coming through. The reports carried a more optimistic tone to them which lifted Nathaniel's spirit somewhat. In the situation he was in, he welcomed that despite its minuscule amount.

"...I've stabilized this one just in time...there is nothing but a scratch on this little boy, he'll be fine...I'm hoping the worst was behind us...minimal bleeding at worst...all of them are uninjured so you don't need..." That was the end of what he could discern. Although the signal was unreliable, there was a definitive picture painted by the broken relays that did make it through. Nathaniel was willing to place as much or as little info into a positive perspective as he could to contest everything he'd seen and experienced up to that point. He happily categorized what he'd heard as good news. Briefly, he forgot himself.

He paid for that lapse in urgency with a sobering reminder.

Ahhhhh!!

A shrill cry echoed toward him as if it was itself trying to escape some horrible thing. His temporary respite was abruptly ended. The sound cut through the darkness as well as his calm. Throughout all of his years as a doctor, he'd never heard anything that compared to the degree of distress in that scream. It froze him where he stood. Initially, he was unable to discern the direction it had come from. Then, he realized that it had originated from ahead of him. There was no going backward regardless.

His eyes were wide, and his breath was bated. Despite that, he took off at a run toward the source of that scream. He moved as fast as he dared to through the intermittent darkness, confident of where the sound had come from. He'd already been in the middle of the section when he'd heard the cry and sped through the remaining part. At the end of the corridor, around a corner, was the hospital's Burn Unit. That had to have been where the sound originated.

As he reached the end of the shadowed hall, he felt relieved to be leaving it. He hoped that he'd be able to avoid any more areas as forbidding. The moment he turned the corner, that hope became unrealistic. What stared at him then was worse. He immediately came to a dead stop, reluctant to go on through the total depthless darkness that barred his way.

He looked forward into nothingness. It was as if existence had come to an end directly in front of him. An inherent fear overcame him despite his age and despite his reasoning. No person blithely ventures into the utter unknown without bringing their own past distress as an unwelcomed companion. Those pasts always retain their potency, if even for a very brief time. Nathaniel felt his distinctly just then.

The thing that snapped him out of his spell was a second horrific scream. The sound came from directly in front of him. There was no mistaking it. He began to move forward cautiously. Subconsciously, he began to talk out loud to himself either in an attempt to strengthen his resolve, or more probably, in an attempt to refute the reality of the situation.

"Take it slow-you don't want to trip on anything. It's not that far-"

As he went forward, he progressed using a kind of slow sliding, unwilling to lift his feet too far off of the ground. He stretched his arms out in front of him and bent low to steady himself. Vertigo was unavoidable in that blackness. But his apprehension strengthened his awareness. Then, another plaintive scream shot through him like a bolt, taking unfortunate advantage of that awareness.

"Can't be too much farther..." he heard himself say. He was amazed at how confining emptiness felt. One more step forward-one more step forward. He simply urged himself to continue on. Naturally, the darkness he moved through made it seem as if he was surrounded by a threat, a threat that intended to toy with him just long enough to convince him that he was secure, when in fact, his safety was completely immaterial.

He of course had no way to truly gauge his progress. All he could do was just keep blindly lurching forward. Then his outstretched hands came to the solidity of the wall. He knew through experience to follow it to his left. He pressed his back against it and side-stepped his way on, reluctant to look backward for fear it would dissuade him from continuing. Another scream came, and he stepped up his pace.

The area he'd entered was the Burn Unit and he knew that directly ahead of him, somewhere, was the main isolation chamber. It was a wide room of glass with a single entrance. The large room was routinely used for burn -victims for the purpose of controlling their environment as fully as possible so that their wounds would not be subject to infection. There had been no doubt that what he'd heard had come from that room. The wall he'd been using ended at a corner, and he continued ahead because he knew that he'd reached the Iso-Room. The large chamber would be directly in front of him, a short distance across a narrow hallway. It was the only room in that part of the hospital, kept apart to provide a completely controlled environment. His extended hands slapped the cold hard glass in front of him, confirming the fact. To his surprise, something inside slapped back.

"Oh shit!" he said shocked.

"Ahhhhh!" came from the other side of the pane and directly in front of him. Nathaniel was startled out of his wits! He believed he'd caught up to the man he'd been chasing there in the B.U. The problem was that the darkness obscured the man's face to the point of complete anonymity.

The desperation of the moment poured out of him as he tried to communicate through the glass of the Iso-room. He heard his own voice reverberating loudly as he spoke. No indication that he was being understood at all was given. No further recognition of the person on the other side presented itself either. Every effort to communicate by Ash was obscured by a hideous outcry from inside the chamber.

"Can you under-" Ash would attempt to say.

"Ahhhhh!!!" would echo from inside.

"Listen to me! Can you-" he would persist.

"Ahhhhh!!!" mirrored in response.

"I'm coming in. Just stay-" he insisted.

"Ahhhhh!!!" was hollered in tandem.

For every attempt he made, a simultaneous and wretched yelling would begin so that the two sounded as one. He didn't understand it and couldn't determine the cause of the distress of the figure in front of him. Abandoning the verbal, Ash moved to the door.

His urgency was no help in getting the door opened at all. The critical nature of the moment meant nothing to the locked area. Ash struggled with and pounded on the entrance futilely, not knowing what to do to help the person trapped inside. Rushing back to the glass, he started to yell through the pane again, as if he'd forgotten the lack of success he'd already had with it.

"I can't get-"

"Ahhhhh!!!"

"The doors won't-"

"Ahhhhh!!!"

"SON-OF-A-!"

"Ahhhhh!!!" was echoed back at him.

"Ahhhhh!!!" Ash shot back in complete aggravation, only to be mirrored from the other side again.

Then he spun around with the intention of trying to find something substantial enough to break through the door. Of course, the darkness hindered his efforts. As he felt around blindly for possibly a chair or a small table, he noticed a change around him. He realized that there was a slight difference in his sight. That realization came from his peripherals. Then, his attention shot back toward the Iso-room instantly in panic. The change he'd noticed was in fact a slight glowing coming from inside, deep in the room at the figure's back.

That glow was the beginning of a flickering fire!

By the time Ash fully grasped what was happening and turned to face the room, the person he'd seen inside had already been moving away, retreating further into the dimness. In a panic, he threw himself forward on the glass, slamming his fists against it in an attempt to coax the man back. Ash then went back and forth between the glass and the doors trying in vain to gain access.

Nothing worked as the amber light increased steadily. In a short time, the fire grew large enough to spill a little glow into the hallway Ash stood in. That fact urged him away from the locked doors he struggled with and back to the window for a look inside.

Ash was staggered by the speed at which things had devolved. The fire had spread and threatened to become an inferno. A mass of heavy smoke obscured everything inside at that point. Nothing discernible could readily be seen through that smoke, or so he thought. Just then, he was proven wrong. He would have wished it otherwise.

The light of the fire had brightened so much that it revealed twisted silhouettes, contorted on and behind the smoke inside. The figure he'd trailed was not at all alone! As Ash began to fully understand the severity of what he was seeing, a chorus of howls and screams began. The sound was torturous. The distress was   pal-pable. His helplessness was infuriating. Frantically, Ash raced back to the door, slamming his fists against it with a string of obscenities to accompany each hit. There was no movement, there was no give.

Light began to brighten the darkened hallway. As he went back again to the glass, he started throwing his body against it recklessly, un-cognizant of the damage he might do to himself. All the while, the fire's brightness grew. As that light spread further out from the Iso-room, a lone passive figure, seemingly lurking, was revealed, looming behind Ash.

"Where did you come from!!"

"From where you are going."

Nathaniel was taken aback by the sudden appearance, from out of nowhere and from out of total darkness, of Aegis. The ironic and distinct calmness displayed on his face was also surprising considering the circumstance. On the other side of the glass, the fire which had erupted further revealed the frenzied panic of the multiple figures trapped inside. Nathaniel looked on helplessly as they were suffering torturously. Then, he turned back to Aegis angrily.

"Why aren't you helping me? Why are you so calm? We have to do something to get those people out of there now!"

"No Nathaniel, you don't." was the sober response he was offered.

"What!? You're afraid...? Is that it? I don't blame you. We'll all get out of here safely, now please come over here and help me!" Nathaniel said trying to sound as reassuring as possible.

"I don't know fear Nathaniel; I only comprehend the pointlessness of what you're attempting. I am well aware of the fact that you are reacting to this manufactured situation in the best possible tenor of humanity, but what you can't be aware of, at this time, is the detrimental effect of those actions on your outcome."

"I'm not thinking of myself now!"

"We agree. We differ on the understanding that that is your only beneficial recourse. The point of affecting another Remnant has passed. This is a distraction from the process that requires your full attention right now. You're only witnessing the appearance of suffering. It's a show being performed for your benefit alone. Well, it's actually better to say it's for your detriment..."

"SHUT UP!" Nathaniel yelled as he turned away to throw his effort back against the heavy glass. The sight he looked in on horrified him as figures thrashed and howled and knelt pleadingly before him. Bodies scattered and then collided with one another in hysterics. All the while, Nathaniel suffered vicariously.

Aegis continued as if he hadn't heard the disgust in Nathaniel's outburst. "I'm sorry, but this is beyond you.

There is nothing you can do here. Let me be direct with you-they are already dead. Don't misdirect your finite energy towards what you have no ability to affect."

"They're not dead already! There's still time! I was warned about you! I know that you have some ulterior motive here! I don't care about that! Can't you see what is happening right in front of you? Either help me or get the hell away from me!"

With that, Dr. Ash turned away in desperation again, working furiously but futilely to break through the barrier in front of him. He kicked and beat the doors with no effect. Then, lost in panic, he began calling out to anyone for help. The strangeness of his own voice didn't register with him as it echoed away in all directions. He called out repeatedly to no one, mixing the pleas with curses for the situation he was in; all to no response.

His mind raced to find an answer, but none came. If his desperation had had substance, he could have used the weight of it to shatter the glass. But it was just another ineffectual part of him and proved useless.

All the while, Aegis stood motionlessly near him displaying no expression at all on his face; for good or ill. That fact only served to infuriate Nathaniel more. But he put that aside necessarily, single-minded in his struggle to help.

Inside, the flames rose high enough to obscure any movement within. To his mind, nothing could have been done at that point even if he could have finally gained access. The scene was almost identical to the one in the ambulance bay where everything had begun. No optimism could possibly be reserved for the situation.

"They were never yours to save Nathaniel."

Reluctantly, he stopped his attempts, not because he accepted what he was being told, but because his every effort to access the room had proven to be totally ineffective. Although he knew that turning away from the anguish was the only thing left to do, he found himself spellbound. There was a beauty in the destruction he was witnessing that dug its claws in, so as not to be easily discarded. He felt that somewhere just beyond the point of the willingness of acknowledgment. He hated liking it.

"How did this happen? Who are all of those people?" he asked out loud rhetorically.

"They are only silhouettes of something actual and substantial Nathaniel. This is a deceptive theatre with an audience of one: you. It is the underside of the truth. If you'll just listen to me now, all of the exertions you're wasting can come to some good for that truth."

"I have no intention of listening to anything you've got to say." he said through gritted teeth. "Rather than helping me, you chose to stand there and do nothing. What have you got to say to me...huh? What could you possibly say that would convince me that you're any-thing other than a soulless evil coward?" Nathaniel challenged.

"I'll be what you make of me."

"I'm not going to make anything of you! You've shown me what to expect from you!" Frustration exploded from him as he lashed out at Aegis. "Who are you!? What the hell do you want!? What are you doing here!? Are you really the cause of all this? Tell me!" With that, he started forward without thought, unsure of his own intentions at that moment. His usual stoic character was quickly erased by unusual aggression. "I don't care if we have to throw-down right here and right now- you're gonna tell me the truth!" He moved toward him then, but Aegis stood immobile. No amount of aggression mirrored what was directed at him. Then, with the short distance between them closed, Nathaniel lunged.

What happened then was incomprehensible.

Before he could reach Aegis, his peaceful stance was replaced by a blur of motion, first receding rapidly, and then shooting forward again blindingly, directly at Nathaniel's ill-advised aggression. Nathaniel felt his body impact the heavy glass behind him awkwardly. He'd been lifted from his feet by the flash of motion that had been Aegis and realized that his head had, in fact, cracked what had seemed to be shatterproof just a moment ago. It had all happened so suddenly that he didn't register the pain of the initial hit if there had in fact been any. But he immediately began to suffer from the wound at his temple. It was the same injury that had been throbbing intermittently since he'd set out from the ambulance bay. Now, the discomfort was intensified by the blow he'd just taken and by the heat that licked anxiously at it through the fractured glass. For a perceivable but unnatural length of time, he hung there against the glass surface of the Burn Unit, stunned and afraid. Then, suddenly he dropped to the floor excruciatingly, in a heap. Disoriented and pacified, he struggled to get up but only managed to turn over, pressing his back against the B.U. in fear.

Aegis began to speak then almost consolingly. The degree of sincerity in his tone of voice was palpable to Nathaniel.

"I'm truly sorry about that Nathaniel. It was purely defensive. I would have never initiated that. But there was no other option open to me. What did you really expect would happen if you attacked one of the Etherium?" Aegis asked.

"...What...?"

"Maybe you'll take a moment or two to listen now?"

Nathaniel Ash cowered away from him, preoccupied with his confusion and disbelief, not as much unwilling as incapable of listening at that point. Although he realized that something profound had been revealed, he was in no condition to grasp it just then. He froze feebly where he was and waited for understanding. He waited there dumbstruck and wide-eyed, staring at something or someone that defied explanation. He simply stared forward, transfixed.

Something in him reverted to a primal state of self-protection that warned him not to take action. The   notion of getting up never occurred to him. The idea of saying even a word was never considered. The only things that moved at all were his widening eyes; stretched with shock. Nathaniel stared up at Aegis who stood stationary there in front of him. His face lost the look of threat it had taken on. His tone had returned to its original calmness. His apology had been given. Whether or not Nathaniel would accept that apology was yet to be determined.

After a short but tense time, Aegis began to take a step forward. Aegis's move toward him snapped him out of his mute haze. Reflexively, Nathanial pressed hard against the pane at his back, trying to maintain a distance between them. He began to speak shakily.

"Stop! What the hell just happened!"

"Again, I'm sorry about..." he replied with new pre-occupation sounding in his voice.

"Damn the sorry, man! I don't understand what's happening here...What are you?"

"As I've intimated already, I am what your frequency refers to as an Angel-despite the sentimental inaccuracy of that title. But in the end, I'll be what you make of me." he responded with an unhidden distraction in his tone.

Aegis took another step toward him at that point but before Nathaniel could react in any way, he stopped and stood as still as a statue. Just that quickly, his appearance seemed transformed. His face hardened and his posture stiffened. Fury was the mask that he was wearing then.

The brightness behind the thick glass at his back intensified as the fire flared. Then inexplicably, Aegis ignited in a brilliance of his own somehow, matching the furnace opposite him. His body burned white-hot and though there could be no rational understanding of it, Nathaniel instinctively knew that he was witnessing Aegis enraged!

Ash began to rise to his knees, trying to position himself for whatever was coming. The prospect of that rage being directed at him was terrifying!

Without warning or apparent cause, the clear and heavy sheet he'd been pressing so closely against cracked and exploded outward like a thousand weapons aimed at Aegis. Ash threw himself down protectively and instantly. Then, the inferno behind him came over his head in a torrent, out like a second wave.

Awkwardly flattened against the floor, Ash looked up to see that Aegis hadn't been impaled like he reasonably should have been. He had, in fact, not moved at all or been touched in any way! He stood tensed where he'd been before, suddenly engulfed in brilliance and with a look of ferocity across his face. Then with a soundless scream, the light that was emanating from him pushed back. The shards stood suspended where they were in the air, then, spun, and were hurled back toward the fire which appeared literally to recede from the back-lash as if it were animate!

With that, Ash fought through his fear and disbelief for the sake of self-preservation. He pulled himself shakily from the floor and scrambled away rapidly, without daring to look back.

By not risking that look behind him, he never saw the eyes that had been there, directly over his own shoulder glaring out at him; the eyes that seemed to derive from the flames themselves.

Endgame Trilogy

PART II: THE RESONANCE

Panic was a distinct reality only a heartbeat away.

That reaction had to be expected following the chain of events that had taken place. It began with waking up confused and injured in the middle of a fiery ambulance bay. No memory of why, or reason explaining it, presented itself and that led possibly to impeded decisions. Each subsequent incident contributed evidence to support that possibility. Every inexplicable happening compounded it. The sum of it all led him to his present position.

In the midst of that confusion, an unknown and desperate figure dove headlong into smoke and darkness, luring the doctor in the wake. Need and obligation drove him. So, with a leap through fire, he wandered unknowingly toward what was becoming a disastrous outcome.

The facility he'd worked in for so long appeared to be in ruin. Everything seemed dark and devoid of life. Each person he'd come across was completely beyond his abilities and un-savable. That fact ate away at him, making his anger grow. Then, the separate appearances of two distinctly unusual men ushered in the rapid decline of an already deteriorating situation.

Those encounters with Aegis and Riven pulled him unwillingly in different directions, leaving him confused and vulnerable. The most profound feelings had been elicited by his run-in with Aegis outside the hospital's Burn Unit.

There was nothing that feasibly explained what he'd seen or what was done to him then. In an instant, barely within his capacity of perceiving, a seemingly ordinary man standing in front of him moved inhumanly fast and with inhumanly strong force, threw him helplessly against the thick solid glass at his back. Nathaniel was sent tumbling to the ground like something broken and stayed there, trapped in yet another intense emotion; abject fear. He'd been told that it was a defensive response to Ash's own aggression but that answer satisfied nothing. That answer failed to engender even the slightest bit of trust.

The effects of what he was in the midst of began to manifest in ways that clouded things. Consequently, the instability around him evoked a degree of paranoia. He began to feel pursued, but he had no idea of why or by what.

The range of emotions Nathaniel Ash experienced had one common thread running through them; profound inadequacy.

At his core, he believed that he was equal to any task that could be placed before him. Training had taught him that. Experience verified that fact over time. But the product of his recent efforts drew a different conclusion. This new and compelling situation was slowly erasing his confidence in his ability. Through everything that had occurred, he felt distinctly inadequate.

That fact made him reconsider his original intention and instead focus on his own interest. Self-preservation became the foremost thought in his mind. He wanted to get out of that place intact. He chose to believe that when he did, explanations for everything he'd experienced would come readily. He was willing to put aside his inherent curiosity, the very thing that made him become a doctor in the first place, and allow himself to stay uninformed, pacified, and ultimately, safe.

He'd accept that delusion if he could get out. He would actively convince himself that anything outlandish that had occurred was just a product of over-stimulated imagining. He'd, in fact, already begun the rationalizing of it.

"These surroundings alone would make anyone pull from their subconscious..." he tried reasoning. "Any first-year Psych student would know that stress and environment can make you misinterpret things." He said it but it was unconvincing. Despite that fact, he'd made his choice.

So, Nathaniel stopped looking for people left

behind and sought a way out for himself at that point. Going back the way he'd come was out of the question. He had no choice but to continue in the direction he was headed. His intention was to make it through the few remaining areas between him and the rear of the building without distraction.

Nathaniel had been running blindly after the incident in the Burn Unit. Profoundly shaken, he'd been making his way haplessly, moving as if he was being pursued.

The part of the facility he found himself in was the ICU. The darkness around him seemed alive and willful to him despite his stubborn rationality. The cast of the emergency lighting left things two-dimensional and devoid of depth. That was a parallel to his state that he'd failed to notice at the time.

On either side of him, extending the length of the hall, were rooms grouped in twos. All of the rooms had sliding doors and clear glass walls with ceiling-to-floor blinds. As Dr. Ash entered the section, he noticed that those blinds were all left open. He soon found himself struggling to lock his eyes down the center of the hall, loathe of catching sight of anything or anyone disturbing that may be behind those clear glass walls.

He found that keeping his eyes from those rooms would be a challenge he might not be equal to.

To his right out of the corner of his eye, he thought he caught sight of something. He saw whatever it had been so briefly, it stayed undefined. To a large degree, he wasn't opposed to that. It was something that he actively chose to dismiss.

The goal of locating the person he'd been chasing, or rescuing any other person was discarded, replaced by the singular task of escaping intact.

"Look straight ahead-keep moving." came from him tensely.

Moving at a quick step, he tried to put it behind him. On his left, a little farther down the hall, he thought he perceived movement inside one of the rooms. It worked to hold his attention. He refused to let it. Again, he reminded himself to keep moving forward toward his goal. He kept his vision pinpointed in front of him.

Apprehension surrounded him as he walked on. An un-named fear teased him from each room he passed. Soon, he struggled to distinguish if he was, in fact, seeing those things, or if his own anxiety was to blame. The uncertainty made it so much worse.

Then, as if induced by his apprehensions, flashes of lives lost throughout his career turned the ICU into a nightmarish theatre. He began to witness his Hell.

On one side of him, he perceived a withered elderly lady. Then, he saw bodies with peeled and seared skin. Each image was vividly clear, yet momentary to him. How could it be so intensely real and at the same time so intangible? The next thing he saw was a young man curled up and wracked with pain. Then that too dematerialized. Moving quickly away, he saw an emaciated, pale form with sunken eyes frantically beating his own arm the way one does when trying to raise a vein. Farther down, a man with a gunshot wound looked down at his own partial head in his hands. A young girl stood eerily, impassively still across the corridor from him, soaked through, water gushing from her slack mouth and down her body like a faucet. Her black eyes traced his quivering steps.

Despite his better judgment, a part of him struggled to assign a name to each figure he saw. Something in him insisted that each apparition be identified. Something wouldn't allow him to disregard. Some vague recognition for each vision he saw wanted to be acknowledged. A familiarity licked at the edge of his mind as he worked desperately to resist each new scene. That familiarity was on his heels, chasing him, pushing him on, and threatening to make him abandon his own prized, rational senses.

Although he needed no additional incentive, it made him move with an even more urgent purpose through the section. Nathaniel knew that if he could make it through the ICU, he'd be close to a way to exit the building. He drove himself on, as single-minded as he was before, but with a contrary objective.

He found himself so harassed by the images that assailed him that he began to walk with his head down, his arms raised and cradling his face and ears like blinders. The attempt was only minimally successful. Glimpses of death pried their way in.

Determined nightmares aren't so easily discouraged. New and equally disturbing images continually made their way through his inadequate defenses, refusing to be shut out. That fact began to erode his composure. Unknowingly, he started muttering out loud - to push back at the threatening things around him.

He was saying, "...not real...don't believe...doesn't add up...leave me the hell alone!" If he'd have been able to disconnectedly gauge his condition at the time, he'd have assessed himself as definitively imbalanced.

Nathaniel moved on determinedly, working towards the rear of the section, resisting as best he could all the way. As he went, his muttering became louder, and then it took on a more aggressive tone. Ultimately, he found that he'd begun to scream at the top of his lungs as if he could use that as a weapon against what assailed him. His head was raised again, and his words were directed balefully at the disturbing things that flashed so menacingly at him. Each word was like a stab. Every phrase was a slash. No consideration was given to whether or not it was effective at all. It was purely defensive desperation.

One effect of those outbursts was that he began to feel emboldened to some degree. There was a power in forcefulness that his circumstance had almost beaten out of him. Remembering himself, he was spurred on.

"You're in my head! You're only in my mind!"

Nathaniel had worked to apply a kind of selective memory regarding what he'd experienced with Aegis. He reminded himself that he was far too rational to accept any unsubstantiated explanations. He fought aggressively against infusing some comforting non-reality into his core. The farther away from each moment and occurrence, the less significance it would retain. Or so he felt. He chose to take the same approach to all of the sights he was being confronted with.

For the moment his apprehensions began to subside. He'd always been able to find confidence in the strength of his conviction, and he clung to it.

The better part of the ICU was behind him and he was fighting his way through the remaining distance, although he was unsure if that fight was with some outside source or in truth within him. All that he could do was to concentrate on getting out.

Beyond that remaining section of the ICU, and a short distance more, he would soon get to a side exit and make his way to the others who, he believed, were undoubtedly waiting safely outside. He allowed himself to feel some slight amount of encouragement.

The apparitions began to subside as Nathaniel's confidence surged. Some of the rooms he was passing were empty and held no horrid scenes in them at all. With only a little farther to go, a growing but dubious comfort began to settle over him, lulling him back into dropping his guard. Mistakes like that are never without repercussions.

Loud popping like the sound of glass bulbs erupted behind him. Newly panicked, he spun to face whatever fresh threat made its way toward him then. What he saw, was the darkness coming toward him, like something stalking.

The emergency lighting was exploding one by one, completely obscuring an already shadowed corridor as it crept forward. Then, the sounds began. The sounds of all the suffering he'd just witnessed filled the blackness behind him. Each flash of light as each bulb blew brought it that much closer. That was the end of his courage and confidence. It didn't matter that nothing he had seen and nothing he was hearing made sense or could be explained. The visceral reaction to it was manifest despite that. Something in him implored him to run.

It seemed to him that his upper body had turned to escape but in fact, he hadn't moved at all. Looking down verified that. He stood there frozen. Fear had anchored his feet in position and his legs shook violently. The effort it took to break the hold it had on him almost allowed the darkness to reach him. With an obscenity, he pulled himself away, just before he was overtaken.

The rooms of the section flew past him as he moved. The thought of being enveloped by enshrouding emptiness drove him on. Glances behind, meant to reassure him that he'd distanced himself, instead, forced him to see more of those scenes in the brief burst of every bulb. He saw, but he refused to accept. How could he?

"Hallucinations with or without names- They're all unreal.", was his vain and hollow reassurance.

"The surreal images could only be projections-stress induced and dismissible." he thought to himself without conviction.

As he continued on, he couldn't gauge how long he'd been moving. In some sense, he believed that he'd been running forever. Then a conflicting feeling told him that he'd only just begun. The truth didn't matter to him just then; he absolutely wouldn't stop either way.

The pursuing darkness was equally as determined. It came on, moving toward him as if it had purpose and reason. In reality, Nathaniel wasn't putting any distance between himself and it, despite his efforts. A look over his shoulder as he rounded a corner showed that it wound through the halls behind him relentlessly. Absolute bleakness followed behind him and affirmed his need to stay ahead of it and in the light, to survive.

Un-defined sounds still followed him from out of

that bleakness. The combination of the things he'd seen and the sounds he heard left him distraught. There was no explanation for any of it! No explanation sufficed other than his slip from reality. That possibility was not something he was willing to concede readily. To a degree, his training had in fact taught him to manipulate reality, and to forge it to his discretion. So, to his logic, that meant that he could be distracted from it, but not separated from it. His rational mind wouldn't be so easily derailed.

He was moving only just ahead of the power failure at that point. Another corner was rounded when a familiar sound stopped him where he was. As he spun, he saw that the darkness had halted too. Dr. Ash stood defensively at the boundary of the ICU, looking back into nothingness. Then, it sounded again, loudly and urgently.

HSSSSSSSTT!!!

Static filled the corridor. Another transmission was coming through over the radio he carried. His posture remained guarded as he stared back into what was literally chasing him just a moment ago. Like a thing huffing from exertion, the blackness expanded and withdrew almost imperceptibly; paused before a second strike. But it held where it stopped.

With wary eyes, he slowly lifted the partially damaged radio up, closer to his ear, working to hear the anticipated message.

Only the sound of his trepidation filled the bleak hall he'd paused in. No report was conveyed over that damaged little speaker pressed to his ear. Stopping for too long a time was not something he was willing to risk. The decision to move on was an easy one to make. Then, as he began to turn away, footsteps from the darkness echoed toward him.

"What the hell...?"

Nothing other than those footfalls sounded. Nothing inside that darkness could be seen. The bleak setting made something ordinary like footsteps take on a more ominous implication. Nathaniel stared, his body partially turned away, unwilling to face the unknown fully.

Then, a figure began to take shape. The silhouette of a tall man was moving toward him.

As if he had been a part of the dark, Aegis strode forward, separating himself from it. His expression was serene; his arms calmly held behind him.

Considering the way things went down the last time he was with Aegis, Nathaniel looked at him in complete disbelief. To say that he felt apprehension wouldn't suffice. He was trembling. That fact held him where he was, quietly waiting for Aegis to act.

The two stood face-to-face without a word for a time. How long remained undetermined but it was long enough to begin to un-nerve Dr. Ash. Aegis, on the other hand, seemed unmoved. That contrast didn't help

Nathaniel's composure at all. He took a step backward, hesitantly, to gauge the reaction. None came.

Aegis didn't flinch or change expression. He looked on passively as if he was waiting for something. Strangely, he showed not one single sign of the confrontation from the Burn Unit. There wasn't a wrinkle or singe on his clothes and there wasn't an ounce of distress on his face. It was as if nothing had taken place at all! That was something that couldn't be. Nathaniel thought he knew what he'd seen! He didn't understand at all and that fed his unease.

Still, Aegis did nothing.

He wasn't sure if he expected another bizarre encounter or if Aegis meant him harm. All he was sure of was that he didn't truly know what that man was, or wanted. He found that he feared getting the answer. He was intelligent enough to realize that he was at a disadvantage. That meant that he'd lost the control that he always strove to maintain. That meant that he'd also been bereft of self-determination.

"It's quite the contrary Nathaniel. You still have determination. You have decisive control. I've been endeavoring to make that point clear to you." Aegis stated, breaking the deadlock between them.

Somehow, again, Aegis perceived his line of thought! Yet again, he'd been confronted with something that seemed unequivocally impossible. Had he guessed? Could he be that perceptive? Those explanations were too improbable to consider. All he could do was file it away as another piece of unsolved confusion. He turned to continue toward his ultimate destination in hopes of escaping another confrontation.

"There is no avoidance at this point.", Aegis claimed.

"I'm not listening to you."

"My point will be made at one expense or another."

"It won't be at mine.", Nathaniel said defiantly.

"If it is, you'll know after it's too late."

No response to that came. Nathaniel kept moving. His stride never changed. As he went, he was aware that Aegis stayed with him. There was nothing to be done about that. He had no power. Moving on, toward the way out remained the focus.

"It is not hidden from me that you have questions you choose not to ask." Aegis began. "Too much has been experienced to go unexplained. It's alright...you need not voice what you want to know. I am aware..."

"How...!? How is it that you know!?" was blurted out involuntarily. It was reflexive.

"You know but haven't yet accepted. I've used the term "Etherium" before. That refers to any one of us within a range of frequencies within The Nature. The Nature is Totality. We are its essence. We are positive and negative- brightness and bleakness-creativity and destructiveness-emancipators and subjugators. You'll soon come to understand that there are "systems" for lack of a better word that we all work within. Those systems all have purposes and functions. They have rules and parameters. They are completely interconnected. You're close to gaining that first-hand knowledge."

No opposition was voiced. Not a single word was said to express the total lack of comprehension that was felt. Without a sound, Dr. Ash simply turned and continued walking away from Aegis.

"Your Resonance is in jeopardy, remaining ignorant is not an option any longer."

"Ignorant?" came from Nathaniel indignantly. "I'm not ignorant-you're un-hinged! I tried hard not to encourage you but what the hell are you saying! "Etheri-what"? What game are you playing? Reso-nance...? Nature...? You're telling me you're an Angel!?"

"No-I said that I was what *you* might call an Angel. I wouldn't refer to myself so narrowly. The Etherium can't be constricted to the antiquated identities that were assigned to us by those in the physical. I am a function of the whole that is The Nature. You, too, soon will be. That is the only reason we're communicating now. You must be prepared. My intention is to facilitate a proper choice.", Aegis affirmed.

"Oh, really…? I've heard different. What is the Anathema? I was told that you…"

"You were told only what Riven felt would influence your judgment. I know what was relayed to you. That term is biased as well as misdirected." Aegis interrupted. "The question you should've asked me instead is "What choice are you referring to?"

"You've apparently decided to speak for me. Answer your own question.", Nathaniel replied.

"Impudence doesn't serve your needs. The choice you have to make is before you. Do you know where you're going? You're walking blindly now, despite the belief that you are headed in the right direction. Your saving destination isn't simply the rear of some building. The edifice is euphemistic. The destination you've been working toward is fundamentally condemning. Riven would have directed you toward that end shrewdly and you would have been converted before you could fathom what you'd betrayed in yourself. You've veered off of that road slightly now, but not away from it. I encourage you to continue away from that road. But, know that I'm not what Riven has misled you to believe. I'm not some trivial egocentric opportunist fighting for a fleeting political or religious faction-I am *Etheric*. Called by the name of Inimical or Chimerical, Angel or Demon, Anathema or Abhorrent, we are Etheric. We are your eventuality. No amount of denial or resistance will alter that fact.

The choice you have to grasp is that one of us is malignant and one benign."

Trying to feign disinterest was Nathaniel's only response. What Aegis was saying affected him of course but he couldn't get beyond the things he'd seen. How could those things be explained? How could he put aside the fear he felt after what he'd witnessed from Aegis?

"Your fear is unwarranted.", Aegis tried to reassure.

"How...!? How can you be picking up on what's going through my mind!" Nathaniel blurted out, unable to subdue his own curiosity any longer.

"Thoughts, like all else, are energy. Energy emanates in a pattern and resonates within a range of frequency. The entirety of the range is within The Nature. I am attuned to The Nature wholly. So, of course, your thought is not excluded. That frequency, like all others, is perceptible with the right equipment. I am that equipment."

"You are saying you read my thoughts? That is..."

"*Not*... impossible-Actually.", Aegis concluded. "It is actually rudimentary."

"I'm sorry I asked! Forget it. Moving on to the exit..."

"As I've said, I encourage that fact, but the problem is that you don't fully understand why or what is required once you get there.", Aegis stated.

Somewhat exasperated, Nathaniel responded with, "What am I supposed to understand?"

"Thanks for joining the discourse-You need to understand that you will choose your place in the larger "system" of things. You will ultimately affect the conversion to The Nature by the summation of your choices. The ultimate and last choice is very near now and will determine your resonance within the Totality. That equates to a future of condemnation or of preservation."

"Why do you make it sound as if I'm being damned to Hell?"

"Can you be sure you haven't been already? Know that what you refer to as "Hell" doesn't actually correspond to your indoctrinated understanding of it. The reality is that it is your own energy corrupted. The full and clear comprehension - that it is Anti-Nature and inharmonious - is haunting to you throughout and further fueled by the inability to act to change it. "Hell", is you at your worst, thinking your worst, believing your worst, experiencing your worst, and accepting your worst. That existence is self-inflicted and perpetuating. There is no doubt that you can be persuaded and corralled toward it though. That is Riven's intention. Following his urging is a direct line to ruin."

"You're wrong. I don't know what he's trying to gain any more than I know what you're working toward. But I do know that he encouraged me to HELP- which is more than I can say for you. You're telling me that's bad?

That doesn't seem Hellish. All you've done is try to dissuade me. That doesn't seem Heavenly! To be blunt, it seems to me that your efforts place you in a negative light and make it seem as if you are in fact the very thing, you're trying to convince me Riven is. Either way, it doesn't matter. I'm just getting out of here in one piece."

"The negativity of helping becomes clear with the acceptance of an essential falsehood. You cannot be of help to anyone in this manifestation. Subsequently, you can't be of harm to anyone either. For that reason, I've told you to disregard what you've seen and may yet see."

"I don't care. I'm not doing anything one way or the other anymore."

"That is incomplete Nathaniel."

"What do you want from me?"

"Only that the right choice is made."

"What's your stake in this? What's it to you? If I was to believe anything I've heard, then it's my ass on the line, right?"

"Your ass…? Yes, but not only yours Nathaniel. Your fate will be my fate and my fate will be reflected in the Totality. The inter-connection is inescapable. So, you might say that my "stake" in this is parallel to yours; existential."

As he walked on, Nathaniel shuffled through his thoughts for possible lines of attack to contradict what he'd heard from Aegis. He couldn't help but engage him. That was how his mind worked whether he liked it or not. The scientist in him honored the default positions of skeptic and Devil's Advocate. Without turning, he sneered over his shoulder to Aegis, "Prove it."

What he heard in response was unexpected. An amused laugh echoed in the passageway behind him. His irritation began to grow.

"What's funny? The fact that you've been called on your delusions and can't respond? That shouldn't amuse you."

"I would think that the number of inexplicable things you've been through lately would preoccupy you enough. Or have you already found a suitable rationalization to satisfy yourself?", Aegis asked.

"Yes actually. You're insane - I'm satisfied."

"How enlightened...! *My* insanity causes your delusions!"

Another amused laugh sounded behind him.

That made the intimidation he'd felt earlier turn to aggravation. So, he moved on defiantly. The ICU was left behind, and the Rehabilitation Center was before him. Nathaniel knew that just beyond that was the exit he sought. A short distance through that section was all he needed to navigate to get himself to his final destination. He thought, 'It's almost over.'

"You'd like to think that wouldn't you?"

Again, he found that his mind was open to his unwelcome follower and not exclusively his own as he'd always believed. The inaccuracy of that continued to be proven wrong.

"I want what you want whether you accept that or not Nathaniel. I want you to make it to the other side intact. The problem is that we can't seem to agree on what that means or how that's achieved."

"We don't have to."

"True enough. But believe me when I say that I'd prefer it if we did.", Aegis asserted.

"Why?"

"Aren't you listening? Your Resonance is in question...Simply put, you're coming to your terminus and your services will be solidified on one side or the other. Riven is working diligently to ensure that you fall on his side of the conflict. The potential ramifications of that can be deciphered in the frequency. Your essence is far more critical to this region than you know. Your abdication would be destructive. That would be most unfortunate. That would be unfortunate for you and for The Nature and also for the many others that you will have condemned. Yes, despite your disbelief, your alignment, as well as others like you, could possibly have very detrimental consequences. What will you serve?

Would you be a guide through grimness, helping to liberate or would you convict?"

That question went unanswered. Nathaniel considered the exchange to be little more than a futile intellectual exercise and chose not to expend any more energy on it. He continued silently toward his goal. Although he was aware that Aegis remained only a step behind, he fought against engaging him further. But he did wonder immensely at his incredibly strange situation in spite of that effort.

His limited psychological training and experience did remind him that what he was hearing from Aegis seemed too complex and intricate to simply be a contrivance.

Aegis was convincingly urgent. He was fervently persuasive. The fact that he also had no apparent motive to deceive had to be considered as well. What would be gained? The answer escaped him.

'His convictions seem too solid to dismiss easily.', Nathaniel reasoned. He understood then that the enigma following him, fervently believed what he was espousing. Even if that were true, Nathaniel refused to buy into it so easily.

He weighed an alternative possibility. What if Aegis was exactly what Riven had implied? Could he be the cause of the damage surrounding him? That couldn't be ignored. Following the lead of someone responsible for the chaos he was in, even in any slight way, would make him complicit. There was no real evidence that Aegis bore any responsibility, but the suggestion resonated just the same. But there truly was no way of knowing. So, an agnostic tact had to be taken.

"That strategy won't get you far I'm afraid." Aegis said breaking the silence.

The degree of intuitiveness Aegis displayed repeatedly, couldn't be reasoned away. That was a puzzle piece that went unplaced. Could perceptiveness be enough of an explanation? That seemed unlikely. It was possible that Aegis was very capable of following a predictable line of thought to a rational conclusion. The appearance of seeming like he was in Nathaniel's head could be just theatrics. Aegis seemed even more duplicitous to him then. Yes, he was smart, that was clear. That fact worked against him in Nathaniel's mind. He maintained that pure intelligence was not enough to acquit the man. He went on, using the seeds that Riven had planted as the basis of doubt in Aegis.

"So, tell me, Nathaniel, what criteria are you using to draw your conclusions? Is it your depth of knowledge of my counterpart? I'm sure your experience with his kind is extensive. Could it be the grasp that you have for the visceral? No, I don't think so. After all, you've spent the better part of your life in cerebral pursuits, right? Oh, I know! Could it be that self-preservation is coloring your decisions? Yes! That's exactly it. But, again, that is good but only a part of the equation. You are presented with and must make the same choice that is before you all when the time arrives. Not expending your vital energy on phantoms of your own making is the prep-work. Making your way out of your present perception is the primary procedure, but the final suture is your choice of alignment. That is what you're unprepared for. It may seem contrary, but you must be concerned with yourself alone at this point. Deviating from that will only redirect you back toward an untenable position. You've stated that you've chosen not to attempt to save anyone else. That is your best option. Attempt to save yourself. When you're enticed by Riven to do otherwise, you have to disregard him for your own sake. Why would you do so? Choosing to do otherwise is equitable to choosing to follow Riven. Following Riven won't save you or anyone else. You will fall and everyone you lead beyond that point may follow. This is true because those you try to help here are presented only to misdirect your attention. Therefore, they aren't worth your efforts. Your intention won't count for anything at all. Only the outcome will be lasting. What will you serve?"

With that question posed, Nathaniel spun on his pursuer, "Stop asking me that! I won't serve anything or anyone! I don't work for Riven and I don't trust you any more than I do him."

"That fact hasn't made you completely abandon the intention of helping anyone else you may come across though, has it? That's the point I'm trying to emphasize.

You've stated that you only want to move on, but I can still perceive a deep desire in you to assist. That may be your undoing."

"You have no idea. You're not..."

"...in your head? Can you claim that definitively Nathaniel?"

"Son-of-a-bitch!" he blurted in frustration.

"Your confusion is understandable. Don't let your benevolence be converted in such a way that it becomes the weapon most effectively used against you. That scenario isn't so impossible to imagine, is it?"

"Maybe not. But the person who's actually attempting to do that may be harder to nail down.", was Nathaniel's counter.

"Clever-but distracting."

Unconvinced, Nathaniel turned away and continued to make his way through the Rehab area. He was in the first large section which, unlike where he'd come from, was brightly lit and orderly. Everything seemed in its place and undisturbed. The contrast to what was behind him was stark.

For the meantime, Aegis remained silent. That suited Nathaniel just fine.

As he looked around, no indication of the ruin he'd been making his way through presented itself. The section he was crossing was large and fully lit. It wouldn't take long to get through and he thought that he'd be able to do so without any trouble. He could only hope that the areas ahead would stay as unaffected. That would make for an easy transition out. That was all he desired at that point after everything he'd just been through. Those experiences unfortunately taught him not to expect any degree of ease in the midst of his situation.

When he made it to the far side of the room and reached for the door, anxious to gain his reprieve, he heard Aegis echo his own apprehension when he said, "You can't expect your path to remain unmolested."

Despite the fact that he was already considering that possibility, the blatant pronouncement of it by Aegis was unwelcome. The statement engendered resentment, regardless of whether it was intended or not. Nathaniel also felt some slight but potent degree of fear surface. The possible and likely fulfillment of that dour prediction gave him pause. Lost in thought, he hesitated there, positioned to turn the doorknob. To his dismay, when he opened the door, that warning proved to be all too accurate.

In contrast to the relief he'd allowed to come over him only moments ago, the passageway on the other side of that door led to pure despondency. The threshold he'd crossed was like the difference between life and death. Unfortunately, he'd become overly familiar with what he was entering. That did nothing to allay his concerns. He deeply desired a reprieve from that darkness.

Edging cautiously forward, he took note of his surroundings; the empty and lifeless rooms on both sides, the foreboding atmosphere, the discouraging stillness. Nothing invited him to proceed. But that was what he chose to do.

He moved cautiously, aware of Aegis' presence directly behind him. A vague but imposing sense of desolation seemed hidden somewhere in the dark ahead of him, waiting to fulfill itself.

"You can't expect your path to remain unmolested."

That probability repeated itself incessantly like a hated but memorable song. That statement was quickly joined by a nagging thought. Had he been cautioned or threatened? Aegis stayed quiet and revealed no indication one way or the other.

Nathaniel made no effort to examine the rooms around him. Inside, he feared that he was being negligent. His own feelings became another adversary then. He could have reconsidered his intentions, but he didn't. He chose instead to ignore what he felt. He sought diversion. The only possible distraction for him was following behind; Aegis. He was the only option available. The problem was that Aegis had inconveniently fallen silent.

"What, nothing to say anymore?" he attempted over his shoulder.

"You may be my captive audience but you're lacking in receptiveness.", Aegis challenged.

He walked on, annoyed by that response.

"What am I missing? I've heard what you've said. You're claiming that you're more than you seem and that you're attempting to get me to make a choice. That choice will supposedly save me and others. The one problem is that I can't directly act to save anyone here according to you. Does that even make sense? Not acting will save but acting will damn..."

"Yes, fundamentally correct."

"But even though I've already said I'm just trying to get the hell out and have no intentions of helping anymore, I'm still not grasping something. Is that right?"

"Well, yes. The only reason you're not taking action is because you're afraid. There's been no conscious decision reached by following the proper line of reasoning."

"*Your* line of reasoning! Whatever...The end result is the same, isn't it?"

"No. You can still be swayed. Riven's line of reason still presents a threat."

"That's your take. He'd tell me the same thing about you.", Nathaniel said.

"Thus, the conscious choice that's before you."

"Who is Riven to you? There seems to be a very personal conflict between the two of you."

"He is the Abhorrent. We differ intrinsically. Our conflict is the result of opposing polarities. Light erases dark, heat beats back the cold, ignorance cripples wisdom, and we clash eternally. All of those things are intertwined. One is because of the other, but is also in effect, controlled by that other. Our kind is no different than those examples. And so, we struggle.", Aegis offered.

"To what end?" Nathaniel pushed.

"That answer relies on perspective."

"Fine-What would his be?"

"He would claim an innocuous goal. He'll state that your protection and freedoms are his sincere priorities and that whatever actions he'd take would be for your benefit."

After considering that response, Nathaniel asked, "Are you claiming something different?"

"No, not exactly. But you have to understand that those reasons are only part of the whole...", Aegis began.

"You're not helping! You've just stated that you and he are opposites, but you've contradicted yourself now by saying that you both basically have the same agenda. You see the dilemma I'm in here? How could I possibly know which of you to believe? But no, don't bother trying to answer that question. It's all academic now."

"Is it?"

"Yes, it is. Soon I'll be out of here. There's no need to listen to this. I've indulged you long enough and you've served my need by preoccupying my mind. I'm simply going to make my way through this next section and then I'm out. Once we're out we'll get you examined. There'll be no ominous choices and no damning mistakes to be made. Now, my secondary objective was to lead you out of here as well. I've gotten you this far so just stay close and don't say another word unless it's to thank me."

The inherent arrogance he possessed flared up because he'd seen a spec of light ahead of him on the far side of the second large room. Unlike the other side of the Rehab area he'd just come from, which was still brightly lit and functioning, that side was a tomb. He worked his way cautiously toward the light at the opposite end, only vaguely aware that Aegis still trailed him. His thoughts turned inward at that point.

Had he done all that he could have? Had he been sufficient to the task and performed as well as anyone could have? Should he be so resigned to leaving? A part of him felt above reproach but at the same time, something in him complained that he was simply cowering.

As he walked on, those questions he'd raised brought to mind the choices Aegis referred to. He'd been told that he had a conscious decision to make. The fact of that was true but the reasoning given was rejected. There was a depth to the situation that was escaping him. Vocally he denied that possibility but internally he lacked conviction. He chose to dismiss that completely and to simply make the most logical choices he was capable of. In other words, he intended to trust his instincts.

The area almost seemed to brighten as he went. He wondered if it was the likelihood that he would soon come to the exit that lifted his spirit. Whatever the reason, the atmosphere had changed for the better. He stopped doubting himself and began to notice the slightest bit of relief growing in him. The ominous cast of the darkness had begun to perceivably withdraw.

He was nearing the way out. The glimpse of light that he'd seen at a distance was becoming clearer. It had in fact been light shining around a doorway. The brilliance of it grew as he got closer. The door was only partially open, but the light seemed as bright as the sun compared to the lifeless dimness he'd been walking through. Although it was unintentional, he realized that Aegis was about to get what he wanted. But, when he turned with the intention of goading Aegis, he found himself confused by the look displayed on his face. Aegis seemed disturbed. He appeared anxious and almost pained.

"What's the problem? We're almost out of here. See that light up ahead? That's the door to the east exit. The sun must be coming up." Nathaniel reasoned.

"That isn't daylight you see."

"Oh really? Look, we've been in here for a while I'd say. Of course, we lost track of time. What else could be shining through the doorway?" he asked, turning back toward it.

"An unprepared-for eventuality." Aegis responded.

He found that cryptic answer irritating and spun angrily to face Aegis only to find that he was alone. How could that be? He was behind him less than a heartbeat ago.

Quickly, he scanned behind him for a darkened corner or overlooked passageway that could have been taken. But there were none! He'd just dematerialized.

Nathaniel turned back around to second guess himself then. But that didn't last. His instincts told him to just keep moving. So, he moved to the beginning of a long corridor, toward the light in the doorway.

Behind him, footsteps sounded loudly. Someone was running through the Rehab rooms he'd just come from. Immediately he thought it was Aegis stupidly giving himself away, spoiling his own attempt at theatrics. So, he became determined not to play along. Then, a series of crashes rang through the area suddenly. His attention became fixed behind him as he stopped in his tracks. If it was Aegis, then he was doing a terrible job of being surreptitious. Was he trying to lure him back into the facility for some reason? That didn't add up. He'd been trying to get him to abandon the idea of helping. So, it couldn't have been him.

It was possible that someone else was back there and that they were trying to get attention. He hadn't seen anyone as he passed through. But then, he realized that he specifically hadn't been looking. He'd intentionally turned a blind eye. Was he being made to regret that just then?

Nathaniel turned back toward the light he'd been making his way to. He was so close. He was near enough to make the risk of going back foolish. Rationale ran through his mind. He told himself that he could get out and get help quickly and come back en masse, which would better serve anyone he'd missed. He also tried to convince himself that Aegis was still behind him and that if it was truly necessary, he would abandon his ridiculous request for passivity. Besides, Aegis had chosen to wander off on his own. That alleviated Nathaniel of the responsibility for him. That rationalization refused to take hold though. There was a conflict in him. It was all he could do to turn away.

But he did.

The brilliance of the light ahead of him swelled and stole his attention. He walked as if he was being seduced by it. What he was actually doing was using it to his own ends.

Concentrating on that light was a sufficient enough diversion to distract him from what might be behind in the dark. That light was his reprieve and focusing on it allowed him to dismiss his own conflictions. He was a stone's throw away and intent on getting out. At that point though, the footsteps he'd heard earlier sounded again; they were moving quicker and toward him.

Soon he found himself motionless, being tempted to turn for a look behind. Although he reasoned that he should continue and wanted to, something made him stop where he was. He questioned if it was his conscience? If it was, it was overriding his self-interests. He wasn't allowed the time to dwell. The sound had gotten close enough to demand his attention.

Still reluctant to turn away from the exit, he listened to gauge the distance of the steps behind him.

With his back to the sound, his anxiousness took control and colored his perceptions.

But it still wasn't enough to divert him completely. He reaffirmed his belief that getting out was the best course of action. His attempts to help up to that point had all proven to be futile. His confidence had been shaken somewhat and buried insecurities were re-surfacing in him because of that. It was the fear of that growing feeling that kept his back turned.

But the situation wouldn't allow that bravado to go unchallenged. Just as he began to force himself forward again, what he'd been trying so hard to ignore became critical and urgent. A hoarse and grating cry, undoubtedly directed at the Dr., came down the corridor that was impossible to disregard.

Nathaniel spun around; compelled.

At a distance, down the hall, was the same figure that Dr. Ash had seen before in both the O.R. and the I.C.U. How was that possible he wondered? After the fire, could anyone have survived? The proof was there a short distance away facing him! Then, the questions began to stir; had he tried hard enough? Had he just been unequal to the task? Did anyone else survive? Should he go back?

The figure opposite the Dr. kept his distance for some reason. He seemed to stoop a little where he stood but didn't advance. As Nathaniel looked down the dark hallway, he took notice of what looked like smoke rising from the unknown man! He had to have undoubtedly been hurt very badly. Instincts over-rode at that point, forcing the Dr. to action.

He urgently began waving and gesturing to the man saying, "My god! I see you! Come down here, the exit is right here. Come on!"

No response and no movement followed from the shadowed form. Nathaniel reasoned that there was a state of shock responsible for that. He'd seen it before. He knew what he had to do and didn't hesitate. His assistance was vital. In that moment, he forgot about himself and began to make his way back toward the man at the opposite end of the corridor. He said, "I'm coming to you don't move..."

What he got in response to that was a similar and demoralizing throaty cry, as hoarse and scary as the first. Then, the shadow figure turned ungracefully, awkwardly lifted an arm, and pointed back toward the inner area of the hospital that Dr. Ash had come from. Then, with speed that defied circumstance, the figure was moving away from the Dr. at a rate that made it difficult to keep up. Quickly, he lost sight of him and the echoing footfalls were all he had to try to locate him again.

The thought of his moving away from potential safety did not go unacknowledged. He was back on auto-pilot again, just that quickly. The urgent need he'd seen propelled him. So, he followed, maneuvering through the same areas he'd thought and wished he'd left behind.

He lost sight of the shadow he chased more than once. No matter how he moved, he never seemed to make up any ground. Someone seriously injured and shocked like that shouldn't be able to remain a step ahead. But that was exactly the case. The figure remained inexplicably elusive.

Then, the thought occurred to him that he was being led somewhere. The where and whys of it was a mystery, and the potential consequences were even more so.

He'd been forced to retrace his steps through the facility to a point before he lost sight of his bleak guide. Motion caught his eye again. A door was closing off to his right a short way ahead of him. That door opened to a stairwell. Nathaniel moved toward it decisively. As he crossed that distance, the vision of the collapsing ceiling he'd escaped, flashed through his mind like a warning. Knowing the danger of fire and collapse was ahead of him, he checked his courage. Neither he nor the figure he worked to catch could be afforded hesitation. He threw open the heavy double doors with a purpose.

If he'd have thought it through, he would have moved more cautiously. When he threw open those doors, a wave of heat and smoke rushed out like an attacker, singeing him and blinding him. He gasped, affected by the stifling air. Recovering somewhat after a moment, he fought for a clear view up the flight before him. Small fires burned dully where debris fell. A thin veil of smoke wafted around him. What sounded like labored footsteps above confirmed where he had to go.

Nathaniel began to climb, feeling weighed down with fear. Another attempt was made to get through to the one he followed, "Come back! What are you doing! You're going to get us both killed!" Again, he went unanswered.

Some of the distance separating them was made up which allowed the Dr. to catch a glimpse of the man further ahead. After that glimpse, Nathaniel wanted assurance that he wasn't hallucinating. What he thought he saw was impossible.

More intense but scattered fires burned at the higher levels and it appeared that the silhouetted man was making his way through those, stepping recklessly through each without caution, coming out of the other side intact and unburned! Nathaniel couldn't believe what he was seeing. Then the rational mind took command again and attributed what he'd seen to his own smoke inhalation and blurred vision. No doubt, he was mistaken about what he thought.

All he could do was to continue the chase.

Although he'd allowed himself to be convinced that what he'd seen was a mistake, to him the pockets of fire around him were a very real threat to navigate. He'd already experienced a lot and had made it through relatively untouched (with the exception of the initial head wound). He had no intention of getting immolated.

So, he made his way very slowly then and more carefully.

There was good reason for him to be afraid. How many times had he recently side-stepped death he wondered? He felt like a kind of macabre escape artist. But he also knew that his luck could easily take a turn. Just then, he imagined that eventuality would prove much more likely. He followed despite it.

The first flight was behind him. He hopped over debris where he could and scaled the railing when the fire got too intense. Soon, the second flight was behind him. He wondered how it was possible that the figure he followed had made it through without using the same methods.

At the third level, he saw that the door was left partially open. For a moment, Nathaniel hesitated unsurely. He scanned above him up the stairwell and saw that everything beyond that point was impassable. A collapse blocked everything above that level and left no other option for him. He went through the door.

The contrast was stark.

On that third level, there was darkness and stillness. As strange as it seemed, no fires were burning there. A look to both his left and right showed that he was totally alone. The area was lifeless and bleak. Stepping out of the stairwell, he let the door shut behind him with just a quiet hint of metal scraping. Hesitantly, he called out, "Hello?" to no response. His eyes shifted around the area warily. For some unknown reason, he found himself tiptoeing around as if there was someone there to disturb.

Only sparce lighting filled the room. There were no windows in that part of the building to look out of. He was deep within the facility then. The room led off in either direction toward double doors.

There was a seating area in front of him lined with multiple pieces of what appeared to be small hand-prints, taped or pinned to the walls. To him, each tiny hand looked exactly alike. Each one seemed like the last. He found himself staring. It was difficult to pull away, but his attention was soon stolen. To his right, down the short hall, a radiant glow began to grow that demanded his attention.

What was it? The fire...? Not likely he reasoned because the light was brilliantly white, not amber. For the moment, he was satisfied with the distance he was at. But that moment quickly passed because the longer he focused on it, the more drawn to it he became. It was spellbinding! Despite that fact, he found himself reluctant to investigate further. In the midst of all he'd experienced, that glow struck him as an inexplicable thing. Regardless, it drew him in. The Dr. was becoming oblivious to all else without realizing it. His concern for his safety faded. He lost interest in his pursuit of the unknown man. His desire focused solely on the brilliance he was seeing.

In the opposite direction, a slow stalking movement went unnoticed because of that light's distraction. That figure Nathaniel had been chasing regarded him curiously, his one arm raised as a shield against the same brilliance that held Nathaniel entranced. Then, he laboriously inched further down the hall, escaping acknowledgment from the doctor.

Abruptly, that hold was broken when a thunderous pounding rang out. Nathaniel turned with a gasp to see that the shadowy figure was responsible. He watched as the man purposefully threw his body against the heavy doors ahead of him. They were directly opposite from the others but were bleak and void of any brilliance. With three forceful efforts, he managed to break through to the dense darkness on the other side.

"Hey wait! Stay where you are." Nathaniel urged.

The lack of response that he got was expected by that point. So, he turned his back from the light reluctantly and started to move quickly.

He started after that evasive figure again, wondering where he was being led. Soon, he realized that he'd lost sight and was moving through the darkness, without direction, as he had been for too long. Still, it was impossible to abandon the mystery he'd been pursuing. He was resolute.

What the doctor desired was to see through what he'd started. That seemingly aimless and wandering figure became the embodiment of that desire. So, he followed determinedly.

Moving through the doors, he took note of where he was; Pediatrics. He entered the section with some degree of mixed emotion. Throughout his tenure at the hospital, he'd spent the majority of his time in that area. Some measure of fondness and sentimentality mixed with a vague hint of regret and remorse. There was a purpose behind each, but there was also a purpose for subduing them. He'd become adept at the practice.

The normally cheerful section took on an ominous mood in that dimness, and whatever liveliness there had previously been, faded to indistinct greyness.

The desk where his colleagues worked was deserted. The waiting area he'd ushered so many parents and children through looked much bigger and lonelier than he'd remembered. The atmosphere accounted for most of that perception. The situation itself did everything it could to magnify the mood. Putting that aside as best he could, Dr. Ash continued searching for the man he followed.

"Where have you gone?" he said out loud, his own voice sounding thin to him. Despite the gravity of the situation, a game of hide-n-go-seek came to mind. But that was quickly reconsidered and exchanged for the more appropriate Ghosts in the graveyard. His chuckle was more ironic than humorous. Purposefully, the searching continued.

"I should name you man!" he yelled out to no response. "I can't call out to… "Mysterious Unknown Shadowy Aimlessly-Roaming Trauma" can I? So, now you're…MT. That's what you are - MT."

"MT! MT! MT!" he yelled never really expecting any acknowledgment. It echoed through the blackness.

The detour he'd taken disturbed him. The feeling that he'd been steered away from what was believed to have been the best course of action made him a little angry. The decision to make his way out quickly and intact had been the right decision he believed. Nothing had changed. His desire was still to get out stat but seeing the one he now called MT, forced him to reconsider.

He continued because he felt he owed it. MT had almost been overlooked once before. Doing it twice was unthinkable.

Like before, the doctor remained unable to make up even the slightest bit of ground. Each time he'd spotted him, the distance couldn't be closed. The frustration of that fact only added to an already overly infuriating situation.

The attempt was worth the risk but there was a limit to his sacrifice. If his task at hand couldn't be accomplished relatively soon, the effort would have to be abandoned. Nathaniel told himself that he would go no farther than that department. If nothing came of the search, he would look for an out as soon as possible. He told himself that if it came to that, he'd have to be content with the amount of energy he'd already expended.

As he walked, his mind wandered. The thoughts of what he'd experienced since coming to, mingled with the disjointed disturbing images that he'd worked so hard to suppress. The significance behind those thoughts and images was something he felt the need to evade. Distractions that strong would hinder progress. Unfortunately for him, those distractions were persistent. His wounded head couldn't have been the cause he felt; he didn't believe he was hurt that badly. The things he'd seen were not hallucinations. The amount of stress he was under was the next consideration, but he'd been trained thoroughly and was experienced in high-stress situations.

With those things ruled out, reality- no matter how improbable it was- was the only possibility. The logic was there but acceptance wasn't. He had his doubts.

Some vague correlation seemed to be drawn for each apparition he'd seen. That same vagueness also left each of those undefined. No names came to mind and no other details lent themselves to those images.

Just as expected, his distracted thoughts forced his eye off of his goal. He'd been looking for the man he'd named MT., which was in-of-itself a separate enigma.

The obvious questions persisted: Who was he? Why was he still there? Why hadn't he made his way out? Why had he been non-responsive?

Other puzzles resurfaced in that stillness. Those remained unsolved as well. Those questions were even more difficult to rationalize. What could possibly explain what he'd witnessed Aegis do back in the Burn Unit? The things that happened back there were unnatural!

The fire and shattered glass actually seemed willful. Aegis had reacted inhumanly. The thought of taking Aegis at his word was initially rejected, but viable explanations were elusive. Aegis used the term "Angel" to describe himself. That seemed absurd at first, but a doubt had been raised.

Nathaniel had always considered himself to be a pragmatist. Empirical evidence and the scientific method were what he believed in. The provable interested him not the improbable. He had little patience for thoughts of that kind.

The afterlife was in a way the enemy in his mind. Hours and years were expended trying to help people avoid it. The suggestion of it from Aegis was easily dismissible at first but then the fire and glass argued otherwise.

...Aegis- an "Angel"?

That thought screamed absurdity to the doctor. He had to maintain that reasoning. It was necessary in his situation to stay the course. There was a task to accomplish before he could extricate himself. That task allowed no distractions. He was a doctor in a crisis; someone was depending on him. Angels were reserved for the domain of desperation and sentimentality. That was a way of thinking that he'd abandoned. He'd lost his childhood qualities a very long time ago. Aegis would have to remain something other than an "Angelic" being for now.

But the fact that he questioned his strength to hold to that resolution remained.

Suddenly, his attention was stolen away from his indecision. Although he couldn't pinpoint its position, a sound caught his ear; bare feet on cold tile. He froze where he was in an attempt to hone in on their direction. He found it hard to determine if they were moving away or toward him. All he could tell was that whoever it was, they were moving fast.

He circled around, believing that he was sure of where it was coming from, but he was mistaken. Suddenly, at his back, a blur moved past him like a piece of the dark separating itself. Realizing it, he spun just soon enough to see a figure moving away quickly, farther into the section than he'd ever intended to go. Pure instinct compelled him to pursue.

There was no attempt to call out because all others had gone unheeded before. Catching the person was his intention. The Dr. wasn't far behind, but he did have some ground to make up. Every turned corner prevented a clear view of who he was chasing, but it became quickly obvious that this wasn't the same person he'd been after earlier. This was a much smaller body than before. It almost seemed to him that he was chasing… a child! He was, after all, in Pediatrics. That suggested that some poor child had been left behind in the wake of whatever mayhem had gone down.

The kid moved through the halls hastily. Nathaniel reasoned that he himself wasn't the cause for that because the little one was already running from something. Something else had been responsible for that apparent panic. As he began to make up ground, he couldn't help but look warily backward over his own shoulder.

Down one hallway and then another he followed. The child seemed to be running blindly. Whatever set the child off must have been overwhelming. Nathaniel worked hard to keep him in sight. He decided to take a calculated risk by cutting through offices. He knew the layout and felt sure that he could get ahead. He maneuvered around tables and chairs, and nearly went down after stumbling over something unseen in the darkness. When he burst through the outer door on the other side of those offices, he found that his gamble paid off, but a little too well.

Dr. Ash had come out just steps ahead of the shadow he'd been pursuing, enough to have positioned himself in the perfect spot for a collision. Exactly that happened and they both went down in a tangle. A high-pitched short scream came out then, informing the

Dr. that he'd in fact been chasing a girl. He'd tried to absorb the brunt of the hit by allowing her to land on top of him and not the hard floor. He thought he'd protected her. It became very apparent that she didn't see things that way. A series of sharp screams cut the quiet as she fought to separate herself. The girl was panic-stricken. For all he knew, she believed that he was some un-named menace she'd been running from the entire time. Reassurance to the contrary was going to be difficult for him at best. "Stop, please! Wait! I'm not trying to..." Nathaniel began.

He couldn't finish that plea because from behind him, a different cry sounded. Still struggling with the little girl, he could only spin enough to partially catch sight of another figure pulling itself from the dark, heading straight for them.

Then they collided.

Another child had appeared and attacked him for some unknown reason.

Angry grunting was mixed with fearful screaming, leaving the Dr. thoroughly confused and besieged. With the girl's thin wrists clamped in his grasp, he turned to defend himself against what he found to be a smaller boy trying his best to bludgeon him with a bedpan.

The boy's small size didn't hinder the pummeling he was able to inflict. He was clearly very motivated. Trying to defend himself, Nathaniel let go of his grip on one arm ofthe shrill young girl to fight off the assault from behind.

That mistake cost him exactly two kicks and a handful of slaps from her newly freed limb. Trying to protect himself made him release his grip on her completely. She awkwardly slid backward, almost crab-like, to separate herself from the Dr. as the boy continued his attack.

The corridor was filled with the sounds of the girl's screaming, the boy's grunting, the Dr.'s groaning, and one metal bedpan ringing out with each hit. One good shot to his temple reminded him of the wound there he'd been downplaying. That provided the two little ones an opportunity and they exploited it. They took off down the hall as quickly as their legs could move them.

"Son-of-a-…!" he began and then censored. "Wait! I only want to help!"

The fact that the two were unconvinced was quite clear. So, Nathaniel pulled himself up and took off after them again. The distance between them wasn't as great as before which allowed him to keep pace. He found himself on an unanticipated tour of Pediatrics as the children maneuvered their way through the area. It didn't escape him that every time he found someone that he thought he could help, everything about those situations turned for the worse. He did not want that past to become prophetic. Protecting those kids became especially important to him.

He tried to reason with them again saying, "Don't be afraid of me, I'm a doctor here!" But that wasn't persuasive. One more corner brought them all to a set of sealed doors. Frantically, the two threw their little bodies against those heavy doors and began to struggle to get to the other side.

The Dr. came to an abrupt stop so as not to add fuel to the fire. He saw that the two had their backs pressed against the doors, possessing the expression that anything or anyone cornered like that would have. Between breathless pants, he did his best to calm both his voice and the terrified kids.

They remained guarded, poised to respond to any movement from Nathaniel defensively. Escaping was their more obvious desire though. They would have broken down those doors if they could have, trapped as they were and staring wide-eyed.

"I'm sorry. I didn't mean to scare you. I'm a doctor, I work here. I don't believe I've seen either of you before. Are you new here?" The only response to that was   wariness. "Never mind, that's not important. Why were you running from me?"

"Why were you chasing us!" the girl said accusingly. The younger boy leaned toward her and said something inaudibly then, which made her reply protectively, "You won't get burned up."

That was puzzling. The doctor took that brief moment to have a good look at them both. The girl had striking faun-like eyes. Those eyes were large, alert, and innocent but they also contradicted her determinedly clenched mouth. Her long black hair was tightly pulled back in a ponytail and her form was thin and fragile looking. Despite that, she stood defensively in front of the smaller boy.

Like the girl, the boy's complexion was similar to Nathaniel's. His hair was curly and a little messy. His face was expressionless, but his posture conveyed his fear. The young boy's eyes never lingered too long on the Dr. Whatever inner strength he'd used in defense of his protector moments before, seemed to have dissipated. He'd become passive. He stood behind the older girl as if he was used to the position. The two of them had a haggard appearance and seemed to be working to maintain their composure. Of course, they were all in a very desperate circumstance, but it seemed clear that wasn't the lone cause for the kids' distress. Something specific seemed to have them terrified. It was reasonable to believe that for all either of those children knew, that horrible thing was Nathaniel. They were certainly acting as if that was the case. He awkwardly tried to engage them again.

"You don't need to be afraid of me. Like I said, I'm a doctor and we're all going to be Ok now. We're in this together. What are your names?"

The two stared distrustfully back in response. The young boy let his eyes shift over to the girl for direction but hers never wavered. She was undoubtedly weighing his risk to them. After a time, it seemed she reached a decision because her determined and protective expression softened somewhat. Then, quietly and cautiously, she chose to answer his question. She said, "Gabby and Trace."

"Ok...those are your names then? Gabby and Trace...?"

"Yes. I'm Gabby, he's Trace." she affirmed.

"Alright, that's a start. My name is Nathaniel. Why are you here alone? How could you have been left behind?"

He got no response. They stared with a little less apprehension than before, but they hadn't dropped their guard completely. He looked back at them and thought that they looked like a combination of both strength and fragility. Then, he reasoned that it didn't matter why they were there by themselves. What truly mattered was how he planned to keep them safe from that point on.

"Gabby, do you know if anyone else is still here? Have you seen any other people?"

Breathlessly she replied, "Not people..." Trace stared down at the floor distractedly but managed to shake his head in agreement with her curious assertion.

"What do you mean? Are you saying there is something...inhuman...here?"

She seemed unable to answer that question. But their fear and seriousness about it told the Dr. all that he needed to know. They believed wholeheartedly that there was some significant threat to them there. They believed it, but they were also very young and in a very menacing setting. It would be unusual if their fears hadn't gotten the better of them. It was all he could do to keep his own from getting the better of him. Although he'd seen some things in the darkness, keeping those things to himself was his singular option. He knew he had to lie to them as best he could, the way that adults often do. It was meant to protect.

"There's nothing to worry about." he began calmly. "Shadows play tricks. The smallest sound becomes gigantic when you're alone. I understand. But we're going to get out of here, Ok?"

The kids looked at each other briefly and then back at him. They seemed to come to some silent agreement. Then Gabby simply said, "Ok."

"Good. You guys must be tired after all that running. Let's take a breath for a minute." He gestured for them to sit on a short wooden bench across from where they were standing, and they moved over gingerly. When they finally sat, he knelt in front of them, trying hard not to be imposing. The thought occurred to him that if he could get the two children to talk about what they feared, that maybe they'd be able to see those fears as insubstantial after all. So, he made the attempt.

"Can you tell me what you were running from Gabby?"

The girl seemed to weigh her answer. Then she said, "You."

"I know you thought it was me, but something had to have scared you even before I saw you. You were already running like you were terrified. That's when I started trying to catch you. So, what scared you so bad?"

"It was you...but it wasn't. I guess it couldn't have been- could it?" she said.

"So, was it a man then?"

"Not exactly..." Gabby cautioned. "He was more fire than man."

That answer shocked and worried Nathaniel. The obvious impossibility of it confused him, yet the sincerity she conveyed worried him. That sincerity seemed to rule out some clichéd childish nightmare. That and the fact that whatever scared her also scared the boy. Trying to reason away whatever degree of imagination they may have added to the situation seemed like the best way to calm them.

"More fire than man..." he repeated. "How can that be possible? I can understand if maybe you saw someone whose clothes were burning...or...maybe the flames were lighting their face in such a way that..."

"No, you're wrong." Gabby maintained.

"You both probably..." he tried to continue.

"The fire was alive!" she insisted.

"Listen, kids, I'm going to be honest with you. There has been some sort of -accident- here. What you saw may have been someone that was unfortunately hurt, possibly very badly, in that accident. I can imagine how scary that might have seemed, but I promise that it wasn't anything really bad."

"I know grownups are supposed to make us kids believe that bad things don't exist, but that's not true. There is something bad in here and when you see it, you'd better run just like we did.", Gabby warned.

The incident outside the Burn Unit came back to him then. That thought was followed by still unexplained images throughout Intensive Care. After some of the things he'd seen, the doctor had to make a conscious effort not to legitimize her fears, by adding his own. So, he did what he could to suppress them, and he did what he could to allay theirs.

"Ok, whatever you were afraid of is behind us now. We're in one piece and we're going to stay that way. Now, I'll admit to being a little scared of the dark, so it would be great if the two of you would stay close to me, you know, just to be on the safe side."

Trace again leaned in to share something quietly with Gabby. A whisper went between them and then a nod of agreement. With that, Gabby turned to the doctor to fill him in. She said, "You're fibbing again, and he knows it. You're not scared of the dark. You're just trying to make us feel better. We're not babies."

A slight smile of appreciation formed on the doc's mouth. He'd worked with a lot of children throughout his practice and preferred not talking down to them if it wasn't necessary. He acknowledged their sensibleness and decided to be forthcoming with them from that point on.

"Listen, I saw someone too. I've been trying to catch up to him. For some reason, he is always moving away from me. I have to assume that he's not well. But this was just a figure, just someone alone in the darkness. There wasn't anything unusual about him, he wasn't scary, and he wasn't chasing me. Isn't it possible that you saw the same person and just got a little frightened?"

Trace shook his head without hesitation. Gabby stated, "No." definitively.

"Tell me what happened. Tell me what you saw."

The two kids turned to each other for reassurance and then back to him. For a moment, Nathaniel didn't think that either would answer. They both stared at him somewhat distrustfully. To push the issue could only work against him he believed. Just before he made the decision to drop the matter and find another approach, he began to get an answer from the girl.

Tentatively, she began, "You know how you can tell if something is real or if it's a dream...?" The question hung in the silence unanswered for a moment. Dr. Ash had no clue.

"Blink." That was Gabby's one-word answer. "You never blink when you dream."

The Dr. thought about that revelation and wondered at its significance. It was something he never would have considered. But the assertion also seemed to intriguingly resonate in him.

Then the girl continued softly.

"I put my hands over my eyes and closed them tight, but it didn't help. It was still there when I opened 'em back up again. That was how I knew it was real. I've never seen anything as scary as that before."

"What...? What did you see?" the doctor broke in anxiously.

"We saw you, burning alive, and chasing us!" She went on, relaying her nightmarish experience in detail. Her description painted the picture of a man-like monster, burning from head to foot, hunched over slightly. Overly long arms extended widely across the width of the hallway and grasped menacingly for the children as they ran. Gabby related the ghostly way that he moved; that apparition wasn't running after them in some human-like way. The thing that pursued them hovered inches above the ground with the billowy distortion of heat under it. It used those long, burning arms like hooks, driving them into the sides of the walls and pulling its hideousness forward menacingly.

"Gabby, you know that's not possible. It wasn't real, and it wasn't me. I'm not a demon. There is no such thing.

Look at me. I'm not burning, and I wasn't chasing you. You had to have imagined it."

Trace's face twisted in anger at that. Gabby's expression hardened immediately as well, and she protested, "I told you I blinked! I told you I blinked, and it was still coming for us! That means it was real! You never blink when it's only a...!"

"OK, I'm sorry! I'm sorry." Dr. Ash said quickly to calm the situation. "I didn't mean to upset you. But you have to admit that that is incredible." He also had to admit to himself the impossibility of them both having the same delusion. Something was seen. Some truth was buried in what they believed. But it would've been wrong to encourage their fears, so he kept that thought to himself.

"Listen, guys. We're together now and we're going to stay together. If we all look out for one another, we'll all be perfectly fine. I promise not to let anything happen to either of you. But I'd appreciate it if you would also look out for me. You two are obviously very smart and brave, so will you watch my back too?"

The Dr. looked down at the children and smiled warmly. His intention was to ingratiate himself to them. He wanted to establish a dependency between them. It was a technique that he'd learned throughout his tenure. Like before, it proved to be effective. Both of the children seemed to be slightly bolstered by his need and their response to him was eager nodding and bravely putting on smiles.

"Good. I feel safer already." Dr. Ash said.

A quick look around them then informed Dr. Ash that they'd actually gone further into the building than previously believed and farther away from the exit he'd been making his way toward. Here was one more instance where he'd been turned around.

He silently wondered if he'd ever make it out.

The difference this time was that he'd be able to lead these two to safety, unlike the previous failed attempts. Whatever amount of time he'd lost became negligible with that realization.

They'd taken a momentary rest, but they weren't in any position to become lax. They needed to keep moving, so the doctor suggested that they continue on. The kids had no desire to linger and followed readily. As they moved, both Gabby and Trace kept their eyes wide. Their heads turned in all directions alertly and they repeatedly bumped into each other and into Nathaniel. To distract them, he tried to get them to open up a little saying, "So, you don't talk too much huh? You're kinda the quiet type, aren't you Trace?"

The boy answered that question with a shy glance and a brief nod.

"Trace talks all the time. He talks a lot. You just

have to listen close. Trace is really smart and funny too." Gabby offered. "He's very good at puzzles and knows tons of riddles-don't you Trace?" she asked for the most part rhetorically. "I can never remember jokes and riddles. I guess I'm not very good at games. I'm good in school though. I make sure to always do all the extra credit. But I was talking about him, wasn't I?"

"You definitely live up to your name, don't you?" Dr. Ash said teasingly.

"Huh? Oh yeah. I've been told that before. You're funny. But anyway..."

Gabby went on for some time, which was OK because it not only kept the kids' minds off of their immediate situation, it also gave the Dr. time to think. He was understandably preoccupied with the things he'd seen and been through. He was usually very good with puzzles himself but the answers to the one he was in just then escaped him. Solving a puzzle requires an understanding of the rules. He'd been provided with only some of the pieces he'd need and none of the rules as far as he could tell. The things he'd seen couldn't be possible. The damage and abandonment of the facility couldn't be explained. Exactly how either Riven or Aegis fit into the scenario was still unclear. The most definitive things that were spelled out for him were the penalties. What little information he did have wasn't enough to even attempt a guess at the larger puzzle that surrounded them. Any additional bit that could be gathered might lead him to a resolution.

"Where are your parents?" He interrupted Gabby in mid-sentence.

The question immediately quieted the girl. She may not have liked him asking.

"Not here." she replied.

The doctor began to pursue it further but then thought better of it. He could tell by the way she responded that she had no desire to clarify and he didn't want to upset either of them any more than they already were. So, he took a different approach by asking, "Can you tell me why you're here in the hospital?"

That question didn't seem to have the same effect on them and after Trace whispered to Gabby, she gave her answer.

"I don't know." was all she said.

There didn't seem to be any deception or avoidance in that answer. She'd just stated it as simply as she could it seemed. The fact that they didn't appear to know the basics of their own situation didn't bother the doctor much. The failed attempt to solve the conundrum had only provided yet another disconnected puzzle piece. That bothered him more.

They introduced their own personal riddle to the mix. Putting aside his unanswered questions would be necessary. But he'd hoped that answers would lead to answers. Instead, he questioned if there was in fact a single mosaic comprised of all of their puzzle pieces.

He made another attempt. "So, how long have you been here?"

"A while." was her simple answer.

"Now is not the time to clam up on me Gabby. Is there something wrong? Did something happen to make you forget? Isn't there anything that you can...?

"Where are your parents?" Gabby blurted out.

"What? Why would you ask me that?" the doctor responded with confusion.

"How long have you been here?" she said instead of an answer.

He paused for a moment, questioning her motivations. "You're asking strange questions Gabby. I can't help but wonder why. What are you trying to get at?"

"Why am I asking strange questions? They were the same ones you asked."

It was unclear to him if she was somehow confused or if she was being purposefully evasive. No progress was being made, so Nathaniel backed off. He said, "It's OK if you don't want to talk about it."

"Do you?"

"Do I? Do I what?"

"Want to talk about your parents?" Gabby probed.

At first, the suggestion seemed unusual, but the thought quickly arose that she may have been reaching out to him in an unconsciously round-about way. He'd seen it before in his practice with troubled children. He'd have to reveal something of himself if he was to draw them out at all.

"Quid pro quo then I guess. My parents huh...? Well, I don't even know where to start. They are... complicated. You see, I was raised by people that weren't my biological parents. My Aunt and Uncle took me in when I was around your age I guess."

"Where did your real mother and father go?", Gabby inquired.

"That's a long story that I'll save for another time, I think. Suffice it to say, they were out of the picture, and in came my Aunt and Uncle."

Trace leaned in a little to mumble something to Gabby, and then she relayed his question, "Were they nice?"

"Well..." the pause in his answer would have revealed so much to older listeners, "... they were fine, they were probably like anyone else's parents." he said half-heartedly.

"That doesn't sound so nice to me. Were they mean? They sound mean to me." Gabby said despite the Dr.'s attempt.

"They were strict. That's different."

Trace quietly weighed in again and allowed Gabby to translate his comments. She relayed, "How were they strict? Did they take away your video games and your cell phone?"

A chuckle came out at that suggestion. "Gabby, when I was your age, I didn't have one to take. My-parents - didn't have much tolerance for those kinds of extravagancies-for those kinds of extras. Those things were distractions to them."

"Why?" the girl questioned.

"They were distractions because they expected me to spend my time studying. See, my aunt was in medicine, a surgical nurse, and my uncle was an administrator in a college. So, their idea of playtime didn't include video games."

"Lame!" Gabby said in agreement with Trace. "That's sad. No fun!"

"It wasn't so bad. I've made it to where I am now right?"

"Where are you?" she said.

A short chuckle was the response to that question. That revealed his uncertainty.

"I'm not sure how to answer that to be honest Gabby."

"I think you're in a bad place. If it wasn't so bad back then, wouldn't you be in a good place now?"

"Things aren't so cut and dry ya know. It may have been hard at times but..." he began.

"When was it hard?" Gabby cut in.

"What? I...don't know. Everyone goes through times when..." Nathaniel started.

"When was it hard for you? What happened?"

He would have been content to let the matter drop but the children had different ideas. Several questions were asked in rapid-fire about the Dr.'s parents. Being candid was never his instinctual reaction to probing questions, but he chose to play along. To his mind, they were seeking a distraction from the situation they were in.

"Well, to answer your question, I guess it was hard when I didn't do as well as I was expected to. Like anyone, I'm imperfect despite the public face I wear. Doing well was a requirement that I sometimes fell short of. When that happened, my parents didn't react like the ones on television. Thinking back on it now, I guess that could be difficult on a kid. Ya know, to your own mind you never age much at all. Your perception of yourself stays basically unaltered as you go through life. You just experience new things through the eyes of the person you were when you became first aware- at whatever age that may have been. I was pretty young when I started to feel the pressure from them to excel."

His speech had become wistful and detached.

"I'll never forget the time when I was made to try out for the debate team in school. I had no interest in that at all, but my mother thought that it would make me strong and unafraid to confront anyone as I grew up and went out into the world. Well, I did horribly and didn't make it. Maybe it was subconscious, but I paid for it just the same. They made me debate them and called it instruction. I called it punishment though. Man, having to debate with your own parents for hours on why I in fact *wasn't* a loser is not what they would have done on all those old TV shows... I think it actually had the inverse effect though. My arguments weren't sincere. I believed the opposite of what I was saying; I believed that I was inferior. What else could I have believed? Their arguments rang true and were easier to believe. Then, after all that, dad used his influence to get me onto the very same team that already considered me to be inadequate. I don't know, maybe I was." His voice trailed off and the sudden quiet pointed out how much he'd been revealing. He'd allowed himself to be more vulnerable with them than he'd been with anyone in recent memory. Something about those two allowed him to speak freely. Something about them didn't make him regret it.

"Trace doesn't think that's all. That didn't sound so bad to him. He thinks you haven't said the worst of it yet." Gabby relayed.

"Oh really…? That's what you think huh?"

"We think you're holding back." she continued…

"Well, even if that's true, I'm not sure this is the time or place for…"

"Why not?" she pressed.

"Because the truth is, it's none of your-"

"Didn't they love you?" was relayed by Gabby. It had in fact been Trace's question.

The answer came pensively, "I'm sure they did. I always had a warm bed and I was never hungry."

"Wow, don't get all emotional." Gabby teased.

"Yeah, I know- pretty under-whelming huh? I guess it sounds like I'm selling it short, but I don't mean to. It was fine. Why don't we talk about something else? How about you tell me…"

A quick exchange between the two kids and then an interruption from Gabby decidedly stopped the Dr.'s attempt short. She'd stated, not in so many words, that his talking abated their fears and distracted them from their situation and that they only wanted him to ease their passing. Her argument was convincing enough to persuade him. So, he asked, "What do you want to know?"

That question was answered by Gabby with, "Why are you so sad?"

The perceptiveness of the girl's question was something the Dr. didn't want to admit to. There are instances when a complete stranger calls out your secluded truth as if they had some extra perception that one couldn't guard against or predict. That was one of those times. It suggests that maybe those so-called strangers, aren't that at all.

Regardless, rarely would someone who'd experienced that occurrence readily play into it. Denial is a much more convenient and defensive position to take. That is exactly what the Dr. chose to do. "That's a strange question. I didn't realize I was so sad."

"You had to say that, I know, but now what is the real answer?" she responded.

"How do I answer something like that? I don't know. Why is anyone really sad? A puppy dies-a contest is lost-you get rained on-you feel abandoned and alone-you're..."

"That's how you answer a question like that-with the truth." she stated simply.

"What?"

"You said you feel abandoned and alone."

"No, I didn't." he protested.

"You did. You just said you did." Gabby insisted.

"No... I was just talking...I didn't say that was what *I* felt."

"I know I may be young, but I know what sub-consciously means. I'm pretty smart. You let it slip out and I heard it. No take-backs." She insisted.

Her manner was disarming to him. Maybe it was her age, maybe it was their surroundings and circumstance or maybe it was a combination. Whatever it was, he let his guard remain down when he would have otherwise maintained it.

"I guess you got me huh? Fine. The truth is, I've spent a lot of time on my own; more than I've allowed myself to think about until now, to be honest with you. I was physically abandoned by two people as a child and I was emotionally abandoned as I was growing up, which in turn only served as training for me to do the same thing to anyone that put themselves in the unfortunate position of possibly caring for me. All that, adds up to me being isolated and alone. I'm sad because I have a good reason to be. So, there's your answer."

At that point, Trace leaned close to Gabby to whisper his usual input. Dr. Ash had become accustomed to their way of communication and waited for their exchange to end before asking, "What did he say?"

Gabby looked up with sympathetic eyes and conveyed Traces comment. He'd said that he understood. The boy claimed to know what it was like to be alone and wished it was different. The inference was that the wish applied to both of them.

"I can see I won't be able to put anything past you two huh? Your parents must have their hands full." he said in a baiting way but to no response. "How is it that I've never seen you before today?"

"This is a big place." Gabby replied.

"That's true, but I think I'd have noticed you."

"Why?" was Gabby's response.

"There's something about you..." Nathaniel stated, his thought trailing off.

There was specifically something about Trace that stirred some undefined feeling in him. He struggled to identify that elusive feeling the boy elicited. What he eventually came to realize was that, despite the fact that they'd just met, there was a vague familiarity about Trace that was undeniable. His mannerisms, his demeanor, and even his features evoked something akin to recognition. Nathaniel saw something of himself in that quiet boy. What he saw was a profound reticence that he himself had struggled against in his past. That fact made him realize how he would have prospered from someone, figuratively, diving in to pull him out of himself. He projected that need onto the boy. So, naturally, he made the attempt.

"Hey, big guy, you doin', OK? Why so quiet Trace?" There was only a non-committal stare in response. The Dr. searched for some in-road to get beyond Trace's reluctance. Then, he noticed something. The boy had a very colorful fake tattoo on his arm. He tried but was unable to make out what the image was.

"What's that on your arm?" he asked but got no answer. "I can't make it out, but it looks cool. Can you keep a secret? I know I'm supposed to be all stiff and professional, but I am a big fan of ink. I like tattoos. Don't tell on me, OK?"

At that point, Gabby spoke up again saying, "You're a doctor, you're not supposed to like that kind of stuff."

"Oh really? Well, maybe I should have been told that before I got mine done."

With that declaration, the two kids smiled widely, obviously impressed with what was shared with them. He'd been able to lower the defenses the kids displayed earlier with that smile. Nathaniel saw an opening and made another attempt. "I'm still a little curious about..."

"Was it just you and your...mom and dad? That's why you were sad too." Gabby posed the question refocusing on Nathaniel.

"Listen," he began.

"'Cause that seems lonely-just you and them. Was it just you and them?"

"Right... I'm not gonna get much out of you, am I?"

"I don't know.", she said.

"How about if we start moving again.", he suggested in hopes of a brief respite from probing questions. Gabby and Trace nodded somewhat hesitantly and then took up positions on either side of Nathaniel. Their pace was cautious and steady. Some measure of acceptance had been reached between the three, but they'd come to no such agreement with the shadows they moved through.

The plan was understood without being stated. The three of them would get through Pediatrics as quickly as possible and leave the building without looking back. To Nathaniel, that also meant cutting earlier losses and counting two kids' lives as a significant win considering the situation.

Their breathing came loudly with their urgency, and the backward glances continued to increase in frequency. Occasionally, one or the other of them would lean in, whisper something, and then resume their watch. Nothing more could be said to reassure either of them or to allay their natural fear, so no effort was made. They moved quietly for a short time, but that didn't suit the children. Their imaginations were beginning to overtake their confidence in the doctor.

What started as a slight tugging of his arms by the children soon turned into them urging.

"What's wrong?" Nathaniel asked them both. "Why are you both so jumpy all of a sudden?"

"Trace has a bad feeling. So, do I. This place is scary enough already, but something seems even scarier now."

"Did you hear something? I didn't hear anything.'"

"No, it wasn't anything I heard or saw. It was something I felt; like one of those pre-ignitions." She insisted.

"Like one of what? I think you mean premonition, don't you?" Nathaniel corrected.

"Yes, one of those. You knew what I meant. We just feel like something is really wrong. Don't you feel it?" Gabby asked.

"Actually, I don't feel a thing, to tell the truth."

"Is that natural?" was her follow-up.

Lost in the search for the meaning of that question, a corner was turned blindly. The three of them nearly collided with the backside of an up-ended gurney blocking that turn. Maneuvering around it, all of them caught sight of what was on the other side simultaneously.

Gabby's scream was almost immediately muffled as the doctor swung an arm around her mouth to mute her.

He'd reacted quickly but that sound still escaped and echoed down the hall for what seemed an unnaturally long time.

Each of them felt a moment of intense apprehension that the sound had betrayed them somehow. They waited motionlessly for something ominous to happen.

The reason for that scream was very real. There, staring back at them was the body of a hanged woman. She was slight and pretty; her eyes wide. Her expression was distressed. Fresh and haunting tears slid from those eyes. Obvious questions ran through Nathaniel's mind. Why was it done? Who was she? How could this be allowed to happen? Gabby looked as if she was going to ask some questions of her own but thought better of it. The Dr. didn't need to investigate any further. The girl was gone. The scene was yet another unexplainable occurrence that had to be suppressed.

The two young ones turned their backs away from the sight and allowed themselves to be guided forward and past it.

Gabby spoke then in a muted tone, asking, "What do you think happens when you die?"

That particular question was counter-productive at the moment. The thought of death was not something Nathaniel wanted to entertain, and it definitely wasn't something to be discussed with children. So, he avoided the question by answering rather feebly, "I don't know."

"I know what I believe." She replied. "I know that there are people just waiting to be born in Heaven. They're all in line waiting for their turn. When we die, we all go back and the next person in line is born."

"That statement is incredibly facile!"

To his astonishment, the doctor heard Trace's first words. He was startled as much by the sound as he was by what was said. The look on his face as he turned to Trace gave it all away.

"Don't look so surprised doctor. Her infantile beliefs have always been a bane to me. Gabby, despite my affection for you, your nonsensical thought process in this matter is intolerable." Trace continued. "What you said is illogical. Are you suggesting that there are countless entities, fully developed astral psyches, holding tiny red numbered tickets somewhere, just idly standing by until their opportunity to fill in the gap of some random deceased soul comes to fruition? Is that what you want to subscribe to?"

"Well..." Gabby began.

"Trace, how in the world...!" Nathaniel interjected.

"It would seem so rudimentary..." the formerly stoic boy cut in. "Our bodies are hardware. That hardware is useful for one purpose; acting as an antenna. That antenna's sole purpose is the harnessing of the energy that makes us recognizable as human beings. Our minds collect, focus, direct, and store all those biochemical impulses that constitute the trite lives we lead. When the body dies, to swing back to your earlier question, the capacity to effectively contain those identifying energetic puzzle pieces is lost entirely. That energy becomes un-tethered and intermingles with the omnipresent miasma. Understand?"

Both Gabby and the doctor remained silent.

"So," he went on, "The thought that our personal essence leaves at the point of death and goes through some "universal turn style" to make room for the next person doesn't seem plausible, does it?"

Nathaniel found himself astounded by the eloquence of the boy who'd up to that point, displayed nothing to indicate that he was anything more than a scared child.

"I told you he was really smart Doc. I didn't mention that he could get on your nerves though, did I?" Gabby said.

"Remarkable. Outstanding. Can you tell me..." the doctor began but cut his question short. The reason he stopped was his sudden perception of a rise in temperature. It came so rapidly; it demanded his attention. The specific threat remained unidentified for the moment, but he believed the source was obvious. Again, he'd permitted himself to linger too long and al-lowed the fire chasing him to gain ground. His priority became the children again. His one recurring and urgent thought was to help them immediately.

The moment that desire came to his mind, a wall of heat rolled into them like waves against rock. A growing and familiar panic began to overtake him. He suggested that they continue on toward the exit.

As they walked, several attempts to open them up were made again. Each was only minimally more successful than the one before. He found that the children were very guarded all of a sudden. Trace, inexplicably reverted to his barely perceptible whispers. Something made him reticent again. Gabby was talkative enough for the two of them but only so long as nothing became overly personal. She had no hesitance to go on about the usual things that interested young kids, but direct questions were avoided. The Dr.'s experience taught him that forcing the issue would never work. So, he listened patiently and waited for opportunities.

The Dr. led them through the facility as urgently as he could without scaring them any more than they already were. They did their best to keep stride, but their little legs had their limits. From where they'd literally bumped into each other, it was a matter of a few corridors standing between them and the nearest exit. They made their way steadily. Without realizing it, he'd become preoccupied with his own thoughts. Trying to make sense of all that had happened up to that point caused Gabby's voice to become droning background noise. He found that he was frustrated.

Nothing had been in his control in any way since he'd come to. People were lost; people he considered to be under his care. That fact brought up feelings of inadequacy in him which only added to the frustration. Not a single reason presented itself for the chaos they were all in. Confusion was burrowing into his usually structured and disciplined mind. Maybe fatigue was the cause. Maybe the stress could be solely responsible. It was possible that his wound was to blame. Regardless of the reason, Dr. Ash felt that he was becoming hazier. Despite that, he never considered taking the time he would need to evaluate himself. The flaw in that remained to be seen.

As they moved, the heat at his back seemed to intensify. He felt sure of it but didn't know if the children had realized. They gave no indication. He let himself lag behind a bit and snuck a look over his shoulder to see if there was any immediate threat. Nothing was behind him but that heat. That was enough. The thought of what he'd already been through angered him but also kept him moving.

When the doctor turned back around, he nearly collided with Gabby and Trace who had stopped in their tracks for some reason. Dr. Ash immediately tried to get them moving again without questioning what had immobilized them in the first place. He tried to urge them on by saying, "This isn't a good place to stop guys. C'mon..." But there was no response. He tried again with, "We really need to keep..." but didn't finish.

The looks that were frozen on their faces seemed like their worst fears had just materialized from nothingness. Only then, did the direction of both their stares catch his eye.

Down a long passageway, the thing that they'd described to him earlier was crouching threateningly.

That sight was what left Gabby and Trace petrified, just as it left Dr. Ash at that point. None of them so much as twitched. What they were seeing was too impossible to accept but too real to dismiss. A "thing" hovered above the ground like a fiery specter. Its body was long and hunched with a distortion of heated air surrounding it. It seemed to heave its chest as it breathed a hoarse and disturbing noise. This was what the kids claimed to have seen before; this was what they'd been running from. The thing was exactly what they'd described and what he'd previously discounted. That was then.

Things had changed. He didn't allow himself the luxury of denying his eyes. He didn't waste time trying to rationalize it away. A complete understanding of what he was witnessing wasn't necessary to know the trepidation it evoked or the danger it posed. It took a moment for the Dr. to realize that its back was turned to them and they hadn't been spotted yet. He felt that they might be able to backtrack and remain unseen. They could circle around somehow and take another route out of the building. Cautiously, he began to lead them away by inches at a time.

HSSSSSSSTT!!!

They were spun upon.

"No! Not now!"

They'd been given away by the radio Dr. Ash was carrying!

The doctor didn't need to tell the kids to run, he needed to keep up. None of them risked a look back when they heard the shrill cry. For that reason, none of them identified the figure that had been silhouetted in the darkness, his presence hidden by the monstrous form.

Not one single thought of where they were running came up. Trace led the way, the doctor quickly caught up and Gabby followed close behind. They wound their way in any direction that was away from what chased them. Becoming lost wasn't a consideration. That could never override their fear.

The doctor watched Trace burst his way through a pair of doors just ahead of him. When he went through them himself, he hesitated just on the other side, realizing that Gabby had lost ground and wasn't right behind him. He spun to collect the girl at the risk of losing Trace; who had continued without them both. He began to call to Trace but was drowned out by the sound of the beginnings of something crumbling. Ahead of him, a section of the wall came down into the passageway, cutting off the doctor from Trace. The boy had gotten too far ahead and was on the other side of the rubble, alone. The doctor feverishly began to claw his way through the debris to get to Trace, calling out his name for affirmation that he was unhurt.

"Trace! Trace! If you can hear me, just stay where you are. We've lost Gabby! But I'm going to get her! I'll be right back! We'll both be back for you!"

Turning desperately, going back for Gabby, he saw the ceiling collapsing on the other side of the doors. He could see Gabby running toward him. But she was too late. She became a shadow in the dust and debris that fell around her, her little body crouched down as she tried to protect herself. Dr. Ash pulled frantically at those doors but couldn't get back through to the other side for some reason. Through the small window, he watched helplessly as Gabby tried to recover, realizing that she was alone and still pursued. He saw the brightness grow behind her as their stalker came closer. Gabby began to panic, searching for a direction to escape. He watched as she did the only thing she could. She ran to an elevator and began to push the button in frantic desperation. She kicked and slammed her tiny hands against the door repeatedly between fearful glances over her shoulder.

"Gabby! Gabby!" he yelled pointlessly, beating and struggling with the doors.

With her back pressed against the closed door of that elevator, he watched her extend her arms pleadingly, defensively out to the threat which remained outside of his own line of sight. Then, with a scream that went unheard through the heavy doors and the collapsing ceiling, he saw the elevator door suddenly open and watched as Gabby fell backward and down into the darkness.

Dr. Ash was struggling with the barred doors that were preventing him from going back for Gabby, as well as the realization that it may have been futile to attempt going back at all. He couldn't allow that possibility to take hold. So, he struggled on.

Dust obscured the other side of the window, so much so, instead of seeing any indications of what happened to Gabby, his own haggard face was reflected back at him.

He tried. He tried extremely hard, but his efforts got him nowhere. Things had deteriorated so quickly. Without giving up in any way, Dr. Ash turned to the rubble that was behind him; he redirected his efforts to where Trace had gone.

Covering the distance quickly, the doctor began clawing at the barrier that had fallen between him and the boy. He had no idea how thick it was or if he could get through it. He dug and called out Trace's name repeatedly, never seeming to make any significant progress. Then, out of the corner of his eye, he heard and then saw a small arm force its way through.

"Trace!" He moved immediately, but Trace's arm withdrew before it could be grasped. Only a small dark hole marked the breach.

"Trace! Trace! Can you hear me? I'm here!"

For a moment, there was no response at all. Falling pieces of the building were the only sounds to be heard. Dr. Ash called out again, desperate for some reply. He remained still, very still, for what seemed too long a time, straining his senses, until the slightest breathy- "Ouch"- came from the other side.

Only an ounce of comfort could be taken from the sound of the boy. There was only enough relief in it to allay his fears momentarily. Gabby was separated from them. He felt so responsible for that loss; to lose Trace too would be just like losing himself.

"Are you alright? Are you hurt at all? Are you hurt Trace?" Dr. Ash got only a whimper in response.

"Can you pull yourself free?" was his next question and the answer sounded like the first. That made the doctor start pulling at the fallen debris urgently. A creaking and a sudden shifting began which froze him where he was. He stopped his efforts because he realized that it could possibly make the situation worse by bringing the weight of the boy's surroundings fully down on him.

"You heard that, didn't you? I don't want to lie to you- I don't think I could get away with it even if I did- so here's the truth. I can't get you out of there just yet. There's no telling how stable this pile is. But don't panic, I'm not leaving you alone. I promise I'll think of something."

From under that rubble, sniffing could be heard which signaled the beginnings of tears. Although that was completely understandable given the state of things, it wasn't helpful at all. He needed to be kept calm.

With sincerity in his voice, the doctor started with, "I know this is scary but don't worry, I'll get you out of this I promise. Stay strong."

Then, quietly, he could just make out the one-word response to that. He heard Gabby's name; Trace was asking about the girl. He hadn't seen what happened to her. How could he be told that she may have been lost to him? Trace would wither.

Dr. Ash was already fighting to contain his own remorse. He chose to believe that she might still be found safe. He might have also chosen to attempt to convey that hope to the boy, but he didn't. Despite his earlier misgivings about lying, he found a slight deception to be easier.

"Let's concentrate on getting you out of there OK? Then, we'll all get out of here together." No sound came from the boy to signal acknowledgment. That was a bad sign. For all he knew, on the other side, Trace might have slipped away.

As he stood to find a way to get through, his world went unsteady around him. Things became unclear and darker suddenly. He reached up to rub his head and brought back a red-stained hand. That haziness he'd been feeling was getting worse. His wound was getting worse. He considered whether it would affect his thought process and his decision-making. He was unsure. Had it already?

He stood there, distracted and directionless, for an undetermined length of time. He'd drifted suddenly. Only the sound coming from that damaged radio he'd been carrying began to cut through the fog. "We're losing him." was all that he heard come through. Still somewhat dazed, he failed to recognize the sounds around him that should have been a warning. Cracking and creaking sounded all around.

The creaking was the beginnings of another disaster. At first, there was only a sudden but slight drop of the floor around him. That was the first indication of the complete collapse which happened a moment later.

He fell.

"OH, SHIT...!"

Everything under him lost solidity as he and the floor he'd been standing on came down onto the level beneath him with a crash. The minor daze he'd been in before was replaced by complete disorientation. He laid there where he'd fallen for a time, unable to focus enough to assess his own condition. When the dust settled, he slowly sat up and looked to where he'd come from. A familiar red glow of flames washed over everything above him.

The structure under his feet had come down almost like a kind of trap door, sending him sliding recklessly, separating him from Trace. He'd landed abruptly and got up cautiously. Then, he turned from one direction to another. There was no sign of either child and he was on his own again. Through muddled thoughts, he blamed himself for not being up to the task. The next move wasn't clear. But the fact was there was only one direction open to him: straight ahead.

He'd lost both children.

PART III: THE DISSONANCE

Nathaniel Ash had both literally and figuratively lost ground.

The collapse that had overtaken him was devastating in-of-itself, but he realized that he'd also fallen into an unfamiliar area as well. There was no doubt that he'd been irrevocably waylaid. Now, dimness surrounded him, dulling his path forward.

With one real direction to choose from, a few cautious, furtive steps were taken. The lighting and his solitude forced him to revisit his previous mood. But now there was a coldness as well, that was a distinct difference. A pervasive sadness welled in him that clouded his focus. He continued on, aware of the depth of that sadness without fully acknowledging its origin.

Murmurs to himself began then.

"This isn't happening! How can this be happening? None of what's happened can happen. There's an explanation somewhere for it all. It must exist, but what is it? What's the differential for seeing dead patients clearly?

Concussion...hallucinations brought on by...hypoxia...due to...gas leak...which caused the explosion..."

"Yes, maybe. No. I don't know. Maybe not...I'm losin' it! That's it. I've gone absolutely insane. No, I haven't. I'm still completely stable, aren't I? Well? I'm as lucid as I've ever been, I'm sure of it. Possibly not completely."

Chaotically, his formally rational thought process sought answers. The area he was in was vacant, which was just as well because he'd lost the clarity of purpose he'd had before. He wasn't searching any longer. Without realizing it, he'd turned inward drastically.

At the end of the area was an unfamiliar room. He was less than coherent as he entered. It was moderate in size and dimly lit, as expected. Seating lined either side of the aisle leading to the front. He'd found himself in the facility's prayer room.

Bypassing the seating, he headed for the stark all-purpose dais ahead of him. He took one step up and turned to peer out at all of the empty pews. In that moment, all he was, seemed hollow.

Imagining that all of his perceived failures were opposite him, staring back, he mocked himself with an affected drawl saying, "Forgive me, I have sinned against you." Then, after a self-debasing chuckle, he put his head down remorsefully, as the weight of the loss of two innocents fell on him.

The sound of an unexpected hissing burst out of the radio he carried, followed by a familiar voice forcing him to focus his attention again. He'd heard, "What sin could you have possibly committed Ash?" It was Riven asking.

"The sin of inadequacy... Where the hell did you come from?"

Riven's response ignored the question and posed one of his own. "Have you forgotten where you come from Ash?"

"What's that supposed to mean? And don't call me Ash, it's Doctor.

"A destination can only be plotted from a starting point. Since you seem to have veered from your end, your purpose, I have to conclude that you've forgotten your point of origin."

"How would you know what my purpose is?"

"I gave it to you of course." Riven stated matter-of-factly.

"Oh, really...? Remind me, that purpose was what again?"

"Of course, Ash. That purpose was to help."

"Ok, first of all, you didn't provide me with that purpose. Secondly, I've been totally ineffectual so far. So regardless of the source, I haven't fulfilled that role. I've failed!"

"You fail by not persisting Ash."

"I'm persistently failing Riven! You have no idea of what's been happening. I've lost the...!" he stopped short. Then he attempted to continue, saying, "I can't do this anymore. Maybe there's just no succeeding or maybe I'm just not up to the task."

"You're mistaken in the belief that you are not capable of helping further. Imagine for a moment. Imagine that there is something prized, like a beautiful car, buried under mounds of snow. You know it is there and all you must do is dig. Now, a given individual may dig at a given rate faster than you. But you are capable of exhuming the prize as well. Yours may be more of an exertion but the end can be the same. So, you're wrong in the assertion that you are inadequate."

"Clever-"

"Accurate." Riven countered.

"Who *are* you?"

"I'm exactly who you think I am.", Riven said simply.

"...Enough with the cryptic shit!"

"Cryptic to you is forthcoming to me Ash. All things are relative, including my imminent reaction to your tone.", he cautioned in his usual, somewhat stilted, inflectionless drone.

"Now, I'll spell this out for you. You have a definitive choice in front of you. It's unavoidable and it's immutable. As I've told you before, a side must be taken. What do you believe?"

"Was I right before? Is this all about some... theological struggle? Am I really just the object of some religious recruitment of yours?"

Riven responded quickly with "Not in the way that you're referring Ash. Religion is only a single syllable where an epic is required. No, it's about something grander. This is about *Existence*."

Ash sobered somewhat at the realization that Riven wasn't who he'd thought he was. He said, "So, you don't work for the government, do you?"

"No, I don't.", Riven replied.

"What am I involved with? What am I in the middle of?"

"More accurately, what are you near the end of Ash."

"And the answer to that is **what** Riven?"

"The answer is; the end of your rotation."

Before his lack of understanding could be demonstrated, Riven clarified, continuing with, "You're at a juncture and you'll have to choose between Aegis and what he serves or myself. The next obvious question is "What do we serve?" The answer to that is;

The Nature. We serve in our own ways. Our ways are disparate."

"I really can't deal with this now Riven."

"Because you believe you have another option, Ash."

"I know we're in a prayer room, but I'd rather not get into a debate on theology. I did my time, Ok?"

"Yes, I know you have. But I'm not interested in your grasp of dogma. You believed at one time, strongly. What about now? What has changed in you?", Riven probed.

"Seriously, this isn't the place or time. Well, maybe it is the place, but I don't want to have this discussion."

"Why? Don't you believe in the Devine anymore Ash? Can't you see beyond your own intellect? Do you *really* believe that you're the sum of the equation?" Riven pressed.

"Do I believe in the Devine? How the hell should I know? I neither believe nor disbelieve. I simply don't know. Listen, I'm not some self-approved militant atheist and I'm not devout by any stretch either."

"Agnostic...? Or is that a lack of conviction?", Riven challenged.

"That's a simplistic, familiar trope; I refuse to commit so I cower in the middle of the road? I'm not lacking in...Never mind. Why are you pursuing this?"

"I'm doing this because this is necessary Ash."

"Drop it. I just need to get out-I just need to survive now, after everything that's happened." As he moved toward the door to remove himself, Riven defiantly blocked his way.

"You feel that's enough, don't you? Well, your survival is very subjective, whether you believe that or not. What if that is no longer possible?"

"Listen Riven, I appear to be intact, don't I?"

"You appear transparent to me. You also appear to have a crisis of faith. How and where did it develop?" Riven's question was leading.

"I don't know, OK?"

"You do know. This is important Ash."

"I don't know. I just want to forget this and get out, OK?"

"You think that would be enough? Step back to leap forward. Getting out is dependent upon that."

"Do you know what I've been through already Riven? I'm not even sure it was all real, but I know I'm drained from it."

"Where's your faith, Ash?"

"Leave it alone."

"Where is your faith? Why do you set it aside?"

"I don't need it OK? Now let it go."

"Is it that you don't need it or that you don't want it, Ash?"

"*I'm* not wanted!" the Dr. blurted resentfully.

"And we finally reach the foundation of your momentary disbelief Ash. Feel free to expound."

"I've heard it put in more than one way but the idea remains the same; only the good die young. The contention is that if God truly loves someone, they're given an early release. Well, I can only assume that even God doesn't want me. I've actually thought this through. That is the summation of a series of realizations. When you do believe in Him and then surmise that even He is avoiding you, the rest all adds up. It's a strange realization too because even if you choose to call yourself an agnostic, you can reason it out. Even if your doubts were unfounded and He exists, the fact that you're able to even perceive yourself as unwanted makes it just the same as if He in fact- didn't."

"Compelling logic but viscerally biased I'd say." was Riven's counter.

"I'm speaking analytically, not emotionally. Sometimes you hear people say, "No man is an island". Bullshit! Many people are islands. With billions of people in the world, we meet or come into contact with thousands throughout our lifetimes. In that number, we make and then lose hundreds of relationships. They range from the quickest of interactions to the most intimate of friendships. That's the norm. There are some people who sail alone through long pointless and unfulfilling empty lives. Many people are islands. It doesn't matter how you became one once you are one. I am one."

Riven posed the question, "Do you revel in that perception?"

"No, I don't. There was a rebellious almost romantic notion about it when I was young. That cliché was told to me by people that I hated then. If those bastards that said it weren't islands, I didn't want to turn out like any of them anyway. It seemed logical. But I don't romanticize it now. What they should have told me, and everyone else they alienated, was that no one could live without love or even the delusional illusion of it. I've never experienced that illusion by believing in any tome or practicing any chant yet."

"It's possible you're doing it wrong. You claimed that no one bereft of that love could live on. You've just stated that you're intact. How is that?"

"It's because I'm a survivor Riven. I'm intact, yes. But am I living? I've gone my whole life fighting to varying degrees with various opponents. Sometimes it was against adults four times my age who were supposed to be in a position of mentoring. Sometimes it was against myself. Either way, I was never one to cower from a confrontation.

My nature always set me apart from most people around me without any efforts of my own. I'm not an angel, which may be why I'm still here. No, I'm no angel but I'm no demon either."

"Despite the fallacious labels you cling to, that determination is yet to be made. Aren't you stronger than this? Don't you have any more fortitude than this?"

"You think I'm shrinking from responsibility? You think I'm weak? I don't think so. You know, one of my first memories is a fight. When I started school in the city, it must have been kindergarten- maybe first grade... I remember vividly being in the lunchroom. Another kid walked over to me, tapped me on my shoulder, and when I turned around, with a huge smile on his face, he took his full carton of milk and poured it all on top of my head. I didn't know him and absolutely did nothing to deserve what he did. He either just got the idea in his head or was encouraged to do it-the bottom line is that I looked like someone who should have been harmed to him. Maybe I looked like someone that was set apart or someone he wanted to set apart. Either way, it doesn't really matter. That was my introduction to being unwanted."

Riven asked, "You mentioned a fight. Am I to assume that you..."?

"...Quickly and thoroughly beat the shit out of him."

"A similar inclination would be helpful now Ash."

He continued on, oblivious to Riven's remark. "I can't remember ever having fought before that. I was maybe five or six! That kid tapped into something that we're taught, exactly at that age, to suppress. My instinct for survival was on autopilot. That kid wanted to hurt me for some reason that I couldn't rationalize. I reacted. There was only hurt and not hurt, black and white, ones and zeros. So, I "survived" that encounter, which was only the first of many. I instinctively understood pride and embarrassment. Fighting to be equal became a full-time job. So, don't tell me I am weak!"

"You're putting up a slight fight now. You're almost convincing, with the exception of the fact that you are giving up."

"What do you want from me?"

"We're re-covering ground here. We want you to do what you've been conditioned to do Ash; continue to help!"

"Riven, what universe do you live in?"

"Technically, there is only one since all variances are relative to a coinciding totality which means they are each interwoven throughout and traversable within the whole of the Nature." he matter-of-factually stated.

"That question was rhetorical! I don't even know what that means!"

"What that means, Ash, is neutrality is not an option for you any longer. There is his side and my side.

There is benign and there is malignancy. He and his kind are egregious! You're already playing into his hands by shying away from your responsibility. He wants you to readily embrace self-preservation. You're performing for him exceptionally well. You're just this close to giving him exactly what he wants."

"Are you still talking about Aegis? Again, I'm not sure what you're getting at, but he's gone, alright? He's gone! Give it a rest."

"Consistently, you're off the mark Ash. He is anything but dead. In fact, with your complicity, he's working toward an apogee."

"Ok, I understand the words but not the context Riven."

"Ash, you persist in thinking in small terms and that he can be harmed in the common sense of the word. This is not the case. I've tried to warn you not to accept him as he seems. Aegis is immortal energy just like I am."

"What reaction are you expecting now? I'm tired and I'm confused, and I'm convinced now more than ever that I really should have taken a look at my own head a long time ago. ... Immortal energy? I doubt you know what you're talking about any more than I do right now. Just show me to the door and let me call it a night."

"Try not to act as if you've forgotten what you saw in the Burn Unit. You saw what he did, how he moved.

Believe me or your own eyes, whichever you prefer. Aegis is something very wrong. His intent is wrong and his motives are misguided. Logically, following his lead is also wrong."

"Well, like I've said, I'm not following anything now. I'm only interested in getting out in one piece. I just want to wake up from this dream."

"You think this is a dream? Maybe it is in some small sense but not entirely. Dreams are apertures. A dream is the intersecting commonality of all the myriad possibilities of you. While immersed in one, you can witness and sometimes even communicate with your own personally created micro-verses. You are in the space between everything behind you and everything ahead. But there is no waking at this point. There is only alignment and experience."

"Do *you* even understand you?"

"What I understand is your situation Ash, even if you don't yet. I understand where you are, what you are, and what you need to do."

"Look, it's been a tough few hours for me. I've lost...I've lost more than I want to think about right now. I can't help anyone else if I can't even help myself. Why can't you either leave me alone or guide me out if you know the way Riven?"

"What exactly have you lost?"

"Apparently, my mind is first on that list."

"That's the only thing you have at the moment and exactly what you refuse to utilize Ash. What have you actually lost?"

"What have I lost…? What have I lost? Damn it! Let's start with my recent memory, the girl I'd been seeing and planned to…Any sense of time, a hospital's worth of staff and patients, multiple trauma victims that I should have been able to help, a stable grip on reality, possibly a few IQ points, my way and…"

"Now you've come to it." Riven interrupted.

"What?"

"You've lost your way, Ash. What you've really lost is your way."

"I get that you're speaking figuratively but I'm being literal, and you know that."

"I'm being more literal than you want to believe. You're facing the wrong direction now and I'm attempting to correct that for your own benefit."

"Don't bother, alright? I don't need it and didn't ask for your guidance. I still don't even know who you really are. I know what you've said but I'm unconvinced. I'm   unconvinced and I'm uninterested. I am going to take a minute to compose myself and then I'm getting out."

"Well Ash, your conceit notwithstanding, I would never have characterized you as self-serving."

"I've done everything that could have been done under these conditions and accomplished nothing. In fact, I've only been detrimental up to this point. My head hurts, and I've lost too many battles in a row today."

"You may think so, but you're surrendering before the decisive battle."

"No Riven, there won't be any more. This has been too one-sided for me. "...Live to fight another day" right?"

"Is this the same resolve that you drew from when you went into practice?"

The Dr.'s mind reflexively drifted away at that remark, back to his earliest thoughts of pursuing medicine. His parents lived next to a family with a boy the same age. His name was Jeremy Roman and naturally, the young boys met and played together. Although the future doctor was much too young to perceive or comprehend the basis for it at the time, there was a distinct condescension directed at him continually from the Romans. Jokes about smiling so that he could be seen at night went over his head and beyond him because of his age. Comparisons between the two boys meant to establish some degree of worth or lack thereof were also constant. Because it was all masked behind the smiling faces of the Romans, Nathaniel simply took it as a shortcoming of his own rather than concluding that it was malice directed toward him. The people seemed pleasant enough, but their subtle disdain flowed freely yet unperceived. That was true until a very informal stay for dinner one day shined a light.

Nathaniel was a child and was unthreatening, so the parents of Jeremy Roman had him over often. Jeremy, his parents, and Nathaniel sat down together innocently enough it seemed. They ate a bland modest meal and the conversation turned to school; probably by design.

Mrs. Roman asked, "So, Nattie, (she always called him that to marginalize and emasculate him despite being corrected repeatedly) how are you doing in school?"

"Fine." was the normal non-committal answer any kid would have given.

"...Just, "fine"? No, I mean how are your grades?"

"They're OK I guess."

"C'mon Nat, you can tell me. I'm just curious. What kind of grades are you getting?" she pursued.

"I don't know-they're OK." he replied, growing more uncomfortable.

"What's wrong? You don't want to tell me?"

"No, that's not it..."

"Jeremy's getting all A's."

"That's good." was all he could think to say.

"What is it? Are you embarrassed to tell me you're not doing as well? Nobody expects you..." Mrs. Roman revealed.

"No! That's not it. I just don't want to talk about it." Nathaniel protested not capable of pointing out to an adult the fact that it was really none of her business in the first place.

"Why not...? It's a simple question." she chided with a one-sided smirk.

"I don't know-it's personal and I just don't want to talk about it."

"It's because you're embarrassed. I understand. Jeremy's smarter than you and you don't want to admit it. It's OK, you don't have to. We can drop it."

That was the first time that he saw their perception of him for what it was. That was yet another instance of an inferiority that someone tried to convince him of early in life. When his parents heard of the incident, rather than being upset by it, they were somewhat embarrassed. Well, despite not being able to define pride and determination, those were actually possessions inherent in him. He realized his mother was equally as critical of him, as she was accomplished in the medical field. He saw the respect that she commanded. He craved that from her. He was vying for her acknowledgment as well so he had to achieve even more than she had if he hoped to get it.

The best way to do that to his mind was to become a doctor.

Luckily for him, he began relatively young so that he could progress naturally. In the beginning, he struggled and was somewhat average. But applying himself paid off. He learned that the more you know, the more you *can* know. He started to excel.

Eventually, the initial impetus faded away and only a fervent self-interest survived. He'd succeeded in achieving his MD without a second thought to the Romans and how they'd settled into indistinctness and gluttony, or to his belittling parents.

He'd been asked by Riven if he was drawing from the same resolve that he'd begun with. Despite the fact that he did view his resolve as unfaltering, he never gave an answer to that question. His motivations had changed along the way. If he would have answered "yes" he would have been somewhat deceitful in a way.

He'd found some reservoir of determination to go farther than his mother had in medicine but in the process, had abandoned the very real need for approbation from his pseudo father and mother. What had once been self-preserving had become self-serving. Everything that he'd been doing was coming from a place of ego. None of his achievements and accolades were done out of benevolence or the demands of a boy for acceptance. They'd been twisted into self-gratification and conceit.

But that reality was lost on him. That degree of introspection wasn't something he afforded himself. The Dr. simply followed the course he'd set along its natural progression. When opportunity presented itself, he took advantage without questioning his original motivation.

Right at that moment, he was being forced into self-examination. That reaffirmed something that Riven said. It went unheard at the time but became clear then. It was undeniable after reflecting on it.

He'd lost his way.

Dr. Nathaniel Ash had been misdirected somehow at some point. It was unclear who was responsible for that. He had in fact lost his way. Riven had somehow known that and he tried to convey the message. That made it seem as if Riven had been attempting to help in some way. But logically that also meant that he'd had some fore-knowledge of things. That couldn't be possible!

Then, the unsettling series of events he'd been through filed through his thoughts, discrediting doubt. There might have been something to what Riven had been trying to convey.

Nathaniel was wrenched from his musing, having forgotten that Riven was present, by an affirmation.

"Well, I'm glad you're catching up Ash.", Riven said breaking into the Dr.'s thoughts.

"What? What do you mean by that?"

"Yes, there is very definitely something to what I'm trying to convey to you. I'm glad you're beginning to see clearly."

"How could you possibly know what I was thinking? Never mind. It's not important right now."

"You know that answer anyway. It's been covered. Let's get back to you being self-serving."

"What? Who said that I...?" Ash began.

"Don't. We both know your line of thought. By looking for the easy way you're not fulfilling your necessary role in things. There are many in the balance. That won't end well for anyone."

"Oh, really...? This won't end well? If you haven't noticed, this isn't going well right now! I'd like to get out before that trend continues. And what was that you said? I'm not fulfilling my role? My role isn't to be self-sacrificing at all costs. I have an idea. Why don't you stay here and be the martyr? Isn't that your duty? What about it? What's your role in this?"

"It's not very different from your own. You need to be directed. You need guidance. I'm in effect showing you how to do what you have to. I'm saving you, Ash."

"I can see that. Look how well you're doing. Thank you."

"Your sarcasm isn't lost on me."

"I don't care Riven. I've been here too long already. I'm leaving now!"

"You're not ready Ash."

"I am. I'm past ready to get out of this hell." the Dr. declared.

"You're not ready Ash.", Riven repeated.

"Don't tell me I'm not ready. I'm not even going to ask you why you think that because I know you're on a different page. I'm moving on with or without you."

Then he saw something.

From where he stood, something over Riven's shoulder caught his eye. The darkness of the corridor outside was being altered. The hue of flames was creeping and growing with every second. He'd lingered too long again. He'd been distracted by Riven. That had to end.

"Riven- look. Do you see that? We've got to move."

"What do you see Ash?"

"What do you think? Let's move!"

"Look again.", Riven warned ominously.

Dr. Ash moved beyond Riven toward the door. Just then, a figure sped awkwardly past, too quickly to be recognized. Before he could get any closer, the heat and glow of fire grew. Then, the thing that separated him from Trace and Gabby shot past the doorway. That thing was chasing the first figure.

"Holy shit! Did you see that Riven?"

No answer came.

When he spun for validation, Riven was gone, like he'd dematerialized; as if he'd never been in the room. But Nathaniel's confusion gave way to urgency. Spinning back toward the door, moving cautiously into the hall, the Dr. began to follow.

At a distance, farther than he would have expected, he saw light from flames moving through the corridor, leaving dimness behind as it went. He followed quickly despite his misgivings. There was something in him that insisted that clarification was ahead.

It was all he could do to keep up. Stumbling through the darkness like he was, became more familiar than Dr. Ash would have ever believed.

He moved as quickly and as safely as that darkness allowed. The Dr. made up ground with the hope of resolution pushing him on.

After everything he'd been through, Nathaniel had lost the presence of mind to take note of where he was being led. He simply followed thoughtlessly. Without realizing it, a very real disorientation had come over him. That haze was worsening.

Ahead of him, the glow he'd been chasing came to a stand-still. So, he stopped reflexively. At first, there was nothing. Then, he heard something muted. Forcing himself to inch forward was an effort. As he neared, the sound of a struggle drew him in. He inched closer to the far end of the corridor. What he was hearing began to paint a stark picture of a brutal conflict. Easing to the corner, he risked a look. That was all he was willing to risk after seeing what was unfolding ahead of him.

With their faces obscured, two bodies fought with each other in a large intersection of the building's corridors. There was no doubt that he was seeing that same fiery figure he'd run from earlier. He was witnessing something impossible! The rationale had to wait. The struggle demanded attention.

The other figure remained unrecognizable in the confusion. There was nothing artful about how the two fought. The few chairs that lined the walls were used as both shield and projectiles. The sound of glass breaking mixed with crashes from thrown furniture, as well as hoarse, throaty gasping from at least one of the two; possibly both. That second figure was obscured by the fire engulfing the first and was doing all he could to hold off the other. It looked like a losing effort from where the Dr. stood. Then, the realization hit Dr. Ash like a stone; he was watching the one he'd named MT struggle for his life.

Despite it being a sincere impulse, the thought of intervening withered in the face of fear and self-preservation. He watched from a distance in presumed safety. He watched as they moved farther into the dark. That darkness was soon replaced with firelight.

The two mercilessly battled. Their conflict made it seem as if they'd been at odds for a very long time. It became obvious that MT wasn't a match for the other. That fact, combined with Nathaniel's own animus toward the beast, made his choice not to help completely unreasonable.

With a small table held in front of him like an inadequate shield, MT began to give ground to his fiery attacker. Relentlessly the figure beat his arms against the table, driving MT down first to a knee and then tumbling backward. He'd lost his balance and was left helpless in fear on the ground. At that, the figure on fire threw its head back, taking a momentary celebration before the kill. But before he could take that action, urgency put the Dr. in motion. He reacted without thinking.

"No!" he roared as if his will was a weapon.

That demand, inexplicably, rendered that attacker a statue. He stood immobile in the position he'd taken; his arms raised and poised to strike, and his head thrown far back, directed toward the ceiling. No further prompting was needed for MT. He recognized his opening and took it then. He was on his feet and hobbling away from the danger in an instant.

Nathaniel wasn't sure what action to take next. He knew that he wanted to keep MT in sight and catch up to him, but that meant putting himself at risk. MT was already moving farther into the darkness and would quickly be lost to him. There was no time. He had to move.

Crouching low, he exposed himself in the open and crept toward where the figure stood motionless a short distance ahead of him. Anxiousness made him shake and stutter-step forward cautiously. He inched closer with the intention of bolting past once he was near enough. His eyes were locked, scanning for the slightest indication that the figure was aware of his movement. But that never came. It seemed oblivious to him; only the flames engulfing it in motion.

Nathaniel found himself unable to look directly at it for fear that that would somehow awaken it. At the same time, he also realized that he didn't want to find anything identifiable in it. He wanted nothing more than he'd already been exposed to. He wanted nothing more of It to solidify in his memory. So, he crept up to it, preparing himself to turn and run in an instant.

A foot, then pause. Another step and then another pause. It seemed like it took eons. Within five feet of it, the heat it produced was stifling. What exactly was it and what allowed it to exist as a living immolation? No one was there like before to perceive that thought or offer an answer.

Pressing himself against the wall just in front of it, he got to a point in his mind where he felt confident that he'd remained unnoticed. A small amount of resoluteness mixed with panic sent the doctor bolting away. He straightened himself and allowed one look over his shoulder, only to see its head begin to turn malevolently in his direction.

That was more than he could bear. It was more than enough to push him through that dark recklessly. All he wanted and needed was to put that abomination behind him.

With no sign that he was being followed he turned his attention back to finding MT. There were a very limited number of places he could have gone. They were deep within the facility at that point. Even when it was at its peak, normally there was little to no activity where he was just then. That section was used for patients with disorders, sleep disorders. The sleep lab was affectionately referred to as "The Museum" by the staff because odd and unique pieces were sent there to be studied. The area consisted of four small rooms laid out around one small central observation and control area.

He called out, timidly, into the unlit lab to no response. Then, he started to his left, going around the observation desk, checking the first room on that side. The next attempts at calling out to MT went unanswered as well. It took no time at all to go from the first iso-room to the next and the next. At the fourth and last room, an intense light suddenly filled the space, blurring his vision as his eyes worked to adjust. Ahead of him in that room, he saw, unclearly, a figure facing him. Assuming that it was the hiding place of MT he approached cautiously.

Nathaniel took a step forward through distorted sight.

The door slammed violently behind. Spinning, he threw himself against it. At his back, the light suddenly went out. Defensively, He turned quickly to confront the figure there. The movement from the other side of that room put him on guard. Understanding sobered him as his vision cleared. Bizarrely, it was his own reflection opposing him.

"Assess yourself."

The doctor jumped at the sound of an intercom system and at the words he heard. To his astonishment, he was hearing a low, almost mumbling voice addressing him-demanding something. The assumption of who was talking was made.

"I've been following you." the Dr. began. "Every time I got close you managed to slip away. Didn't you realize I've been looking for you and calling out to you? Or is that the point? You realized but intentionally kept avoiding me. I just wanted to help. I mean, I still do. I'm..."

"I-know you." The voice cut Nathaniel off.

"Then you're ahead of the curve.", Nathaniel responded. "I'm sorry. I had nothing else to go on, so I've just been calling you MT. That was short for..."

He wasn't allowed to finish his explanation. He was cut short with, "So it's MT, huh? Say that five times fast for a measure of true irony." The meaning of that eluded Nathaniel and he chose to look past it.

"OK, I'd appreciate it if you'd let me out of this room, right now."

Again, in that disaffected half-mumble, MT claimed, "I had no part in that.'

"Really? Who did? Never mind, that doesn't matter, just open the door."

"You have that key. Assess yourself, Doctor."

"I'll play along. That seems to be your fee for letting me out. What aspects, exactly, am I assessing?" No answer came from the other side of the glass. "Fine, I'll set the parameters. Let me start with the physical. I am experiencing all of the expected reactions to my circumstance; elevated pulse, tension, anxiety, and a throbbing headache most likely associated with the minor laceration I sustained. This environment is enough to cause anyone an enormous amount of stress so none of those things are surprising."

"Moving on, I'm mentally sound.", he reported without elaboration.

"Lastly, I'm trapped in a burning, crumbling edifice crippled by instability and wreckage!"

Nothing was uttered in opposition to that assertion.

"I think that about covers it.", he said summarizing.

The response to the doctor's patronization was immediate and intense.

"Lie of omission Doctor!"

Scanning quickly, he strained to identify the figure in the shadowed observation room beyond the glass. Nathaniel couldn't make out features. Who was he? Where did he come from? Why was he detaining him? Then the elusive figure that had been MT leaned forward, still only partially in the light.

"I don't understand..."

MT cut him off by saying, "You haven't understood much for a long time, have you?"

The frustrated doctor silently peered into the shadowy outer room, weighing his response. He chose to call upon a lesser relied upon aspect of his training.

"I'm not sure how you came to that conclusion, but I suppose that could be true. Tell me what exactly I need to grasp."

"The depth of ignorance requires me to answer, All things."

"That kind of vagueness makes me feel like I'm being prepared for a sales pitch."

"Then you'd only be selling to yourself. You are the perfect salesman, aren't you? Yes, you're accomplished at selling yourself a manufactured product, aren't you? That's something you take pride in."

At that, Nathaniel spoke up saying, "What makes you think you know anything about me or what I take pride in?"

MT's response was, "I know you - I know myself."

He then continued saying, "Listen to me, I'm trying to help."

"Listen to you? Who are you? What are you trying to help me with?", Nathaniel questioned.

"I am a necessary mirror.", MT answered.

He followed up by stating, "I need you to see your fatal flaw."

His words were riddles but Nathaniel had no leverage to bargain for clarity. The other continued on, leading him to some unknown destination.

"Are you a good doctor?" came from MT.

"Well, I..." Nathaniel began.

"Hubris is your nature!" was shouted in annoyance. "Don't equivocate."

"Yes! I'm good at what I do! Does that satisfy you?"

"I'm ashamed to say that I don't agree." came from him in opposition.

The doctor was more inquisitive than injured by that. He responded with, "How do you come to that conclusion?

Are you trying to say that you're a former patient that I somehow... mistreated?"

"I would say a present patient Ash.", MT replied. "And if by, mistreated, you mean that you've been woefully neglectful, then I'm sorry but the answer is yes."

"You're sorry? Listen, this has to end now. We're in danger here. Do you understand?" Nathaniel tried to reason.

"I say that you've been a neglectful doctor because you've misdiagnosed and mistreated your primary patient.", MT accused. "I'd have to call it willful ignorance on your part. Symptoms were ignored, and treatments were overlooked."

In a moment of clarity, Nathaniel realized what was being implied. "You're referring to me, aren't you? I have no idea how or why, but I get the distinct impression that you're talking about me."

MT chimed back in at that point saying, "You think everything is about you, don't you? This time you just happen to be right though. But then again, it's not just about you. It's about something much bigger. It's about something much nobler than anything you could pry out of yourself."

"If I knew you or knew what that has to do with me in any way, I might take that as an insult. Actually, your tone was pretty undeniable, so - screw you." Nathaniel shot back.

"It's too late. You have already." came in retort.

"How…? How have I done anything to you? I'm the one locked in - trapped here! I'm the one being imprisoned. The way I see it, I'm the victim here. I'm staring out from the inside, wondering how I got here and why, and at the same time, I'm being forced to defend myself against something I'm not sure of and can't fathom."

"You know me well enough." MT offered.

"How could I possibly…? Don't answer that-don't bother.", Nathaniel said.

He disregarded that request and responded with, "I'm sorry to say that you need to be shown certain things and need to *accept* those things as well."

"What things? Make it plain!" Nathaniel demanded through waning patience.

Then, from the other side of the glass, his answer came unexpectedly, in an accusatory voice- "YOU ARE DEVOID."

"How would you know?" he asked, unable to fully hide his self-consciousness.

MT spoke up saying, "I recognize myself in you I'm sorry to say."

It occurred to him that he was again at the wrong end of yet another unsolicited edification. A defiant protest instantly began to form, but then a momentary reflection stopped Nathaniel in his tracks.

"What exactly are you suggesting I'm lacking?"

It didn't seem helpful to question specifics, even as the words passed his lips. The answer was potentially disturbing and not something to be disregarded. That could prove to be extremely difficult to do.

"Look to your spirit. How much of your will have you forfeited and how many times? What are you passionately fighting for? You've been submissively domesticated. You're a non-participant. You are on cruise control as opposed to plotting your own destination. Look to your withered spirit."

That type of command hadn't been given at any time in the doctor's past. No one had ever demanded that type of examination from him and it had also never been self-evident. He'd never had that capacity. Recrimination filled the doctor's mind. Then, almost submissively, he questioned, "What do you want me to do?"

"You have to act decisively."

With that said, Nathaniel watched MT's shadowed form shift; he'd pressed something which opened the door with the sound of an accompanying buzzer.

MT and the doctor moved at the same time, but the doctor was quickly halted and lost sight of the other as, again, an intense and blinding light obscured his vision. After the necessary adjustment, Nathaniel bolted for the exit.

The speed with which he was moving enabled him to dodge a barely perceived attack to his head. Avoiding that was an ungraceful feat. Forcefully, he slammed into and then off of the corridor wall.

Spinning away and back a few feet, Nathaniel witnessed the beast on fire that he'd been running from. It had been just inches from taking his head off with a baleful strike. That miss caused its crooked talon-like fingers to be embedded in the wall. With a wrenching tug and then a second, it became clear that the thing was stuck. Then, its attention shifted to its intended target.

The deliberate turn and damnable stare forced the breath from Nathaniel's lungs. No further urging was necessary. He sprang away and was off instantly just as a throaty rasp and the sound of plaster being pulled forcefully away sounded.

Straight was his direction; away was his only goal. Now free, that thing was right on his ass. The doctor's attempted escape was only seconds long when, at the end of that short corridor, he saw a door swinging shut. With haste born from abject fear, he caught that closing door with just enough space for one finger to be slid in and he threw his body beyond it.

The confusion of the moment bred carelessness, causing him to fall. He'd bounded through the entrance to a long stairway. Missing the first step, he went down with suddenness and surprise. He tumbled, and he impacted. At his back, the crashing, the heat, and the rasping indicated he'd gained no safety. Behind and above him, he could still hear the din he'd barely avoided, but it had taken on a furious volume. Ironically, the only thing that may have saved him was falling.

Unfortunately, he hadn't been spared the physical toll. The throbbing of his temple came first. Disorientation was running a close second. It was worsening.

It was terribly dark.

Where ever it was he'd landed, it made him wish for that glaring light he'd previously tried to avoid. The irony wasn't lost on him. 'Need breeds clarity' he thought.

His fears were pulling him between desires erratically. The desire to escape the perpetual bleakness conflicted with his need to remain hidden. The darkness or the light...Which would provide for him best now?

He then realized that if he was hindered, then so might that thing be.

The distinct desire to call out to Riven for guidance came to him. He also considered MT's loss. Yet again, he'd been forced to abandon him to the grievous conditions surrounding them. His intention to help was derailed by his need to evade his raspy antagonist. Regardless, he considered calling out to the pale intim idating pseudo-Angel that was Riven.

HSSSTTT!!

The decision had been taken out of his hands. Again, he was betrayed by the sound of the radio he'd been carrying. His hope of hiding was eliminated just that quickly. The doctor fumbled for his hissing betrayer in the blackness to prevent it from giving his position away completely, but the attempt was in vain.

Realizing that his surroundings were clearing, becoming brighter, he feared the implication. He spun then to see his pursuer peeling from the dark nothingness directly behind him.

He hadn't advanced from where he'd fallen, so the threat forced Nathaniel to begin a hasty scamper. With outstretched hands, he tried to feel his way. He was only somewhat successful as he bumped and bounced his way through an unknown area. A forced glance over his shoulder revealed that everything behind him had become a torrent of flames.

Distressed, he scanned in every direction. He'd lost sight of the source of that pyre. That fact was more unsettling at that moment than if he'd actually been within its reach.

That conflagration began to consume everything, consequently lighting the way ahead of him as it did. That allowed him to pick up speed. He moved hurriedly but without a clear destination. He moved urgently without knowing if he was effectively distanced from danger.

Nathaniel felt that he wasn't but actively tried to suppress that impression.

The area he was in unfolded before him as the light spread. Hasty looks around revealed that he'd fallen into an area like a basement boiler room. Around him, machinery that appeared old and unused became alight. Still, the source of the spreading flame was lost to him. Winding through that furnace room became increasingly more dangerous because the fire had sped past him and set the area ahead of him ablaze. The doctor's retreat continued out of necessity.

Fire and fright were the whole of his world.

As the doctor frantically wound his way, the surroundings changed, at first, gradually. Then, things hastily became inscrutable. The basement-like area he'd been in began to resemble an intermingled nightmarish landscape.

A quickly stolen swivel to his right revealed, not the flooring that would be expected, but a rocky and jagged terrain. The damaged brick walls that should have been the hospital's lowest level let a ruddy hazy light beyond show through. Over to his left, somehow escaping his notice, the wall dropped away and had become a crevasse with shards of broken rock and fire leading perilously downward. It was inexplicable to him. He attempted to calm himself by clinging to his sense of stoic logic and tried earnestly to reason things through.

"This is explainable! I've stumbled into an area of ... uncontained fire damage. This is just the foundation being consumed. Chemicals being ignited...fumes flooding the air...flames engulfing the structure. Don't inject your anxieties into this! There are enough things to worry about without resorting to irrationality!"

He tried to berate himself into sensibleness.

He tried and failed.

His fear hadn't abated and likely would not

The unexplainable amalgam of stone and steel that was thought to be the furnace room, stretched all around him now. Pits boiled in the ground near metal structures that were pipes to nowhere. Above him, a crimson and charcoal sky replaced the expected tiled ceiling. In the distant landscape that should not have been possible, spouts of fire furiously erupted.

"What the hell...?"

Moving franticly, the doctor stumbled over the uneven rock with no gage of how long he'd been moving. One phrase was repeated breathlessly: "This doesn't add up... This doesn't add up..."

In his haste, he'd lost all sense of direction. It almost seemed that where he'd come from had been erased. Simply saying that he'd become lost struck him as inadequate. Regardless, he couldn't go back if he'd tried.

Then, in a crystallizing moment, he realized that the stubborn grasping of his rational mind did nothing to lessen the seriousness of his situation. His understanding wouldn't remove him from where he was. The rejection of his circumstance wouldn't eliminate the danger he was emersed in or fled from.

A sudden burst, an eruption, ahead and just to his left, forced him to the ground recklessly. Scrambling to regain his footing, Nathaniel found that he was now completely removed from that shell of a building and was exposed and in the open.

Above him, indistinguishable sounds began to make themselves heard. Disembodied wails reverberated both around him and through his head at once. What started as a very few and random, became something like an unnerving symphony.

The sounds of dismay he'd been hearing took on a profound urgency. The volume of those wails penetrated. To his right and behind him, one of those cries demanded his attention. Then, recognition came and the familiarity of it horrified him completely. It was nearly upon him.

With one look ahead, he weighed his options. A steep incline stood before him, and behind was the despair he'd heard. He was set in motion. The landscape was treacherous shale and obsidian and resisted being climbed. But he fought out of relentless desperation.

He climbed recklessly. Clawing his way up and over those black rocks was exhaustive. But still, he fought.

Before much progress could be made, the harsh, throaty rasping that he'd been trying to escape sounded beneath him. One tentative glance revealed that the thing was closing the distance and threatened to be upon him quickly.

Quite naturally, Nathaniel panicked.

Looking up, he chose his path and began to scramble feverishly.

His speed came from need. His energy was terror-driven. As he moved, the rocks under him fell away unevenly, making it hard for his pursuer to gain any further ground. He looked down to see an outstretched limb, intent and striving toward him.

The disembodied wailing above his head grew louder and demanded attention. The tone of what he heard above concerned him almost as much as what chased him from below. In the space between his lunges, attempts to identify the source of that clamor were made. His neck strained almost as much as his arms. But he was in no position to see clearly. Whatever it was, it would have to remain unidentified for the moment. His imagination would be forced to design its worst.

Further and further up, he strove. Had it been minutes or hours? He'd become uncertain. Nothing at all was clear to him at that point. Numbness had become a part of him. The impossibility of what was happening and of what he was experiencing dominated his thoughts.

With his handhold continuously breaking away, he fought for footing. When that began to give way, the only recourse was to take a leap. With a thrust, he was able to pull himself up to what amounted to little more than a thin ledge.

Below him, where he'd just been, the rock loudly tumbled down. Assessing his situation, he found that there was nowhere else to go because the summit protruded outward above him, to either side. The rock had become void of handholds.

Nathaniel was standing on the only spot that could support him.

He was too close to fail! His pursuer was making up ground. Stubbornness in him flared up and compelled him to tear away bare rock to use as projectiles. With each small handful, a defiant scream followed those rocks down.

The only thing that could drown out all that was going on around him sounded just then.

HSSSSSSSTT!!!

There it was again. The damaged radio broke through the turmoil.

It distracted him momentarily, and he fumbled for it if for no other reason than to heave it down as his last weapon.

"You actually have one final weapon and it's not that affectation Nathaniel."

Aegis' voice caught the doctor by complete surprise. It surrounded him, clearly and loudly.

He continued, "There is no time left for the obvious questions that you would assail me with, so you must work to accept that what I'm saying is factual. You have only one weapon left at your disposal now and believe me when I assure you that it is the most vital. It will deliver you from the perception of danger and confusion that you are mired in at this final moment. It will ultimately provide you with the mechanism of change that will propel you forward. Hear me when I tell you this for the benefit of The Nature and of you. Your last weapon to wield is "choice"."

A new sense of urgency sounded in Aegis' tone. An air of finality was conveyed. The combination of that tone and the imperiled position he was in forced Dr. Ash to be attentive.

"Nathaniel, you are astute enough to determine the gravity of the situation you are in. The Endgame is well underway. A single crystallizing choice is the only measure left to be taken."

The Doctor listened attentively despite not being able to see the man speaking.

Nathaniel pressed himself against the jagged rock face, staring back at a harsh crimson and blackened sky, fearfully clinging to a disembodied voice. Searching above him proved futile. That view showed him only more sky, rock, and the cliff's edge that was inaccessible to him. A furtive glance down verified that the pursuit was still on.

"Tell me what to do Aegis!"

"Do nothing." was the response.

"Please..." Nathaniel heard himself quietly say, a step away from surrender.

"Do nothing Nathaniel, except surrender."

"What?"

"Your active resistance is, in actuality, causing the dissonance that you're experiencing right now. You can end this now of your own volition by letting go. The struggle will cease, and the vision will clear. Stop feeding the flames and the fire will die."

"That's not helping me! Look around! Look at where I am and what's below me!"

"Yes, I understand quite well. I see clearly what is before you." Aegis offered.

"If it's so clear to you then why would you tell me to give up? Where are you? Show yourself and help me!"

"You regard what I'm advising you as unhelpful, but it is quite the opposite. Your decisive refusal to perpetuate the construct you're witnessing is the one and only means of progressing."

"Do you not see what's down there?" he asked angrily.

"I see only your personal manifestation."

"Aegis...!"

"What you are cowering from now and what you have been fleeing is the manifestation of your ruin Nathaniel. That thing, as you see it, is your fear, regret, anger, and disillusionment made manifest into a beast worthy enough to terrorize you. You are the constructor and you are the keeper. Accept that and then release that. After that point, you will have no need to struggle and no question as to direction."

"There's no time for this. Drop something down or something. Give me a hand Aegis! It's getting closer! C'mon, I'm going to die!"

"That much is certain Nathaniel." Aegis calmly confirmed.

That response elicited a harsh reaction from the doctor.

"Riven!" The doctor called out in frustration and desperation.

"Riven show yourself and help me!" he pleaded.

With a violent cracking and the usual disturbing hiss, the radio sparked violently and sounded for the last time before it was launched downward, missing the mark, and doing less than nothing to prevent his pursuer's ascent.

"That...Nathaniel...was a MISTAKE!" From the cliff's edge above, Aegis' voice sounded with an uncharacteristic amount of anger. His tone held a challenge. That validated what was actually a misguided assessment that Nathaniel had been resisting.

"Was it? I ask for help and get a threat? Your façade is fading Aegis. I thought you meant no harm."

"No Nathaniel, I have never had any intention of harm. That threat was most definitely intended for another.", Aegis confirmed.

"Truth! That threat was never intended for you, Ash." Riven's voice broke through then, seemingly in response to the call.

Looking beneath him, clawing fiercely at the jagged rock, the threat was closing in.

"Fuck this...! Riven!"

Nathaniel called out in the hopes that an alternative outcome could be exploited. His mortality was in the balance and his faith in Aegis had become thread-bare.

Perhaps Riven was well aware of that.

"Ash, surely you see that all of the experiences you've had to endure of late were direct efforts to harm you? Surely you can grasp the threat that is posed by what you see now. Do you believe that the passive and flaccid act of doing *nothing* will release you from the danger you perceive? Don't be misled!" Riven exhorted. "These things are tangible examples of the need for pushback. I would argue that your passiveness is what's in fact feeding these perils. Therefore, DO something! Start by rejecting the misguided words of my nefarious counterpart. Continue to resist! Continue to seek ways to offer yourself." Riven said commandingly.

The words came like pointed weapons yet, for some reason, Nathaniel seriously considered them.

Riven continued, accusingly, "The one you called MT is not at all what you think. That is every bit of the stagnant inactivity that you left in your wake. That was the very coalescing of your indecisive avoidance."

"No, I tried..."

"Did you?"

"I TRIED...!"

"Listen to your own tone now. Is the situation resolved? No! It isn't! So, don't tell me that you "tried"! Your trying hasn't ended. That is the point that you must see!"

The doctor attempted to pivot on the tiny rock ledge, only to lose his balance. His fingers clawed inadequately, as he struggled for footing. With a sudden slide, the distance between him and the one below was dangerously narrowed.

"Riven! Are you up there? Do something!"

As the doctor looked down in fear, he stretched his arm above him blindly, hoping for assistance.

An arm below him grasped at his leg and missed by mere inches. Until that point, the creature's face had been averted. But, with a wrenching motion, it twisted its head and neck, most un-naturally, and their faces met.

Dr. Nathaniel Ash was staring down at his pursuer in horrified disbelief as sunken, hollowed sockets stared back and yet still managed to bore through him. That drawn and gaping mouth shot a baleful roar at Nathaniel as recognition ripped through the doctor.

He was staring down at a monstrous version of himself.

Another attempt was made to reach his leg just as the rocks conspired against him and began to give way.

Calmly, Aegis offered, "The misleading nature of his twisted words confuses the identity of Chimerical and Inimical to your detriment Dr. Nathaniel Ash."

"RIVEN!"

Nathaniel fell.

He still had his arm outstretched and, although he didn't see who'd done it, he felt someone clench his hand, pulling him forcefully upward, with only the very slightest window of opportunity left.

With the cliff's edge behind him, Nathaniel Ash found himself sprawled on the ground, looking up tentatively in an effort to identify his savior.

Some distance away, he watched as Riven took a step toward him, reasoning that he'd been the one to pull him over the ledge. Riven separated himself from a devious-looking individual at his back that Nathaniel didn't recognize. Then, noticing movement opposite Riven, he realized that Aegis had been standing there with a shadowy and unknown figure at his back as well.

The doctor looked at Aegis then back to Riven repeatedly. From where he was lying, each of the assembled men seemed incredibly imposing. That group stared down on him for a brief but decidedly unnerving beat of time.

Then, everything erupted.

Aegis and Riven both closed the distance and engaged each other in a blinding motion. Their partners behind them moved as if they were intending on matching what had just taken place, but instead assumed a defensive posture. As they met, the energy between them flowed out in a palpable wave that altered his perception.

Momentum violently overtook him.

He was ascending, but it seemed to be too far and much too fast. The sensation was disorienting and utterly overwhelming.

His rational mind dismissed what his eyes were witnessing. The tiny ledge he'd been on moments before fell in the distance beneath him. The cliff's edge that had been out of reach now appeared distant.

Seemingly in the beat of a heart and the span of a life, he'd moved from unsure and dangerous footing to an inexplicable circumstance.

All around him was dark, billowy, and threatening. He'd found that the crimson sky and black clouds he'd been under now surrounded him.

It was astounding! Then the realization that one threat had been exchanged for another became clear.

Responding to movement in his peripheral, he turned toward a sight that was beyond explanation.

Riven and Aegis were there, struggling with each other in what should have been the atmosphere - as if it was no different than the ground they'd been standing on.

The two were separated by only a small distance but appeared to be engaged in some kind of powerful resistance that defied reason. One would push, and then the other would pull. One would retreat as the other advanced. An attack from one would elicit a defense from the other. Each movement brought a counter as the skirmish continued. It was a brutal exchange.

With no law of gravity constraining them, the whole encounter was taking place on a non-linear plain. They traveled in logic-defying directions. Aegis and Riven were circling Nathaniel in wide arcs in front of and behind him but also both below and above him.

Although he was suspended in nothingness, he found that he was capable of movement and able to follow the struggle revolving around him.

Aegis' and Riven's counterparts held their respective stances all the while. As the conflict between them flowed and glided through the atmosphere, the other two counterbalanced them, revolving in the opposing direction and at an identical rate.

All of that was happening in sweeping arcs around a singular point; Nathaniel.

As their fight went on, Nathaniel realized a similar conflict raged internally. If only he'd understood that the fuel for that struggle was his own pride. That was beyond him then. He was determined to berate himself.

The first barrage came in the form of what he considered to be his recent failures. His perception of the emergency he'd witnessed in the ambulance bay and throughout the building provided him with extensive ammunition as well. To his mind, he'd failed repeatedly.

He'd allowed MT to go unsaved. He failed to lead the patients he'd come in contact with to safety. Most regrettably, the children he'd been responsible for were both lost.

What eluded him was the fact that his feelings were comprised as much of his self-involvement as they were of any concern for others. Thoughts of various shortcomings flew through his head. He'd begun to feel a swell of anger and then the distinct reminder of the pride that had buoyed him for much of his life.

He'd allowed his attention to be diverted with his own self-reflection long enough. The doctor sought vindication and required closure. Doing nothing would not expunge his failure. Being passive ensured that they would damn him. Although the full understanding of his situation escaped him, Nathaniel began to believe that his passivity would cement his ineptitude.

Re-focusing, he located Aegis and Riven, still in the midst of their own battle. Riven looked as if he was losing ground and faltering.

Nathaniel acted.

With affected authority, he shouted, "Stop this!"

That outburst generated an immediate reaction as the group that had been encircling him and fighting intensely an instant before, imploded in on his position like missiles. Aegis, Riven, and what was presumably their Seconds in battle, all met at his position; crashing together blindingly. That impact was seen, felt, heard, and imprinted on Nathaniel.

They all began to hurdle downward. Like a comet, complete with a fiery tail trailing in its passing, the group sped toward the ground dangerously.

For him, momentum didn't exist, but the perception of distance did. As they all fell, he heard himself pleading his case. Nathaniel spoke, not audibly, but rather, from an internal place that had somehow been accessed. Those thoughts, he instinctively understood, were perceptible to the others around him.

"I don't know why any of this is happening, but I know this can't go on! This has to end now!"

"Quite right!" Riven agreed.

At that point, their spinning freefall made contact.

Then, on uneven and jagged solid black ground, the struggle continued. Riven and Aegis became a blur of motion as each attacked the other.

Blindingly fast, the two fought furiously. When one or the other was forced back, their counterparts seamlessly leapt in to continue the battle. The imposing figure that fought on Aegis' behalf had searing black eyes under a stern brow that was nearly as dark. His opponent, fighting at Riven's side, was conversely pale and slight in comparison but seemed to be equally matched. Nathaniel watched intently as Riven, Aegis, and their companions battled inhumanly on.

As the conflict intensified, all four combatants engaged each other. The war dance between them became both stunningly beautiful and captivating as it was horribly intimidating. All the while, Dr. Nathaniel Ash stayed out of the fray; his own capabilities yet undefined.

His part in the struggle had been unclear to him up to that point. That clarity came in the realization that he was in fact the crux of the conflict. He had been pressed to act decisively by Riven and he'd been advised to accept a kind of passive inaction by Aegis.

He'd been swayed to either side at several points throughout his ordeal. But he was fundamentally divided. Although he had always tenaciously believed that he was the sole initiate of his fate, no definitive course of action had been chosen up to that point.

Their urgings left him wavering.

Just then, a swing occurred as Aegis and his dark partner took the momentum from Riven and his sallow ally. With furious aggression, the two began to overtake their opponents, weaving in and out, attacking one, and then switching to the other like artful choreography.

Riven tried to counter but he was being methodically pushed back. All of the exhortations to action rang through the Dr.'s head. He watched as Aegis and his companion beat back the other two and he replayed the bidding he'd gotten to simply-do nothing.

That reasoning became contradictory to him at that moment. That counsel seemed hollow and self-serving to him as he looked on at Aegis' exertions.

The attempt to stave off ruin had been a life's pursuit for the Dr. The desire to push back against the seemingly insurmountable, was a continuous exercise that he'd committed to long ago. The equation began to take form inside of him, and the conclusion that he came to was one that he'd been attempting to, although half-heartedly, reach all along. The encouragement to submit by Aegis had become wholly counter-intuitive to him.

Looking on with emotion boiling up, Nathaniel felt himself warily moving forward. With tentative steps, he inched closer to the fray. He allowed his intentions to remain ambiguous in the moment for fear of disclosure. He still refused to acknowledge an allegiance, even to himself.

As the distance between them was closed, he saw that Riven and his counterpart were fighting back-to-back. Their opponents had truly gotten the upper hand. They were both almost simultaneously forced to one knee, and the outcome of the fray seemed inevitable.

Riven's voice cut through the fray in a beleaguered tone, "You would have them meekly go into servitude!"

Aegis responded passionately, "Dissembler! You've worked to portray corruption as virtuousness throughout this remnant's alignment!"

Riven shot back with, "I've done nothing but extol the virtues of self-sacrifice! What have you professed other than narcissism?"

"That very attribute is at the basis of your insurrection! Relent and succumb to the Balance that preserves us all!" Aegis bellowed authoritatively.

To Nathaniel, there was subtle oppression detectable in the demands of Aegis. The call to submission didn't sit well with him. It never had.

Had Aegis been deviously leading him to betray his own interests the entire time?

Just at that moment of revelation, despite the tenuous position Riven and his partner had found themselves in, a Machiavellian smirk curled the corner of Riven's mouth.

Nathaniel was oblivious to it; focused on Aegis' aggression. Riven's outcome looked bleak.

That outcome, however, was changed irrevocably by the Dr.

The protestations began weakly, unsurely, but grew vociferously with the imminent peril.

"This isn't right...He only encouraged my help... Asking me to disregard the afflicted is monstrous..."

Still consumed with his struggle against Riven, Aegis attempted to clarify his stance. "Allow me to illuminate the deception that you've fallen under. You have been manipulated..."

Nathaniel's denial came without hesitation, "No..."

"These Abhorrent here work toward ends that you remain blind to..."

"You're wrong..." Ash countered.

"Your resonance is inherently meant to be synchronous but has been driven to dissonance! The elimination of this malignancy will prove curative!"

"Aegis you're wrong, I won't let you!" Nathaniel screamed thunderously.

A strike intended to be the terminus of the aggressions was begun.

With his declaration still ringing, Nathaniel leapt forward and with palms pressed together, drove his hands through the back of Aegis like a scapel. There was no resistance as he plunged them through what appeared as flesh, but was in fact incorporeal.

He held his stance as Riven seized the opportunity by simulating the move, thrusting his own hands through Aegis' chest. The two clasped hands within his breast and a glaring radiance began to spill out of the breach. Then, a wail like hurricane winds and a howl like thunderous echoing washed over the totality of everything around them.

With that, all that Aegis had been, seemed to unceremoniously cease and disperse.

Nathaniel had most definitely acted intently.

The ones that fought alongside Aegis and Riven ceased their combat, as it was clear that an allegiance had just been solidified.

Resolutely, and reverently, the companion of Aegis assumed a dignified stance, his hands clasped behind him as he spoke.

"Although your alignment has been chosen Nathaniel Ash, redemption can be reclaimed. Call on me when you conclude that you've been misled. You may call me Sheperd."

Instantaneously, he took to the sky like a blinding beam of light.

Stillness replaced the melee.

Battling through distorted perception, the Dr. struggled to identify where he was. Unsure if it was mere moments or an eternity, he fought for clarity. Gradually awareness came. He slowly began to realize that he was in familiar surroundings.

The ambulance bay encircled him, still in fiery ruins. As he spun slowly, his returning there eluded him. Every experience he'd had since his initial waking, raced through his mind's eye and came into question. His disorientation was unbalancing.

"I can eliminate your confusion." he heard Riven state from somewhere behind.

"How did I get here?"

"You never left." was Riven's answer. "The shroud over your perception will fade soon. You will come into your own in a very short time. For now, you have the opportunity to witness the beginning of your transmutation. Look..." he instructed.

With hesitancy, he turned to witness an unbelievable sight; himself, as he was before the fiery incident ever began. He watched as the flames receded and died down to nothing as if time had been turned backward.

As he saw himself standing under the archway just outside of the hospital's entrance, the familiar piercing sound of an ambulance filled the air. He witnessed his own face grimace as the vehicle came to a stop near him, and he struggled to recall what the cause for that grimace was. Then, it became obvious as the driver stepped out and around, and that same expression was returned in kind.

Daniella Ramirez was driving that rig that day.

It began to become clearer to him. He began to reconstruct what happened. Transfixed, he saw his past begin to unfold.

"Hey D..." he witnessed himself attempt awkwardly. Then her unmistakably intentional lack of response followed. The sight was distressing to re-live.

"Listen..." he began.

But the EMT seemed to have very little interest in that when she interrupted saying, "What you did was shitty as hell Nate." Her lowered tone did nothing to mask her anger.

"I know but you have to hear me out." the doctor countered.

"I really don't."

"Are you telling me that you can't see my side of things?"

The only response to that question was an incredulous look from Daniella.

"Nate, you can't act like a kid and then demand to be treated like an adult. If you had a problem with us, then that's fine, we could have talked it out. But you tried to avoid the situation by changing my shift? You can't manipulate people like that." she admonished.

He looked on at the situation as a third-party observer as it played out. The vaguest of feelings pushed at his awareness as he began to recall what he was seeing. He started to voice the same response that he had used at the time, his voice sounding in unison.

"I can, and I will again." he echoed, but vacantly that time.

"You were naïve to think that he could just be a friend without a hidden agenda D! I told you from the start that the guy was after something."

"And I told you that I could handle it myself."

"Well now you don't have to." he retorted.

"I need this job Nathaniel and I can't afford to push back. But what you did means I have to rearrange my life. I have classes that are built around my work schedule.   Because of you, I have to upend everything to placate your fears."

"I did you a favor even if you don't realize it. First of all, that guy was just an orderly. He was sniffing around you like a dog. I just wanted to look out for you."

"You just wanted to assert your power, Nate."

"Yeah, I have pull, and I used it. It's better now this way because I'll see you more." he insisted.

"Oh, it's better now? It's better for you? How can anyone be so arrogant? You didn't look so excited to see me when I pulled up. Why is that? Is it because you know you were wrong whether you want to admit it or not?"

The doctor that he had been in that re-enacted moment, knew the truth in what she'd said. Even then, the third-party observer he was, watching himself re-live the day, knew he'd been wrong. He continued to watch the past as it unfolded before him.

"I saw a problem and I fixed it. I acted. What did you expect? I shouldn't have to apologize for looking out for you D."

"You can't control every outcome Dr. You can't affect any selfish change to things as you see fit. Sometimes doing nothing can be the best thing to do. Did you ever consider that?" she challenged.

"Doing nothing...? No, that doesn't sound like me."

"I guess not." Daniella agreed. "I have a patient in the back. We can finish this later, can't we?"

"What if I come over later with a nice bottle and your favorite take-out and we find a great movie to ignore? I want to talk to you about something else. Sound good?" he said with a smile.

"It sounded good...but you had my schedule changed...remember?"

Daniella ended with a barb and the doctor felt the sting of his mistake for the first time.

He'd been through so much since that scene in the ambulance bay that he'd just re-lived. Guilt was an unfamiliar emotion to him, but his recent ordeal had made him reconsider its validity.

That regretful scene hadn't played itself out completely though. There seemed to him to be something more. A vague and troubling thing played at the fringes of his memory...

Back in that moment, Daniella turned to attend to the patient in the back of the ambulance. She unlatched the doors and began to swing them open as she'd done so many times before. Then, there was a spontaneous moment when the memory of the event and the perceived re-occurrence of it instantly coincided.

Just then, the Dr. Nathaniel Ash that he was in that instant, and the one that he had been previously, spoke the same word.

"Wait…"

That request went unheeded.

Daniella Ramirez opened the doors to the ambulance and the last receding sunlight poured in, highlighting the occupied gurney. On it, a frail, elderly indigenous woman was reclined. She was weakly struggling with both the covering on top of her as well as something underneath them.

As Daniella started to climb up into the rig, the lady pulled the item she'd been fighting with from under the blanket. It was a little pink lighter that had somehow escaped notice.

With one hand pulling at the oxygen mask on her face and the other shaking, the familiar "Flick, Flick" of the lighter sounded and a tiny flame was lit. That fire was small, but it was more than enough to set alight the free-flowing oxygen that was keeping the woman alive.

Before any action could possibly be taken, an explosion consumed the back of the rig and then the whole of it as the gas tank became engulfed.

Although his perception was altered due to his disembodiment, witnessing the explosion from his newly detached vantage point did little to lessen the distress.

His form moved ethereally through the disaster untouched. Newly aware of heightened capabilities, he experienced the explosion with inhuman perceptions. The speed of the blast responded to his desires to either slow it or speed it. Because of that, he examined it with awe from multiple angles.

In one instance, he focused on the living fire. In another, his attention went to the beautiful but doomed Daniella. The lovely woman lying on the stretcher exposed a thin brown wrist that revealed a metallic medical tag wrapped around it reading: Eyote, Winona.

Then, he shifted his gaze to the one that had been him. His intent in the moment was observable. In the minuscule time between the thought of some imminent, undefined danger, to the explosion itself, Nathaniel's thought process became transparent.

Movement suggested that he'd intended to spring toward the EMT, toward Daniella. His intention was to help. That effort was futile in many ways.

As he continued to watch things unfold, the blast rushed out toward them, sending debris out dangerously, as if the fire needed an accomplice at all. A piece of that debris, a pair of scissors, buried itself deeply in Nathaniel's temple as if being resigned to the fire was not enough, that second sentence had been carried out callously.

Full comprehension of his irrevocable end was reached as he watched himself and the woman he loved being consumed by the conflagration.

Dr. Ash witnessed that death with increasing dispassion.

"So now you see the whole of it.", Riven stated.

"So now I do." came in reply.

Riven continued by saying, "Your ending only led to your proper alignment. All that you have witnessed, was the Endgame playing itself out."

"I see. It's becoming clear to me now. Aegis was continually telling me to do nothing. Daniella was asking the same of me... But you, you implored me to act. I did. I injected myself into your battle, and - here I am."

"Yes, here you are. You are now as I am and have been.", Riven said eagerly.

"And what is that Riven? What have I become?"

"Inimical, you've become Inimical.", Riven stated reverently.

"I - was a doctor..."

"Whatever you *were*, you are now Ash."

Endgame Trilogy

Symmetry

Endgame Trilogy

For days and weeks, medications were obediently taken with no positive effect at all. Why should there have been a change? They'd placed their desperations in the hands of someone who lacked any real insight and prescribed per quota.

Raf watched helplessly as his sister's loving essence deteriorated in front of his eyes. But without a different strategy, he knew, the situation would only become more and more untenable. He left work agitated and sought distraction.

He wanted to take the strain from her. He wanted to relieve his sister of the trauma she'd been going through, even at his own expense. Sacrifice was a minor demand. He'd done so willingly in the past and nothing would make him want to undo it. Rafael was more than prepared to do it again if it meant his sister would be unburdened. His intentions were in the right place. But unfortunately, at that particular moment, he was not.

Without a better alternative coming readily to mind, he found himself at the corner of a bar, in the corner of a room, of a dive on the corner of a street.

His search for inspiration turned into self-indulgent recrimination. The need to soak his concerns if even a little before heading home had become habitual. For an hour or so, a drink or several would be nursed in pensive silence. No one was ever confided in. No one was ever there. Raf's thoughts remained his own. That much was customary. But he could never look on himself from outside of his burdens. He wore his state-of-mind on his face like a warning.

"What's wrong? You look as if you have a target on your back."

Startled out of his preoccupation, Rafael spilled a little of his drink and then turned to answer whomever it was that seemingly snuck up on him to offer that unsolicited and trite observation.

"Where did you come from?", Rafael asked in legitimate bewilderment. He was shocked at the degree of fixation he must have been overcome with that would allow someone so close, at his elbow, to go unnoticed.

"From where you are going...", was replied by the brooding man beside him. His eyes were diverted and buried under a heavy and furrowed brow. How long had he been there?

Rafael turned away and attempted to dismiss the statement as barstool rambling. Then he responded to the original question posed. "I would gladly wear that target if I could." Then he completed the thought under his breath, stating, "Better me than her..."

"We feel the same way.", was almost growled back at him.

The statement felt like a threat and Rafael responded. Turning to face the man, only an empty stool was there to receive his scornful intent. Rafael's mouth dropped in disbelief and then his drink followed.

A quip about the spill came then, "See, that's just alcohol abuse..."

No one was in that seat, or that corner, or that entire bar but him and the bartender. Had he succumbed to voices and visions as well? Before he could dwell on that, something else proved to be more immediately concerning

Three men came in as if on cue, spouting several incoherent things about their politics. The way they looked, their dirty baseball caps, and woefully inappropriate slogans on their T-shirts, said all anyone would need to know about their leanings. They decided to turn up the volume at first sight of Rafael.

They weren't alone. A woman came in with them possessing the same raucous spirit. She was, as Rafael saw it, marginally attractive. He thought that she was obvious and loud and that she would benefit from a little modesty. But, despite not really being his type, he could see that she had some appeal. He was never the kind to hide such appraisals.

The immediate problem was that she, quite obviously, felt something similar toward him. The asshole she'd come in with was quick enough to spot it. That kind of slight was intolerable to someone like him. The thought of it alone was enraging. That insulting failure to mask her desire was the tipping point that sparked the distinctly problematic and unwanted attention they chose to direct his way.

Rafael began to prepare himself. Then, his promise to his sister came suddenly to mind. This was an opportunity to live up to her request; to not fall short. So, the decision was made to finish what was in his mug and leave without incident. That decision wasn't unanimously agreed to. Intent and outcome can sometimes be inverse.

"Hey, kid!" the largest and loudest of the three shouted toward Rafael. "Did you do the right thing? Huh? Did you cast the right vote today?" he prodded.

The fact that it was an election day didn't register with Rafael until that point. Politics were only meant to be a passive control of the obedient, where active resistance was called for in his view. Right or wrong, that was his belief. So, no, he hadn't voted and would most likely not have voted to their satisfaction if he had.

"No." was all Rafael simply stated.

"That's un-American son! Where's your pride?"

"I might have lost it back in Brazil..." Raf pondered, not quite under his breath. Then, reaching a conclusion, he finished his thought by saying, "No, I didn't really, I just don't give a shit about your politics or your candidate."

How quickly he'd forgotten to leave quietly.

The perceived insult those three men felt couldn't be hidden even if they'd wanted to. They came in with bad intentions, and to them, those intentions found a justification.

"Sounds like you should go back where you came from." another of the group said.

A come-back played on Raf's lips for only a second. Wrestling against it, he drank what he had left, stood up, and agreed with those men instead.

Walking past them, he almost made it to the door without escalation.

All he'd wanted to do was to consider the best way to help his sister in peace. That wasn't meant to be.

From behind, one of the men, disastrously for him, dropped a forceful hand on Rafael's shoulder with the intent of stopping him. One blindingly fast and aggressive armbar was applied and one knee met nose with a "CRACK!".

For the briefest moment, everyone stood frozen.

SMASH!

A glass flew past Raf's head, barely missing before the other two men were on him. He was not participating in an exhibition. Class was not in. He found himself fighting to stay in one piece.

The men were burley and might have intimidated the average bar patron, but they were showing themselves to be prone to throwing hay-makers, and Rafael wasn't prone to falling for them.

Not outmatched by any man, in particular, Raf was though, in fact, outnumbered. That reality allowed one of the men to land a stunning blow that did bring some dimming to his sight, even if only briefly.

One of the chimps got behind Raf and applied an amateurish half nelson. His pungent body odor was almost enough to turn the fight in their favor. Rather than subduing Rafael, it gave him recovery time as it lulled them all into thinking he'd succumbed.

A fast-shifting of his weight, a twisting of the hips, and a subsequent strike to the man's groin bought his freedom.

The next aggressor changed the rules drastically by producing a rather small but still lethal pocket knife. An otherworldliness came over him as his perceptions compressed to pinpoints and his actions responded compliantly to many years of training.

The first knife strike missed. As did the second. Undeterred, that man struck again, and un-like the effortless disarmings in the movies, Rafael chose to use his best defense; he leveled the man with a barstool. Only then did he apply a wristlock that separated the man from his blade.

The pummeling began in earnest then. They'd crossed a line.

As Rafael unleashed upon that man, he'd drifted dangerously away from himself, and the knife he'd stripped made its way to an exposed neck. The others he'd been fighting worked to extract their man, but Rafael was largely detached, he was outside of reason. He brushed off their every strike. He'd regressed to another time and to another country; he regressed into an unsuccessfully repressed remembrance.

That day in Brazil, when the Dos Santos children had the nightmare of the Shadow Man towering over them, Rafael and Raquel had seen, experienced, and understood more than enough to assess their situation. It had been life and death.

Raquel fought with all that she was to escape his grip, to no avail. Rafael's pleading only managed to send the situation into ruinous freefall. O Homem Das Sombra's intent was to punish; with finality.

He'd reached for the serrated weapon that he carried at all times. That blade had indiscriminate blood upon it. It had a vast tally of souls stolen. The two of them were meant to be counted among those.

His ham-like hand sought the blade but came back empty.

When Rafael attacked the Shadow Man earlier, the thought was never that he would be able to overpower him. Rafael Dos Santos was quick-witted and talented. He turned the skills that he'd been forced to ply against the unwitting, against the very beast that taught him.

When Raf wrapped himself around the man, he lifted that fearsome blade right off of him, expertly, and he now presented it threateningly, demanding the release of his sister.

O Homem Das Sombras didn't show the slightest trepidation, he didn't hesitate, and he didn't release Raquel. Instead, he mercilessly dragged her off of her feet and violently shook her little body in front of him, declaring, "I will kill you both where you fall! Give me the knife! Give me the knife!"

Even through fear and screams, Raquel lashed out. She dug small but claw-like fingers into his eyes, causing him to, deservedly, wretch with pain and drop her. As she scrambled away, Rafael reacted when he knew she was separated.

Two little hands enfolded around that weapon and two little legs planted themselves as two little arms drove that hideous blade deep into the Shadow Man.

That beast died quickly and unceremoniously.

"Irmã! I had to Irmã! I had to!"

And now, he held another man's life in his hands at the point of a blade. It sickened him and he sent the knife spinning away furiously, to bury itself in a wall.

That act should have been seen as a juncture to peacefully part ways; as a ceasing of hostilities.

It was not. They fell on him.

Raf took a little punishment before he could separate himself with a few well-placed blows. He had no desire to continue the fight and he backed out of the place hastily, but not before he noticed the look of satisfaction on the face of that only marginally attractive woman, that it could be argued, was the cause of the entire debacle.

At a jog, he made it to his bike, started it up, and began to peel away from the brawl, only to be chased and cursed violently. The sound of a muffled pop and something stinging followed him as he sped down the street. His only thought then was to go home.

Raquel was there by herself, resisting panic. Raq rarely showed a glint of her vibrant nature at that point; she'd almost completely succumbed. Her stare was too often vacant. Her mood was always detached. On more than one occasion, her brother watched from a distance as she rocked where she sat, muttering and moving in ways that appeared to be meant to guard herself against some unseen assault.

Fortunately, she'd been able to take time away from work, so none of her students had to see her in that condition. Rafael couldn't afford to do the same, which meant that there were periods when she was alone. In those times, she suffered.

Diva had a sadistic predilection for abusing Raquel with her losses. Those losses included long-forgotten family and the culture and land they lived in. The loss included old and newfound friends that were ripped away. The loss, most regrettably, included her love and the future they'd have had together.

In those instances, Raquel curled up defensively as she was verbally beaten. It had become, regrettably, familiar.

She considered calling her brother in the hopes that he could reassure her. She felt that she knew what might be coming and she desperately wanted a reprieve.

Reprieves were seldom granted. When they were, Glori appeared to Raq and could be credited for them. Glori's presence was much less haunting than her severe counterpart. Glori's words were always spoken with encouragement and softness, but the fact of her, the manifestation of her, was unnerving despite it all. Still, her comings were preferable.

While lying on her side, on the floor of her bedroom, that voice she'd heard many times before came over Raq's shoulder. With a shudder and the conscious decision not to face it, Raq felt herself tighten with fear. She questioned what she'd heard inwardly, but refused to ask for clarity out loud. Fearfully, she raised the shiny black face of the phone she'd been clutching, to see what was reflected at her back.

She then heard Glori pronounce, "The curvature of circumstance has quickened the outcome, Raquel."

With no acknowledgment offered, she continued, "What you've been through thus far can be turned against you or to your defense child."

To Raquel, that statement almost sounded like an offer of deliverance. That was something she couldn't ignore.

"W...What...?" she asked aloud, stammering. Her own voice sounded unnatural to her.

"A resolution plays itself out as we speak. The time and space of your disposition, as well as your brother's, doesn't creep, it races. He will require more fortitude than you are displaying at the moment."

It took that critique to force Raq to turn, to face her. It was a monumental but necessary effort. Slowly, Raq sat up and managed to turn her head to peer over her shoulder. The familiar beauty of Glori looked down on her placidly.

"You won't leave me alone; either of you. You won't stop coming to me and *she*-she *rips* at my mind..." Her voice shook as her eyes began to well with tears. The frustration of everything that she'd experienced of late had built to a breaking point. She released it with a scream, "What do you want!"

"Peace little one- I encourage more resolve like that which you've just displayed. This is for the benefit of your brother."

"What does he have to do with anything that I'm going through?"

"I assure you that he will need your support and affirmation presently.", Glori stated in her accented, lilting tone.

"Do I look like I'm in any condition to hold him up? I can't think straight! I can hardly- talk straight. These drugs aren't helping me!"

"You've lived your lifetime with him girding you, as it should be, and he will continue to do so. But, recognize when that must be reciprocated and don't fail to act."

"He's *my* strength...he's *my* anchor...it's not the other way around." Raq offered meekly.

"The two of you work very much as a vessel; as one. Conception, delivery, and development all correspond. You have a concurrent role to play. He may act as an unbreakable hull, but you-you are the compass. Diva's goal is to disrupt. Her efforts have had the desired effects have they not? You are unmoored. If you remain adrift, how can your twin hope to stay afloat?"

'I'm talking to myself...I'm just talking to myself... and I'm telling-me- that I want to hurt my brother?' Raquel silently put words to what she thought was her inner struggle. The words never left her lips but they elicited a response from Glori just the same.

"The struggle that you're involved with is only partially inside of your essence Raquel Dos Santos. It is quite comprehensive."

"Doesn't that prove it? I'm talking to myself here and I heard...*you* heard what I was thinking! I don't know, maybe I..."

"...just need stronger drugs...?" Glori continued, completing the statement that Raq began. She elaborated, defying Raq's previous logic, stating, "If this is all, in fact, a manifestation of your damaged psyche and we share one mind, then kindly duplicate what I've done and tell me of my purpose."

Raquel was at a loss.

"Thank you for indulging me. Now, I tell you, sincerely, that I want you to be a buoy to Rafael when the time comes. The structure of events is turning toward that very necessity. Your testament can provide firmament under his feet. That, my dear, is the emancipation.", Glori declared ominously as her typically pleasant tone shifted abruptly.

The meaning behind that very drastic change wouldn't remain hidden for long. Raquel took no solace in that belief though, knowing that it would undoubtedly cause her more distress. Her fears would soon be realized.

A roaring engine, gravel under tire, and the sound of countless insects broke through the otherwise peaceful night, followed by the squeal of brakes and an angrily slammed tow truck door.

Before entering the isolated and dimly-lit house, Flay inspected the door as he always did, looking for the same piece of string he routinely placed in the door-jam before leaving each day; a premeditated trap to indicate that   anyone entered the house while he was gone. His mind saw cleverness where others would have seen paranoia. Finding that string right where he'd left it, he entered satisfied.

One lone bulb was turned on. That one light was all that was allowed to counter the dimness. Comfortable in the gloom he lived in, he set himself to his standard routine.

With delicateness, an exquisitely cared for violin was retrieved and soon, the sound of the most magnificent playing filled the stale air. His melody was slow and plaintive. His technique would have been unpredicted if anyone else had actually been present. However, all of his ability could not entirely transform him from the wretch that he was.

Flay stood before a make-shift alter resting on a decrepit-looking table, comprised of two unlit white candles, one unopened Bible, and, gruesomely, six black-feathered corpses that were splayed out, pinned in a line to a tattered piece of wood. They received the serenade he offered. In time, his song wound to an end and he moved to his next nightly task.

In the kitchen, which was tiny, cluttered, and smelled of something rotting, he placed one plate and one knife down before him. From the shelf, he pulled down a large oval-shaped can with the unappealing picture of a chunk of meat; ham.

The smell of it mingled with the other odors. With coaxing with the knife and the typical sound, it slid out of the can and fell on the plate in front of him, the jellied goo all over it splattering.

Quite strangely, he retrieved one more utensil from a drawer before sitting down.

An absent amusement settled on his face as he took a cutter in the shape of a gingerbread man to the pink slimed slab in front of him. Six un-cooked figures were cut out and laid on his plate. Then, before a bite was taken, something took precedence.

The door to the basement was to his right. First, deliberate footsteps echoed behind the door. Then, one creak sounded and the slightest of gaps appeared.

Urgently, Flay leapt up from his chair, sending it crashing, and threw himself at the basement door; not to slam it shut in fear, but to open it in anticipation.

In the blackness staring up at him, three figures stood, somehow, just apart from the shadow.

He immediately fell to one knee fawningly without being instructed to do so. Flay recognized the first figure and both craved him and feared him. He knew him as Forge. The second man was larger and imposing with the threatening stance and heavy-looking brow of a fighter. Lastly, a woman stood with them with contrasting bleach white on brown skin. Flay had never seen her before and ambivalence toward her presence began to fester in him.

For that moment though, he wisely held his biased tongue.

Forge regarded him with an unreadable expression for a time. Then, he began to address his minion, saying, "Flay, you've been attentive thus far. Good boy. We're pleased with your effort-for the most part."

"There is a deficiency in your offering. It remains incomplete." The large man's accusation was damning.

"My companion has a point. Riven can be a bit of a stickler about expectations. You have let one of the intendeds go un-gathered. If you aspire to be one of us, close the gap!"

Those words reverberated within Flay. A line of drool fell with the slightest of whimpers.

"I see by your, pitiable reaction, that we've sufficiently impressed the requisite urgency upon you, but something goes unsaid..." Forge posed.

"I...I'm sorry...I will close the loop. She's as good as cut! All I need is the right opportunity and her influence will be pruned." Flay sought to reassure as well as to forestall punishment.

Having stated his intentions, he hesitated.

Flay had no capacity within him that could hide his misgivings from his visitors. Having the ability to decipher his thoughts wasn't necessary to see that more needed to be brought to the surface.

"And...? State what you must." Riven prodded.

"Why is that here with you!? I don't understand! Isn't she the opposed? Isn't she unclean? Ain't I superior?"

His indignation was directed at the woman in their daunting trio. His worldly prejudices were brought to the conversation with these otherworldly visitors. He should have thought better of it.

Calmly, the one called Diva addressed his ire.

"Is the blind worm in a position to condescend to the majestic swooping down upon it?"

Then, blindingly, she ascended with a gaping maw, breathing a hot acrid wind on him, singeing hair and skin beyond bearing.

Her point had been made indisputably.

"Fulfill your purpose.", Riven commanded.

"Reward requires execution, my friend." Forge said in his patronizing tone.

"Try my patience again..." Diva left the threat hanging in the air.

With that, the door slammed forcefully enough to bend inwardly.

Flay fought to contain what he felt. He'd been enticed by the promise of a position among them and he was failing to meet the requirements. Anger built in him as he seethed where he still knelt.

Awkwardly, he stood, moving quickly to the front room in search of an outlet for what had been evoked in him.

Absently, his hand went to retrieve the violin he'd been so delicately playing earlier, and with it, he began to furiously smash the altar that he'd held in such high regard. Blow by blow, each of those decaying birds was attacked until the very table gave way. The remains of the beautiful instrument were thrown aside and he rushed to fulfill his promised tithe to them.

The front door slammed behind him and the truck door followed that. A diesel engine broke through the night as the tow truck moved, lurching down the road recklessly toward the promise of an overdue victim.

At the Dos Santos house, the atmosphere had changed severely. Glori had become uncharacteristically hostile. Raq learned the reason for it harshly.

BUZZ!!

Her heartbeat in her chest to break free.

Raq jumped as her phone, once again, startled her with urgent and unexpected alarms and vibrations. She'd had enough! With a grunt and the full force she could muster, that phone was hurled down with destructive intent!

Still facing Glori, Raquel noted that her outburst got no reaction at all from her ethereal visitor. The calloused expression on her face was directed behind Raq.

From over her shoulder, she heard, "Save your energy- you're going to need it, Thing!"

With her focus set tenaciously on the one called Diva, Glori directed her words to Raquel, saying, "Undue influence by this one will be the ruin-and not only of yourself."

"Sage advice from the Anathema! Abandon her now, whelp, and let the worthy be heard." Diva had the unmistakable tone of entitlement in her voice; as if contradiction would be impossible.

That was not how Glori saw things.

"Speak to me of worth when you produce it rather than extinguish it."

Witnessing them interact, the hostility between the two was a first for Raquel. They'd never materialized at the same time. Individually, each was difficult to bear. Together, she felt herself cower. Their animosity filled the room and overwhelmed her.

Diva perceived that discomfort and goaded her further.

"You wallow in your feebleness. You're a disheveled husk of a thing and I'd weep if it were in me to do so!"

Glori countered, "Her every word is a misdirection. She'd have your spirit hobbled so that she and her kind could profit…"

"You may not reveal…!" Diva commanded in vain.

"There has never been an instance that I required direction from you! What insight could you possess that I have overlooked? Don't presume!"

Diva spoke then, attempting to appear as a rational advocate, "Raquel Dos Santos…! Listen to me! This one is mistaken. I only comment on your current condition because I desire your fulfillment. Truly. For too long you've attached yourself to the disloyal; Rafael."

Diva's accusation forced Raquel to face her.

"No." she defied.

"No? No!?" Diva raged. "His self-interests have led you around like an ankle-dog for half a lifetime. Should I innumerate your losses?"

"Why are you doing this?" Raq asked without expecting an explanation.

Glori offered a response, "Recognize her attacks as what they are; a diversion. Her every urging is counter to your true necessity Raquel."

"Your presence offends! Our conflict can begin prematurely if you insist dank whore!" Diva lashed out and assumed an aggressive stance in anticipation.

Glori stood defensively but disregarded the threat. She wouldn't be baited. Her attention never turned from Raquel.

Raquel was experiencing complete panic. She had no way to counter the threat she was surrounded by and had no escape from it. She was bereft and alone.

"Yes!" Diva exclaimed. "You are alone!"

The thoughts Raquel had, were not her own. She chalked it up to self-delusion, erroneously.

"I know your mind, Thing, but not for that reason. Continuing, you are very much alone! Why deny it? Why fight against it? Even an iota of wisdom would make you embrace that fact and capitalize on it!"

"What are you saying?" Raq managed.

"You can do for you! Stop relying on another and get yours! Abandon co-dependency and excel! You don't prosper with your brother. You are self-contained-just exemplify your power!"

Glori saw the gambit for what it was but could not forcibly convey it to Raquel. Reason was her only available tool.

She began with, "Ask what is to gain by driving a wedge between Rafael and yourself. The answer need not be apparent; the question itself should provide pause. Symbiosis is the nature of you both."

"Where is he now?" Diva demanded of Raquel.

"What?" came from Raq with a whimper.

"Witless Bitch, I asked you of his whereabouts! You don't know. Regardless, where ever he is at this moment when you are so desperately consumed with anguish, he's not where he's needed is he?" Diva accused.

Glori reaffirmed her position, saying, "Don't allow lies to mislead..."

"But..." Raquel countered, "It's not a lie. He's not here."

"That's right, little Thing.", Diva said in a tone that was nearly affectionate.

Raq continued, "I don't know where he is now but I do know that he'll be back. He always delivers when the time comes."

The slightest ease of tension came over Glori after hearing Raquel's words. Perhaps Diva's attempted corruption had in fact fallen short. Glori offered encouragement.

"Yes. Good. Disregard being led by the iniquitous. You have a role to fill..." Glori urged.

"*You* have a hole to fill!" Diva spat in frustration.

With that, the stale-mate that had endured was broken. Fierce stances were struck by both of the beings as they squared off in front of Raquel.

A piercing, shrill cry came like gale-force from Diva then; presumably a battle cry. Her appearance began to change dramatically as her back hunched and her arms elongated.

Glori responded with a show of force of her own.

Unseen winds from behind blew her garments forward as her hands glowed white-hot.

For a moment, Raquel was petrified. For so long, she experienced more fear than she thought she could stand. The conflict between Diva and Glori now made those times pale by comparison.

She didn't know what would happen next and whether or not she could bear it. Desperation overcame her. It began with an attempt to will the situation away, followed by far too passive urgings of, "No, no, no, I can't, I won't..."

With a single step taken toward each other, Raquel's anxieties erupted from her.

"LEAVE ME ALONE!"

She'd screamed that demand loudly enough to overcome the sound of Diva's wailing. Their confrontation immediately ended as the two then shot upwards and out, as if the ceiling was immaterial; disappearing entirely.

That was exactly the moment Rafael pulled into the drive recklessly. With the growling motorcycle turned off, the shrill scream it had been drowning out suddenly came through.

Raf got off of the bike unsteadily and broke toward the door, stumbling before righting himself. Even from outside he recognized his sister's voice, but he'd never heard such terror in it before.

Once inside, he scanned the room cautiously. Then, the urgency of Raquel's cries sent him frantically to her. At the top of the stairs, he saw his sister backing out of her bedroom, arms held above her head defensively, and moving erratically as if she was fending off an attacker. When her eyes landed on her brother, there was no recognition in them. She backed into the nearest room, the bathroom, and sought to slam the door-to ward him off.

Rafael pressed against the door as Raquel fought to slam it shut. He was struck by the amount of effort it took. Even as she abandoned the struggle, her screams never ceased. Blindly retreating, she fell into the tub rigidly, tearing down the shower curtain as she went.

With gentleness, Raf tried initially to soothe his twin, calling her name, his hands held out, gesturing for calm. That attempt failed. His voice turned, harshly.

"Raq! It's me, stop! Raq! You're having another episode! He tried to take her firmly and shake her but she fought him.

The disconnection from her felt agonizing.

With patience and time, he was able to lead her back to him. She began to acknowledge the familiarity of her brother's face and of his tone. She hugged him in a death grip and he tried to right himself but their position was awkward.

"It's not enough to ignore them..." Raq began to plead.

"I hear you. It's over..."

"I can't shut them out! I can't push them away."

"Focus on me now, you're safe."

"Threatening...powerful..." she gasped.

"Raq, let it go! There's no one here to hurt you."

"You don't see...You don't hear!"

"The pills-have you been taking them? Have you taken them today?"

"What? Pills? Uh...Yes...No! No! Pills don't help!"

"Raq! Listen to me!"

"No! You don't understand! But she told me..." Raquel let the thought go unfinished.

"What did you say?"

Raquel stood, mechanically, and vacantly wandered out and down; muttering.

Rafael heard pieces of her incomplete thoughts as he followed her downstairs. She said something about his disloyalty and she stated something about being misled.

Dedication to his sister made any thought of her believing such things incredibly painful to him. He withered a little where he stood.

"Rafael-where have you been?" Raquel posed the question with a disturbing coolness.

"Raq..."

Without turning to face him, Raquel pointed out the fresh wounds that were readily apparent.

"What did you tell me? What did you promise me!" She'd spun on her brother at that point and for the first time in their lives, all of the anguish she'd been experiencing was directed like a weapon at him.

"You don't know what is happening to me! Dancing was my passion and that's gone now! I've lost Casey! My mind is in shredded little painful bits! I'm fuckin' insane! You get that? And this was the worst day ever! I'm being attacked and no one else can see or hear it-but everyone thinks force-feeding me never-ending chemicals will sort that out at any moment now. The one person that I have left on the face of the Earth to turn to is supposed to be you. YOU! And where were you-again?"

"Raq..." Rafael began meekly.

"I said where were you when I needed you!? You were doing the one thing I asked you to stop so you could look out for me. Why? You were fighting...WHY!!"

"I DON'T KNOW WHY! There is nothing but anger deep down-I accept that but I'm not fighting for laughs. I'm good at it! And people need to be protected!"

"*I* need to be protected!"

"I've been protecting you your whole life just like Sao Paulo!"

"You won't stop or be satisfied 'til you kill again!" Raquel blurted before she could think better of it.

Up until that point, the mention of any past tragedies they'd been through was forbidden by an understood but unspoken contract. It was sacrosanct. It protected them both and allowed them to endure.

Raquel, entirely because of anguish, had just broken the pact between them; with malice.

With head lowered and without a word, Rafael turned and left their house. He offered no excuses or retaliation. His soul very well might have been ripped from him and left on the ground behind. He felt weak. His thoughts were cloudy. He was hurting.

Once outside, hesitation gripped Raf. He found himself directionless. The night air was cool but comfortable. The moon was full and high providing extraordinary clarity. It was only his spirit that was unstill.

Almost involuntarily, he reached into his jacket, as he had so many times before, with the initial intention of dulling the stinging feelings washing over him. His consoler, his flask, was chill to the touch. His thoughts of late were focused on the servitude he willingly pledged to that little metal container. The most immediate disappointment he'd just inflicted on his sister solidified a need.

That need had, up to that point, been to obliterate his responsibility; to obfuscate his role. That line of thought had run its course and proved unsustainable.

With the kind of sound that is generated from the limits of a tormented spirit, a violent hurl sent that flask far down the street. It landed with a metallic echo repeating itself as it bounced.

He'd, internally, just made a new covenant with his sister.

She had been watching just inside the doorway, concealed by the dimness, through tears and understood the importance of his gesture.

Maybe it was because he was so agitated, maybe it was the otherwise stillness of the night; but for some reason, Rafael's intuition was triggered.

Something caught his ear.

Coming from somewhere close, the only sound echoing in the darkness was that of an engine; a diesel engine. Scanning without fully knowing what drove him to, Rafael spotted the slow creep of a truck halfway up the street. Its lights were, dubiously, turned off.

He froze and that truck followed suit.

Rafael remembered vividly what his sister described to him regarding her attacker. He was well aware of what he'd been driving that night. Raf had his suspicions and he intended to act on them. Only one step toward that truck could be managed before, abruptly, that diesel thundered to life, bolting like a hiding animal being discovered.

Rafael's will outweighed his ass though, as he moved to block the truck from escaping shouting, "STOP!" without any way to enforce that demand.

With murderous intent, a swerve toward Rafael sent him dodging across the pavement and into the grass with an uncharacteristic sprawl. He was somewhat slow to get up, but he quickly reached down to his reserves in determination. With a snarl, he reached into his pocket, still possessing the keys to his bike, and started to pursue the stalking tow truck.

Raquel tensed at what she was witnessing.

Whether it originated within her or behind her was unclear-but Raquel heard Glori's distinct voice insisting, "This is the pivotal instance dear one, what would you do? His Endgame is unfolding and your role is inseparable. Aid or abandon?"

No consideration was needed. No coercion was necessary. Raquel spun on her heels, grabbed her car keys, and leapt from her home with purpose. Even from where she was, she took notice of the dark spots on the ground that remained where Raf had fallen. Cool clarity may have been the impetus, but she maneuvered that car skillfully and flawlessly as she pursued her brother.

10,000 pounds of truck careened through the side streets that led away from the disrupted "cleansing" that Flay'd sought. To him, the loose end that was Raquel Dos

Santos, left him seething. He'd missed another opportunity to harvest. A tantrum was thrown in the cab of that truck as he pounded the seats and frothed at the mouth; barely containing childlike whimpering. The would-be savior that followed him then was a very immediate concern, and he had to be dealt with.

Raf rode feverishly behind. All the while he battled to keep a balance between his adrenaline-fueled aggression and a distinct haziness that intermittently tried to overtake him. Riding harder became a dubious antidote. He had only one opportunity, as he saw it, to eliminate the threat ahead of him. The singular drive he possessed had served him in the past and it would do the same then.

The sounds of grinding gears, chirping brakes, and skidding tires echoed off of homes and then buildings for miles as the chase went on.

Raf had no way to compel that rig to pull over and could only hope to stay with it; knowing that it couldn't continue forever.

Raq trailed from a distance, intent on keeping up and supporting her brother. She watched as the driver of that truck attempted to initially lose his pursuer. Side-swipes came horribly too close when that failed. Attempts at forcing a rear-end collision were resorted to after that. No traffic light or sign was considered and no parked car or curb was guaranteed safety from any of them.

At that time of night, the streets were empty and the sounds of the chase carried; echoing through the business district they'd been led to.

Flay wove through familiar roads and alleyways, frantically trying to elude Rafael and culpability. But he couldn't manage it. Nearly manic at that point, a wrong turn at a wrong corner resulted in a violently blown tire that sent the truck careening into and over low hedges that were hiding a very solid brick wall behind them. The front end met it thunderously and fought against conceding, but lost the fight decidedly.

With the passenger-side twisted and suspended on top of the broken bricks, Flay drove a desperate foot down on the gas, hopelessly trying to free the truck.

Rafael witnessed the accident but he'd been too near and moving too fast to pull out of his turn safely; he began to go down painfully- low-siding.

For a moment, disorientation blurred everything that Raf could see or hear. It was as if a dark hood had been pulled over his perception. The moment froze the way moments like that do. Then, the thud of his body hitting pavement and the exhalation of everything in his lungs surprised him with their distinctness.

Failing to dislodge the tow truck, Flay opened the squealing door and fell from the up-ended seat gracelessly. Scrambling to get to his feet, sure that his pursuer would be on him, he realized that he was in fact dazed and presumably pinned under his motorcycle. Jagged teeth bared themselves as Flay took a step toward Rafael in over-confidence.

One step was all that Rafael allowed him.

He righted himself almost immediately and turned his attention to the scarecrow-looking cause of his sister's distress. With a scowl that promised punishment, Rafael stopped Flay in his tracks.

The true and cowardly nature that lived in Flay showed itself when Rafael's glare pierced it. He, sheepishly, took a step back and tried to turn; both cowed by the look in Raf's eyes and unable to readily break it.

Watching Rafael get up forced Flay into action. He bolted.

A resonating grunt of frustration and physical discomfort came from Rafael as he got to his feet to follow. He'd been able to scare Flay with his anger, but the truth was that he was bluffing; he was diminished.

She'd been trailing from a distance, driving only somewhat less recklessly, when Raq saw her brother go down forcefully. Involuntarily, she slowed, distracted by her concern. As she watched him struggle to rise, her urgency returned and she sped forward again. She watched as her attacker, wisely, fled. She watched as her twin followed unsteadily after him.

By the time she reached the corner where the wreckage was, she'd lost sight of them both.

Exiting the car, the smell of hot and burning engines wafted in the air around her. Although she wasn't sure which direction they'd gone, she made a decision and moved off quickly to find Rafael.

The area they were in wasn't residential, it was more industrial. Empty roads led between businesses and truck bays. Street lights were spaced evenly along the main road but the back alleys remained dim.

The situation was scary and that made the night oppressive. Raquel heard her own heavy breathing and questioned the route she'd chosen. Then, some clamor in the near distance told her she was close. She found herself behind a row of businesses. A tall fence lined one side and the back doors and receiving areas were on the other. Glass broke somewhere at the end of that area, urging her to move in deeper. So, she started toward the far end; toward the main road.

Something caught her attention and Raquel turned into fearful darkness down a narrow pathway between two corner buildings.

Her quick pace changed to measured steps as the light abandoned her. Her need grasped her and she, hesitantly, called out to her brother.

"Raf?" she said in a muted tone to no response.

"irmão...?" she attempted again, trying to project, but failing.

"And the noose slips around you."

The familiar voice chilled Raquel in all ways and she froze where she stood. Behind her, the echo of footsteps bounced off of brick. That forced her to spin and face him. She'd found a killer rather than her brother.

He stood there in a guarded pose, lanky and pale, with the intention of springing on her if she tried to retreat. When he spoke again, his words were rushed with giddiness.

"This is art! This is an homage to...to...murderous geometry! Do you know where we just happen to find ourselves? Don't speak! You'll cheapen this. Do you know where we are standing at this very moment? Here-is hallowed. There-is hallowed! This is the alter of my first!"

His giggle was repellant and unmasculine.

"You don't understand- (he said it aloud as a realization, not an accusation). This is the very spot where I rid this world of my first tithe to my liberators. With your death, I'll have closed the circle just as I promised them I would."

Remarkably, Raquel believed she understood what he was boasting about. The story of an unsolved murder a little more than a year ago came to her. It happened in an alleyway, between corner buildings, in darkness just like she was in then.

"You were denied me that first night by that- savior. Is that who you're calling out to now? I'd love to X him from my list as perhaps a bonus."

Enraged, Raquel spat, "That was my fiancé and he's dead, you sick piece of..." but she was cut off.

"EWWWW". Flay mocked her like a child while doing a silly little dance. "Saves me the distraction I suppose. Now, I have an appointment with transcendence. Will you just submit to the cuts now please, and thanks?"

Complying was never a thought. Raquel braced herself for the fight as Flay produced two severe-looking blades and took an eager step toward her.

That one was all he was allowed.

Flay's weak form folded when Rafael tackled him without warning. He was rag-dolled initially by the much more adept fighter and his knives flew out of his grasp. Raq watched with relief and moved closer to join in if her brother needed her. She didn't expect that he would. But, shockingly, both the surprise and Raf's edge were expended before her eyes. Flay gained the upper hand!

The thin man didn't have fighting skills. Yet he somehow managed to get on top of Rafael and began to pound his head on concrete with a desperate grip on his dreadlocks.

There was no question that Raf was far from being himself-but why? There was no time to consider it further before Flay retrieved his blades and set himself on Raquel again; the threat of Rafael only temporarily postponed.

Raquel Dos Santos acted before her stalker could. She bared her teeth and hefted a garbage can with a spinning move; hurling it at him like an Olympic hammer thrower. She hit her target as he and the metal can went down with a loud thunderous noise. She set herself to charge him, knowing that he might turn on her dazed brother and that he was, for the moment, defenseless.

"Why! Why! Why do you persist?" Flay pleaded. "This is my place to fill! Know yours! You're lost! No intervention can save you! Now DIE!"

Raquel screamed defiantly as the attack was begun. Her intent was more than simply survival; it was his complete ruin.

The totality of her courage was extinguished before that could be managed as the imposing figure of Diva appeared behind him, as if to bear witness to Raquel's ending.

Although he seemed oblivious to her appearance, he took notice of Raquel's dismay and took pleasure in it.

Flay raised his blades and made his killing move.

In that instance, time crawled as she thought about her brother, then her imminent death, then the malicious smirks on the faces of both Flay and his apparent benefactor.

Rafael stirred and struggled to rise, painfully aware of what was about to happen when his vision blurred. It wasn't from fatigue or pain but from brilliance.

At his sister's back, a beautiful and frightening figure materialized, shining radiantly and striking a defiant stance directed at the would-be killer. An unfelt wind blew her elaborate clothing and braided hair wildly. She framed Raquel like a protector and he had to shield his eyes, even for a moment, against the light. Rafael was enthralled.

Flay responded quite differently; harshly. It was as if the most unmeasurably horrific thing had appeared to him. His scream was shrill and reverberating. His fear was evident. His subsequent action was irrevocable.

In the midst of that piercing scream, the demonic man that called himself Flay drove his own hateful blades into his eyes in order to block what was, to him, the disdainful and painfully benevolent vision that was Glori.Horrifically, he dropped to his knees; writhing. That seemed inadequate to ease her assault and he went berserk, inflicting multiple stabs upon his own chest. Even in the darkness, his blood could be discerned as it pooled under his dying body.

As he withered, he posed a last question, "Is this the way?" Then, he slumped and ceased.

The satisfaction that Diva displayed went unseen by Flay because of the self-inflicted ruin he'd caused. She'd made no attempt to intervene. She held no regard for his leaking carcass. His defiled form was simply the briefest moment of entertainment to her perception. The sound she made as she allowed the shadows to enfold around her was barely a chuckle. Her presence was gone silently.

The light behind Raq faded. Rushing around the body, Raquel went to her brother. One arm went behind him for support. With her help, he began to rise.

They began to speak simultaneously, talking over each other; neither of them getting answers to the questions asked.

"Did you see that Raq?"

"What's wrong? How could he take you out like that?"

"Who was that...woman?"

"Did he stab you, Raf? I didn't see him..."

"But did you see that?"

"Yes, Raf, I saw it! I've seen her before. Haven't I been telling you that?"

"Yes, Ok. You told me. I never said I didn't believe you. I just never saw it- too."

A beleaguered expression passed between them and a firm embrace followed. They believed they'd survived a nightmare and come out the other side; intact. As they ended their hug and began to turn to leave that alleyway, something became urgently apparent to Raquel.

"Bro, what is this...?" Raq solemnly asked.

Raf looked down as she pulled her arm away; the arm that had been helping to support his inexplicably weak frame. There, on her hand, was something crimson reflecting in the moonlight. It became too clear to him just that quickly.

"You're bleeding! What happened? Did he cut you?"

"No. I meant to tell you back at the house..." Raf began before succumbing. He lost his balance and began to go down- only stopping it with the remainder of his will.

"I had a little run in-you know that corner bar the guys and I went to about a week ago...? No? Well, anyway...I was there again, just having a drink and... I think... I got shot."

Gripped with hysterical panic, Raq searched her brother's torso until she, in fact, found a wound. It had been roughly an hour since he'd returned from that bar and their chase began. All of that time, he'd been steadily losing blood and exerting himself; worsening his condition!

Preoccupied, neither of them initially grasped the sound of sirens that rang around them; nearing. Their struggle hadn't gone unnoticed. Someone made a call.

"Raq, we have to move."

With some effort, they gathered their strength and began to leave the scene. Nothing good could possibly come of them being discovered.

If only they'd had more time.

Without enough time or information to accurately decipher the situation, the first two cops on the scene saw a dead white man and immediately drew conclusions.

"Don't move!"

"Don't fuckin' move or you're dead! Show me your hands-both of you!"

Raquel separated herself from her brother and moved slowly forward with the intention of pleading with the police. That might have been somewhat naive.

With what could only be described as malicious intent, a large and overly aggressive man pushed past Raquel and confronted Rafael; gun drawn.

"Hands where I can see 'em Muther Fucker!"

"All right! All right! I didn't do anything! Easy Bro..."

"Don't call me Bro! Get down on your knees, now!"

"He's hurt, he needs help." Raquel pleaded.

That was the excuse needed. Non-compliance demanded harsh consequences. Some would refer to it as justified; some would refer to it as brutality.

Ingram struck at Raquel violently, unnecessarily, with the heavy flashlight she'd been blinding them with. Staggering backward, Raquel fell as her brother intercepted the subsequent impact that Ingram had intended for her. Multiple blows were landing as Rafael began to buckle. The punishment was something he'd withstand if it kept his twin from pain. He endured willingly as he always had. But then, Ingram attempted to attack Raquel again in the same manner. That was unacceptable.

"WHAT ARE YOU DOING! Don't touch her!" was blurted angrily by her brother. He launched himself toward the abusive cop determined to protect his sister. The look on her face was a combination of abject fear and disbelief that anyone would oppose her. Ingram tried to fend him off in vain.

First, it was a shove and then a wildly thrown punch, and then the struggle to take him down to the ground began. It happened in the span of a heartbeat, then her partner reacted; a look of malice twisting his face. Donaldson pounced on Rafael with unrestrained force. The butt of his gun landed against the base of Rafael's neck. That was enough to separate him from Ingram who retreated to allow her partner to subdue Rafael.

The burly, mannish woman moved back, and redirecting her attention, stood guard near Raquel, shouting orders repeatedly not to move.

Rafael was already weakened beyond the ability to defend himself effectively. Even though he wanted to resist, it simply wasn't in him.

Yet he struggled through pure necessity.

It was the natural struggle for survival. It was instinctual. Even in his weakened state, that cop didn't present much of a challenge. That was when his partner stepped away from a hysterical sibling and began to tase Raf; no warning given and no quarter given. The two of them took turns doing a brutal dance with an unwilling participant.

Tears flowed freely down Raquel's face as she struggled to rise on quivering legs. Soon, those tears were mirrored on the identical cheek of her brother.

There was no way that it could continue.

With the full weight of the malicious cop Donaldson sprawled on top of him, his arms locked in an awkward chokehold around a defenseless and innocent neck, Rafael Dos Santos faded.

She began softly, plaintively, "No...No...No...We're the victims here. That monster tried to hurt us. No...No...No...No..."

Then, the wave of grief that swept over her came crashing out. "What did you do? NO!!! We were almost free of him! NO!!! He didn't do anything! He killed himself! Do you think his evil eyes could stand Glori? My brother didn't do anything! NO!!!"

Several responders arrived and were witnessing what they thought was a definitive breakdown. The area was now bathed in flashing lights and bystanders.

As Raquel sobbed; beside herself in loss, she was being forcefully restrained by the partner of the man that was still choking her brother. That woman yelled angrily to a young paramedic that was rushing toward them.

"You! What's your name?" she demanded.

"Reese, it's Reese..."

"Shut up and listen!" she berated. "Can't you do something with this one? She's freakin' lost it. She's hysterical and I need her to shut the hell up! Give her something to calm her down!"

"Well..." Reese began.

"Now kid! I've seen it done before. Do it!"

It happened occasionally; he knew. He knew what she wanted done. With a little more time on the job, a little more experience, he might have refused. But he was not that confident yet.

So, as he was instructed, a syringe was pulled out of the case that he'd brought and a dose of ketamine was injected into Raquel to calm her as she was roughly restrained and pleading sorrowfully for her brother.

Whether it was an improper dosage or the degree of distress, Raquel succumbed. She stopped fighting, she stopped speaking, she stopped weeping and-she was still.

PART III: ADJUDICATION

"And thus, we are brought to our current disposition."

With the circumstance of their demise laid bare, Rafael and Raquel Dos Santos heard the Thrice, the body that they understood to be of a judicial nature, speak in chorus.

Then, the realization of where they'd found themselves hit him; they, along with the Thrice and an ominous group of adversaries, were suspended in the Heavens. Raf was being inundated with comprehension.

Without any evident cause, Rafael's perception expanded, instantaneously, to encompass the enormity of all. The vastness of what he'd united with was fully apparent to him. Somewhat to his surprise, he still had the capacity to be profoundly awe-struck; and he most definitely was.

The entire cosmos was spread before him, yet nothing felt distant. Everything unknown to him before and everything that was intimately familiar to him then was one and the same.

He would have expected fear, but there was none. He would have imagined loneliness in the dark bleakness of space, but that was not what he witnessed or experienced.

Anywhere Rafael turned his attention, clarity leaped forward, regardless of any amount of distance. Energy flowed visibly as an undercurrent all around and through everything imaginable. It was astounding!

Then, he turned to Raquel. During the entire time he had been working to convey his sister's and his account, she'd been immobile as if all that she was had somehow been rendered inert. It seemed his newly acquired and expansive knowledge had limits because he didn't know why.

"All unveils in time. You have not yet achieved your decisive frequency and so, we will extrapolate." the Thrice offered.

"Eventualities spring forth from developed and undeveloped potentialities providing access to options which subsequently spur choices that determine station. Raquel Dos Santos has been subject to an inordinate amount of distress and one of her potentialities is the inability to acclimate; leaving her unable to exercise options to determine any eventual station; as would happen organically in the vast majority of transitions. The collective gathered among us has had and will have a part to play. There is a divine interconnectivity between all of the aspects representative of the Nature present now;

both Chimerical and Inimical. You are all on figurative "Lay-lines"- a "Power-hub" in a sense. This body, which is Judicial and not Combative, will preside and adjudicate the Endgame and the disposition of all those concerned and involved."

"ONCE."

"TWICE."

"THRICE."

Comprehension and then acceptance came easier than Rafael would have imagined. Although no outward acknowledgment was required, a nod and an "I understand." was offered with newfound stoicism.

That was the very last moment without turmoil.

Flay was the initial source of it.

"He understands? I do not! I received inspiration. I received reassurances! The station of both of those murky trifles should be the stepping-stones to my ascending." Flay ranted as if transcending the flesh did nothing at all to enlighten him and in fact, solidified his earthly prejudices. He was thoroughly corrupted.

As Flay railed against the judges, behind him at a distance, four figures smoldered, seemingly in anticipation. Rafael instinctually knew them to be known as Forge, Riven, Ash, and Diva.

In formation, opposing them, were luminous and intimidating creatures that he, again, without foreknowledge, knew to be called Sheperd, Goode, Aegis, and Glori.

All of the players were known to him. The most prominent of that collective moved forward to address the Thrice with a resonant, penetrating, and accented voice.

"Sheperd, you have something to submit to us?"

"Good Judges," Sheperd began, "The very influence of these Abhorrent upon these two before us should negate their claim. Their approach was both premature and torturous. Would she willingly choose to align with them given a lucid essence?"

Sheperd's line of reasoning seemed rational to Rafael and he believed that their welfare was better served with the Chimerical. But others present disagreed; harshly.

"This perpetual charade of the Anathema gets old!" It was Forge that voiced his objections, adding, as a procedural afterthought, "O' Good Judges."

That sent a surge of anger through the gathering; the Chimerical bristled at it and the Inimical seethed in agreement to it. He continued, "The question was posed of who would choose to align with our righteousness? The countless. Look there, one stands with us now!" he gestured to the one at his back known as Ash. "Choices were made and opportunities were interrupted by them; I heard no definitive denials from that remnant!"

"Choices? Opportunities? Mine! Mine! I chose to follow and align! I saw my opportunities withered! Why do we continue to do this sad dance with these obsolete bureaucrats? Why!" Flay spoke out of turn and was near frenzy.

That only spurred others to do the same.

"Don't think that I don't know you." Goode directed his ire at Flay. "I know, intimately, what kind of thing you are. I know what you did to my family in life... I had no way to get to you then. But you're only a thought away from me... Now, the only opportunity coming your way is to beg me not to beat you into redemption!"

Flay responded vehemently, "My redemption will come when our overthrow of this pathetic anachronism called the Thrice is done and I am awarded my standing with these GODS!"

His words inadvertently revealed more than he intended; a sign that he lacked the sophistication of his would-be companions. The Thrice had been prematurely alerted to their planned treachery. The Inimical gathered there were well aware that they'd been exposed but were unmoved. They were greedily anxious.

"Your machinations are now transparent." the Thrice asserted. "Turn away from this course before...", but they were denied completion of their warning.

Riven cried, "For the Eonian Inimical Rule!"

Diva shrieked, "Damn them all to oblivion!"

Forge simply offered a shrug of inevitableness.

And with that, there was open rebellion.

Rafael hovered, astonished by the spectacle as warfare erupted around him at every turn and on multiple levels.

Raquel remained unmoving-heedless to everything around her. The Thrice were grouped dispassionately as always, just observing the fighting. It was Rafael that craved involvement. He knew that he had a part to play and that the outcome, whatever form it took, would likely determine his sister's fate. Despite his will, movement was difficult for him. Then he considered his twin's vulnerability and suppressed his urge. He tensely watched the individual clashes unfold.

For each member of the Chimerical, a counterpart in the Inimical engaged and peeled away in a personal skirmish; some were above where he watched and some beneath. They were like multiple bolts across the sky; entangled and explosive.

Their forms and appearances altered as each sped away and engaged with their rival. HIs gradual "tapping in" to shared sentience allowed him to distinguish between which of the vaguely human-like figures he was witnessing.

Above them, Sheperd and Forge met forcefully. Forge's billowy form swelled and attacked with gouging limbs and fearsome wings. Sheperd was blindingly glowing with energy that pulsed and flowed; coursing around and through him and his own expansive wings.

Below them, Glori and Diva glided through the dark ether surrounding them, gracefully and terribly, the way a manta moves through the ocean. They would, in turn, attack, retreat, and then turn and attack again. Glori had a fearsome grace to her. Diva's transformation, in stark contrast, was striking; revealing a form akin to a hideous bird of prey.

Turning his attention to those on his level, Rafael saw Goode charge Flay with ruinous intent. He moved like an arrow towards a target. It seemed as if Flay retained the same spinelessness he possessed in the flesh because he backed away fearfully, turning from side to side, trying desperately to find an out. In all the openness of Eternity, no out appeared available.

But then another intervened.

Ash intercepted Goode without warning and the intensity of their meeting sent a wave through their surroundings. Flay was given a sudden reprieve.

The two of them impacted and then deflected off of each other repeatedly. Once they separated, Goode gestured, throwing his arms wide which initiated a concussive pulse that sped toward Ash's position. One after another was sent out, targeting Ash. Resounding booming filled the air as they struck and the ones that missed the mark sailed on into the distance with an almost musical tone.

Ash countered and maneuvered away deftly until he found an opening and began his own offensive. As his hands moved up to touch his temples, a brilliant beam shot from the crown of his head like a laser toward his opponent. As Goode had done, so did Ash. One by one those beams sought their target. Some streamed away with crackling intensity and some hit their mark with stunning impact.

They railed against each other tirelessly and were not above verbal attacks. Goode's rang clearly as he searched Ash's motives, urging him to reconsider his allegiance.

"Examine what you're doing Ash! You've been deceived!"

"You only think you understand me! A shared perception does not equate a mutual comprehension Goode!" was Ash's answer.

"I detect the value you placed on your intellect. How 'bout you try to comprehend what that abhorrent devil did. You have at least that much capacity, don't you? Search your vast understanding!" Goode jeered.

"Can't you tell the difference between indoctrination and self-determination? I was given a choice to act on my own behalf and not to accept placidity. Can you say the same, Goode?"

Their discussion ended and their striving continued.

Back and forth they fought for an unknown measure of time. Through it all, Rafael observed, still guarding over his sister, in silent concern. Then, the struggle beneath them drew his attention away.

Glori lashed out furiously and it was captivating. The edges of what she'd become sailed gracefully, but they emanated destructive energy outward, set on the eradication of Diva. Her form flowed like a dancer swirling many willowy skirts. With rapid succession, those glowing shards were aimed and hurled with malicious intent. Had she been aware, the perception Raquel had gotten of any placidness or frailty would have been dispelled by Glori's newly-revealed ferocity.

Diva, on the other hand, exceeded the perception she'd presented. She, in essence, took on the appearance of a Harpy; bird-like with a leathery maw and, curiously, possessing several holes along her ragged wings and body. As they circled each other, her cries elicited shivers. Those shrieks were not meant as a warning; they were her weapon. Rafael watched as one hit its mark, but grazing, separating a small part of Glori from herself.

Diva spat a curse at her in a shrill scream, repeating "Wretched! Wretched! Wretched!"

"Your aggression against The Nature is the offense. Did you think we would let this go unchallenged? Insipid!

Vacuous! Mutineer! The Totality will remain despite you.", Glori vowed.

"There is more of this design yet to be revealed Chimerical!" Diva alluded.

That threat reverberated through the air and all of those present and was ominous. Despite that fact, no pause in the hostilities could be afforded by either side. Their collective warring continued with no sign of abating.

While some of the fighting had an almost visceral grace to it, the struggle between Aegis and Riven was baser; more of an exercise in brutality. Aegis had appeared peaceful in the past. The situation didn't allow for that type of vulnerability any longer and his aggression toward Riven bore that out.

Aegis had taken on a fluid characteristic. He wasn't rolling like a placid tide though. He was crashing like violent waves against Riven's defense. With each strike, arms shot forward like spouts and tore away pieces of what Riven was.

Riven responded by swelling to an even more opposing stature. His entire form became like a blood-red inferno and two arms like battering rams pummeled Aegis relentlessly. In short time, he began to gain the upper hand.

Rafael noted the barely masked disdain Riven exuded and voiced.

"Concede now Chimerical. Concede and allow your unavoidable ruin to enfold around you." Riven's words were level and filled with overconfidence.

"You lack clarity of vision insurgent. Your individual momentum can't move the entirety of the ocean. The Balance will persist. The most you can hope for is a merciful edification." Aegis displayed his own profound confidence in defiance, and that enraged Riven.

The conflict escalated.

Nothing that Rafael had ever seen or experienced remotely prepared him for what he was witnessing. No dream or imaginative moment measured up to what he and his sister were involved in. Their very existence was under threat. He fought to influence that outcome. Moving became easier for him as he continually attuned to everything that was. The physicality he possessed in life started to become analogous as his will and his form aligned. The realization that he'd have to contribute was not lost on him. That led him to a second realization; he hadn't accounted for Flay for some time.

Panic began to grow and then it swelled as he spun to see Flay, relentlessly stalking then as he did in life, closing the distance between himself and the prone essence of Raquel.

Rafael lunged to her defense.

His desperation made him more mobile, but Flay had somehow gained an advantage over him just large enough to be disastrous. The distance would not be made up in time. Flay turned to glare in triumph for what he, irrationally, believed was both inevitable and deserved before attacking. Entitlement surged out from him.

Rafael relentlessly fought forward as he braced for tragedy.

Flay hesitated long enough to gloat before striking.

"My directive is realized! This stabbing elevates me! Your end is overdue, darkish sacrifice!"

Flay's hands transformed into serrated weapons and swung toward Raquel Dos Santos but they did not connect.

Like unexpected saviors, three gleaming phantasms swooped in to protect Raquel; denying the killing blow that Flay believed was owed him.

Rafael was ecstatic; Flay was incensed.

As if they were shields locking into place, those three formed a protective barrier that defied breaching.

The attempts that Flay made were beaten back in an almost imperceptible manner. It was blindingly fast.

It took a moment for Raf to fully comprehend what happened.

Then, it became crystalline.

The ones shielding his sister were known to him. The first was her friend Kristina; wife of Goode and heinously murdered by the same pale butcher she stood against then. The second was Sophia; the daughter of Goode and Kristina, robbed of life too quickly. The last was recognizable but, if not for the interconnected knowledge that they shared, would have gone un-named. But he knew her as Daniella Ramirez. He'd seen her driving an ambulance one fateful day in the recent past. Her role to play hadn't been revealed.

As they protected Raq against Flay's onslaught, Rafael made headway and sped up his advancement. The distance wasn't much, his acclimation was the issue.

One slash was parried after the next as Flay reenacted the awkward display he'd performed so many times before in the darkness of his home. But he couldn't breach their defense.

As he struck, Kristina would break off from the others, retaliating furiously. As he attempted another cut, Sophia would separate and hurl her form at him blindingly, only to return to her original position. That dance continued relentlessly. They were more than a match for him.

When Kristina Goode addressed Flay, raw disdain was directed at him. Even through her soft, feminine tone, it penetrated damningly.

"Do you feel that you demonic fraction of a man? That is your reckoning barreling down on you! Your weakness is plain. Your licentious desire drove you to hurt what you were never worthy of and that's clear now."

Kristina's accusation wounded him visibly.

Then her daughter weighed in with a tone far more mature than her earthly age would have dictated. She condemned him saying, "You were allotted the role of a simp and a loser in life, and you will be judged even more harshly here and now!"

Flay was incensed and retaliated furiously.

The continuous opposition he'd come up against pushed Flay beyond what he'd been. With a scream born out of the frustration of failing, he transformed, sprouting several twisted and knurled arms; each ending in one form of sharpness or another. He'd become unexpectedly more horrid than he'd already been.

Beating down upon Kristina, Sophia, and Daniella, he began to taste his first measure of success. He began to wear them down with unrelenting blows. A gaping jagged smile elongated his features.

That eagerness was short-lived though.

The urgency of the situation forced Rafael to immediately find a way to overcome his limitations and throw himself into action.

Rage and determination launched Rafael toward the malignancy that was Flay as if unseen restraints had been broken. A shockwave shot out as he propelled himself into the fight.

Thunderously, Rafael Dos Santos impacted against the thing that Flay had become. It had been almost imperceptibly fast. The essence of his twin remained guarded by her three protectors. The adjudicating body of the Thrice remained dispassionate, detached, and non-combative as they observed the fullness of the conflict all around them.

The proficiency Rafael had achieved in life in the art of combat was without question significant. But it was a shadow of the possible. It hinted at the promise of what could be accomplished. With his transfiguration and grave necessity, he'd unlocked the fullness of his nature; and it was astounding.

He had transformed into a shining silver form of human perfection with flowing tendrils trailing behind him in place of the dreads that he'd sported in life.

Unbridled hatred was unleashed on Flay in a torrent of twisting kicks and blows too rapid to be counted. Raf had gained full mobility as well as an other-worldly capability and he used it with elation.

His body flipped, leapt, flew, and twisted in every perceivable direction, landing hit after hit against Flay as he flailed. Amazingly, Rafael even displayed the ability to disappear and to reappear in another position; a kind of teleportation. He used that strength to attack from disparate and unforeseen directions. He'd become incredibly formidable.

Despite the opposition, Flay would not be deterred. He'd become even more manic than he'd been in the flesh and, to some slight dismay of the Chimerical, he'd also become more proficient himself. He unleashed a barrage of slashes that were largely intentionally aimed and effective. Flay too had achieved a degree of what would be his personal perfection; treacherous as it may have been.

Their battling continued for possibly a moment or millennia; there was no differentiation. intermittently, a jagged limb would be thrust toward Raquel, which forced Kristina, Sophia, and Daniella to remain where they were as her defenders.

Flay sought to antagonize Raf then by posing the question, "How long can this persist? It's only a matter of time before I pierce the barrier of these sub-creatures and fulfill my assigned task-the tithe-the sacrifice!"

"It's only a matter of time before I pierce your hollow corpse-like soul! Look at the face of newfound clarity, you wannabe. Your failures have been monumental! Your ineptitude will be a testimony!" Rafael promised.

"You lowly, unworthy piece of shit!" Flay raged, void of any further pretense of elevation.

They fought on tirelessly and the would-be Inimical continued his attempts to harm Raquel, sure that   accomplishing that would provide the key to his attaining a position alongside Forge, Riven, and Diva. With so many flailing and stabbing limbs, one regrettably did find its mark; but it wasn't Raquel that had been damaged. It was Daniella Ramirez.

The unified comprehension that each combatant was attuned to allowed all those present to share knowledge. In this instance, that knowledge penetrated a previously estranged and preoccupied individual; Ash.

His awareness was triggered by the injury Flay had inflicted on Daniella and by her subsequent reaching out to him.

Ash broke off from the ongoing hostility he'd been engaged in with Goode and hastily redeployed himself toward the direction of Daniella. Goode was in tow, focused on his intention to enact retribution.

The other combatants fighting around, above, and below them never disengaged, although it was clear that they took notice and began to close ranks to some degree.

As Ash neared, Daniella separated herself and intercepted him peacefully. When they met, their joining took them out of time. Their parlay occurred wholly separate from the fray around them. Although there was pleasure in the joining, some measure of remorse came upon Ash. The circumstance of their deaths in the ambulance bay began to overcome him.

But their time apart didn't change their affections.

Daniella met him with softness and reassurance, saying, "Nate, don't."

"Don't? How can you ask me that? I'm doing what I must now. You must see that!" Ash attempted to rationalize.

"You've been manipulated, sweetheart. Only regret keeps you from seeing clearly." Daniella assured him.

"...How...?"

"Unclench your emotion, Nathaniel. Breathe-figuratively speaking." She laughed.

At her request, Nathaniel Ash initiated an openness, an accessibility, that he'd fought against for so long. He'd had it beaten out of him, in a sense, on so many occasions that, until his passing, he couldn't access those attributes.

"Yes, now you're seeing..." Daniella encouraged.

Images of his life and also his troubled Endgame scrolled across his awareness then. Congruencies between himself and others were beyond concealing at that point or on that plane.

Eyes that stared at him scornfully from inside fire in a Burn Unit; a living, stalking inferno that had been, in fact, Riven disguised. Those fires were a continuous, symbolic, mocking of Nathaniel's past and path. Even the base tormenting of an innocuous Native woman was unveiled to him.

As if Nathaniel had actually been present at the time, events rolled back to a stifling hot apartment where Mrs. Eyote, regrettably, overexerted herself. In opportunistic fashion, Riven appeared to her illicitly.

His objective was treacherous and also readily accomplished. Her fear at the sight of him traumatized her. The impetus of her cardiac distress had been Riven!

The amount of deceit that Riven had perpetrated was damning. The way that he'd presented himself as some kind of reasonable and sincere type of guide to Nathaniel was infuriating.

Coming back to the moment they shared, Nathaniel posed one heartfelt question to the woman he'd loved in life; a newly achieved liberation overcoming him. He asked, "D, what would your answer have been?"

"What do you think? It would have been "YES", Jackass." Daniella Ramirez teased him lovingly. She beamed with joy, and then, wistfully dispersed.

In the span of a blink or, for untold hours, unadulterated clarity had been absorbed into him. Daniella had been the bridge between Inimical deceit and redemption. Then, a conclusion was drawn and a new source of ire was called out. His allegiances turned.

"Riven...!" he declared angrily.

He hurled himself back into the fighting, careening toward Riven and retribution.

At the same time, Goode, who had been trailing Ash, understood the enlightenment that Ash had achieved and was perfectly attuned to the redirection of his hostilities. With a knowing acknowledgment, the two signaled agreement to each other as they passed; their erroneous fight behind them. Unburdened from the wrong battle, Goode sought to engage the true, definitive source of contempt; Flay.

The melee that Rafael and Flay were engaged in never waned. Their enmity had been profoundly cultivated and neither gave way. But, being consumed by the display of force that was unleashed against him, Flay perceived the imminent threat aimed at him too slowly. That's when Goode collided with him ruthlessly.

The two were sent spiraling; Rafael pursuing closely.

Twisting in a death-roll, Goode received multiple piercings and slashes, but none of them critical. Flay's cackling rang out all around them as they flew, proving exactly how imbalanced he'd been all along.

Separating himself, Goode countered with rapidly thrown pulses leveled at Flay. Many hit the target, impacting brutally, leaving Flay reeling.

Goode held his position firmly, offering a curse with every pulse thrown. His disdain was a weapon in of itself.

"This-is for my sweet girl! This-is for my exquisite wife. This-is for the torment I went through for six mutha-fuckin' months! Oh, and this one's for my cat!"

But, no matter the intensity, Flay's own chaotic frenzy refused to relent. Some of his twisted limbs were used to shield him while the rest struck out desperately.

But there was another that had more than a little fight left in him close at hand; Rafael had his own reasons to end his sister's stalker and he acted on them.

Between them, the fury Goode and Rafael unleashed was awesome. They circled and parried in concert flawlessly, as if they'd rehearsed. Flay struggled to withstand the barrage. He began wildly, blindly swinging out at them, spinning like a dervish.

Another conflict nearby was reaching a fever pitch.

Glori pursued her overmatched counterpart relentlessly through the dark expanse. Shards of light were shot like rapid-fire daggers.

Diva was in retreat. Despite that fact, she never stopped taunting. She never ceased her derisive jeering. Her attempts at provocation were only intensified with the unrelenting punishment she received from Glori.

"Your kind is nothing! Nothing! Sham whores all! The Chimerical dissemblers will be shown their worth before long! The debasement will be EPIC! YOU THINK THAT YOU ARE PREVAILING?"

Glori trailed her antithesis aggressively like a fighter pilot in flight, listening to the delusional ranting being spewed. After a short, soft but mocking laugh, she responded.

"The full measure of the Balance will be the prevailing force Abhorrent one. Consider your debt to pay at that time in dread."

"Damn you, bitch!" was Diva's frightened response.

As Diva was being routed, her attempted evasion forced her to fly erratically in the direction of Raquel's listless form.

"Riven! Riven! Deceiver!" Ash vehemently roared through the heavens as he moved toward the position where Aegis struggled against him.

The duplicity Riven had used against Ash had been uncovered and a price to pay for it was owed. Ash intended on collecting regardless of the risk. He neared the fight and saw the advantage go to Aegis. While Aegis lashed out continuously, Riven swelled more than he was dispersed and he pressed forward. Nearly upon them, Ash drew Riven's attention.

With a rapid motion, Riven spun from Aegis to send a piece of his burning form at Ash like a missile. Aegis reacted. He separated himself and extended a limb, flowing more rapidly than Ash could have moved; intercepting that projectile and deflecting it away from its target.

Deftly avoiding a mistargeted assault that Ash unleashed in return, Riven swooped beneath Aegis, rose up behind him, and entwined two scorching, snake-like limbs inescapably around his torso. A snapping, electric, burning static began to ring out loudly; the beginnings of an incineration. Ash witnessed Aegis falter.

With that action, Riven, Aegis, and Ash all hesitated; be it in exhilaration, defeat, or dismay.

As Aegis slumped in Riven's grasp, Ash unleashed his anger with an immense beam of energy fired from the crown of his head, borne on the sound of his screams.

That intensity cut through Riven's chest, penetrating and exiting the other side. That brutal trauma caused him to release Aegis and to retreat from his limp form as it slowly descended. At a short distance, he waited, guardedly.

"Aegis!" Ash called out. "Aegis...?"

Ash caught him and held him upright with ease, attempting to assess his condition; a remnant from his past profession.

With some effort, Aegis lifted his head to regard him.

"Aegis, I...apologize. I should have listened to you from the beginning. Now, look at what I have caused."

"The introduction of an antigen into a system may sometimes result in deleterious effects. The greater health is ever the goal though, is it not?"

"...I...I've failed you a second time Aegis."

"No. Your actions haven't failed me; *my* actions have fulfilled me. The goal that you did not know to acknowledge was to be-*directed* - efficaciously Doctor. All that you've done has enabled that outcome. Nathaniel Ash, the opportunity for learning is near completed. Remove the barrier of hubris from the process and accept your instruction. You have not, will not, and cannot control the myriad calculations that equate to the immense sum of experience! You act as an integer in the equation-a *factor* in the diagnosis. I serve The Nature. What will you serve?"

Previously, in his figurative infancy, in the realm of the Endgame where he'd first encountered Aegis, that statement would have defied understanding or gone unheeded. But he'd grown since then. He'd begun to recognize the part he had to play and that all of his past experiences were necessary to bring him to that clarity.

"Thank you. I understand Aegis. I only wish that I'd..."

"...Come to the enlightenment before the end?" Aegis completed the thought.

Nathaniel simply agreed, "Yes."

Aegis then answered with, "Endings are subjective..."

He'd offered his last lesson and faded to mist.

The fury of Ash's condemnation bore into Riven where he'd been suspended; attempting to reconstitute his essence. Then, a second destructive beam followed that look; negating any progress he'd made toward healing. Riven recoiled and withdrew. His path led directly toward the spot Raquel was hovering.

Nearer to the position of Raquel and the Thrice's neutral observance, Flay's treacherous whirling kept Rafael at bay; at least for a time. While Goode launched concussive hatred at Flay, Rafael sought an opening.

Flay was beset on all sides. Goode attacked ceaselessly, Rafael inflicted punishment and sought his end, and the victims he'd taken such pleasure in harming while he was seeking his ascension, were guarding his desired final testimony to the promotion he'd coveted.

He sincerely wondered why no one pitied him.

Then, a vulnerability in his defenses appeared and Goode struck with intent.

The blow successfully landed; leaving Flay reeling. That opportunity wasn't wasted. Rafael appeared directly in front of his lurching, detestable form and delivered several strikes before they could be countered. Quickly, he dematerialized and repeated.

Goode never let up and the impact of their combined efforts began to be apparent. Any semblance of intent or skill Flay had shown in his attacks began to fade as his many jagged arms took on more flailing motions.

Desperation sounded in his voice as well, when he could be heard letting something near a whimper slip into the void.

The pity he'd sought became ironic.

Still, he pressed toward Raquel.

Coming up behind Flay, Rafael sought a decisive conclusion to the struggle. His now silvery form brightened where he hovered and the tendrils that replaced his dreads extended, shooting forward at his express command. One by one, they sought out and restrained the arms of Flay with whip-like speed.

Flay was bound; held vice-like and prone. Goode

swooped in closer at the sight of it; anticipation propelling him forward.

As Rafael tightened his hold, Goode glared at Flay, directly in front of his panicking twisted grimace. When he spoke, he conveyed the calmness of victory.

He offered him the chance to deny his defeat.

"Let's hear your pleas of entitlement. Tell us how your motives were justified..." Goode said in a mocking tone.

When Flay responded, it wasn't directly to those that held him. He directed his imploring to those he'd sought to join.

"Don't abandon me to these lesser things! I should be one of you! I've sacrificed toward your purpose! The stains mark the streets where I've proffered." The meekness that had always been his true essence poured out of Flay in a pathetic whine.

Resolutely, Rafael stretched Flay's multiple captured and writhing arms wide and said, "Smile, it's dark out..."

Goode began to build his energy, intent on amassing a tremendous amount of power to deliver a death blow capable of ensuring the disintegration of Flay.

Flay understood and he cried.

As the other engagements were being waged in separate hostilities, a distinctly singular and perpetual conflict played out simultaneously.

Sheperd and Forge were bitter and enduring enemies. Their disdain for each other was immemorial. This contest was one of the innumerable others that they'd enacted, each time contributing to the aggregate sum of the Balance.

Much more often than not, Sheperd prevailed.

On occasion, Forge overcame. Either way, the reconstitution of the defeated occurred in the proper measure of time; allowing the Totality to endure in the intended state of Balance that was so very integral. Forge had become disillusioned by the inescapable and designed function of reiteration.

That longing for a disparate outcome infected several other of the Inimical with the same conceit and initiated the insurrection that they were undertaking.

Forge fought Sheperd with a self-prescribed devout purpose.

Sheperd fought for something larger; he fought for Eternity. He fought for the Totality.

These particular Chimerical and Inimical combatants were experienced and familiar with each other's ferocity. The last time they warred, another present there now influenced the outcome in Sheperd's favor. Forge twisted in hatred.

Their fight covered vast distances instantaneously. There was no border or restriction that contained the aggression.

Sheperd's brilliance seared Forge's murkiness when they came into contact. Forge's bleakness sought to engulf Sheperd; to quell his energies completely. Over and over, they exchanged blows, slashes, impacts, and derision.

Violence between them, atypically, had a beauty to it.

From one end of the expanse they dwelled in, to another, they traded damage. The shared perception of their circumstance provided awareness of the struggles around them between their allies and enemies.

As they re-entered the vicinity of the fray, Sheperd felt Aegis succumb. That occurrence bred grief in him. His energies ebbed, and Forge eagerly lashed out.

In like manner, when Riven was run-through by Ash, the un-foreseen betrayal enraged Forge and allowed for a similar distraction that Sheperd exploited;

resulting in a minor loss of essence.

Diva's decisive retreat was noted, but concern for her defeat never developed. To the Inimical, success was never contingent on individual combat.

Around the periphery of the larger warfare, Sheperd and Forge raged against each other's objectives; neither conceding defeat and neither pulling a blow.

Flay's feeble, anemic pleas were heard by all as his ending was shown to him. With both Diva and Riven in a strategic retreat, one that none of the Chimerical had yet divined, only Forge was in a position to attend him.

He had no intention of doing so.

Even Flay's depthless, limited perception gleaned that he'd been misused. He'd been assured a place next to the select and elevated superiors. He believed that he deserved recognition as an elite and in his own estimation, his killings and fealty earned that position.

Flay implored his deities for help.

"What have I done that is lacking? I am one of you! Pay my balance and exterminate these mud-things! I'm of your ilk! Destroy! Destroy! Free me!" he raged.

Rafael held the raving Flay securely as Goode amassed his energies and offered one last bitter condemnation.

"Say hello to oblivion."

Goode's power exploded outward like a cannon, directly from his chest, engulfing Flay as he singed away to nothingness; his pitiable wail filling the expanse that surrounded them all. He was ended and swept away like dulling embers.

At that moment, Diva raced past them from below, followed by Riven, shooting like a bolt, in a similar trajectory.

Ash had been pursuing him but broke off when he neared Goode and Rafael. Realization struck him and he needed to communicate what he'd worked out to them.

As if momentum had no bearing, Ash stopped instantaneously near Goode and began speaking with urgency.

"Listen, both of you! That little display won't be sufficient!"

"What?" Rafael asked.

Ash posed the question, "What is the first law of thermodynamics...?".

A wordless, confused glance passed between them. Goode was an artist, and Rafael was a fighter. Neither of them remotely understood what was being asked of them.

With a hint of his earthly aggravation and ego still present in him, Ash answered his own question.

"The law of conservation of energy states that energy can neither be created nor destroyed - only converted from one form of energy to another…"

For a moment, their expressions remained. Then Goode, who was not unintelligent, understood.

"That pale, soft son-of-a-bitch isn't dead and gone! His energy has only been dispersed-not destroyed. He can be reconstituted!"

Ash affirmed Goode's statement with a, somewhat, sarcastic, "…And the winner is!"

Rafael grasped the dilemma and sought an answer.

"What the hell do we do? How do we prevent his re-… re-grouping…or whatever? How to we "dead" this bitch?"

With the remnants of Flay visibly floating around them, the solution became apparent to Ash.

"I have an answer. We have to absorb him. We cannot destroy what is already in existence, we have to convert it by consuming it and making it part of each of us."

Rafael began to object, "Wait, what? I don't like the sound of that and I don't think I'll like the taste of it either!"

Goode conceded the logic to Ash and respected the intelligence that he perceived in him. So, he chose to make the attempt.

"It makes sense. This is the only path forward, the best guarantee we can have that he won't reconstitute and inflict more damage. Let's do it."

Ash and Rafael nodded in acceptance and voiced their agreement in turn.

Ash said, "I concur."

Rafael said, "Let's get some!"

Before it became too late to act, they encircled the whole of Flay's energy and began in earnest, to consume it. The collaborative concentration of Goode, Ash, and Rafael allowed the Inimical to tactically maneuver themselves around the area where Raquel Dos Santos had remained immobile. The Thrice had remained impartial and at a minimal distance from her.

That left Raquel vulnerable.

She was much more vulnerable to those seasoned Inimical threatening the Balance than she'd been when Flay incompetently attacked.

Kristina and Sophia remained as her guards, but they would be inadequate against any one of the three, let alone all of them.

The Chimerical were present and pursuing, but each of them was trailing their targets. Neither Sheperd nor Glori was positioned between the Inimical and Raquel, and Ash had broken off his pursuit to eliminate Flay's threat.

That was an opening that the Inimical had manufactured and absolutely sought to exploit. Their manipulation had been as masterful as it was hidden.

Forge roared, "USURPATION!"

That exclamation was a signal to the others. It had in fact been a command. Coming from another source, it might have been an accusation. From Forge, it was intended to be the death knell.

Driven by spite, the Inimical dove forward.

Consumed with the absorption of each minuscule particle that remained of Flay's repugnance, Goode, Ash, and Rafael found themselves transfixed. The effort was a strain on them and required the full measure of their intensity. They'd committed to the judgment unanimously and none of them faltered. But, then the awareness of the Inimical aggression became jarringly evident. The threat to Kristina and Sophia caused Goode to hesitate.

Because of his concern, Goode began to separate himself. Defending his family was paramount to him. Even the briefest amount of disengagement sent a critical tremor through the atmosphere around them. The conduit that had been established by Goode, Ash, and Rafael faltered; but it didn't fail.

"Goode! Don't break the link! It's almost done! He's nearly contained!" Ash bellowed over the booming, sizzling cacophony that they'd initiated when they encircled Flay's remains. Their attempt was violently energetic.

"My family is in the line of fire! We've sacrificed enough!"

Rafael implored him, "I understand you! We've almost eradicated him Bruh! Don't make this for nothing!"

Torn, Goode twisted in indecision. Fortunately, just long enough to complete the task. With a single and final crackle of energy, what had previously been Flay, was absorbed.

Goode exploded away from the others in desperate urgency. The other two sped behind closely.

Kristina Goode and Sophia Goode remained tenacious. Their guard never dropped, regardless of the peril, as they sought to protect their friend. They were unmistakably clear with regard to the imminent threat that barreled down on them and they set themselves firmly; defiantly.

Forge, Diva, a damaged but still potent Riven, Sheperd, Glori, Goode, Ash, and Rafael all raced in a magnificent formation toward their position.

With a look at the immobile form of Raquel, and then at each other to solidify their resolution, Kristina and Sophia braced to be set upon.

That never happened.

As if a celestial reprieve had been granted, the three almost imperceptibly fast Inimical bypassed their defenses, revealing their true objectives. Raquel had never been the intended victim. The misdirection was encompassing.

Like shots to a target, the Inimical struck in succession, each of the passive, exposed, and unguarded Thrice that were standing by in neutral observance.

Their deceit had been flawless. The treachery had been perfectly orchestrated. Even with all of the well-known duplicity the Inimical were capable of, that cavernous level of betrayal was unprecedented.

A shiver billowed through the very essence of all who were present and resonated through all of vast existence. An assault against a designated judicial arm of the Totality had been executed brazenly. All present and witnessing stood immobilized; aghast.

Like a grisly replication of what was done to Flay, the assimilation of the Thrice was undertaken. The violation was strenuous and destructively potent. The energy expelled became a barrier that none of them could individually breach.

No word was uttered; the ramifications not being lost on any of them. Sheperd and Glori appeared to stand down, ceasing their aggression. Goode, Ash, and Rafael looked to them for any hint of direction but none was offered. The uncertainty passing between them all felt torturous.

Diva was the first to fill the abyss with her usual scorn. She stabbed at them saying, "You were told that there was more to be seen! Look intently you loathsome, inferior dupes!"

Riven joined her jeering in an uncharacteristically triumphant voice, boasting, "Conquest began here and now! No deadlock or impasse will stand! The Balance wavers!"

Elated with what was deemed an irrevocably decisive maneuver, Forge welcomed the conceitful derision being directed at the Anathema and joined in.

"This treason is savory to me. Your bewilderment will sustain my, admittedly, covetous ambitions throughout our ascent. Regard and then venerate the inception of the Ageless Inimical Reign!"

Forge's rant echoed maniacally.

"Sheperd! Glori!" Goode implored over the furor the Inimical initiated, "Don't let this happen! Do something!"

"There is an imbalance impeding us. With Aegis rendered inactive, we would neither affect a change nor survive the attempt." Sheperd responded with regret in his voice.

Rafael broke in then, "What does that mean... an imbalance?"

"Your neophyte ways amuse.", Forge chided. "But you won't have an opportunity to come to the necessary enlightenment so I will, graciously, spell-it-out-for-you."

Still immersed in the effort of consuming the Thrice, the three Inimical bristled at their nearing victory as they relayed the ramifications of what was happening.

There was a thought that their forthcoming was a tactic to stall; but without a decisive course of action, the Chimerical were left in check.

"You three have rather organically, begun to maneuver yourselves into an Etheric frequency. We travel in packs, or haven't you noticed? Forge-Riven-Diva. Sheperd-Aegis-Glori...And then we come to you;

Goode, the traitorous Ash, and lastly Rafael. It is a Triumvirate of celestial making. Right? Well, guess who crashed their party?" Forge allowed a childish mocking to come to his tone with that jibe.

Rafael broke in by stating, "So you have beef with them, fine. What do we, my sister, his wife, or Daniella have to do with any of it?"

Forge answered without restraint, "Distractions-all."

Maddened, Goode raised a question of his own, "What about Flay? What was his part in this?"

"He was a barely useful blunted tool.", Diva sneered.

"A tool! To what end?", Goode demanded.

"To what end...? To our end.", Ash surmised.

"Ah, yes. And the intellect asserts itself.", Forge offered in some slight appreciation of Ash's mind.

When Ash continued, his clarity was conveyed to Goode and Rafael precisely.

"It's become obvious to me now. All things fall in an order. He's stated that we are conjoined-allied, in some specific way."

Rafael listened intently and began to grasp.

Ash concluded, "We-the three of us, were the targets all along."

Riven, struggling with the effort to convert the Thrice and still impaired from battle, simply acknowledged, "You were."

Pushed to his limits, Rafael roared, "You want to do battle-Fine! Why not just come for me? Why involve the others?"

Forge revealed, "Who are they to you? A wife, a daughter, a fiancé, and literally the closest possible ally to you; a virtual duplicate. Each of them is inspirational to each of you. They were the fuel to each of your inner tenacities. You were each primed to oppose us per the measure of your frequencies. That couldn't stand. To hobble them is to hobble you, but even more critically. What better impedance could be positioned in your paths than the elimination of those brilliant lights?"

"Daniella was sacrificed! For what?" Ash raged.

"We've tired of the ceaseless teetering of a maintained Balance. Where is the supremacy in that?" Riven asked.

Diva asserted vainly, "Dominance is preferable and warranted. Let your eyes see me and know that!"

Forge continued, "By actively working to gain said supremacy, I-the Inimical will achieve direct access to the harvest-or people if you want to be pedantic- for the purpose of corrupting them before death, *before* their Endgame, so that imbalance can be achieved. Riven defeated Aegis and now their company's potency is diminished. Their third, their "Body"-Aegis, is gone. Our third is functional enough to ensure our triumph. The detestable Sheperd's Triumvirate is broken-Imbalanced! But be assured, that overdue accomplishment is only the principal imbalance!"

He then offered his full sanction by adding, "When this exertion is completed, and the Thrice has been supplanted, we're going to rain reprisal down on your withering husks as the Balance itself succumbs!"

The consumption of what had been the Thrice was almost complete. The energies that comprised them were dwindling. The consequences of that void being created became critical. As Goode, Ash, and Rafael looked in every perceivable direction around them, turmoil began to manifest.

On the Earth beneath them, a tidal wave battered down on a Caribbean Island relentlessly. The once distant Sun, now readily accessible to them, erupted with spouts of fire that would be too immense to fathom for most. The human toll became evident with the sharp escalation of violence that mirrored the celestial unrest that was unfolding above it.

Their heads spun at what they were perceiving. They bowed them solemnly in what the Inimical took to be tacit acquiescence of defeat.

But they understood that the assertion made by the Inimical of their interconnectivity was the key. The vague association that had begun between the three, worked its way to becoming a unification. They weren't defeated; they were silently conspiring.

With the remainder of the Thrice flittering, near failing, as if they were straining against the Inimical in an effort to endure, Ash, Rafael, and Goode came to a conclusion and struck.

In a thunderous, intermingled voice, they commanded, "Noooo!"

Squaring up against the Abhorrent ones before them, the inception of their resistance began. Side by side, Ash and Goode unleashed the full force of their animus on the Inimical; Rafael at their backs, anchoring them, bracing them with all his strength against the backlash. The crown of Ash's head burned white-hot while a concussive force, fueled by the knowledge of their betrayal, burst from Goode's core.

They'd unleashed hell!

When it hit, a seismic impact reverberated through them all. The sound was deafening. The antagonistic energies scorched and seared. Glaring, blinding forces from both factions pushed against each other in a struggle to overcome.

Cutting remarkably through it all, was the euphoric cackling of Forge, Riven, and Diva. They'd become completely untethered. The conflict that had been unleashed against them seemed ineffectual and the perception of victory was inebriating. They raved.

The forms of the three Inimical began to swell as if the power they were converting was enabling the truest and most potent iniquity in them to be brought forth. Based upon the chaotic disruptions that had been incited up to that point, allowing the completion of that transformation promised nothing short of cataclysm.

Nothing penetrated the barrier the Inimical had erected and the last vestiges of the Thrice were fading. Precious few moments stood between those remaining pieces and total eradication.

Over the din, Goode sought alternatives.

"We're not having any effect on them. We need another option!"

Ash challenged, "They will break! I can't see another way. We're hitting them with all we have!"

"NOT ALL! THERE IS MORE IN YOUR POSSESSION."

The statement came from behind them. The voice was familiar but-altered. The implication was of a weapon and a resolution.

Without conceding their position, Rafael turned to regard the unidentified source of hope that had presented itself.

Raquel looked back at him, delightfully offering him a signature wink.

"IRMÃ!" Raf shouted in his native language.

"Yes, but not alone." Came in response to her brother's elation. He came to understand that her voice had become a strange entanglement of the Thrice and her own soft tone. Somehow, they had merged.

The happiness that Raf experienced at the sight of his sister's recovery took on a wholly different, much more profound quality apart from the flesh. He'd become joy. He was regrettably forced to subdue that in the midst of the skirmish they were waging.

Ash and Goode noted the abrupt awakening behind them but never wavered from their bombardment.

Raf called to his sister then, asking, "What happened to you? I couldn't gauge anything from you or even sense your presence."

His question was necessarily bypassed in the urgency of the moment. The combined voice he heard urged him to focus, saying, "Clarity may come lazily, but it will come. For now, Brother, Body, Chimerical, an alternative presents itself. Attune and enact."

As she spoke, Raquel's voice alternated between each individual member of the Thrice and her own. More astounding than that fact was what became of her features.

With every sentence, her appearance transformed to mimic that of the individual Thrice that was speaking at the time, and then it would revert back again.

Goode broke through at that point, alerted to the potential alternative that had been referenced. Through his exertion, he demanded clarity.

"If there is another weapon to use against these bastards then make it plain!" he shouted.

Ash added, "They've nearly achieved critical mass!"

"Now or never Raq! What's the move?" Raf implored.

Raq's form stiffened where she hovered and with her head thrown back, she responded with that intermingled voice.

"We are the remaining vestige of the Host of the Thrice, speaking through the vessel Dos Santos. Her form shuttles our will. Now, we will instruct. This is the means to an undoing. This is the armament that will neutralize malicious ascendancy."

The roar of the tumult swelled. Precious few specs remained of what had been the Thrice as they dully diminished. Forge, Riven, and Diva were rejoicing. The desperation had peaked.

Ash endured but the resistance weakened him.

"My strength is failing! I can't maintain..." he began but couldn't complete. Goode was experiencing much of the same. Rafael lost ground as the feedback emanating from the Inimical lashed against their position. In short time, they were cast like dice.

The remnants of the Thrice completed their instructions as the three opposing the newly empowered Inimical gathered themselves.

"There is no in-fighting between the parallel frequencies of the Etherium for a reason. This is plain; use the malignancy within you as a bludgeon against itself. There is no immunity to the contaminate that they are. They succumb just as readily!"

A knowing consensus passed between them. Inspiration had been cunningly imparted!

Attunement for them was no longer an ongoing process. They'd thoroughly comprehended what was relayed and set themselves to the task.

Rapidly, Goode, Ash, and Rafael arranged themselves in formation and launched like projectiles at the position of their nemesis.

Alacrity and the immense hubris of Forge and his allies combined, providing a means of gaining unhindered advancement. The three vain dissenters against the Balance estimated themselves to be beyond the censure of such inexperienced Chimerical.

To an extent they were correct. But they had also underestimated their opponents.

Each of the Inimical, newly bolstered by the presumed consumption of the Thrice, was set upon violently.

Goode impacted with Forge, Ash impacted with Riven, and Rafael impacted with Diva. Each like a constrictor, they entangled their foes with relentless resolve.

Sparks of contradictory power arced violently. The sound of a baleful and eternal division filled their surroundings and were perceptible light years from where they fought by many disparate counterparts as well as many very much like them.

Through it all, they held firm.

Not sated in the least with the energies he believed he'd stripped from the Thrice, Forge and the others beamed with the assumption of what they presumed was the Anathema's folly.

"Inane!" Forge spat.

"Asinine!!" Riven agreed.

"Witless bitches!" Diva spewed.

Their manic laughter thundered around them. No initial resistance was offered as they were struck. The belief that they'd in fact been saved the exertion of capturing their prey dulled their collective perception. It was a momentary conceit that they hadn't yet realized they couldn't afford.

Ash disabused them of their belief.

"We gather your mindsets. I especially do, having once, if only fundamentally, been one of you. But you miscomprehend! Greatly!"

Goode continued to enlighten them stating, "You believe we've delivered ourselves to you naively, don't you? You're only somewhat wrong. We most definitely have something for you. But it won't be what you want."

Forge attempted to break free but he wasn't able to overcome Goode's virtual stranglehold.

Ash glared into Riven and tore at his wounds with his mind's eye until he'd carved him masterfully, driving a limb through his defenses like a scalpel through flesh.

Diva screeched madly until Raf extended what were once dreadlocks to engulf her jagged straining maw. Then, he pried them apart with the sound of breaking as he held her panicked body securely.

The reality of their abrupt restrictions fell on them. The previously belittled Chimerical were not acting alone in their attempt to arrest them. There was a hidden collusion. The fact of it incensed! They'd received illicit assistance!

Forge screamed, "What is this? The frequency of the Thrice is still prevalent! You're being directed covertly!"

The three demons began to desperately flail, attempting to extricate themselves.

Diva perceived the deception she'd fallen under as unjust treachery. No correlation to her own past foulness was recognizable to her. Somehow, her entitlement overrode her merit.

She screeched, "You're unworthy! You simply cannot handle my stature! It is your own weakness that prevents your acceptance! Honor me as you should!"

"Shut it!" Rafael demanded, intensifying his hold.

"Your intent is only somewhat hidden from us. Pouring your fledgling energies into us, even with an effete Thrice as back-up won't prevail. You've hit us with all that you are already. We shall just devour it hungrily! Even if you actually had aptitude, we are not permanently bound. We will shake you off quickly. What do you expect will come of this brief interlude, little infant Etherics?" Forge posed.

"The arrogance is astounding! And look who's calling you on it!" Ash accused, with a humorous nod of agreement from his cohorts.

"We simply want to deliver a message." Goode began. "Once, you told me that I was intended to identify the "remorseless doomed-do you remember that?", his question was rhetorical. "Your assertion was true. Can you feel my concentrated gaze, ZEROING in on you!? Your Inimical uprising hadn't completed the destruction of the Thrice entirely. Their vast understanding remains woefully underestimated by you even now. They were able to communicate the method of your eradication..."

"...And we have the means." Ash completed.

"Bottoms up, Fucks!" came eagerly from Raf.

With that, the entirety of animus that they'd absorbed from Flay was balefully redirected. Like a monstrous wave, Goode, Ash, and Rafael released the potent betrayal Flay'd received from his would-be deities directly into their cores.

The Inimical took the impact directly and they suffered.

What Flay had been, sent a ripple of disharmony through the Inimical. A disruption of the frequency had been introduced. He was only an acolyte of the Inimical and hadn't achieved any measure of their capacity. By releasing Flay, they'd essentially initiated his reconstitution. His inclinations would be intact. His immense cravings would demand fulfillment. Thus, Flay was intentionally released in a position to *take* his coveted elevation from them. That would not be something achieved through passivity.

Discord surged through the three bound Inimical as well as the bleak, awakening remains of Flay as he writhed through them. With reproving intent, Goode, Ash, and Rafael unlocked the totality of the anguish that had been experienced by Flay's victims like a sudden deluge. The depths of despair obey no boundaries and the Inimical found the chastising to be unbearable. The willful neglect of such sentiment was previously within the control of the Inimical. But they'd been caught without that capacity. At that point, their combined resolve was under assault and wholly inadequate. They suffered and they succumbed.

Forge perceived the terminal decree imposed on them all and he roared in defiance, monstrously.

Although Flay was not wholly sentient, his consciousness was clear enough for the Chimerical to interpret. Even in that state of being, he raved. Mistakenly, Flay perceived his release as a form of acquittal, brought about by his Inimical hosts' ultimate triumph. Once the actual situation unveiled itself, Flay railed furiously, in essence, razing Forge, Riven, and Diva from the inside of their essence out.

Nothing previously heard during their conflict compared to the sound of their devastation. Nothing mirrored the pall of the rebelling Inimical's gruesome obliteration.

The Chimerical shuttered with the effort of holding their adversaries at bay until the infection they'd introduced was complete.

The bystanders, Raquel, Kristina, and Sophia were awestruck by the forces that were unleashed before them. Even in their elevated state, what they witnessed was previously unheard of. Then, the energies on display rapidly expanded; becoming an existential threat.

Without hesitation, Sheperd and Glori swooped down on their position and enveloped them protectively; bearing the full brunt of the disruption.

With their intermingled screams, deriving from enormous strain, the Chimerical and the Inimical were separated violently. Goode, Ash, and Rafael were thrown clear and fought to regain their stability in the wake.

Forge, Riven, Diva, and Flay had come to nothing. They'd been undone. No ember or shard remained that could be discerned. Only the resonating aftermath left in the spanning surroundings indicated that they'd ever existed. What they'd been was dispersed; far-flung, presumably unable to be reconstituted again.

When the deed was done, Sheperd turned his perceptions outward in the wake of the wave as it swept through the heavens toward the earliest emitted spots of light. Variations of the entities around him were expressed throughout existence and they each witnessed what had transpired with intense interest. A symposium on the inviolate sanctity of the Balance had just been displayed as a definitive edification.

Though it was yet to be understood by most of those present, that was in fact, the first judicious act done by the newly promoted Thrice.

Righting themselves, the three unified and newly more experienced Chimerical approached each other with some esteem. It was the kind of reverence that soldiers reserved for each other. In a very real sense, they had in fact become Veterans. Their mutual salute remained silent though.

That acknowledgment shared; each sought their respective loved ones.

Goode, Kristina, and Sophia raced to each other and in an expression of their familiar union, touched and brightened with beaming incandescence.

"I told you that was only the beginning didn't I sweetie?" Goode jested with his daughter.

"I think you may have undersold that Daddy." Sophia countered, sounding more wizened than the last time they joked.

Ash was alone; Daniella having been a casualty to the treachery of Flay's ambitions. Their victory was regarded more pragmatically through that loss. The joy those around him shared was separate from what he experienced then; though sadness was left to the domain of the physical form. The most Ash could exude was profound satisfaction. His remembrance of Daniella was   symbolized in a meaningful way as he willingly separated a fraction of his own essence to form a perfect and radiant circle; a replica of the engagement ring he'd intended to give her the night of their demise. With a kiss, he allowed it to hover in the expanse they'd last shared, as a monument. Then, he turned away to move off toward his companions.

As he moved away unaware, the slightest filament of energy slipped itself through the opening of that symbolic ring. An unseen tinge of hope began to intermingle with Ash's gesture.

Rafael glided to Raquel and stopped short to regard her. They shared a look of contentment. They'd fought for and achieved a degree of security like they'd never felt before and they reveled in it for a time.

"You sacrificed yourself for me, Raf. Thank you."

"When I said "I got you" I meant it and I intended to fulfill that promise one way or another at some point.", he stated.

"You did. You always have." She said generously.

"Well, I always attempted to."

A knowing laugh passed between them.

"Thank you, brother. I'm so grateful to you."

"Thank you for being the one person I'd do all of that for, sister."

"What can I possibly do now to compare to this? Freakin' overachiever!" Raquel hurled the phony insult at him wryly in her typical manner.

"Interesting that you should ask..." he dangled.

Some slight remnant of the Thrice still communicated through Raq, and Rafael recognized her need to reacquaint herself with her nature. He suggested that they join everyone else.

Regrouping with the others from across the starry battlefield, their veneration continued. The atmosphere was decidedly pensive.

The gathered regarded each other quietly, in mutual admiration. Until...

"CAN YOU BELIEVE WHAT JUST HAPPENED!"

Rafael shattered the solemn mood with his unbridled enthusiasm. Laughter and relief spread through the group then, as the last remnant of the conflict flowed away from them like rolling thunder.

Sheperd hovered there amidst the others expressing pride and satisfaction. He understood profoundly the import of what had transpired as well as what had been prevented. He reflected on the breadth of his experiences and allowed himself only the most fleeting moment of self-deference. Then, his characteristic manner returned to him. He beckoned the others to redirect their attentions.

"We have played a role in averting a very dangerous insurrection. None more so than the Regional Thrice that were nearly overthrown. The implications are self-evident." he added thoughtfully.

Continuing, he added, "If you extend your perceptions, you'll note that the Thrice has not yet untethered completely. If you would turn your attention to Raquel."

Turning, all present noticed that she was somewhat separate from them all. Her stature was noble and still.

Then, Sheperd's statement was validated when Raquel began to address them; the intermingled voices of the Thrice and her own flowing placidly.

They said, "Gratitude is voluminous in this Judicial Body. The averted upheaval and attempted acquisitional subjugation that was surreptitiously..."

"Just say 'THANK YOU' and give us a pound, BRUH."

Rafael again succeeded in dispelling formality. No one minded the lightened mood.

"Thank you." Raquel/the Thrice said in response.

With that, Ash sought what he usually did; answers.

"This is astounding! How did this come to pass? How is it that your essences survived the Inimical corruption?"

The others gathered turned back to Raquel/The Thrice in agreement of the questions. There, in her grin, was the beginning of the answer.

"The Thrice are of a higher attenuation by necessity. We divined the transgression that was directed at us with little time to act against it."

"Providence asserts itself and it is our duty to exploit the opportunity. We did so with the proximity of Raquel Dos Santos' dismayed frequency. What began as the Judgement of her derailed alignment, was usurped by devious ambition."

"I can vaguely feel an unsettled aspect to her energies but It's not completely clear to me. What do you mean by derailed alignment?" Goode inquired.

"My sister was a victim of police brutality in the same incident that I transitioned..." Raf informed them.

They continued their telling, "That is the tragic truth of it. The ending of Raquel was not organic, it was violently enacted at the improper time by malicious actors; leaving her essence -undesignated - in a manner of speaking. Her distress was overwhelming to her. She was detached, in a Limbo of sorts, awaiting alignment. That state necessitated the need to gather testimony on her behalf and subsequently assign a disposition."

"But that function was hi-jacked by Forge and his conspirators before that purpose could be fulfilled.", Kristina noted.

"Thus, requiring our intervention.", Sophia added.

"So, you chose to..." Ash's intelligence began to interpret what had occurred.

"...Inhabit her unoccupied vessel." The Thrice finished his observation. "As we stated, the perfidy of the Abhorrent became transparent to us with no more than an instance to enact a countermeasure. We may be inherently passive, but we are not helpless. The eventuality of their successful consumption could have possibly played itself out, so we allowed them to cooperate, unwittingly, in our performance. While they accepted that their absorption was succeeding, we very covertly, repositioned our frequencies within the vessel that had been fortunately provided. That deception, furthermore, afforded the three of you the opportunity to assert our energies in a concentrated effort against their myopic objectives. The transgressions identified were many: the conspiring against their purpose, the numerous premature contacts resulting in extensive and harmful instigations of the Earthbound. The unscrupulous influence directed at the ill-equipped and the lasting consequences of that. They provoked adjudication. Their verdict was rendered; a conviction administered. And thus, we are brought to our current disposition."

The impact of everything that had occurred was profound. From where they were, they each looked down on the surface below and knew that they'd played a part in the stabilization of existence; and no one would ever know about it.

Goode spoke up then to pose the unanswered question, "So, what now?"

The Thrice's voices responded and were becoming less prominent and less intertwined with Raquel's own, it became clear that they'd lost some degree of vibrancy. Attentively, they answered Goode's question saying, "It is interesting that you should ask..."

There was an undertone of weariness in their response.

"These occurrences have led to a vital consequence. There is a vacuum that has been left. A reassignment is necessitated with alacrity."

Rafael asked, "You can't mean the Inimical..."

"No. We refer to the Thrice."

Confusion passed between all present with the exception of Sheperd and Glori. Then, they all calmed and wisely waited for elaboration.

"With our duties concluded, and the exercising of the larger part of our energies, our position as the regional Thrice will be vacated, immediately to be assumed by the obvious successors."

"Wait," Ash interjected, "Why wouldn't you simply continue?"

Goode asserted then, "Sheperd must be who you're talking about as your replacement...As well as Glori...?"

"You aren't implying that my sister is remaining?"

"You've all fallen short of understanding. That may bode well; it speaks of selflessness. To answer each question; Sheperd and Glori are a disrupted Triumvirate. Reconstitution of Aegis may take place, it is unknown. They are essential Harvesters nonetheless and will continue to attend the Nature as they most effectively have. We, are of a higher attenuation and with our duties fulfilled, we await transfiguration."

A glimpse of their intentions became clear to Goode, Ash, and Raf then. Grasping their shared line of thought, the Thrice confirmed, "Yes, the three before us are the intended successors to our post."

Acceptance came to them with ease. Their time in the vastness surrounding them and in the Etherium relieved them of the want of past familiarities. They'd ascended. The positions the three would inhabit were suited to them. That fact was verified by the fading voices of their predecessors.

"The Thrice derive from an elevation of the Triumvirate: The Mind, The Body, and The Spirit. You, Ash, Rafael, and Goode were always existentially conjoined as that configuration of Mind, Body, Spirit. That is why those Abhorrent sought your demise; because you were rightly perceived to be the foremost direct opposition to their Triumvirate in this region. Forge's mind, Riven's body, and Diva's Spirit. They failed and were dispersed. You ascend. That is the Nature."

"Once."

"Twice."

"Thrice."

It was thought that it was their final decree. Having said it, they went silent and were conclusively seen gently billowing away. They were dispersed.

The Balance remained.

As if she'd been tranquilized, Raquel's consciousness had been drifting in the periphery, at a distance, for the entirety of the ordeal. That detachment lessened with the influence of the Thrice leaving her.

With their absence, she became fully aware. Every instance she'd been privy to was intact and she marveled at it all.

Raq never questioned the extraordinary experiences that she'd had because the veil had dropped; her Earthly restraints had been untethered by her passing. Despite the brutality that had been inflicted on her mortal self, a degree of contentment filled her. The misgivings of her sanity had been dispelled. The anguish of a devilish and covetous stalker had been eliminated. And, she had remained with her brother.

"Sorry Raq, but that's not entirely accurate."

Her brother's voice had taken on a more mature aspect to it. Clear-headed, she faced him eagerly.

"What are you saying, Raf?"

"I'm saying that we are not intended to remain together. Our paths diverge at this very point. While I attend to the Nature in my new capacity, you have much to do back in life."

"This is the point where I'm supposed to go into hysterics but, honestly, I can't help but see the clarity of purpose that's in front of me."

"It's the vicissitudes of misguided worldly efforts that create impaired vision." Raf asserted.

"Look at you, Mister Phil Osefee!" Raquel joked.

"Yes, I've really grown..." Raf joked back.

"I-*know*-that we both have. Listen, I just want to say..."

Prescience caused Raf to break in saying, "... I feel the same overflowing gratitude as well Raq. The only way that I can embrace the station that I've inherited, is by acknowledging the part that you played..."

"You mean, how I helped by being the Thrice's Trojan horse?"

"No, I mean how you helped shape the person that I was Sister. Every test we faced was an opportunity for me to hone my essence. All of those obstacles we *soared* over, were only overcome because you were so special to me, any other alternative was inconceivable."

The sincerest of emotions passed between the siblings as they shared what might have remained unspoken were they still earthbound.

"Rafael, there was never a time that I can remember that you weren't protecting me; even when I didn't realize that I needed it, even when I didn't want it, even after we ascended to a freakin' higher plane of existence! Eu te amo, irmão."

"Eu te amo, irmã.", her brother said in return. Then, he added, "What are big brothers for?"

A short but silent pause passed between the two before their laughter erupted and became contagious. Raq pulled back a hand, primed for a customarily playful slap for her twin, but she thought better of it.

"So, what now?" his sister asked unsurely.

"Now, a loving goodbye, a kiss, a hug, and... this."

A touch on her shoulder sent Raq speeding away.

The momentum of Raquel's descension took her by surprise; a thing she didn't think possible any longer. As if her consciousness had been propelled at the speed of light, she sped downward, toward the previously familiar world she'd been expelled from.

Any previous stoicism about returning that she'd exhibited faded with the proximity to her more natural, earthly station. Resentment began to swell in her.

Approaching the location of her most recent trauma initiated a flood of emotional content. She found the capacity for the more negative feelings to be a consequence of being Earthbound.

Although it was a momentary transition from the heavenly position she was in, the sensation was timeless to Raquel.

Perceptions of the ghastly situation she was bound for flooded Raquel with an intensity that couldn't have been predicted or prepared for. With a distinct and jarring visceral impact, she descended through immeasurable brilliance, back to the frequency of the living.

By contrast, the darkness that encompassed that alley was both literal and figurative. Monsters were among those present. Although flashing lights spun throughout the area, those particular beasts hadn't been illuminated; yet.

Raquel tensed immediately, but she did not rise.

Initially, only her eyes shot open with panic. For the moment, prudence cautioned her to remain still and to gauge her surroundings. She did so and went undiscovered.

Quickly, Raquel deciphered the circumstances. All around her was chaotic. She'd been left alone, unattended, covered, and supine on a gurney. Conversations around her were unguarded because the presumption was that she was deceased. Those conversations varied. Several police officers engaged in speculation of the crime scene. A pair of EMTs were debating their potential culpability. Spectators that were being fended off by overly aggressive cops objected with raised voices. A single individual was heard questioning the impact on his business after the second homicide to take place on his property in as many years. Most disturbingly, the chattering of two vile conspirators drew her in and begged for exposure.

Unseen, Raquel rose leisurely, maneuvered between those present but unaware due to their self-absorption, and made her way to where her courageous twin remained.

The thought of his contribution to those people's banal enduring and the obliviousness of it that they all shared surged through her. The disgusting brutality he'd received at the hands of the corrupt police and the undignified spectacle that was breeding from it disgraced them all; even without their awareness of it.

Knowingly, Raquel bent and delicately shifted her brother's jacket to reach inside for something. Retrieving it, she stood up, and turning toward the congregation there, with intent, she aimed it like a weapon.

That was when someone noticed the empty gurney, searched, and alerted the wretched gathered authorities present with a resounding profanity.

Everyone halted in their tracks.

They regarded Raquel and she regarded them back; although much more disdainfully. For an instant it held; silent and contentious. Then, Raquel moved to assert her intentions, slowly raising her arm.

With predictable and cowardly overreaction, panic erupted through them all as one of the police began to shout, "GUN! GUN! GUN!"

Weapons were drawn blindingly; aimed at a petite, lovely dancer, incapable of being a threat to them, that had recently been thought to be dead. Demands and commands were vulgarly spat at her; contradicting each other as the situation escalated. Only the span between a single inhalation prevented several of them from opening fire. Then the glowing in her hand became apparent.

An abrupt stillness settled over the confusion in anticipation of Raquel's compliance, and she chose to take that opportunity to reveal what had remained hidden.

Raquel held her murdered brother's phone in her outstretched hand and pressed PLAY.

The sharp night air was filled with sounds of past evilness as they echoed from that phone off of the brick surrounding them. Roughly a dozen witnesses stood stock still and gaped at what was unfolding.

That screen glowed in the dark as an intentionally discarded cold-case unraveled before them all grimly. Those gathered watched intently as a sallow, drawn, rabid man brutally killed his victim.

The footage was clear enough to be distinct despite the obviously unnerved camera work. Barely tethered rambling from the murderer penetrated those crowded nearby. Dying, uncharacteristic, cries from the victim followed those ramblings mournfully. The man had been named Darnell Brown and he was killed in the same alley with the same animus that Rafael Dos Santos had been.   Everyone present could clearly grasp that the deranged killer on that small screen was the same pale man lying not ten feet away.

Soon, the crux of the revelation became clear.

Two officers were seen apprehending the perpetrator, only to inexplicably backtrack. While a few present understood what they'd just seen, a murmur could be heard through others asking, 'Five words...? Fourteen words...? What is that supposed to mean?'. The release of the pale killer sent a ripple of hostility through the bystanders. Then, the identities of the erroneous, conspiring cops became evident.

Eyes darted to the two detectives that had been trying to discreetly separate themselves from the onlookers.

Anne Ingram and Mitchell Donaldson had been implicated.

Guns that had still been drawn and aimed at Raquel, began to rapidly swivel in the direction of Ingram and Donaldson. Shouts that were threatening Raquel only moments ago, were then trained on the formerly unassailable pair of veteran badges. Shouts for their compliance, although from a minority of the police present, rang through the alleyway.

The foremost reaction of corruption is denial, and that's exactly what transpired.

"What the hell are you doing? Don't point your guns at me!" Anne Ingram's entitlement radiated from her like heatwaves. "Do you know how long I've been serving these streets? Don't you know my record? I been cleaning these fly-specs off the streets for longer and better than you bitches for years!"

Donaldson seemed to dispense of his almost legendary façade of dominance immediately as he began to emotionally shut down, wilting as realization weighed on him. Little resistance was offered as he was detained and he, in fact, began to wretch with the effort of containing his whimpering. Tears flowed. He'd been broken, just that readily.

Ingram continued to portray herself as hardened and impervious. Warnings that lacked enforceable consequences were targeted at the few approaching officers. Her mannerisms spoke of someone capable of prevailing in a physical confrontation. She in fact, never had been capable of it. Her authority came from the men around her that proved the muscle to her mouth.

The nearest officer to Anne Ingram reached a hand out, only to be struck, closed-fisted, in his jaw. That sent him into a kind of blind rage that would have normally been reserved for the likes of Rafael. Ingram never truly merited consideration of winning that struggle.

Her aggressiveness was a ruse.

Immediately, uncharacteristic waterworks began to stream from Ingram as she was roughly and unceremoniously taken down. Her sobs were unreserved and put Mitchell Donaldson's to shame.

"Who are you gonna believe? Look at her-and look at me!" Like a perp too dim not to incriminate themselves, she unintentionally repeated the phrase that Flay had uttered.

The astonished stares surrounding them as they were handcuffed ultimately compelled Ingram to hold her tongue. Only judgment and weeping were left in the air.

After the footage stopped, Raquel dropped her head in only a slight acknowledgment of relief. An unknown cop approached her then. Questions needed to be asked of her.

"Who are you ma'am?" he began.

"Don't you see the resemblance?" was wryly answered.

"Do you realize what you just did? Do you know what this will bring about?"

No expression passed between them and no answer was offered. Raquel remained unbreakably stoic having done what she intended.

"Who took that footage? Were you there that night? Was it you?" the investigator pressed.

Raquel regarded him vacantly. Her mind remained entwined, if even infinitesimally, with the Etherium. The man's questions were self-serving, though he didn't know it. Her immediate purpose had been fulfilled.

"Miss... what can you tell me? Was that you! Did you witness that?"

"No... He did." Raq gestured delicately at the lifeless form of her brother at her back.

Questions begot questions, as Raquel's assertion left the cop staggering. He sought clarification by beginning a barrage of inquiries.

"How...What are you saying? If he had no part to play in it, why wouldn't he speak up! If he cared about his community, then why wouldn't he come forward from the..."

"...Beginning?" Raquel completed.

Slightly mystified, the cop's questions paused.

"Now that my brother has ascended, and I'm no longer at risk, I can explain what's unclear to you. The night that man was murdered, my brother Rafael was engaged in an unfortunately typical pastime of his; pissing me off. Our past haunted him. Things that he'd been forced to do burdened him. For some time, he'd been masking his troubles with alcohol and too much of it."

"What does that have to do with..."

"Where are we now? That's a liquor store right there. That's the back door to it right there. For about three years now, he's been buying his alcohol from the back of this place, from...that guy."

Her gesture toward A middle-aged and somewhat round man listening from the crowd spun heads condemningly. The store owner paled. Then he was held.

Raquel continued, "Imagine for even a second if you can, what it would be like to be a black, intoxicated, underaged, immigrant witness to a murder in the dead of night! Then two of the very first "Officers of the Law" that show up, prove to be complicit in that killing by laughing, setting the bastard free, and then conspiring to cover it up! If you're not convinced quite yet, they then threaten to kill anyone they find and anyone that they care about if they dare to speak up and expose them." Raquel paused to allow the gravity to penetrate. She then posed a question of her own, "Tell me-Super Sleuth- how quickly would you have exposed yourself and anyone you cared about to the ramifications of our so very equitable justice system?"

"So, if he was in hiding, what changed? How did we get here, tonight? How do these two come across each other again?"

"Misfortune is a twisted bitch...He chose me as one of his victims but failed. But he apparently just made other choices. You'll find his stench on several murders. Considering that long killing spree, it had to come to an end somehow. Rafael was intended to facilitate that end. Providence asserts itself and it is our duty to exploit the opportunity. At least - that's what I heard."

The bewilderment expressed in the cop's expression spoke volumes. He knew what he'd seen take place on the video, but without other significant pieces of the narrative, he only understood a fraction of the importance of what he was being told.

"Um, What? Why does it feel like I'm getting the run-around from you?

"Perhaps it's because your base attenuation to the more Inimical frequencies affords you only a rudimentary empathetic tolerance with regard to the proclivities of more complex and virtuous resonances."

"What?" he asked; clueless.

"Which what?" Raq mocked him knowingly.

"Let's go! We're gonna finish this behind closed doors."

Amidst the gathered officers that were taking Ingram and Donaldson away, a commotion that initially simmered erupted. The crowd, incensed by the corruption they'd been witness to, pressed the police. Chants about justice were used like verbal bludgeons. Objects were thrown and voices were strained in anger. The citizens expressed their collective betrayal openly, passionately.

That defiance could not be permitted. That insolence incited a callous response from the police and they quickly closed ranks. Historically, the reaction to the denouncement of police misconduct was more brutally suppressive misconduct. That threshold was fast approaching.

The cop that had been questioning Raquel turned away to bark orders regarding crowd control. He'd suddenly become completely preoccupied with the disruption growing behind him. The criminality that he'd seen on that phone only moments ago, seemed to have paled by comparison to the spontaneous but organized expression of criticism of the police. That mobilized the whole of them.

That was also the distraction that Raquel Dos Santos desired. Soundlessly, she backed her petite form away from the commotion, lithely pirouetted, and after honoring her brother with a loving glance, and with a kiss blown toward the place that she was quite sure he now resided, she vanished into the shadows between the two buildings and was gone.

Her immediate purposes, having been fulfilled with the assistance in the liberation of the Thrice, and subsequently, the indictment of the corruption and depravity that was crippling the community, she set herself to the task of her newly unraveling, more intrinsic purpose.

Raquel's gentle influence had only just begun to express itself.

<u>END</u>

Endgame Trilogy

GLOSSARY

Abhorrent (The): The term used by the Chimerical to describe their counterparts; the Inimical

Aegis: One of the Chimerical; initiate of Dr. Nathaniel Ash

Alignment: The resonant frequency within The Nature at the final juncture, post-physical

Amiss (The): The term the Inimical use to describe the multitude of abandoned souls they feel are left behind in the wake of Chimerical misconceptions and unrealistic conclusions that corrupt everything they do

Anathema (The): The term used by the Inimical to describe their counterparts; the Chimerical

Anne Ingram, Officer: Police officer involved in the cover-up of Darnell Brown murder; Mitchell Donaldson's partner

Anthony: The fourteen-year-old would-be car thief Rafael Dos Santos caught

Ascension: The transition from the physical to the frequency sympathetic to the Chimerical range of the Balance at the time of death

Balance: The desired state of existence between the opposing polarities of the Chimerical and the Inimical throughout the Totality

Casey: The college student that died as a result of Nathaniel Ash's negligence; also, the boyfriend of Raquel Dos Santos

Chimerical: The Order identified with the altruistic polarity of the Nature

Consciousness Chorus: The manifestations of the various emotional states of one experiencing the Endgame

Constance: The Endgame manifestation of Devlin Goode's active consciousness as it fades

Daniella Ramirez: An experienced EMT and romantic partner of Dr. Nathaniel Ash

Darnell Brown: Murder victim of Flay

Devlin Goode: Artist and musician who lost his family tragically causing him to commit suicide; newly Ascended member of the Thrice

Diva: One of the Inimical Order; extortionate of Raquel Dos Santos

Dr. Erlikson: The Endgame manifestation of Devlin Goode's self-destructive tendencies

Dr. Larena Ahern: Nathaniel Ash's arrogant, condescending Attending Physician

Dr. Malcolm: Nathaniel Ash's first mentor

Dr. Mia Li: The Endgame manifestation of Devlin Goode's strivings for reason

Dr. Nathaniel Ash: Doctor involved in a tragic accident leading to his corrupted frequency; newly Ascended member of the Thrice

Egon: The Endgame manifestation of Devlin Goode's Ego

Endgame: The means by which a dying individual enacts and perceives their final choice of frequency before passing into The Nature.

Etheric: Of or relating to the Etherium

Etherium: The collective whole of the Chimerical and the Inimical

Extortionate: One belonging to the Order of the Inimical charged with corrupting a transitioning person into their polarity of the Nature

Flay: The stalker of Raquel Dos Santos and serial killer responsible for several deaths intended to advance him into the Inimical

Forge: One of the Inimical; extortionate of Devlin Goode

Gabby: The manifestation of Nathaniel Ash's innocence, with specific regards to his comprehension of death.

Glori: One of the Chimerical Order; initiate of Raquel Dos Santos

Harvester: The Inimical romanticized description of their role of gathering the unjust or corrupted; the title is skewed because the Inimical are responsible for corrupting those very individuals in order to convert all things to their purpose

In-Between: The invisible layer of Existence between the physical frequency and the Etheric frequency that is the natural battlefield of the Etherium.

Inimical: The Order identified with the iniquitous polarity of the Etherium; dogmatically referred to as Demons

Initiate: One of the Order of the Chimerical charged with bringing a transitioning person into their altruistic polarity of the Nature

J.P.: One of Rafael's close friends

Kristina: The murdered wife of Devlin Goode and mother of Sophia

Lopez: The Endgame manifestation of Devlin Goode's effort to inflict punishment on himself

Mitchell Donaldson, Officer: Police officer involved in the cover-up of Darnell Brown's murder; Anne Ingram's partner

MT: The Endgame manifestation of Nathaniel Ash's regret with regard to his in-action

Mateo: One of Rafael's close friends

Nature (The): The sentient totality of all that has been and will ever be.

Nurse: The Endgame manifestation of Devlin Goode's self-loathing

O Homen Das Sombras / The Shadow man: The crime boss that forced Rafael and Raquel Dos Santos and other children to steal from unsuspecting people in Sao Paolo

One Motive (The): As defined by the Chimerical; The process of re-engineering or tainting the spirit of those the Inimical touch, which ultimately results in the corruption of their frequencies and the Inimical propagation

Rafael Dos Santos: Brother to Raquel Dos Santos, Young Capoeira instructor dedicated to protecting his sister; newly Ascended member of the Thrice

Raquel Dos Santos: Sister to Rafael Dos Santos, young dance instructor and intended victim of the serial killer Flay

Rasp (The): The fiery Endgame personification of Death unleashed to stalk Dr. Nathaniel Ash

Reese: Rookie EMT and partner of Daniella Ramirez

Remnant: the essence of one that has deceased while still in the Endgame transitional period

Riven: One of the Inimical Order; extortionate of Dr. Nathaniel Ash

Serenity: Devlin Goode's pet cat

Shea: One of Raquel's close friends

Sheperd: One of the Chimerical Order; initiate of Devlin Goode

Sid: The Endgame manifestation of Devlin Goode's deepest malicious tendencies

Singularity (The): a dubious belief by the Inimical that opposing states and beings are in fact the same; such as God and the Devil, Angels and Demons, and good and bad

Sophia: Devlin and Kristina Goode's murdered daughter

Totality: The infinite summation of everything imaginable; A spectrum; a range of "frequencies" There is a particular range of the spectrum and an opposing range of it as well. The Inimical being on one end and the Chimerical on the other; antitheses. The minutest fissure-physicality-exists as a separation between these particular two "frequencies" of the spectrum; physicality

Trace: The manifestation of Nathaniel Ash's intellect with specific regard to his comprehension of death.

Thrice (The): The non-combative judicial body responsible for mediating the conflicts and instances of dispute between the polarities of the Etherium

Triumvirate (The): A reference to the composition of the Thrice; consisting of representatives exhibiting aspects of Mind, Body, and Spirit

Winona Eyote (Mrs.): Kind Indigenous woman that sold the Dos Santos 'and the Goode's their cats